PRAISE FOR THE BLOOD COVEN VAMPIRE NOVELS

"Delightful, surprising, and engaging."
—Rachel Caine, *New York Times* bestselling author

"Dark, delicious, and full of surprises."
—Heather Brewer, *New York Times* bestselling author

NIGHT SCHOOL

"An action-packed story with appealing characters, dark humor, and a new spin on both the worlds of the undead and the fae. Though primarily targeted to a YA audience, this novel will appeal to adult fans of *Buffy the Vampire Slayer* as well as the Harry Potter series and the 'Twilight' novels." —*Library Journal*

"This book has it all! Vampires, vampire slayers, and faeries, what more could you ask for? . . . A fast-paced book from start to finish. I can't wait to read more about Sunny and Rayne's adventures. This is a must read for anyone who enjoys paranormal fiction and a good story." —*Night Owl Reviews*

BAD BLOOD

"A vampire book so worth reading, with dark humor, a distinctive voice, and a protagonist clever enough to get herself out of trouble . . . A great ride." —Ellen Hopkins, *New York Times* bestselling author

"Mancusi writes with a wicked sense of humor and keeps readers turning the pages, eager for more." —*Novel Reads*

continued . . .

GIRLS THAT GROWL

"An amusing teenage vampire tale starring a fascinating high school student . . . Young adults will enjoy growling alongside of this vampire slayer who has no time left for homework."

—Midwest Book Review

"A fast-paced and entertaining read."   —LoveVampires

"A refreshing new vampire story, Girls That Growl is different from all of those other vampire stories . . . a very original plot."

—Flamingnet

STAKE THAT

"A fast-paced story line . . . both humorous and hip . . . A top read!"

—LoveVampires

"Rayne is a fascinating protagonist . . . readers will want to stake out Mari Mancusi's fun homage to Buffy."   —The Best Reviews

BOYS THAT BITE

"A wonderfully original blend of vampire/love/adventure drama which teens will find refreshingly different."

—Midwest Book Review

"A tongue-in-cheek young teen tale starring two distinct, likable twins, the vampire between them, and a coven of terrific support characters who bring humor and suspense to the mix . . . Filled with humor and action . . . insightfully fun."   —The Best Reviews

Berkley titles by Mari Mancusi

BLOOD TIES

NIGHT SCHOOL

BAD BLOOD

GIRLS THAT GROWL

STAKE THAT

BOYS THAT BITE

Anthologies

THE BLOOD COVEN VAMPIRES, VOLUME 1

THE
BLOOD
COVEN
VAMPIRES

·Volume 1·

MARI MANCUSI

BERKLEY BOOKS, NEW YORK

THE BERKLEY PUBLISHING GROUP
Published by the Penguin Group
Penguin Group (USA) Inc.
375 Hudson Street, New York, New York 10014, USA
Penguin Group (Canada), 90 Eglinton Avenue East, Suite 700, Toronto, Ontario M4P 2Y3, Canada
(a division of Pearson Penguin Canada Inc.)
Penguin Books Ltd., 80 Strand, London WC2R 0RL, England
Penguin Group Ireland, 25 St. Stephen's Green, Dublin 2, Ireland (a division of Penguin Books Ltd.)
Penguin Group (Australia), 250 Camberwell Road, Camberwell, Victoria 3124, Australia
(a division of Pearson Australia Group Pty. Ltd.)
Penguin Books India Pvt. Ltd., 11 Community Centre, Panchsheel Park, New Delhi—110 017, India
Penguin Group (NZ), 67 Apollo Drive, Rosedale, Auckland 0632, New Zealand
(a division of Pearson New Zealand Ltd.)
Penguin Books (South Africa) (Pty.) Ltd., 24 Sturdee Avenue, Rosebank, Johannesburg 2196,
South Africa

Penguin Books Ltd., Registered Offices: 80 Strand, London WC2R 0RL, England

This is a work of fiction. Names, characters, places, and incidents either are the product of the author's imagination or are used fictitiously, and any resemblance to actual persons, living or dead, business establishments, events, or locales is entirely coincidental. The publisher does not have any control over and does not assume any responsibility for author or third-party websites or their content.

Copyright © 2011 by Marianne Mancusi.
Boys That Bite copyright © 2006 by Marianne Mancusi.
Stake That copyright © 2006 by Marianne Mancusi.
Cover art by Shutterstock.
Cover design by SDG Concepts, LLC.
Interior text design by Kristin del Rosario.

All rights reserved.
No part of this book may be reproduced, scanned, or distributed in any printed or electronic form without permission. Please do not participate in or encourage piracy of copyrighted materials in violation of the author's rights. Purchase only authorized editions.
BERKLEY® is a registered trademark of Penguin Group (USA) Inc.
The "B" design is a trademark of Penguin Group (USA) Inc.

PRINTING HISTORY
Berkley trade paperback edition / October 2011

Library of Congress Cataloging-in-Publication Data

Mancusi, Marianne.
    The Blood Coven Vampires. Volume 1 / Mari Mancusi.—Berkley trade paperback ed.
        v. cm.
    Summary: Mistaken for her Goth twin sister, Rayne, sixteen-year-old Sunny is bitten by a vampire and races against time to avoid becoming a vampire permanently. Rayne learns she is destined to be the new Vampire Slayer just as a maniacal member of the undead is trying to spread a fatal blood disease.
    Contents: Boys that bite—Stake that.
    ISBN 978-0-425-24309-1
    [1. Vampires—Fiction. 2 Goth culture (Subculture)—Fiction. 3. Twins. 4. Sisters—Fiction. 5. Virus diseases—Fiction. 6. High schools—Fiction. 7. Schools—Fiction. 8. Single-parent families—Fiction.] I Title.

PZ7.M312178Bjm 2011
[Fic]—dc 23
                        2011020653

PRINTED IN THE UNITED STATES OF AMERICA

10 9 8 7 6 5 4 3 2 1

CONTENTS

BOYS THAT BITE

1

STAKE THAT

191

BOYS THAT BITE

To all those who stepped in to help
when my house burned to the ground.
I couldn't have rebuilt without you. And
to all the Blood Coven Vampires-in-Training
and students at Blood Coven University. You
make writing these books so worthwhile! ☺

Sunshine and Rayne

You know, being bitten by a vampire one week before prom really sucks. On soooo many levels.

Okay, fine. I'm sure it'd be equally sucky at other times of the calendar year as well. Photo day at school, for example. Bad time to sport a two-hole hickey on your neck. Easter would blow, too—imagine trying to explain to your mom that you can't attend sunrise service because, well, you're allergic to the sun. And then there's Christmas. Sure, you'd sport a good chance of running into Santa, but could you resist the urge to snack on his jolly old jugular?

Now that I think about it, there just ain't a good time to be bitten by a vampire.

That said, you gotta understand. Three hours, twenty-five minutes, and thirty-three seconds ago JAKE WILDER asked me to prom! I mean JAKE WILDER, people! The hottest guy at Oakridge High School. The heartthrob leading man in every school play with soulful, deep brown eyes and droolworthy bod. Every girl I know is officially In Love with him—even Mary Markson and she's practically married to her boyfriend, Nick.

But, I ask you, who did the Sex God in question ask to the senior class prom? Uh, yeah, that would be *moi*. Seriously, if you had asked me three hours, twenty-five minutes, and thirty-TWO seconds ago whether Jake Wilder even knew my name, I'd have bet my iPod he hadn't a clue. (And it's a darn good thing I didn't make that bet, 'cause a day without sixteen gigs of music at my fingertips is like a day without sunshine.)

That said, I can't tell you what a total and utter bummer it is to be slowly morphing into a vampire one week before the big event.

I'm getting ahead of myself here. Since you don't have a clue as to who I am, you probably don't care all that much about my imminent Creature of the Night transformation. (Mom always says I have the worst manners known to mankind, so I apologize in advance for my shortcomings.)

So okay, all about me for a moment. My name is Sunshine McDonald. Yes, Sunshine, and if you think that's bad, I dread to introduce you to my identical twin sister, Rayne. I know, I know, Sunshine and Rayne—it makes you a little sick to your stomach, doesn't it? Well, you can blame our cruel, ex-hippie parents who (hello!?) grew up in the disco era and should have been hanging out at Studio 54, dancing the night away, instead of at the Harvest Co-Op broiling tofu. But, sadly, no. They preferred peace, love, and stupid baby names to hot dance tunes and bling.

Of course, these days Dad's probably driving around in a hot red sports car while picking up honeys in Vegas. He left Mom to "find himself" about four years ago and has remained lost ever since. We occasionally get guilt-ridden birthday cards with the sincerest apologies and a crisp fifty-dollar bill stuffed inside, but that's about it. I miss him sometimes, but what can you do?

Anyway, back to me. I'm sixteen years old. Five foot four, average weight, dirty blond hair. I've got muddy brown eyes that someday I'm going to hide with blue contacts and a billion annoying freckles that don't fade no matter how much lemon juice I squeeze on them. Mom says I got the freckles from Dad's Irish side of the family. Dad says I got them from Mom's Scottish ancestors. In any case, Rayne and I were cursed in the womb by the bad gene fairy and can't do anything about it.

At school I do okay—an A/B student usually. I like English. Abhor Math. Want to be a journalist when I "grow up." I play varsity field hockey and have twice tried out for the school play, mostly to be up close and personal with Jake Wilder. I have now twice ended up as Heather Miller's understudy and the stupid girl is never sick. I'm talking winning-the-perfect-attendance-award-two-years-running never sick. To add insult to injury, she also has big boobs and throws herself at Jake on a daily basis.

But anyway, I'm sure you're much more interested in the whole vampire thing than Heather Miller's chest. (Though you should see it—she looks like freaking Pamela Anderson!) Basically, the trouble all started when Rayne decided to drag me to a Goth club.

Now for the record, I'm so not into Goth music or that whole scene AT ALL. Not that I'm a Bieliber, of course. I guess you could consider me a John Mayer type of girl. But Rayne, on the other hand, is a full-fledged Goth chick. If I ever saw her wear anything but the color black, I would seriously fall over in shock and awe. She listens to all this bizarre music that you'd never hear on the radio and loves dark, twisted movies that make absolutely no sense. For example, she's seen *Donnie Darko* fifty times and can quote seventeen *Buffy* episodes by heart. When a new Anne Rice book comes out, she camps overnight to be first in line to buy it. (Even though there are plenty of those sicko books to go around, trust me.)

So anyway, two days ago Rayne tells me she saw this flyer at Newbury Comics for an all-ages Goth club up in Nashua, New Hampshire—about twenty minutes from where we live on the Massachusetts border. It's called, if you can believe it, "Club Fang," which has seriously got to be the most cheeseball name on the planet. Rayne, on the other hand, is so excited, I'm half convinced she's going to pee her pants. (Or her long, black skirt, to be exact—the girl wouldn't be caught dead in pants.) And because, as she reminds me, I've known her since birth, it's evidently my twin-sisterly duty to give up any Sunday night plans I might have had to go with her, since all of her friends are too busy.

Lucky me.

ONE

Goth Me Up—Bay-Bee

"Give me one good reason why I should go tonight."

It's Sunday evening, five P.M., and I'm desperately trying to get out of the big Club Fang outing my sister's got planned for us. I'm not holding out much hope, though. After all, it's a proven fact in life that what Rayne wants, Rayne gets. Period. End of story.

Rayne rolls over from a lounging position on her four-poster bed, props her head up with an elbow, and gives me her best pout.

"Quit your whining. It'll be totally fun and you know it. Besides, I went to see Dave Matthews with you and you can't possibly imagine how painful that was for me to endure. My ears still haven't recovered."

My identical dramaholic rubs her lobes with two fingers, as if they're still causing her pain. Puh-leeze.

"Whatever." I shove her playfully, and she falls back onto the mattress. "As if it's a chore to hear that dreamy voice."

"Chore, no. Cruel and unusual punishment worse than death? Now you're getting warmer." Rayne jumps up from the bed and makes a beeline for her closet. "So you're going. It's decided." She rummages through the hangers, face intent. "Now we need to find you something to wear."

Danger! Danger!

"Oh no you don't!" I cry. "I may be forced to go to this stupid club, but I'm so not undergoing some extreme Goth makeover. There's nothing wrong with what I have on." I stand up and model my tank/ jeans/flips combo, which has always served me well.

Rayne turns to look at me for a second—long enough to give me a once-over and roll her eyes—then turns back to her closet. She pulls out a long black skirt and black sweater.

"I'm not wearing a sweater to a nightclub," I protest. "I'll sweat to death!"

"Fine. Jeez. It was just a thought." She crams the outfit back into the overflowing closet, exchanging it for a black (surprise, surprise) tank top. Now while as a rule, I'm totally a tank top type of girl, I tend to stay away from ones made out of vinyl.

"No effing way." I shake my head. "People will think I'm into S&M and start trying to whip me or handcuff me to the stage or something."

Rayne emits her patented sigh of frustration at my protest, but thankfully returns the bondage outfit to the closet. I, in turn, sit back down on the bed and wonder whether I should be concerned that my twin owns an outfit like that to begin with.

"How about this?" she asks. She pulls out a very cute spaghetti tank with the words *Fashion Victim* written on the front. "It seems rather appropriate."

I throw a pillow at her.

"Only in the most ironic of ways, of course," she amends with a giggle. "Or, there's always this one." She exchanges the tank with another—this one pink with white writing that says *Bite Me!*

"Where'd you get that shirt?" I ask curiously. "It doesn't seem like your type of thing. It's not even black."

She shrugs. "Some vampire let me borrow it a while ago. I keep forgetting to give it back."

"Vampire?" I raise an eyebrow. While I knew Rayne ran with a different crowd, I hadn't realized they fancied themselves creatures of the night. "We're swapping clothes with the undead now?" I guess that would explain all the black.

Rayne snorts. "I just borrowed a T-shirt, smart-ass. But for the record, yes. There's like this whole group of them in Nashua. They look like Goth kids, but they're really members of an ancient vampire coven."

"You've got to be kidding me," I groan. "Why would anyone want to pretend to be a vampire anyway? Like why is that so cool? Do they go around drinking each other's blood or something?"

Rayne gives me a noncommittal shrug, which tells me she actually thinks it *is* cool, but isn't about to admit it to me. I consider teasing her, but then decide the "live and let live" theory of sisterhood is the best plan of action at this point and drop the subject. After all, I have to hang out with her all night. Having her mad at me is only going to make things that much more painful.

"Okay, I'll wear the *Bite Me* shirt," I say to appease her. At least it's not black. "It'll be my standard response to anyone who tries to hit on me." I giggle. "Someone can come up and be like 'Hey babe, what's your sign?' and I'll just point to my shirt."

Rayne laughs appreciatively and tosses me the tank top. "Of course they might think you're pointing to your boobs in a 'have at 'em, big boy' kind of way."

"Ew!"

"Don't worry," my sister says, swapping her T-shirt for a long, black princess dress ornamented with a ton of lace. Where does she find this stuff? "Most of the boys will be gay, I'm sure. All the good ones are, especially in the Goth scene. You don't get many hetero guys who dig wearing eyeliner." She snorts. "So, little angelic twin of mine, I'm quite confident that your virtue will remain intact, no matter which shirt you wear."

Here she goes again. I knew we couldn't have a whole conversation without Rayne's infamous "Sunny the Innocent" digs. My precious little twin lost her virginity last year and has been bragging about it ever since. You'd think she won an Olympic sex medal or something. But I'm sorry. Meeting some grungy skater dude at camp and sneaking out to do it on the floor of the boathouse is so not my idea of a fulfilling first experience. Call me a girly-girl, but I want my first time to be all candles and roses, not splinters and knee burns. To each her own, I guess.

"So anyway," Rayne continues, taking my silence as license to carry on teasing me, "you can be well assured, your innocence is safe at Club Fang."

I giggle in spite of myself. She sounds like a saleswoman. "Is that printed on the flyer?"

"Absolutely," Rayne declares confidently. "Money-back guarantee."

Club Fang

Club Fang turns out to be pretty much what I'd pictured, but mind you I didn't have very lofty expectations for the place. Since it's held in a building that by day serves as a Knights of Columbus hall, there's only so much the promoters can do to Goth it up at night and still be able to tear things down in time for the Veteran's Breakfast at six A.M.

Not that they haven't given it the old college try. They've strung flashing multicolored lights in the rafters and hung large white sheets from floor to ceiling, blocking the windows. They set fans behind these sheets so that they billow in the breeze. Slide projectors across the room cast eerie, nondescript images onto the white sheet backgrounds.

In front of the slightly elevated stage area, they've placed the *pièce de résistance*—a bondage cage. At least that's what it's supposed to look like. I think they just took some wire fencing and spray-painted it black.

Behind the "cage," a DJ type with a scruffy beard rummages through records and large speakers pump out overblown Goth, industrial, and electronica sounds. They even have one of those cheesy smoke machines, which totally makes me start coughing the second we enter.

The other club kids don't seem to mind the cheesiness or the smoke. Dressed uniformly in black, they sway to the music, doing a dance that to me resembles getting one's foot stuck in the mud. They slowly, meticulously pull the foot out, only to have the other foot then seemingly get stuck as well, forcing them to repeat the whole process from the beginning.

"School!" Rayne shouts in my ear.

"Huh?" What does she mean, "school"? Argh—does she see someone from our high school? Oh, man, I'd be mortified if someone I knew caught me here in my current ensemble and word got out to my field hockey teammates. I'd never hear the end of it. "Who's here from school?"

"No, I said, 'it's cool!'" Rayne corrects. Oh. Phew. Not that I agreed with her assessment, mind you, but at least it didn't involve me having to hide behind one of those billowing sheets.

"I'm going to get a drink," Rayne says, pointing to a small, makeshift bar on one wall. Unlike bars in real clubs, of course, this one only serves soda. Too bad. Not that I'm some alky, but in this case a beer might help dull the pain.

"Get me a Red Bull," I tell her. Maybe a megadose of caffeine will be the ticket. Rayne nods and disappears into the fog.

I find a wall and make like a wallflower, wondering why on earth I agreed to this torture. We've been here five minutes and I already have a splitting headache. Not to mention, the stench of the masses makes me want to puke. Seriously, would it hurt to apply a little Secret to your pits before working up a sweat on the dance floor?

I try to give my brain the Pollyanna pep talk.

Okay, try to have a good attitude, Sunny. Rayne has done plenty for you. Stop being so selfish and go with the flow. Who knows, you might even have fun!

Yeah, right. Even Pollyanna-brain doesn't believe that one. Best I will be able to manage is to fake a good time.

"Good evening."

Oh no. A guy. Addressing me. I thought Rayne said everyone was gay here. I look up, ready to point to my tank top, when my gaze falls on the most gorgeous pair of eyes I've ever seen in my sixteen years on the planet. They are literally the color of sapphires. I mean, I've seen plenty of blue eyes in my day, but nothing like these.

Better yet, the eyes are attached to a face equally amazing. I quickly take stock: smooth skin, high cheekbones, sooty black eyelashes. Long brown hair, pulled back in a ponytail. I'm not normally into the long hair thing, but on this guy it totally works. He looks like a blue-eyed Orlando Bloom. (*Pirates of the Caribbean* Orlando, not *LOTR* and certainly not *Troy*, just FYI.) Best of all, unlike the other Gothed-out club kids, he isn't wearing a stitch of black. Just a simple tight white T-shirt and a pair of low-rise jeans. No eyeliner either, thank goodness.

I scan the area, sure that "Orlando" must be speaking to someone other than me. Some supermodel to my right, perhaps. But I see no one in the general vicinity. Hmm . . .

"H-hi," I say, my words sounding squeaky and young. I hate my voice. Makes me sound like I'm ten. Rayne and I are identical twins and yet she has this sultry, raspy voice somehow. Maybe it's due to her smoking, though, and I'm sorry, but if it's a choice between eventual lung cancer and a squeaky voice, you can call me Minnie Mouse any day of the week.

Instead of replying, the guy reaches out and presses his palm against my cheek. His skin is cool, but his touch scorches my skin. His eyes study my face, then roam my body and I suddenly feel naked under his glare. I give an involuntary shiver and I can feel goose bumps popping up all over my arms. Wow. I can't remember the last time a guy gave me actual goose bumps! Maybe never.

I know I should be questioning why this random guy has approached me in a nightclub and evidently feels it's no big deal to reach out and touch me so intimately, but I can't find the words to voice any objections.

"I'm Magnus," he says in a breathy, dangerous voice with a distinct hint of English accent. "I believe you were expecting me?"

My heart sinks. Damn it, I knew he had the wrong girl. He probably has some blind date he's searching for and mistook me for her. (Though why a guy of his caliber would have to go on a blind date is beyond me. Any date with 20/20 vision would snatch him up at first sight!)

Wait a second here. If he doesn't even recognize his date-to-be, what kind of hold does this chick have on him, anyway? They're obviously not yet a couple, which in my book makes him fair game. I look around, making sure there's no crazy possessive blind date type hovering nearby, ready to claw out my eyes for stepping into her territory. But the coast seems clear.

"Hi, Magnus," I say, having to shout over the music. "I'm Sunny."

He cocks his head, a confused look on his face. Then he touches a finger to his ear and smiles at me. Ah. I get it. He can't hear me over the music. Just when I'm about to retry my intro with a louder voice, he takes my hand and pulls me toward the club's exit.

I can feel my heart pounding in my chest—a billion beats a minute would be an understatement of tempo at this point. Where is he leading me? Should I follow or break away? I scan the room for Rayne—to at least let her know I'll be right back—but she's nowhere to be seen.

We step outside into the crisp night air. It's rather chilly out here, even for New Hampshire in May. The club's bouncer eyes us suspiciously for a moment before turning back to continue flirting with the cute blond jailbait to his right. Magnus leads me down the front steps, still holding my trembling hand in his.

"Uh, where are we going?" I ask, stopping short. After all, no matter how cute this guy is, I know absolutely nothing about him. And logical Jiminy Cricket voices in my head warn of the dangers of following a random stranger out of a nightclub.

He turns and smiles again and my defenses crumble. Surely someone with such a beautiful smile couldn't be dangerous, right?

"It's a bit difficult to hear you in there," he says at last. Wow, I so love his accent! "I thought we could come outside for a little chat."

Okay, a chat. As in a talk. Talking is good. Talking doesn't involve anything Mom wouldn't approve of. Not that I care what Mom would approve of, I remind myself. I mean, I'm sixteen years old—practically an official adult. I've really got to stop the goody-two-shoes routine I've got going on all the time.

"So um, do you come here often?" I ask, trying to make conversation. Too late I realize how clichéd I sound.

He chuckles softly, and I feel my face heat. That's another pain-in-the-butt thing about having light skin and freckles. I blush like nobody's business and there's no hiding it. Hopefully the darkness around us will reduce its fire-engine-red glare.

I want to say more, to redeem myself for my idiotic question, but my tongue just doesn't seem to want to work right. What the hell is wrong with me? My brain says I should be freaking out, but my heart says to go with the flow. After all, how often does a gorgeous guy just walk up to you in a nightclub and start talking? I mean, sure, it may be an everyday occurrence for, say, Paris Hilton, but it so doesn't ever happen to little old me.

We walk behind the building, where there's a parking lot and a single streetlamp casting a yellowish glow on the vehicles. Magnus stops walking and smiles at me. I lean against the building's brick wall and give him a shy smile back.

Now what? I hope he's not expecting some intellectual conversation, because I don't think I can manage it at this very instant.

But verbal discussion seems far from his mind as he takes a step closer, his knee brushing against my inner thigh. The sudden body contact invokes a slightly nauseated feeling in the pit of my stomach. But nauseated in a good way, if that's possible.

He brings a hand to my face again, this time tracing my cheekbone with a smooth finger. His eyes search mine, as if they can see into my very soul. The whole thing is so unnerving and dangerous and sexy, I swear I'm going to fall over and faint.

"You're beautiful," he whispers. "And so innocent."

I frown. God, I hate when people say that. I mean sure, technically I am innocent, Innocent with a capital *I*. But what royally sucks is that it's evidently so easy to tell this about me at first glance. Like, what, am I wearing some big *V* on my chest or something? Rayne is my identical twin and NO ONE ever says SHE looks innocent. Oh, no. The boys think she's all seductive. Kick-ass, even. But never innocent.

"I'm not *that* innocent," I declare, too late realizing that I'm quoting Britney. I really need to keep my mouth shut until I can count on it to say something intelligent, witty, and interesting.

"It's not an insult," he murmurs, his finger drifting to my ear and tracing the lobe. "I find it very, very attractive."

Did I mention how utterly hot he is? And how turned on I am? And how utterly incapable I am of responding to anything he says?

"Oh. Well, um. Thanks. I guess." I laugh my stupid laugh—the one I always break out when I'm nervous. It resembles a donkey's bray and I'm not all that fond of it.

He leans in closer, his mouth so close I can feel his breath on my face. He smells of mint and something spicy I can't identify. "Are you sure you want this?" he asks, searching my face again.

I scrunch my nose, puzzled. Am I sure I want what? This whole encounter really gives me the feeling that I'm missing out on some vital piece of information. By the way he's looking at me, though, I'm getting the feeling he's asking if I'm sure about kissing him. And the answer to that question is *hell yeah*.

"I'm sure," I murmur, hoping my voice sounds husky like Demi Moore's. Like Rayne's. "Very, very sure."

He smiles. "Okay, then. Let's do it."

I close my eyes and next thing I know I can feel his full lips brush against my own. Chills erupt in every crevice of my body and the goose bumps return with a vengeance. Now I'm no kissing expert, mind you (in fact, I'm a bit embarrassed to admit I've only made out with three guys in my entire life), but even I can tell this is an amazing, once-in-a-lifetime kiss. The way his lips press against mine, as if he's starving and hasn't eaten for days. As if he desires something that only my mouth can provide. My lips part, and I can't withhold a soft moan of pleasure. I hope he doesn't think I'm total slut girl for letting him kiss me like this. I mean, I barely know him. But something about this seems so right.

His lips abandon my mouth and kiss a trail down to my neck. I love being kissed on the neck. It is a total turn-on for some reason. The ultralight wisp of his lips brushing against my—

OWWWW! "What the—?" I jump back, horrified.

Did he just BITE me?

THREE

The Contract (Signed in Blood)

My hands fly to my neck. I can feel hot blood bubbling from the wound. "What the hell did you do that for?"

He doesn't even have the decency to look apologetic. Just plants his hands on his hips and frowns. "You said you were sure," he says in a decidedly pissed-off voice. "Damn it, I hate when you kids change your mind at the last minute."

"Sure that I wanted to *kiss* you, not let you munch on my jugular," I retort. "What ever gave you the idea that—" I catch him glancing down at my *Bite Me* tank. Oh. I cross my arms over the writing. "That wasn't meant to be taken literally."

"Look, you knew there was going to be mild discomfort during the initial procedure. It clearly states that in the contract you signed." Now he looks exasperated.

"Contract? What freaking contract?" This guy is insane. Gorgeous, but clearly and utterly insane.

To my further shock, he reaches into his book bag and pulls out a thick stack of papers, bound with a black binder clip. He holds them up and points to the bottom of page one.

"*Con-tract*," he says slowly, as if addressing a small child.

When did Mister Tall, Dark, and Charming turn into Major Jerk-Off?

"Look, I don't know what you're talking about, but I never signed any—"

He flips to the last page and points to a signature. "*Sig-nature,*" he says in the same patronizing tone. I barely resist the urge to slap him. My neck is burning at this point. What did he eat before kissing me, wasabi?

I squint at the signature line, trying to figure out what he's talking about. I gasp as I see my sister's scrawled handwriting at the bottom of the contract.

"What the—?" I whisper. I try to yank the contract from his grasp. He holds on tight—guy's got a killer grip. I look up, staring him down. "What is this?"

He runs a hand through his long brown hair, which has come loose from its ponytail. He looks wild and dangerous and angry. "You know damn well what it is. You went through the class. The testing. You signed your name, for hell's sake!"

"That's not my name, dude. That's my sister's. Now why don't you tell me what's really going on here?" Oh Lord, what has Rayne gotten herself into now? Some kind of weirdo cult?

Magnus frowns. He glances down at the contract and then up at me. "Your sis—?"

"Magnus?"

I jump a mile as I hear my sister's voice cut across the parking lot. Speak of the devil.

"Oh, Magnus, are you out here? Rachel said you might be out here. I'm ready, you know. Ready and willing, baby," she says, easily mastering that sultry voice thing I was attempting a few minutes before.

I glance over at Magnus, who has suddenly lost his confident swagger and looks like he's sweating bullets. I mean, the guy wasn't all that tanned to begin with, but now he looks positively glow-in-the-dark white. He stares at me, then behind me. I turn around and see Rayne approaching.

"Sunny, what are you doing talking to Magnus?" Rayne asks disapprovingly as she approaches. "He hasn't . . . told you anything weird, has he?"

"Rayne, what the hell is going on here?" I demand.

"There's . . . two . . ." Magnus the once-smooth lover stammers. "But I thought . . ."

"Rayne is my twin sister," I explain to him, marveling at how in control my voice sounds.

"But you look . . . I thought . . ." Magnus trails off.

Rayne's face drains of color. "Oh no," she cries. "You didn't!" She places a hand on my shoulder and yanks me around to face her, peering at my neck. "Oh no!" she cries. "No, no, NO!"

"Will someone please tell me what is going on here?" I demand, hands on my hips. This has gone way too far. "And I mean, now!"

"Now, Sunny, don't get mad, but . . ." Rayne begins, her voice trembling.

I shoot her an angry glare. "But WHAT, Rayne?"

"I, uh, think you've accidentally been turned into a vampire."

FOUR

A Bloody Bad Case of Mistaken Identity

"A vampire?" I cry. "Is this your idea of some kind of sick joke?"

Rayne shakes her head. "No joke, Sun. But a serious problem." She turns to Magnus. "How could you have screwed this up? You're supposed to be my blood mate. And you can't even tell when it's not me?"

Magnus moans, then leans over and starts spitting onto the pavement. Attractive. I can't believe five minutes ago I thought he was hot and sexy. Someone I wanted to hook up with. At this point, I'd sooner kiss the Cryptkeeper.

"You look exactly alike," he whines. "How was I supposed to know?" He closes his hand into a fist. "Lucifent is going to kill me."

"Um, technically aren't you already dead?" I ask in my sweetest voice. I'm so over this game already.

He turns around to shoot me an evil-looking glare. "I take it you were absent the day they covered 'figure of speech' in school?"

I raise an eyebrow. "At least I showed up when they taught us not to bite the other kindergarteners."

"Guys, please!" Rayne interrupts. "Stop arguing. This is serious.

It doesn't matter why this all happened. Just that it did. And that we've got to make it unhappen. Sunny can't turn into a vampire. She's got field hockey play-offs next week."

For the record, field hockey would be the least of my concerns were I to turn into a vampire for real. I'd be thinking bigger picture: like the fact that the whole "sleeping all day, hunting humans all night" gig might be a deal breaker at all the colleges I'm planning to apply to.

Magnus hocks another loogie on the sidewalk. Ew.

"Uh, do you mind the whole spitting thing?" I ask, backing up to put distance between me and his spray zone. "It's really grossing me out."

He looks up. "I'm trying to remove all traces of your blood from my mouth. You weren't tested first. Who knows what kind of diseases you could be carrying?"

Of all the . . . Gah! This guy is pissing me off big time. It's not like I freaking asked him to start munching on my jugular. It'd serve him right if I did have some weird communicable disease.

Rayne rolls her eyes. "Puh-leeze. Sunny's pure as the driven snow, Mag. Total Virgin with a capital V. So unless she has some hidden heroin addiction she hasn't told me about, I think you're clear. And," she adds with a smirk, "I'm pretty sure she's not a smackhead. After all, she doesn't exactly have that waiflike heroin chic thing going on, now does she?"

"Oh, thanks a lot, Rayne." Now we need to bring up the circumference of my hips as well? This night is getting better and better.

"Right," Magnus says. "No diseases. Well, at least that's something. But still. An unauthorized bite! Do you know how badly Lucifent is going to kill—er, kick my arse? I mean in this day and age no one turns someone into a vampire against their will. It's simply not kosher and an absolute lawsuit waiting to happen."

"I can sue you? Cool." I rummage around in my purse for a pen, wanting to write this down. "Under what? Medical malpractice? Assault with a deadly fang?" I look up. "How much you think the courts would award me for that?"

Rayne frowns. "Sunny, stop being a bitch. Can't you see poor Magnus is freaking out here?"

"*I* need to stop being a bitch? For *Magnus's* sake?" I stare at her, unbelieving. "Uh, hello? He's the guy who walked up and bit me for absolutely no reason whatsoever."

"I had a reason," Magnus remarks, more than a bit sulkily. "I just thought you were Rayne. A bloody bad case of mistaken identity, that was."

"Look guys," I continue. "I don't know what kind of sick little games you Goth kids like to play, and to tell you the truth, I don't think I want to know. So run along and hang out in graveyards, wish you were dead, whatever floats your little Gothic boat. But I am so out of here." I turn to my sister. "Rayne, find your own way home. I'm no longer in the mood to get down and dirty on the dance floor."

I turn and hightail it for the car. But Rayne comes up behind me and grabs me by the shoulder, whirling me around. Her eyes are wide and fearful and her powdered face is even whiter than normal. (And that's saying something!)

"Sunny, listen to me," she cries. "This isn't a game. Magnus is a vampire. And if he's bitten you, then you're going to become a vampire, too. You've got to take this seriously."

I roll my eyes. "Rayne, sweetie. My dearly deluded twin. I know this may come as a great shock to you, but there are no such things as vampires."

"I used to think that, too. But there are. And Magnus is definitely one of them," Rayne insists. "Mag, show her."

I huff and grudgingly turn around. This oughta be good. "Yeah, Mag, show me."

Magnus lets out a deep, overexaggerated sigh. As if he's weary of the world demanding he prove his creature-of-the-night shtick. I'm sure he gets it a lot.

"Fine," he grumbles, reaching into his bag for a pocketknife. "Do you want to do the honors?" he asks, flicking the blade open and offering it to me.

"I think I've been honored enough for one day, dude."

"I'll do it. I'll do it," Rayne butts in excitedly.

"What exactly are we doing?" I ask, as Magnus hands the knife over to my eager twin.

"Stabbing him, of course," Rayne says matter-of-factly.

Of course.

As Magnus lifts his shirt to expose his stomach (and his washboard abs, I can't help but notice) I wonder how they've set up this trick. Retractable blade? Blood packet embedded in the tip?

"You know what? I think I'd like to do it after all," I announce. This way I can better figure it out. Then I can denounce them and get on with my night.

Rayne shrugs and hands me the knife. I run my fingertip lightly over the blade. Ouch! A small bubble of blood bursts from the cut. It really is sharp. Hmm.

I hear a soft moan and look up. Magnus is staring at my finger as if I'm a gourmet dessert and he's a *Survivor* castaway who's eaten nothing but bugs for the last month. I've never seen such lust in someone's eyes and it's kind of unnerving.

"Do you mind, um, wiping your finger?" he says in a breathy, panicked voice.

"Why, does it bug you?" I ask, waving the finger in question in the air. "Do you want to suck it or something?"

"Sunny, don't tease the vampire," Rayne scolds.

You know, I do have to admit, Magnus has got this vampire act down pat. I think I even see a little drool at the corner of his mouth as he stares, entranced by my bloodied finger, following it with his eyes as a dog would follow a treat.

"Okay, sorry," I say breezily. I slowly bring my finger to my mouth and make a great show of licking the blood away.

Magnus gasps and looks for a moment like he's going to pass out.

"Now that's just mean," Rayne rebukes. "Really, Sunny."

I laugh. They're so serious about all of this. "Okay, okay," I say. "The big bad bloody finger is gone. Let's get back to stabbing."

Magnus, seeming to recover somewhat, lifts up his shirt again. Wow, I wonder how many sit-ups he has to do to attain that kind of bod? Too bad he's such a loser. If he could get a personality transplant or something, he'd be the perfect catch.

I examine the knife again. How does it retract? I don't feel any springs . . .

"Just hurry up and do it," he says. "We don't have all night."

"Right. Wouldn't want you to get caught in the morning sun and get all dusted and stuff," I say with a snort. "Fine. Here we go." I pull the knife back, then jam it into his stomach as hard as I can.

"Agh!" He screams in pain and buckles over, the knife still sticking out of his abdomen, dark blood seeping from the wound.

"Uh, um . . ." Wow. That looks really real. How'd they get all that blood to come out of the knife? And how does the blade stick in his stomach like that, if it's retractable?

And uh, why is he acting like it really, really hurts for that matter?

"Uh . . ."

I glance over at Rayne, who's watching the scene with cool eyes. What the hell is going on here?

I look back at Magnus. He's fallen to his knees, clutching his stomach, an expression of agony on his face. His hands are almost purple with blood and he's still moaning in pain.

Fear clutches my heart with an icy grip. Did I screw up? Did the blade not retract when it was supposed to?

Did I really just stab a guy in the stomach?

"Are you okay?" I ask worriedly. Dumb question, really. The puddle of blood kind of gives it away.

In response, Magnus falls from his knees to the pavement—in the fetal position, clutching his stomach.

Panicking, I scramble down to my knees and try to turn him over so I can examine the wound. It's positively gushing blood. I'd be totally grossed out if I weren't so scared.

"Oh my God, I think he's really hurt," I shriek, turning to locate my twin. "Rayne! Call 911. He needs an ambulance!"

I turn back to Magnus, searching for a way to stop the bleeding. Should I take the knife out or leave it in? My breath comes in short gasps, along with choking sobs as my life flashes before my eyes.

I, Sunshine McDonald, have just stabbed someone in the stomach. And now he could die. And I'll be responsible. They're going to charge me with murder. Toss me in jail and throw away the key. Do they have the death penalty in New Hampshire? Oh my God. Why did I volunteer to take the knife? What possessed me to stab a deluded teenager who thinks he's a vampire in the stomach? *Stupid, Sunny. Truly stupid.*

Tears streak down my cheeks as I crouch beside Magnus. "Are you okay?" I ask, sobbing. "Can you hear me?" I lean in closer. "Do you see any white light? If so, I'm begging you, do not walk into it. I've got so much—er . . . I mean *you've* got so much to live for."

"Didn't I tell you?" Suddenly Magnus opens his eyes, sits up, and starts laughing hysterically. "I'm already dead!"

I watch in horror as he grabs the knife and easily slides it out of the wound. Then, incredibly, the gash starts shrinking, before my very eyes. I watch, mesmerized, as an invisible thread seems to sew the skin back together until nothing but a tiny scar remains.

"Oh my God! You're really a . . ." I leap back, horrified. "Oh my God!"

"Sorry," he says, chuckling. "Had to get you back for that bloody finger thing."

I whirl around to find Rayne. She's also cracking up so hard she's practically crying. Like this is the funniest thing she's seen since *Zombieland.*

"Oh man!" She laughs. "You should have seen your face, Sunny. That was classic!"

I stare at her, then at Magnus. I cannot believe this. I simply cannot believe this. "You . . . I mean . . . I thought . . ." Wow, I've completely lost my ability to talk. I may have to spend the rest of my life as a mute. Walk around with a tablet, writing down everything I used to be able to say, before I was struck dumb by a vampire pulling a knife from his own stomach.

"Sorry," Magnus says, scrambling to his feet. He puts the bloodied knife back into his bag without wiping it. "But you said you wanted proof."

I feel like I'm going to throw up. "So you're really . . ."

". . . a vampire?" he asks, raising an eyebrow. "Yes."

"And that means . . ." My stomach is churning at this point. Like I'm on a storm-tossed ship. Or the Superman ride at Six Flags.

". . . my bite has infected you." He sighs, serious again. "Unfortunately, also yes."

I lean over and throw up.

"Ew." Rayne leaps back to avoid my puke. "Sunny, that's nasty."

"Oh, I'm *so sorry* to have offended you," I say in my most sarcastic tone, wiping my mouth with my sleeve. "I guess I'm not taking the fact that I've been accidentally turned into a freaking vampire as well as you hoped?"

Rayne shrugs. "I totally get it, Sun. Still doesn't mean I enjoy getting splattered by your vomit."

Rolling my eyes, I turn back to Magnus. "So wait a sec," I say. "I'm confused. I always thought that in order to become a vampire, you have to drink the blood of a vampire. All you did was bite me."

"Damn Hollywood and its barbaric misconceptions," Magnus says wearily. He reaches into his mouth and pulls something out. He holds it up to me. It's a porcelain fang, half-filled with red liquid. "Through our postmortem surveys, we've learned that most people find the whole 'drinking blood from their sponsor' part a bit on the disturbing side. Plus," he adds, "while our skin is remarkably good at healing, slicing open one's wrist to enable the apprentice to drink can possibly leave scars. And no one wants a scarred vampire."

He holds out the tooth so I can examine it closer. "So Vamps-R-Us.com created these implants a few years back. Bloody marvelous inventions, really. I just prick my finger, squeeze a few drops of blood into the implant, then inject it into the apprentice, at the same time drinking a bit of her own blood to seal the bond." He shrugs. "We could use a syringe to deliver the injection, of course; probably would be easier and more sanitary, actually. But studies have also found that our apprentices enjoy the old-school romanticism of being bitten on the neck."

I can't decide whether I'm more impressed that there are Internet sites that sell blood-injecting gizmos or that these guys ask their victims to fill out feedback forms.

Magnus reaches into his bag and pulls out a small silver case. "Vamps-R-Us.com is the leading manufacturer of vampire supplies. Blood bags, fang sharpeners, body armor, that kind of thing." He opens the case and inserts the fake fang into its velvet lining.

Man, you really *can* buy anything on the Web.

"Okay, gotcha," I say. "But let me ask you this. If I've been turned into a vampire, how come I don't feel like one?"

"How do you know what being a vampire feels like?" Rayne butts in with, unfortunately, a good point.

"Well, I'm not lusting after your blood for one thing," I say slowly. "And, um," I reach under my shirt and pull out my cross necklace. Magnus leaps away. "And the cross doesn't turn me off or burn me or anything." I think for a moment. "And I definitely could go for a slice of cheese and garlic pizza for breakfast as soon as the sun comes out."

Actually the last thing does sound kind of yucky, but I'm not going to admit that to them.

"Could you . . . please . . . put that away?" Magnus asks, gasping for breath.

"So I'm wondering," I say, purposely ignoring him and waving my cross around, watching him dance from side to side to avoid it. "How do we fix this?" I ask.

"F-fix?"

"Yeah. Like stop the transformation. Reverse it. There's gotta be a way to stop it. Right? Maybe suck the blood from the wound like you'd do for a rattlesnake bite?"

I realize Magnus is trying to say something but can't seem to form the words. Oh yeah, the cross. I slip it under my tank. The metal seems a bit warm against my skin, but not uncomfortable. Still, not such a good sign.

"Thank you." Magnus gasps. "Now as I was trying to say, there's no way to reverse it."

"Wrong answer." I reach for my cross.

"Wait!" he cries.

I stop, hand at my throat.

"There . . . might be a way. I'm not sure. I don't know. But Lucifent might."

"Who's this Lucifent guy?"

"My boss. The coven leader. He's a three-thousand-year-old vampire. If anyone knows, he will."

I nod. "Okay. Let's go talk to him."

"We can't. Well, not this second anyway. He's at dinner."

"Yeah, but this is an emergency. Can't we just go hit the restaurant he's at and . . . Oh." I swallow hard. "That kind of dinner?"

Magnus nods.

"Ew."

"Sunny, try to keep an open mind here," Rayne interjects. "Different people have different customs and to ridicule them—"

"So when's he going to be done with his, um, dinner?"

Magnus thinks. "I can call his secretary and see. Maybe he'll have had a cancellation for tomorrow evening, or something. Why don't you meet me in St. Patrick's Cemetery tomorrow at 8 P.M.? I'll be waiting by the big tombstone in the center."

"Tomorrow?" I exclaim. "But that's, like, twenty-four hours from now. I've got school tomorrow."

"So go." Magnus shrugs.

"But won't the sun, like, fry me or something?"

"Look," he says with an exasperated sigh. As if I'm the one inconveniencing him. Jeez. "It takes seven days to complete the transformation into a vampire. So you should be fine. Sun shouldn't bother you too much the first twenty-four hours. Though I would suggest slathering on a little sunscreen, just in case."

Right. Sunscreen and school. This is going to be fun. Not.

FIVE

Boys That Bite: The Blog

You'd think after this drama and unfortunate circumstance, we'd leave Club Fang immediately. But no! When we go back into the club, so Rayne can grab her coat, she insists on doing the Safety Dance before she leaves, saying it's her favorite eighties song in the whole wide world and it'd be cruel and unusual punishment for me to drag her away now. Sure, it's easy for her to shimmy and shake without a care on the dance floor, seeing as she's not the one slowly morphing into a creature of the night. I mean, selfish much?

I'm silent most of the way home, speaking up only to mention that Rayne's selecting the vampire hit "Bela Lugosi's Dead" on her iPod could be viewed as a tad insensitive, given the circumstances. Of course, she points out that technically Bela was only an actor who played Dracula, not a real vampire. As if that should make me feel better as the chorus chants, "Undead, undead, undead, undead."

When I first get home, I want nothing more than to crawl into my bed and sleep. But my heavy feather duvet isn't as comforting as I'd imagined it'd be. I'm wide awake, almost as if I'm hopped up on caffeine. Which is weird, seeing as I didn't even get to drink that Red Bull Rayne was supposed to bring me.

Since I can't sleep, and I have a billion questions buzzing through my brain, I decide my best bet is to go bug Rayne. I push her door open a crack to see if she's sleeping. But she's at her computer, typing furiously, and looking very pissed off. I shake my head. Man, she can be such a freak. I don't know in what Twilight Zone parallel universe we became sisters.

I knock on her door and she calls for me to come in, not looking away from her computer screen. I enter the room and close the door behind me. Luckily, Mom's out at some save-the-planet benefit dinner, so there's no one to overhear us. I'm pretty sure anyone eavesdropping on the convo I plan to have would start speed-dialing the Betty Ford Clinic before you could say *no-I'm-not-on-drugs-I'm-really-an-undead-creature-of-the-night*.

I sit on her bed, marveling how, only hours before, we were joking about what I should wear to Club Fang. If I'd known what repercussions choosing the *Bite Me* tank would have, I'd have definitely swallowed back my good taste and gone with the fetish outfit instead, sweat-inducing vinyl be damned.

After a few more mouse clicks, Rayne turns from her computer and comes to join me on the bed. She's wearing a pair of plaid flannel pajamas and has washed the black makeup from her eyes. With the exception of her tongue piercing, she looks almost normal.

"This sucks," she announces, crossing her legs Indian style.

"You think?" I raise an eyebrow. "'Cause I was totally psyched about the whole thing."

"Not for you, you tool, for me. I've waited freaking years for this night. I've researched, networked, been on waiting lists, the works. And now it's all for nothing."

"What are you talking about?" I know she's speaking English, but nothing she says is making any sense. "Researched and networked for what?"

"To become a vampire, of course."

Of course.

"Why on earth would you want to be a vampire?"

Rayne rolls her eyes, as if to imply I'm the stupidest person on the planet. "Are you kidding me?" she asks incredulously. "Why would

I want immortal life? Why would I want riches beyond my wildest imagination? Why would I want ultimate power over mere mortals? You should be asking why anyone on earth *wouldn't* want to be a vampire."

"Yeah, but," I'm grasping at straws here, "don't you want to finish high school? Go to college? Get married, have a life?"

"No."

"No?"

"No way. How boring is that? To conform to society's rigid rules? To be weak and powerless and beaten down and forced to live someone else's idea of a fulfilling life, only to die, sick and alone, and have your grandchildren fight over your meager life's savings? Bleh. No thanks. Give me an all-powerful, immortal existence any day of the week."

Okay, when she puts it that way . . .

"But . . . you have to kill people."

Rayne sighs exasperatedly. "Yeah. So says Hollywood. In real life, Sun, it's a lot less barbaric."

"Oh?"

"Sure. Each vampire is given a stable of donors. People who are willing and able to give a portion of their blood each day so the vampire can survive. Don't worry, they're well paid for their services, and they can sever their contract at any time, by giving thirty days' notice. And of course, they're completely screened and tested for communicable diseases, drugs, that sort of thing, before being assigned." Rayne shakes her head. "No one kills people like in the movies."

"Okay, fine. But what about the sun thing? I can't go out in the daylight, right?"

Rayne examines her powder-white skin. "Yeah. I'd never have to worry about accidentally tanning. Wonderful."

She's thought of everything, hasn't she?

"What about a boyfriend? You'd never get a boyfriend. You'd never get married. Unless, I guess, you had a night wedding . . ."

"I'd get something better. When someone is selected to become a vampire, he or she is assigned a sponsor," Rayne explains. "The person who has agreed to donate a drop of his or her own blood to aid in your transformation. Afterward, you'll share a blood link with that person forever. He'll be your soul mate. Well, technically your blood mate, as you sort of have to give up that whole soul thing, when you turn." She pauses, staring into the distance, looking a little sad. "Magnus was supposed to be my blood mate. Now he's yours."

Aha! So that's why she's so upset. She thinks I stole her boyfriend. Just goes to show, even in the crazy supernatural world, at the end of the day it all comes down to the green-eyed monster we call jealousy.

"Dude, you can have him," I say, holding my palms out. "I want nothing to do with that jerk."

Rayne turns back to look at me. "You don't understand," she says, her eyes weepy and downcast. "He's turned you. So you're connected. Forever. Whether you like it or not."

"That would be a definite *not*."

"You know, you don't have any clue what a priceless gift you've been given," Rayne says, her voice taking on an irritated edge. "Immortality. The perfect existence. The hottest blood mate to walk the earth. And you're probably more concerned about whether someone's going to ask you to the prom."

"Well, it is this Saturday . . ."

"Man, I can't believe how much this sucks." Rayne angrily swipes her face with her sleeve. Is she crying? Oh man. She *is* crying. She's so totally whacked.

"Look, Rayne," I say, for some inexplicable reason actually feeling the tiniest bit bad for her, "once we get this whole thing reversed, I'm sure you and Magnus can continue your sick and twisted relationship. You can become a vampire and live Gothily ever after."

"I wish." Rayne sniffs. "But no. Even if the process can be reversed, I'll have to start all over. Get back on the waiting list. Find a new sponsor."

"Why?"

"The law says vampires are allowed to turn only one person in their lifetime. Basically so there's never a blood shortage like the Red Cross always seems to have," she explains. "After they turn the person, they're linked to them forever. Blood mates, until one of them dies."

"Er, how can you die if you have eternal life?"

"Oh, plenty of ways. Burned by sunlight. Caught in a fire. Stabbed with a wooden stake through the heart, you know. All the tragic things that happen in the movies."

Okay, let's take note here: blood-drinking movie clichés, wrong. Methods of killing a vampire, should one be in the position to do so, spot on.

Which brings me to the $64,000 question.

"How do you know all this stuff?"

Rayne shrugs. "Like I said. I've studied. Three months ago, when I started my training, I actually created a blog to catalog my research." She gestures to her computer. "You should probably check it out. I mean, at the very least it'll outline what you need to know about your transformation. It's kind of bad how unprepared you are. Everyone else that gets turned goes through an extensive three-month certification program."

She's got her Vampire Certificate? Is it suitable for framing?

"I can't believe how organized this whole thing is," I marvel.

"It's a multibillion-dollar operation," Rayne says. "And very high tech." She jumps off the bed and heads over to her computer, clicking on the monitor. "C'mere."

I come behind her and peer at the screen she's brought up. Sure enough, it's some kind of blog, all Gothed out in black and red. I guess the pastel template on Blogspot.com wouldn't really fly for a vampire site.

"Boys That Bite?" I ask, reading the heading.

Rayne giggles. "Yeah, I came up with that name. Funny, huh?"

"I guess." Vampire humor. Hardy har har.

Rayne moves out of her chair and gestures for me to sit down. "Here. Take your time and read. I think you'll learn a lot."

As I plop down in the seat, she walks over to her bookcase and pulls out a heavy hardcover text. "I also have the Vampire 101 textbook you can read. Thank goodness I hadn't returned it to the library yet." She sets the book down on the desk. "You don't, um, mind picking up the late fees, do you?"

I look down at the massive tome. It's got weird carvings on the front and has to be like three thousand pages. "Wow. This vampire thing has a lot of homework involved, doesn't it?"

"Like I said, it's a three-month course. There's a lot to learn. You're totally going to have to cram at this point."

As if I didn't have enough to worry about, with finals next week. I flip through the book. Darn, not a lot of pictures either.

"So is this a correspondence course, or do you have to actually attend classes?"

"Classes. After all, you can't learn the proper way to administer a safe and sterile blood transfusion over the Internet."

"Right." I shake my head, unable to believe I've somehow gotten mixed up in this freak show. I turn back to the blog and scroll down to the first entry.

> My name is Rayne McDonald. I'm 16 years old and so ready for eternal life. As suggested by my instructor, I've created this blog to chronicle my transformation. Hope you enjoy reading it!

Oh, I will. Believe me.

SIX

Jake Wilder:
Sex God and . . . Prom Date?

After reading some of Rayne's crazy "Boys That Bite" blog and checking out a few links in the vampire Web ring (yes, there really is a vampire Web ring), the bright screen starts giving me a headache. So I say good night to my twin and retreat to the dark safety of my bedroom where I curl up under my duvet and try to go to sleep.

But I can't. I'm too wired with fear and confusion and God knows what else. Plus the spot where Magnus bit me itches like crazy. So I toss and turn and wonder what I'm going to do.

What if the transformation can't be reversed? What if in seven days I, Sunshine McDonald, become a vampire forever? That means no finals. No prom. No sunny trip to the Bahamas with my friends this summer. No college. I'll have to enroll in night school or something. Maybe the vampires have their own university; it does seem like they're pretty organized. I wonder what the SAT requirements are for something like that.

This sucks. Pardon the pun, but it does. I have this whole life ahead of me and now I may not be able to live it, all 'cause of a case of mistaken identity. Damn Rayne and her stupid blog and her stupid idea that becoming undead is the stupid secret to life everlasting. What was she thinking? And why did she have to drag me into it all?

I finally manage to fall asleep, just as the sun peeks over the horizon. In what seems like only five minutes later, my alarm blares me awake with the sounds of the eighties. This morning's DJ chose to wake me with Michael Jackson's "Thriller."

How appropriate.

Groggily, I stumble out of bed and into the shower. It's freezing in the house and the hot water feels good streaming down my body. I try to decide if I feel any different. If I have any urges to suck someone's blood. But no, not yet, at least, thank goodness. Willing donor or not, I'd like to hold off on that part as long as possible, thank you very much. Maybe I could become an anorexic vampire? I wonder if that'd help me shed a few pounds as an added bonus?

I get out of the shower and open the medicine cabinet. A dizzying array of sunscreens stares back at me. From tropical coconut tanning lotions to the no-possible-UV-ray-will-come-within-fifty-yards-of-your-skin-for-three-weeks variety. Damn me for forgetting to ask Magnus the proper SPF for school.

In the end, I decide to go for the middle-of-the-road 15 stuff. Who knows, maybe I'll get a tan out of the deal. Heh. I'd be the first vampire to look like I'd cruised the Caribbean.

After applying sunscreen, I realize I'll also need to address the bruised purple bite mark on my neck. If anyone sees that they're going to think it's a hickey and I am so not ready to get teased about my neck-munching secret lover, on top of everything else. I guess I could tell everyone I burned my neck with the curling iron, like Mary Markson does when Nick covers her neck with love bites, but no one believes her either.

I rummage through my closet, realizing I own very little clothing designed to cover up my neck. Most likely due to the fact that, before this morning, I had no reason to keep it in hiding. Finally, in the back of my closet, I find an old black turtleneck. I think it belongs to Rayne, actually, but it'll do. Of course everyone's going to think

I'm a freak of nature, what with wearing a turtleneck in May. But what can I do? I have become a teenage vampire fashion victim. Ugh.

As long as no one mistakes me for a Goth . . .

SCHOOL IS OKAY, though I'm so freaking tired, it's hard to pay attention. And I seem to have become a magnet for teacher questions. I go rest my eyes for one teensy second and suddenly I'm harassed to start calculating pi or something. (Which I can't even do on a full night of sleep when I'm not transforming into a vampire.)

I eat lunch with a few girls from field hockey, picking listlessly at my salad as I halfheartedly listen to them recount last week's game. My other teammates are so wrapped up in their tales of opposing goalkeeper Jennifer Jack spraining her ankle in the first five minutes of the game that they don't notice I'm barely listening. Which is fine by me. The last thing I need to do is draw attention to myself in my current state.

Luckily, my best friend Audrey is away this week at Disney World with her parents. The girl is so scarily perceptive that she'd notice something was wrong immediately. At the same time, she'd never believe the whole vampire thing and would think I had really lost it. So while I'd love to have some moral support (Rayne so doesn't count!) it's probably better off I don't freak out my friends.

I consider skipping drama practice after school, but Magnus has informed me he won't be up and about till almost eight P.M., so I figure I might as well go and kill time before my big meeting with the head vamp. Besides, this way I can have some quality Jake Wilder spyage time. Bound to make anyone feel better.

Ah, Jake Wilder. How do I even explain the greatness that is Jake Wilder? It's like he doesn't belong in a normal, everyday high school. Like, he should have been born centuries earlier, in Roman times or something—driving a flaming chariot with six white horses foaming at the mouth. He looks like a Greek god, with his six-foot-one stance, slender but muscular body, and high cheekbones. Well, a Greek god or Chad Michael Murray, take your pick. He has short

blond hair and the deepest, darkest brown eyes known to mankind.
I once overheard some girls calling him Bedroom Eyes.

I'd love to see those bedroom eyes actually in a bedroom. Preferably my bedroom. In fact, if I could have me some of that, I'd so re-
tire my Sunny the Innocent status, quicker than you can say "off like
a prom dress."

Problem is, he has no idea I even exist. None whatsoever.

I blame Heather Miller.

You see, Jake Wilder is the leading man, the sexy Conrad Birdie,
in our class production of *Bye Bye Birdie* this year. And Heather is,
of course, playing Kim. No surprise there. No matter what play we
do, Heather nabs the starring role. *Little Shop of Horrors*? She's Audrey. *Oklahoma*? She's Laurey. In second grade we performed *The
Tortoise and the Hare* and Jake got the tortoise and she was the hare.
She's Drama Queen with a capital DQ. Beautiful. Blond. Busty. Even
brainy, if you can believe that. You'd at least hope she'd be an air-
head, but no. No, she's also president of the Honor Society, which is
so not fair to the rest of us mere mortals.

This year, I didn't even get awarded a small part in the play. Not
even some one-line Conrad Birdie groupie role. Nada. Instead, I'm
Heather Miller's understudy. Meaning I have to do all the work,
memorize all the lines, and only if Miss Perfect-Attendance-Award
is sick do I get to take center stage.

Which is actually not as terrible as it sounds, seeing as I have
rather a bad case of stage fright and if I were to be suddenly thrust
into the starring role, I'm not positive I could handle it.

For me, drama is all about permission to stare at Jake Wilder for
hours on end without anyone thinking me Stalker Girl.

So with that in mind, I slip into the second-to-last row of the
school auditorium and pull out my sketchpad. Back here, no one can
see what I'm drawing. I get so much crap for being an artist you
wouldn't believe it. No respect at all.

"Sunshine McDonald? Is that you?"

I look up from my drawing, a rather brilliant sketch of Jake Wilder
if I do say so myself. The drama teacher, Mr. Teifert, is down by the
stage and motioning for me to join him.

O-kay. That's weird. I wasn't convinced he even knew my name, never mind that he'd ever need to get my attention. I slip my sketchbook back into my book bag and trudge to the front of the auditorium, a little wary.

"Sunshine. Thank goodness you're here," Mr. Teifert says, rubbing a hand through his wild black curly hair. He's short and squat and looks like that guy from *Animal House*. "Heather's sick. We need you to stand in for her at practice today."

I stare at him, at first not quite comprehending. The queen has lost her attendance throne? And they need me to step in? Wow. I wasn't expecting that to happen. Especially not today, when I have so much else on my mind.

"O-kay," I say, swallowing down the bubble of stage fright that immediately forms in my stomach and starts traveling up my esophagus. "What scene are we working on?"

"The one where Birdie kisses Kim," says a deep, luscious man-voice behind me.

I whirl around and almost pass out when I realize the delectable Jake Wilder is standing there, in the flesh, not two feet away, actually speaking to me. And using the word *kiss* in a sentence. A sentence addressed to me.

"Kisses Kim?" I manage to speak in my Minnie Mouse voice. *Nice, Sunny.* So very attractive and appealing.

"Don't look so horrified," Mr. Teifert says with a laugh.

I look horrified because I just sounded like a moron, not because of the proposition of kissing Jake Wilder. That's not horror. That's romance. A fantasy dream come true. But I can't exactly explain that, now can I?

"I'm fine. Let's do it," I say, forcing my voice to go back to normal. I hop up onto the stage, my legs literally trembling in a way I hope isn't noticeable. Jake pops up a moment later and now stands facing me.

"Okay, now the scene is, Conrad and Kim are in rehearsals for *The Ed Sullivan Show*. Sunny, you recite your Conrad Birdie fan club speech, then Jake, you're bored with this and want to go party, so you interrupt, yada yada yada, then kiss her. Ronald," Mr. Teifert looks over at the tall skinny boy who's playing Kim's boyfriend, Hugo. "You're on the balcony, glaring at Birdie, really jealous like. After the kiss, Sunny, you collapse in a faint."

Fainting after Jake Wilder's kiss? Shouldn't be too tough to make that look realistic!

Mr. Teifert claps his hands. "Got it? Then places, everyone."

And so it goes. I pledge my devotion to Conrad Birdie a.k.a. Jake Wilder. And he interrupts, then scoops me in his arms and kisses me, hard on the mouth.

Time seems to stop.

I let out an unwilling gasp as he presses his firm lips against mine. I never, ever thought I'd get a chance to feel what it'd be like for Jake Wilder to kiss me. And it feels better than I could have imagined in my wildest of dreams.

He pauses for a moment, as if surprised about something, then takes advantage of my parted mouth and enters it with his tongue. Aghh! What an incredible feeling. I feel like I'm going to explode, it feels so good. Jake Wilder is kissing me. French-kissing me. Is he even supposed to be French-kissing me for the play? I thought . . . Oh, who cares if he's supposed to or not. He is, that's all that matters.

"Hey, guys, okay, already. You're supposed to faint, Sunny." Mr. Teifert's voice sounds a million miles away.

Jake pulls away, reluctantly, it seems. Our faces are inches apart still—I can feel his hot, minty breath in my face. Then he gives me a small grin and whispers, "I think we need more practice," so softly only I can hear. "Don't you?"

Then I faint. Or at least I fake fainting, though actually I feel like I could almost lose consciousness for real after what just happened. Jake Wilder, kissing me. Sure, it was just for the play, but somehow it felt like more than that. It felt like he enjoyed it.

I know I did.

Thank you, Heather, for being absent. Thank you, thank you, thank you. This makes every boring rehearsal, every wasted understudy hour, worth it.

And the best thing is, we have to do it all over again. Several times. Practice makes perfect, you know.

After the rehearsal is over, I climb down off the stage and head to the back, where I've left my book bag. My legs feel like Jell-O.

"Hey, Sunny!"

I turn around, bag in my hands at the voice. I force my mouth not to drop open in shock as I realize who's come up behind me.

"Hey, Jake," I say shyly, dropping my gaze. Gah, he's so cute. I can barely stand it. How can one guy be so gifted in the looks department? I mean, even Zac Efron's got nothing on Jake Wilder.

Jake runs a hand through his hair, for some reason appearing a little nervous. Weird. I should be the one who's shaking like a leaf here, not him.

"You were, um, great up there," he says, shuffling from foot to foot.

I beam at the compliment. I know it's uncool to be so psyched about it, but I can't help it. Jake Wilder has just said I was great. I, Sunshine McDonald, was great in the eyes of Jake Wilder.

"Thanks," I say in my most casual of tones. "You were great, too. I can see why you always get the lead."

He shrugs. "Yeah, I guess," he says, clearing his throat. I look at him curiously. He's not acting like his usual overconfident popular self at all. What's up with that? "But you, you were a goddess."

A goddess? What is that supposed to mean? I know I nailed the dance number, but I didn't think I was especially goddesslike doing it. I narrow my eyes, not quite sure if he's making fun of me. Maybe this is one of those cruel jokes that the popular kids always seem to play in the movies. Bet the football star he can't get Loser Nerd Girl to fall in love with him. Well, I'm sooo not falling for that.

"Uh-huh. Goddess. Right." I snort. "Yeah, I've always kind of thought of myself as a teenage Artemis, now that you mention it." I grab my coat. After all that's taken place in the last twenty-four hours, I am so not in the mood to be made fun of by the guy I'm stalking. "In fact, I've got some goddess-type duties to take care of now, so I'll, um, catch you around." I start to maneuver around him.

He steps in front of me. "Wait," he says.

I wait. My heart is pounding in my chest now. This is too weird.

"Um, I wanted to uh, ask you if . . ." He clears his throat again. Does he have a cold or something? "If you have a date for the prom, and if you don't do you want to go with me?" he blurts out, in one big run-on sentence.

I stare at him, doing everything in my power not to gape with an open mouth. Did he just say what I thought he said? Did he just . . . no, I must have heard wrong.

"Wh-what?" I ask, squeaky Minnie Mouse voice back with a vengeance.

He blushes a deep red. Jake Wilder. Blushing. Have we entered a parallel universe here? I remind myself this could all be some cruel prank. That I may get to the prom and the Populars will pull a Carrie and pour pig's blood on me when I'm voted prom queen. And I won't even have the telekinetic power to burn down the school in vengeance.

But that's stupid. I may not be head cheerleader, but I'm certainly not Loser Nerd Girl either. I have tons of friends and play on the varsity field hockey team. So I highly doubt I'd be top of the list for the Populars to pick on.

Besides, Jake seems deadly serious.

"I just thought, if you weren't going with anyone, that you might, uh, want to go with, um, me," he continues, stammering. "I mean, if you wanted to. I understand if you don't. Obviously you've probably got like three million guys asking you."

I nearly fall backward into a dead faint for real this time. As it is, I'm not quite sure my heart is still beating.

Jake Wilder has just asked me to the prom. Jake Wilder!

"Uh, yeah. Sure. That's cool," I say with a shrug, awarding myself major brownie points for not jumping up and down and doing cartwheels down the auditorium aisle. "Why not?"

He breaks out into his amazing smile, looking oh-so-relieved. "Great," he says. "Really great. Thank you. I'll um, see you around then."

"Uh, sure. Okay," I say at a loss for more intellectual conversation. *Real suave, Sunny.*

He smiles at me again—that infamous brilliant flash of Jake Wilder pearly whites—then turns and bolts out of the auditorium. I stare after him, confused as anything.

Jake Wilder has just asked me to the prom. And I said yes. Before today I would have bet anything that he didn't even know my name. Now I'm suddenly his prom date?

"Hey, Sunny, how you feeling?"

I turn around. Rayne's entered the auditorium.

"Rayne!" I cry. "You'll never guess! Jake Wilder asked me to the prom. Isn't that so amazing? I mean, Jake Wilder! Can you believe it? I'm freaking out here!"

Rayne smiles her favorite patronizing smile. "Ah, the Vampire Scent is already kicking in, huh?"

I screw up my face. "Vampire Scent?" What the hell is she talking about? And what does that have to do with Jake asking me to the prom?

"Yeah, you know. Like pheromones. Vampires give off a scent that drives mere mortals crazy with desire. They can't resist it. It's actually very useful when talking your way out of speeding tickets or scoring an aisle seat on an airplane. Though the old lady the next seat over talking to you about her grandchildren the whole flight can be an unfortunate side effect."

My heart sinks. To my toes.

So evidently Jake Wilder hasn't lusted after me for years and only now gotten up the courage to approach me.

"Damn." I kick the auditorium seat in frustration. "And here I thought he had some secret crush on me or something." I sigh. I knew it was too good to be true.

"Jeez, Sunny, don't act so disappointed. I mean, didn't you read about all this in my blog last night?"

Uh-oh.

"I, uh, didn't finish reading the whole thing. I mean, it was pretty long."

Rayne stares at me. "The pheromone thing is like the third entry down."

"Yeah, but"—I can feel my face heating up—"there were these links and . . ."

"Links?"

"Yeah, to really good stories about Spike and Angel . . ."

"So let me get this straight," Rayne says, crossing her arms over her chest, looking very unhappy. "Instead of catching up on the vital information you need to know about your impending vampire transformation, you instead chose to read *Buffy the Vampire Slayer* fanfic?"

Okay, when she puts it that way, it does seem like a bad decision on my part. But some of those stories were way juicy and . . .

"You know, you shouldn't have links on your Web site if you don't want people to click on them," I say in my defense.

Rayne sighs. Deeply. "You know, I really hope that Lucifent has a way to turn you back into a human. 'Cause you're going to totally suck as a vampire."

I start laughing. I can't help it. I'm going to *suck* as a vampire? Ha!

"What?" Rayne demands. Then she realizes her unintentional pun. "Oh." She tries to frown, but I can see the corners of her mouth turn up. "This is serious, Sunny."

"I know!" I cry, still howling with laughter. The whole situation's suddenly struck me as so absurd that I can't help it. "I'm going to be a SUCKY vampire!"

Rayne bursts into laughter. "Talk about a Freudian slip! I can't believe I said that."

"Yeah, well being a vampire really BITES," I add, bringing on a whole new wave of laughter. We're practically crying and rolling in the aisle, we're cracking up so bad.

"Who's a vampire?"

A deep voice cuts through our laughing and sobers us up immediately. We both whirl around to see Mr. Teifert, the drama teacher, peering at us curiously behind his black-rimmed glasses. I guess we were laughing so hard we didn't even hear him approach.

Rayne smiles wickedly. "Sunny's a vampire," she says. "Well, she's on her way to being one." Then she starts laughing again. I kick her in the ankle to make her shut up. While I'm about one hundred percent positive Mr. Teifert will take her claim with a grain of dramatic salt, I've still got to work with the guy on the school play. I don't want him to think I'm some stupid ditz. Then he'll never give me a good part and I'll be in understudy world forever.

Mr. Teifert raises a bushy eyebrow. "Is this true, Sunny?" he asks in a voice that seems far too serious for the discussion. What's his deal? "Are you a vampire?"

Thank goodness I wore a turtleneck to school so he can't see the bruised, hickeylike bite on my neck. Then he'd really be speed-dialing the guidance counselor.

"No, Mr. Teifert," I say, forcing myself to keep a straight face. "I am not a vampire. We were just messing around."

His serious expression relaxes and he smiles. "Good to know. Especially since we need you for this play. I've just learned Heather has come down with mono and won't be back. So from this point on, you'll be playing the part of Kim."

I restrain myself from giving a loud "Woot!" right then and there and try to look like I'm concerned for poor little Heather Miller. But to hell with her! I'm now the star of the school play. How cool is that? You know, besides the whole vampire thing being a downer, the rest of my life sure seems to be turning around in a big way, go figure.

"Thanks, Mr. Teifert. I won't let you down," I tell him enthusiastically.

"I know you won't," he says with a wink. "Just promise you won't go turning into a vampire on me. We've got a lot of rehearsals and most of them are during the day."

"I, uh, won't," I say, laughing my nervous donkey bray. As if what he's saying is the silliest thing in the entire universe.

He nods and smiles and waves good-bye as he exits the auditorium. Rayne and I exchange looks and then grab our book bags and hustle out.

"That was kinda weird," I say, as we head out into the parking lot toward our car.

"That was more than weird," Rayne agrees. She rummages around in her purse for the car keys. "You need to be careful around him."

"Oh, I'm sure he just overheard us and thought it'd be funny to join in on the joke."

Rayne pulls out the keys by her spider key chain. "I don't know, Sunny. I get creepy vibes off him." She unlocks the door and hops in the car.

I join her and take a seat in the passenger side. "What are you, a vibe reader now?" I ask skeptically. "He's a teacher. He thought he was being funny. You're paranoid."

Rayne shrugs as she puts the key in the ignition. "Okay, Sun, fine. I'm only trying to look out for you. There's a lot of vampire prejudice out there, you know." She pauses. "Actually you *don't* know," she adds, "since you'd rather read the sexploits of Spike and Buffy than research the subject."

"I actually preferred the stories about Angel." I giggle.

Rayne shakes her head. "See what I mean?" she says, sounding more than a little frustrated. "You refuse to take anything I say seriously. I don't know why I'm bothering to help you. I should just leave you to flounder and figure it all out yourself."

She looks seriously mad, so I decide to throw her a bone. After all, I need a ride to the cemetery to meet Magnus.

"I'm sorry, Rayne. I know you're trying to help me," I say in the most sincere voice I can muster. "It's just sometimes I use humor to defuse a tense, stressful situation." Wow, I sound like I should be on *Dr. Phil*. "I do appreciate you helping me, though. More than you know."

"Well, you are my little sister," Rayne hedges.

"Yes, by seven whole minutes. Making you way more older, wiser, and worldly than I could ever hope to be."

Rayne shoots me a look.

I laugh. "Sorry."

"Okay, let's get to the cemetery," she says. "And see if we can't get this vampire thing reversed."

"Sounds like a plan."

Rayne pulls out of the parking lot and takes a left. We're silent for a moment. Then . . .

"Do you think if I change back into a human, Jake will revoke his invitation to the prom?"

"Argh!"

"Sorry." I fold my hands in my lap and make like a good, silent, serious vampire-chick-to-be.

I do wonder, though.

SEVEN

The Coven—
a.k.a. Kick-Ass Underground Mansion

We pull into St. Patrick's Cemetery, driving between two dead-Catholic-guy statues flanking the entryway and down a narrow road lined by gravestones.

"You know, meeting with a vampire in a cemetery seems such a cliché," I note as I stare out the window, trying not to let the gravestones creep me out too much.

Rayne shrugs. "You'd know why if you read my blog, but hey, I'm sure that fanfic was real enthralling."

"Will you cut the 'if you read my blog' crap?" I beg, rolling my eyes at her. "I mean, honestly. I will read the thing. From start to finish, I promise you. But I couldn't exactly have read it between drama class and our trip to the cemetery, now could I?"

"Fine, fine." Rayne turns the steering wheel so the car pulls to the side of the road. She kills the engine. "We're here anyway."

I look around. We're surrounded by gravestones, far as the eye can see, which is, I might add, a tad disconcerting, given the circumstances.

"We're here? Where's Magnus?"

Bang! Bang!

A sudden knock on the window I'm peering out of makes me practically jump out of my skin. I see a head duck down and peek in.

Speak of the devil.

I roll down the window. "Jeez, Magnus," I grumble. "You practically gave me a heart attack. Sneak up much?"

He grins, not looking at all broken up about scaring me half to death. "We vampires are quite good at coming and going without being noticed."

Okay, add super stealth to the list of vampire powers. Probably used to help them hunt humans before they got that whole donor blood bank thing worked out. You know, they should become assassins for the government or something.

Hmm. I wonder if there were any vampires on SEAL Team 6 . . .

"Uh, are you ready to go, or would you prefer to sit in the car making mad faces a bit longer?" Magnus asks sweetly.

"Hold your fangs, will you?" I shoot him a dirty look as I push the car door open, feeling a slight rush of satisfaction when it hits him in the shin. (Even though it probably just slightly tickles, him being a vampire and all.)

I step out of the car and turn back to Rayne. "You coming?"

She frowns. "I'm not invited."

What? She's planning on leaving me alone with this irritating bloodsucker? Annoying twin sister or not, there's no freaking way I'm down with that.

"Yes, you are," I say. "You're totally invited. I'm inviting you. I'll have an invitation printed up, in fact, if that helps. Or how about an Evite?"

"No." That negative coming from the irritating bloodsucker in question, not my poor uninvited twin.

"No? What do you mean, no?" I say, turning to him, hands on my hips.

"Sunny, I can't come. Only vampires get to enter the sacred coven."

"Can't you make an exception? A special dispensation?" I put on my best pleading face. The one that always gets me the car on school nights when my mom thinks I should be studying. "Please? She's my twin sister. And after all, she knows way more about being a vampire than I do. She even has a blog about the whole thing." I turn back to Rayne, giving her a sneaky smile. "Which I totally plan on reading the second I get home."

"No." Magnus huffs loudly. As if I'm a pain in the neck to him and not the other way around. "She can't come. There are rules. Rules that have been in existence for thousands of years."

"Rules, schmules," I mutter halfheartedly. I know I've lost. I glance over to Rayne, who also looks slightly hurt and disappointed. I'm sure she was hoping to get a firsthand glimpse of this coven place. Like seeing Disney World or something to her vampire-obsessed eyes.

"Sorry, Rayne," I say, leaning into the car. "Thanks for the ride, though."

"Do you want me to wait for you?"

"Sur—"

"No." From Magnus, of course. He really likes that word. I can tell. He must have been such fun as a toddler. "I do not know how long we will be. I will take Sunshine home when we are done."

I raise an eyebrow. "Okay, fine. As long as it doesn't involve turning into a bat and flying home or something." Actually that might kinda rock, but I'm not admitting that to him.

"Uh, no. It'd be in a Jaguar XKR convertible if milady dost approve of that," he corrects, in a mocking voice.

Oh. "Uh, yeah. I guess that'd be okay," I say, though inside I'm doing the Snoopy dance. A ride in a Jaguar convertible? How cool is that? Way cooler than bat flying, IMO. And certainly better than our beat-up Volkswagen bug.

Cheered, I say good-bye to my disappointed twin and follow Magnus into the darkness. At first I'm a bit creeped out as we wander through the moonlit graveyard, but then I realize the place's only real-life monster is already on my team, so I'm probably pretty safe.

We come to a huge, ornate tomb in the center of the cemetery. I mean, this thing is big enough to walk in and has a door and every-thing. It totally dwarfs the rest of the cemetery and looks really out of place looming in the center of it.

I watch as Magnus stops at the tomb and produces a golden key from around his neck. I'd been so annoyed before that I hadn't to-tally checked him out. Not that I should bother, but loser or not, he is *such* good eye candy. Tonight he's got this total Euro look going on; he's wearing a leather jacket over a black Armani turtleneck that hugs his perfectly sculptured chest, and distressed, low-rise Diesel jeans that hug, well, you know, everything else. His shiny chestnut-colored, Orlando Bloom hair is pulled back with a black leather tie, definitely giving him the rebellious pirate look. In short, he looks De-lish with a capital D.

It really is too bad he's the bane of my existence and all.

Magnus inserts the key into the lock and the tomb's heavy mar-ble door creeks open on rusty hinges. We step inside and the musty smell immediately takes over my senses. I start to sneeze.

When I do, my vampire guide doesn't say *bless you*, and at first I contemplate berating him for his lack of manners. Then I realize it's probably too religious for a vampire to say and decide to cut him some slack this time. (Though he could have at least ventured a *Gesundheit*, IMO.)

The door closes behind us and for a moment we're blanketed by darkness. O-kay. Kind of freaky. I'm now standing in an actual tomb, in pitch darkness, with only a vampire to keep me company. Last week if you'd sworn on a stack of Bibles that I'd be okay with all of this, I wouldn't have believed you.

Magnus feels around for my hand and then, finding it, latches on and leads me into the darkness. And yes, regrettably, I must admit that his touch sends an unwilling chill up my spine.

Thanks a lot, body. Betray your owner much?

"Watch the stairs," he says as we step down. Are we going under-ground? Curiouser and curiouser, as Alice in Wonderland would say.

We descend. Step after step after step. How deep are we going? It feels like I'm walking down the Empire State Building or something.

They should install elevators in this place. What if they turned a handicapped person into a vampire? Talk about your discrimination lawsuit waiting to happen.

"You all right?" Magnus asks softly, his husky British accent cutting through the darkness.

"Yeah," I whisper back. "I'm good."

Okay, fine. I admit it. The situation is kind of intimate and I'm sort of turned on. I mean, no matter how annoying Magnus is, he's also indescribably hot. And having an indescribably hot guy holding my hand and leading me blindly through the darkness is sort of sexy in a very weird way.

Gah! I can't believe I just admitted that! When I'm done with this vampire nonsense, I've so got to get my head examined. After all, I do not think of Magnus in that way. I think of Jake Wilder, my prom date, in that way. Jake Wilder only. Not Magnus. Definitely not Magnus.

After half an eternity, we finally reach the end of the never-ending stairs and I can hear Magnus pressing some computerized buttons. Like a key code or something. This vampire place has major security.

A door slides silently open and we step over the threshold.

Into complete luxury.

I gasp as my eyes become accustomed to the dim light and I see what we've walked into. It's like a mansion. An underground mansion. With cathedral ceilings, floors made of marble, and the most elegant furnishings I've ever seen. I can see why they need Fort Knox–like security down here. It's a tomb raider's dream come true. Lara Croft would have a field day.

"Holy hot spot, Batman," I whisper.

Magnus grins. "Impressive, no? We vampires like our little creature comforts."

I scan the room, taking in the velvet antique couches and gold-accented lamps. The Da Vinci paintings and crystal chandeliers. This place is like Buckingham Palace. If not more luxurious.

"Guess you guys aren't putting any strain on the welfare system, at least."

"When you live thousands of years, your investments tend to mature and pay off nicely."

"Evidently." Rayne sure wasn't kidding when she said riches greater than your wildest imagination. Maybe this being a vampire thing isn't as bad as I thought. First, you have hot guys throwing themselves at you, then you have enough cash to buy every shoe Marc Jacobs ever made.

Pretty sweet. Too bad there's also the whole blood-drinking and no-going-out-in-the-sun side effects. Otherwise, I'd definitely have to reconsider this whole thing.

"Come on," Magnus says, interrupting my musings. "Lucifent is expecting us."

EIGHT

Lucifent—
King of Vamps and Major Cutie Pie

I follow Magnus across the empty hall, wondering where the other vampires are hiding. Or feeding. *Gulp.* The thought makes me walk faster to catch up to his long strides.

We head down a long corridor, flanked by dim lamps. Nothing in the place is particularly bright, I notice. Probably hard on the vamps' eyes.

At the end of the hall, we enter a lobby where a thin, blond woman sits behind a desk, filing her nails and looking bored. She looks like someone I know, but I can't seem to place her.

"Hi, Marcia," Magnus says, addressing her politely.

That's it! She looks like Marcia Brady from the *The Brady Bunch*. Heh.

Marcia looks up, her eyes widening in delight as they fall on Magnus. "Oh, Magnus!" she cries, her voice high and flirty and American. "It's sooo great to see you! It's been way too long, my darling."

Hmm. Guess this guy's not only hot stuff to us mortals. He's got vamp groupies as well. Go figure. I squash a brief pang of jealousy. Which is ridiculous. After all, blood mate or not, I so don't want to have anything to do with Magnus after we get this vampire thing sorted out. So if Marcia wants him, he's all hers, far as I'm concerned.

I tune back in to the conversation.

"It's lovely to see you as well, Marcia darling," Magnus says in his deep, baritone voice. "How have you been?"

The vampire secretary blushes furiously. Man, she's got it bad! Marcia, Marcia, Marcia! "Very well, thank you," she says and then giggles.

This is all making me feel like I want to hurl.

"Uh, hello?" I interject, to stave off the nauseated feeling. "I don't have all night."

Marcia shoots me an evil glare. "Who is this?" she asks, haughtily. "Another recruit? We *are* going bottom-of-the-barrel these days, aren't we?"

"Excuse me?" I say, raising an eyebrow. "Would you mind repeating that?" Vampire or no, I'm so not taking this bitch's attitude.

"Ladies, please," Magnus says, looking pained. "Marcia, we're here to speak with Lucifent. Is he ready to see us?"

Marcia shoots me one last glare, then sulkily presses an intercom button on her phone. "Your eight o'clock is here," she mutters.

"Send them in."

She nods her head toward the ornate mahogany door behind her. "He's all yours."

I follow Magnus as he opens the door and heads into the rear office, stopping only for a moment to stick my tongue out at Marcia. Childish, I know, but oh so satisfying.

The bee-yotch flips me the bird.

Lucifent's office turns out to be as deluxe as the rest of the underground coven. The only thing missing is windows. I'd hate the no-windows thing, were I to become a permanent vamp. Though the Picassos on the wall might make up for their absence somewhat. The floors are made of gleaming hardwood and a giant mahogany desk lies in the center of the room.

Behind the desk sits Haley Joel Osment, the little kid from that creepy *Sixth Sense* movie.

Okay, maybe it's not Haley Joel himself. But this kid looks a lot like him—has the whole blond hair, wide eyes thing going on. Definitely a cutie pie. Must be Lucifent's kid or something. I mean, who knows, maybe it's Take Your Son to Work Day on the vampire calendar.

"Hey you," I say, crouching down to smile at him. I love children. So sweet and innocent and full of life before age jades them into sullen, sarcastic brats who would sell their own mothers for a nickel bag of pot. "You're so cute. I bet your daddy is really proud of you. How old are you now?"

"Oh, about three thousand, give or take a hundred," the kid snarls, his happy baby face morphing into a very pissed-off look. "Magnus," he rages. "What is the meaning of this?"

Have you ever seen that cartoon *Family Guy* with that baby, Stewie, who talks like he's an adult and constantly tries to take over the world? That's sort of what this kid is reminding me of all of a sudden.

I glance over at Magnus, who looks angry and frightened and nervous all at the same time.

"I am very sorry, my lord," he says, bowing low to the kid. "She doesn't know."

O-kay then. I'm totally lost here. I really should have read that stupid blog.

Magnus rises from his reverential bow and turns to face me. "Sunny," he hisses in a tight voice. "This is Lord Lucifent, Master of the Blood Coven. High priest of the eastern vampire conglomerate of the United States of America."

I raise an eyebrow and glance over at the kid sitting behind the enormous desk. "Haley Joel Osment here is your fearless leader?" I start to laugh. I can't help it. It's just so funny to think of this little Dennis the Menace look-alike as the leader of the vampires. Soon I'm laughing so hard tears are falling down my cheeks. This is who everyone is scared of? The almighty Lucifent? I can barely resist the urge to go over and pinch the little rascal's cheeks.

"Can you please shut her up?" Lucifent demands in an adorable squeaky little-boy voice. Heh. He looks positively livid. So does Magnus for that matter.

"Sunny, listen to me," Magnus says in a snarly voice. A voice way more intimidating than little Lucifent's. "Unless you are happy with the idea of remaining a vampire for the rest of your life, I suggest you stop laughing this instant."

Oh. Okay, if you put it that way . . . I swallow back my giggles and adopt my most serious expression. "Sorry," I mutter.

"Now bow to Lucifent," Magnus hisses from the corner of his mouth. "And pay your respects to our lord."

Oh, jeez Louise! But I guess, whatever it takes, right? I drop a little curtsy, feeling somewhat ridiculous.

"Who is this ignorant woman, Magnus, and why have you brought her to me?" demands Lucifent. "I am appalled by this show of disrespect."

Magnus shuffles from foot to foot. "Well, you see, sir, there's been, a, um . . ."

"Case of mistaken identity," I state, figuring he needs some help spitting it out.

Magnus shoots me a tortured glare, not looking at all grateful for my assistance in explaining the situation. Wow, he seems really nervous. And he's usually so confident. Arrogant even. This Lucifent guy, cute kid or no, must be real powerful in vamp circles. He's like a mafia Godfather or something.

"What do you mean, case of mistaken identity?" Luficent questions in a tight voice.

"Well, th-this is Sunshine McDonald," Magnus says, gesturing to me. "And she has a, um, identical twin sister named Rayne."

"And I care about their family tree, why?"

Magnus swallows hard. "Her twin went through all the training. She was assigned to me as my blood mate."

"And?" Lucifent's face has gone quite pink. I think he's finally getting the gist of what Magnus is saying. For king of the vampires, he comes off a bit slow, if you ask me.

"And I bit the wrong twin," Magnus admits, dropping his eyes to the floor, his face blazing red with embarrassment.

"You what?" Lucifent cries, even angrier now than he was at my laughing. Magnus flinches as if he's been struck. "You bit the wrong person? Someone who didn't sign a release? Who didn't get tested first? Who didn't go through the training?" He slams a tiny fist against the desk and I stifle another giggle. I can't help it, he's just so darn cute. "How could you, Magnus? You worthless bag of bones! You're useless! Why, I should have left you to rot in that Moorish prison. I gave you eternal life. Riches beyond belief. Power beyond a mortal's imagination. And this is how you repay me?"

Magnus looks like he wants to crawl under the desk and die. I almost feel bad for him. I mean, hey, I don't like that he screwed this up as much as the next guy, probably more even, seeing as it directly affects me and my life. But still, we all make mistakes. No need for this verbal bashing. I wonder if vampires have unions. Magnus could so report this guy.

"Look, dude, it's really not Magnus's fault," I butt in, attempting to defuse some of Lucifent's rage. He definitely has major anger management issues he needs to deal with. "I mean, Rayne and I look exactly identical. Even our mom can't tell us apart."

"Shut up, human," Lucifent snarls. Evidently he didn't rise to king of the vampires on the basis of his charm alone.

"I am sorry, my lord," Magnus says, bowing low. "I know I made a terrible mistake. And I'm willing to pay the price."

"That's good of you. Because you *will* pay, for certain," Lucifent agrees with a self-satisfied smirk. As if he's enjoying Magnus's distress. Loser. "You will pay well."

"You know, assigning blame's all fine and good," I interrupt. "But we need to move on here and get more solution oriented. In six days, I'm told I'll be changing into a vampire, unless this whole thing is reversed. So I'm here to find out how the whole reversal thing works. Tell me that, and I'll be on my merry way."

"Anything for that to happen," mutters Lucifent. "Very well, then. I will tell you what you must do."

NINE

Bertha the Vampire Slayer

"So there *is* a way?" I ask, trying not to get too excited. "The transformation can be reversed?"

Lucifent nods. "Indeed," he says. "It's simple, really. All you have to do is—"

Suddenly, milliseconds before he can spit out the knowledge that will save me from eternal damnation, warning sirens start going off. They sound like something you'd hear on a *Star Trek* episode, moments before the *Enterprise* self-destructs. Or after Homer Simpson does something stupid yet again at the Springfield nuclear power plant.

"The perimeter has been breached," a robotic female voice announces, her tone oddly calm and computerized, given her message. "The Slayer has entered the building."

Lucifent utters a curse that no Haley Joel look-alike should ever utter, as it's quite disconcerting to anyone in the vicinity. Then he leaps from his desk, his eyes wide with fright.

"We've got to get to the safe room!" he cries, running toward the door.

"Wait," I call, struggling to be heard over the chaos. "What about turning me back to a human?"

"Later!" Magnus says, sounding just as panicked as he grabs my arm and hustles me toward the door. "We've got to hide from Bertha."

"Bertha?"

"Yes, Bertha," he repeats impatiently, dragging me out of the office. "Bertha the Vampire Slayer."

Hmm. Doesn't have the same ring to it as her TV counterpart. But okay, whatever.

I follow Magnus down the ornate hallway, quickly catching up to and then passing Lucifent, whose little legs can't take big strides like ours.

"Hurry, Master," Magnus begs.

"The Slayer has entered the sanctuary," the female computer announces, helpfully.

"Phew." Magnus stops running, allowing Lucifent to catch up. "She's on the other side of the compound. It'll take her at least ten minutes to get over here."

Lucifent nods. "We should still get to the—"

"The Slayer has entered the east hallway."

Hmm. Either the Slayer is superfast or there's been some kind of glitch in the Matrix. 'Cause suddenly, a woman drops down from a grate in the ceiling, effectively blocking our path.

She's dressed in black leather, but don't get the mistaken impression that she's at all attractive and sexy in it. Let's just say Bertha the Vampire Slayer has evidently been hitting the drive-through a few too many times on her dinner break. And leather sure isn't very forgiving when it comes to super sizing your French fries. Especially tight, low-rise leather pants that allow her stomach fat to ooze out her front. Add a greasy zit-face and the stringy blond hair and you'll get a good mental picture of what this "Slayer" looks like.

I think I prefer Sarah Michelle Gellar.

"Lucifent," she snarls, raising her wooden stake. Wow, she's got braces, too. I can't believe the mortal enemy of all vampires goes to an orthodontist. "Prepare to die."

Then, without further ado and quicker than my eyes can follow, Bertha back-handsprings down the hallway, flabby flesh flopping around like a fish out of water. For someone so anorexically challenged, the girl can really move!

Then she stakes Lucifent in the heart.

There's no dramatic fight scene. No exchange of clever banter. Just stakeage. And dustage. And no more Lucifentage.

I stare in horror as the one guy who knows how to stop me from changing into a vampire goes up in a pile of smoke.

But before I can mourn this fact properly, Big Bertha turns to us with an evil-looking metal-mouthed grin and I realize we may have bigger problems on our hands.

Crap.

"Run!" Magnus cries.

I don't need a second invitation.

We dash down the hall, Bertha hot on our heels. Magnus yanks me into a side chamber and slams the door shut, jamming a chair under the handle. My heart slams against my rib cage as I watch him run to the bookcase on the far side of the room and start scanning it with his eyes.

What is he doing?

I can hear Bertha pounding on the door.

"This is no time for book club!" I exclaim.

Magnus ignores me and pulls out a large, dusty tome from the shelf. Suddenly the bookshelf swings open, revealing a secret passageway leading off into the darkness.

Oh. My bad.

"Hurry," he hisses.

Behind us, Bertha's now hacking at the door with what sounds like an axe. Which is weird 'cause she didn't have an axe on her, just a stake. But I'm not going to ask questions.

I follow Magnus down into the dark tunnel and the bookshelf swings shut, blanketing us in complete darkness. The vampire grabs hold of my hand and starts dragging me down the stairs.

I can't see a thing and my heart is still pounding in my chest. I can't believe that slayer chick just dusted the three-thousand-year-old leader of the vampires in one fell swoop. Dusted him seconds before he could tell me how to avoid becoming a three-thousand-year-old vampire myself.

And now she's after us. Which means I may no longer need to know the 411 on stopping the transformation, mainly due to the fact that I'll be reduced to a pile of gray dust way before it takes place. Instamatic cremation.

Will my life ever be normal again?

TEN

Confessions of a Teenage Knight in Shining Armor

We reach what appears to be a steel door, illuminated by a single torch. Magnus pulls it open and grabs the torch. We enter a tiny room, about the size of an elevator, with no furniture. The vampire locates a keypad panel and presses in a code. The door clangs shut.

Letting out a sigh of relief, Magnus affixes his torch to a bracket on the wall and slumps down to the floor. I join him.

"Are you okay?" he asks, turning to look at me. He's still breathing heavily.

"Yeah, I'm fine," I say, for some reason a bit touched by his concern. After all, he just watched his three-thousand-year-old boss go up in a pile of dust. Probably pretty darn traumatic for the guy. And still, he's worried about how I'm doing.

"That was far too close," he says, still breathing in ragged puffs. "I can't believe she got Lucifent."

"No kidding," I say. I look around the room. It appears to be made completely of some kind of slick, shiny metal. "What is this place?"

"It's a safe room," Magnus explains. "There are a few feet of solid titanium separating us from the rest of the compound. She'll never get in here. We just have to wait it out. She'll leave eventually. After all, she's got school in the morning."

"So let me get this straight," I say, pulling my knees to my chest and trying to still my heart. "That chick was a vampire slayer?"

"Indeed," Magnus says. "Every generation there is born a girl destined to slay all the vampires, rid the world of evil, yada, yada, yada." He shakes his head. "Which is absolutely ridiculous. We're not evil. We don't even kill humans anymore. We keep to ourselves, donate millions to charity, the works."

Interesting. "But the slayers don't buy this, I take it?"

"Please," he snorts. "A few years back, we launched this whole PR campaign. *Vamps Are People, Too,* we called it. We sent the parent company, Slayer Inc., press releases, QuickTime movies highlighting some of the more philanthropic among our ranks, everything. But did that convince them? No. They refused to listen. Insisted it was their *destiny*, whatever the bloody hell that means. It doesn't matter to Slayer Inc. that some of the greatest artists and musicians of our time are vampires. That they are killing off valuable members of society who would never hurt a fly."

"Ooh, musicians? Like who? Marilyn Manson? The guy from Nine Inch Nails? Green Day?" Ooh, I hope Billie Joe is a vamp. Then maybe I'll get to meet him. Maybe he even lives right here in the coven. You know, with riches and rock stars, I gotta admit there may be SOME good things about being a vampire.

"Their identities are secret," Magnus, the spoilsport, explains. "I could tell you, but then I'd have to kill you."

"Technically aren't I already dead?" I ask with a smile, remembering our previous conversation.

"Once again, you fail to grasp the concept of 'figure of speech.'"

"Yeah, yeah. So who are the musicians?"

He groans. "You're like a pit bull with a bone, aren't you?"

I grin proudly.

"Well, you've seen *Behind the Music* on VH1, right? Rockumentaries on gifted musicians who are always dying young in the second half hour?"

"'When we come back, the tragedy that shook their world,'" I quote with a giggle.

"Um, right." Magnus says, rolling his eyes. "Well, do you honestly think every one of these stars just had really bad luck in the tragic accident department?"

Hmm. I never really thought about it that way before. I'd always attributed the multitude of rocker deaths to the live fast, die young, leave a good-looking corpse, James Dean theory of life. But could it be that they were already rocking out as good-looking corpses, only to be killed a second time by a destiny-deluded Slayer with no appreciation for rock-'n'-roll?

You know, if I get out of this, I should write a tell-all book about the vampire world. Maybe I could get on *The Today Show*. Or at the least *The Daily Show* . . .

"Do you remember that program that used to be on TV?" Magnus continues. "The one about the Slayer? That sympathizer Joss Whedon wrote the character to be so noble and good. Always saving the world from this vampire or that demon. But it's not like that in real life. The real-life Slayer is a vindictive ugly bitch with no compassion." He stares up at the dark ceiling. "And now she's killed Lucifent. This is a sad day for vampire kind indeed."

"For Sunny kind, as well," I add, frowning. "Seeing as he was just about to tell me how I could reverse the whole vampire transformation thing. Does this mean I'm going to be stuck as a bloodsucker for eternity? Or until I get dusted by some Slayer?"

Magnus shrugs. "Maybe not," he says. "Lucifent has a whole library of ancient texts. Certainly one of them will have the answer. Once we get out of here, we can take a look."

Okay, that makes me feel a tad better. Maybe there's hope after all.

"Oh, Lucifent," Magnus moans suddenly, banging the back of his head against the titanium wall. That's gotta hurt, even for a vamp. "Why did it have to be you?"

"You seem awfully upset about a guy who was screaming and calling you mean names just a minute ago," I venture, not quite sure how to react to this sudden display of emotion.

Magnus turns to look at me, his eyes filled with bloody tears, which is kind of gross, actually. I wonder if he sweats blood, too. That sure would make for some interesting gym habits.

"Lucifent was my sire," he explains in a slow voice. "My original blood mate, though we didn't call them that back then. He was the one to turn me into a vampire."

"Ah." It's starting to make sense now. I feel an unwilling pang of pity for poor Magnus. Seeing Lucifent, his vampire daddy, go up in a puff of smoke must be pretty traumatizing for the guy. In fact, I'm amazed he had the wherewithal to make sure I got out alive as well.

"So why did you want to become a vampire?" I ask curiously. "Was it the riches and power, like Rayne wants?"

Magnus shakes his head. "Hardly," he says. "Things were a lot different back when I was turned."

He straightens his legs out along the floor and stretches his hands above his head in a yawn. I refuse to notice how this stretched-out position accentuates his washboard abs. Nope, they're not even a blip on my radar.

"Different how?"

"It's a long story, actually."

I shrug. "We've got nothing but time."

"Too right." He grins, ruefully. "Well, it all started about a thousand years ago. When I served as one of King Arthur's Knights of the Round Table."

I do a double take. "King Arthur? So he really did exist?"

Magnus scowls and gives me one of his famous 'are you kidding me, you babe in the woods?' looks. "Of *course* he existed," he says, with mondo indignation.

"Oh. Okay. But I thought—"

"Uh, up until yesterday you also thought there was no such thing as vampires."

He has a point there.

"So you worked for the guy? Sat at the Round Table? Hung out in Camelot?" I try to picture Magnus in shining armor instead of his typical shining Armani. I bet he was pretty sexy as a knight. All the damsels probably went crazy over him. I wonder if he had a wife. Kids. Ugh. Why does the thought of him having kids scar me so much? I mean, who cares? So he had a life a thousand years before I was born. Big whoop.

"Did you know Lancelot?" I ask, to get my mind off the scarring kids thing.

"Lancelot," Magnus snorts disgustedly. "Why is it that everyone always asks about that pansy? I just love how all the legends have been twisted to make him seem like some kind of hero. The guy hardly ever showed up to fight. He was too busy shagging Queen Guinevere behind the king's back. I mean, thanks to him, poor Arthur lost his throne and Camelot was destroyed. So yeah," he says, sarcastically. "Not my favorite person, let me tell you."

There goes one childhood fantasy flushed down the toilet.

"Never mind about Lancelot. How did you get turned into a vampire? Was it by Merlin? The Lady of the Lake? Ooh, I know. Morgan le Fay, the witch. She did it, right?" I'd paid attention in our Arthurian legends unit in history class last year. The stories were too juicy to resist.

"As I was saying," Magnus continues, ignoring my guesses, "we knights were sent to the eastern lands on a crusade. Our mission was to convert the pagans and, more importantly, find the Holy Grail." He turns to look at me. "That's the cup that Jesus Christ used during the Last Supper."

"I know what it is. I'm not stupid," I say. "I mean, I've seen *Indiana Jones and the Last Crusade*. And Monty Python, of course."

Magnus screws up his face. "Um, right. Well, in any case, not long after we arrived, our order was captured by the Moors in the city of Bethlehem. We were thrown into prison. Beaten and starved until we were very close to death. I thought my life would end in that prison. End at age eighteen." Magnus pauses, then adds, "But really, that's where it all began."

I nod. "Okay, go on." This is getting to be a darn good story. For a moment, I almost forget I'm stuck in a deep, dark, underground titanium room with only a vampire to keep me company.

"Back then vampires didn't have donor blood banks like we do today. So in order to get the blood they needed to survive, they were forced to suck it from the necks of unwilling humans. Very un-PC, I know, but what can you do? It was a barbaric age all around. Anyway, one night, Lucifent arrived at the Moorish prison to search for victims. When he saw the torture we prisoners had endured, he was horrified. He couldn't believe such cruelty existed."

"And this from a man who ripped open throats on a nightly basis."

Magnus frowns. "He did it in the most humane manner possible," he insists, shooting me a glare.

"Okay, okay. I'll stop ragging on your sire. Jeez," I say, a bit sulkily.

Magnus shakes his head, then continues. "So, in an act of raw passion, Lucifent murdered all the guards, draining *their* blood instead of ours for his midnight snack. They didn't even see him coming. Then, when he was done, he set us all free."

"Well that was awfully nice of him," I say, trying to earn back my brownie points.

"But I was too weak to get away," Magnus explains. "My muscles had atrophied from nearly a year's imprisonment and I couldn't get up. So Lucifent asked me if I would like to die, or if I'd prefer eternal life." Magnus shrugs. "You can probably guess what I chose."

"Wow. That's some story!" I say, impressed. I try to imagine what it'd be like to live in the twelfth century. To go on crusades and be captured, tortured, with no Geneva Convention to stop them from doing their worst. "So you've been a vampire ever since?"

"Yes. Through the rise of the British Empire, the founding of America, the Industrial Revolution, the Civil War. Through the Roaring Twenties and the Great Depression. World War I, World War II. Kennedy to Khrushchev. Disco and techno. The Electric Slide and the Boot Scootin' Boogie. All of J-Lo's marriages and P. Diddy's name changes. You name it, I've lived through it."

"And are you happy? Do you like being a vampire?"

Magnus is silent for a moment. "In a way," he says at last. "Eternal life is a great gift. I've had so many adventures. So many experiences. At the same time, it's a bit . . . lonely."

"Lonely?"

"All my mortal friends have been dead a thousand years," he says softly, staring at the ground. "And until you're matched with your blood mate, which doesn't happen till you hit the millennium mark and your blood is properly aged, you're not really supposed to get into any serious relationships."

Wow. This guy hasn't had a date in a thousand years? No wonder he's so cranky!

"And now, just my luck, I'd finally been approved for a blood mate. A partner I'm allowed to love and care for and spend the rest of eternity with. And then I go and screw up royally and bite the wrong girl." He slams a fist against the floor. "Now I'll probably be doomed to walk the earth alone for the rest of my life."

I study him sympathetically. Poor guy. All he wanted was a nice girlfriend who appreciated him. Instead he got saddled with whiny, unappreciative me.

"No offense to you and all," he adds, looking up at me, his eyes sad. "You're a sweet girl. But obviously you have no interest in being my companion. And to tell you the truth, I'd rather have no blood mate than one who abhors me and thinks I'm some kind of monster."

A pang of guilt stabs at my gut. This whole time I've been nothing but selfish. Thinking only of myself and what a pain this whole vampire mix-up has been for me. I never considered how much it's probably screwed him up as well. Here he was, finally getting the blood mate he's been waiting a millennium for. A willing partner to share eternity with. (Even if it was just my silly twin sister.) And now everything's all screwed up.

"So do you love Rayne?" I ask curiously, wondering how much of a bond pre–blood mates share.

Magnus shakes his head. "I barely know her. You're not allowed that much contact before the actual transformation. It's sort of like how they used to do arranged marriages back in the old days. The Council decides on your blood mate based on some very complex compatibility algorithms. After all, once you're mated, you're usually stuck together for eternity, so it's something they take pretty seriously."

"And they thought you and Rayne would be a good fit?"

"Evidently. And I think they were probably right. I met her a few times during the training and she seems like a brilliant girl. And call me a shallow male—" he adds with a grin "—but she's obviously very beautiful as well."

I can feel myself blushing down to my toes. If he thinks Rayne is beautiful, that means he thinks I'm beautiful by default, seeing as we're identical and all. Not that I care what he thinks. Really. After all, there's no reason to start getting all interested in this guy. I need to concentrate on finding a way to turn back to a human, not finding excuses to flirt with a thousand-year-old vampire. Even if the vampire in question is an Orlando Bloom look-alike who used to serve King Arthur.

Besides, let's be frank here. Magnus is a royal pain in the butt. Annoying. Self-serving. The kind of guy who only thinks of himself and doesn't care about the needs of others.

"You look cold. Here, take my coat," Magnus says, pulling his leather jacket off and handing it to me. I reluctantly shrug it on.

Okay, maybe not self-centered. But definitely a jerk. Mean and arrogant.

"Don't worry, Sunny," he says, putting an arm around my shoulders and pulling me close to him. I grudgingly fold into his way-too-comfortable embrace. "I promise to find a way to turn you back. No matter what it takes."

Whoa. He's not making this easy for me, is he?

ELEVEN

Garlic and Sunshine
and Raw Meat—Oh My!

We remain in the titanium room for hours. I actually fall asleep for a short bit, waking up with my head on Magnus's shoulder, which is way embarrassing, let me tell you. I hope I didn't drool on him at any point.

Finally, after what seems an eternity of waiting, the computerized female voice announces that, just like Elvis, "The Slayer has left the building."

We exit the room and head back into the main coven. The place is deserted. Magnus explains that most of the vamps were already out feeding when the Slayer arrived and most likely don't yet realize that their fearless leader has been taken from them.

He leads me to the exit, telling me he's going to take me home first, then return to research my reversal in the library. At first I suggest I help him read, but then he admits that he's planning on feeding in between taking me home and researching, which I decide I'm not ready to take part in. I mean, sure, I get the fact that his donors are willing and screened, but the idea of watching him drain them of blood just isn't what I'd call an entertaining nighttime outing. And anyway, Magnus promises he'll text-message me the second he finds something.

So I get home around five A.M. (The ride in the convertible Jag is heavenly, BTW!) I know I should be exhausted, but I'm wide awake. I tiptoe to my room, attempting not to wake up my mom, since I don't think she's going to buy the "I only missed curfew 'cause I was hiding out from a Vampire Slayer who killed Haley Joel Osment right before my very eyes" excuse.

Luckily she's a deep sleeper.

I arrive at my bedroom and switch on the light. My eyes fall on a figure asleep in my bed. Rayne. She must have tried to stay up waiting for me. I crawl into bed beside her and turn out the light. She rolls over with a soft moan.

"Oh," she murmurs. "I didn't realize you were home."

"Just got," I say, pulling the covers over me. After spending the night on a hard titanium floor, I find the bed's softness more than welcoming to my achy, tired body.

"So what happened? Did Lucifent turn you back? Are you a human again?"

I sigh. "No. He was about to tell us how to reverse the process. Said it was simple and everything. But then he got dusted by the Slayer."

Rayne sits up in bed. Even in the predawn darkness I can see her wide eyes. "The Slayer?"

"Yeah, once a generation there's evidently some girl who's destined to kill vampires or something like that. Like in Buffy."

"I know what the Slayer is," Rayne says impatiently. "I just can't believe she got Lucifent! That's terrible. Such a great loss for vampire kind worldwide."

"I don't know." I shrug. "He seemed like kind of an asshole to me."

"Sunny, Lucifent has done so much for the coven. You don't even know. If you'd read my blog—"

"Will you shut up about the blog already?" I know I'm being bitchy, but you'd be, too, if you'd spent your night the way I had.

Rayne lies back down in bed. "I can't believe Lucifent's dead," she mutters, staring up at the ceiling. When we were kids we pasted glow-in-the-dark stars all over it and some of them are still glowing—tiny pinpricks of green light. Such innocent times, then.

"*I* can't believe I may be stuck as a vampire forever," I retort. Jeez. Enough with the feeling-sorry-for-Lucifent thing already. Sunny needs pity, too. "I mean, this is going to put a serious damper on my social life. Not to mention my high school career."

My voice cracks on the last sentence. Damn it, I don't want to cry again. But I'm tired and stressed and afraid and I just can't seem to help it. Once I let one tear escape, the rest start catapulting down my face like a freaking waterfall.

"I don't want to be a . . . a vampire," I choke out.

Rayne rolls on her side and brushes a lock of hair off my forehead, studying me with concerned eyes. "I'm sorry, sweetie," she says. "I keep forgetting how hard this must be for you." She kisses me on the cheek, then starts climbing out of bed. "I'll let you get some sleep."

"Can't you stay?" I ask, the words leaving my mouth before I can stop them. She's going to think I'm such a baby, but suddenly I don't want to be alone anymore. Alone with my tormented thoughts.

She nods and gets back into bed, no questions asked. "Sure," she says, squirming into a more comfortable position. "What are twin sisters for?"

THE DJ RESPONSIBLE for the music playing on my clock radio should be shot. No, that wouldn't be painful enough. He should be castrated and left to be eaten by rabid dogs. Or something. "The Monster Mash" is my morning wake-up song—puh-leeze. Inhuman, I tell you.

I press the snooze bar and pull the covers over my head. I've never felt so exhausted in all my life. I feel like I'm going to throw up, I'm so tired. I don't think I even got to sleep before the sun was peeking over the horizon. And then, I fell into an almost coma-deep slumber until the DJ decided to torment me with this cruel and un-usual musical punishment.

But Rayne, the suddenly evil bee-yotch who's probably in ca-hoots with the DJ, isn't content to let me sleep. She shakes me by the shoulder. "Wake up, Sun," she commands in an overly chipper voice. So help me, if she breaks into the "Good Morning" song my mother used to sing to get us up when we were kids, I won't be held respon-sible for my actions. "We've got to go to school."

"I'm sick," I mumble, resisting her shakes.

"You're not sick. You're just a vampire," she clarifies, as if that makes everything okay. "So it makes sense you want to sleep through the day."

Her words make me bolt upright in bed. Argh, she's right! I *am* acting like a vampire. I stayed up all night and now I'm hoping to sleep all day. Ugh. I don't want to succumb to these vamp urges. For all I know, it might make it more difficult to reverse the transforma-tion if I'm all accepting of it and stuff.

"I'm up," I say, rubbing my eyes. The sunlight streaming through the window feels like fire on my skin. I think I'll be using the 30 SPF this morning. Or maybe the turbocharged 50+ stuff Mom keeps in her bathroom.

I sniff the air. "Ugh. What's that awful smell?" I ask, screwing up my nose.

Rayne shrugs. "Smells like Mom's making breakfast."

"That sure doesn't smell like any breakfast I'd want to eat," I say, climbing out of bed and trying to dodge the scattered sunny parts of the room as I make my way to the bathroom.

I wash my face and notice I'm looking especially pale this A.M. Kind of like what Rayne looks like when she pancakes her face white for the extreme Goth look. Oh well, so much for getting a tan. I slather on the sunscreen, careful not to miss any pertinent parts, then head back into my bedroom. Rayne's left by this point, and I'm more than tempted to crawl back into bed. But no, I must resist the urge. I need to keep acting as normal as possible.

Besides, if I go to school I get to see Jake Wilder. The Jake Wilder who's wildly attracted to me. Talk about motivation!

I look in my closet for something to wear. Something that will impress Jake, preferably. Unfortunately, even though it's meant to hit like eighty today, I don't think my normal tank and flips are going to cut it in the wardrobe department. Too much risk for sunburn. Better to cover as much skin as possible.

So I choose a black sweater with bell sleeves that go over my hands, my favorite pair of Diesel jeans, and a pair of black boots. Now all that's exposed is my face and neck. (The bite mark has thankfully faded!) I grab a pair of dark sunglasses from my dresser and a worn Red Sox cap. I study myself in the mirror (yes, BTW, I *can* still see my reflection; guess that one was a myth), sort of feeling like a Hollywood celeb going undercover to grocery shop. Not exactly the best look to attract Jake, but hey, that's what the Vampire Scent is for, I guess.

Satisfied with my outfit, I clomp down the stairs, ready to face the world. Or at least my mother. But the putrid smell only gets worse as I approach the kitchen. Ew! What the hell is she cooking this time? Fried rotting rat?

Let me just say for the record here, my "yes, I went to Woodstock" mom has made some pretty odd recipes over the years. (Tofu manicotti, anyone?) So I can only imagine what she's cooked up this time around. (And BTW, the Woodstock thing? She neglects to mention that she was five years old at the time and spent more time running around naked in the mud, being chased by my exasperated grandma, than listening to the music. Then again, I guess a lot of adults were doing the same thing, so who am I to judge the cultural influence the event had on her existence?)

"Burning down the kitchen, Mom?" I joke as I enter the room. The smell is almost overwhelming now, and I have to take a step back to steady myself. It's a burnt, decomposing odor that makes me want to vomit. I pause for a moment, blinking my eyes a few times, as they've started watering like crazy.

"What's wrong, honey?" Mom asks, turning from whatever horror she's concocting, a concerned look on her face. "You look awful."

"I feel awful," I say, slumping into a kitchen chair, trying to resist the urge to plug my nose with my fingers. As bad as the smell is, it's obviously something she's slaved over and I can't be that rude. Just hope she doesn't expect me to eat any of it.

Mom wipes her hands on her apron and approaches me. She puts her palm against my forehead. "You don't feel sick," she says, wrinkling her brow. "In fact, your forehead is ice cold."

I pull my head away before she starts wondering about my perfectly chilled vampire temperature.

"What is that . . . smell?" I manage to choke out, wanting to change the subject.

She cocks her head in confusion. "Smell?" she asks. She sniffs the air. "All I can smell is the breakfast scramble I'm cooking up." She shrugs. "Tofu, peppers, and lots of garlic, just the way you like it."

Gah! Realization hits me over the head like a cartoon anvil. That's got to be it. I've suddenly developed the stereotypical vampire aversion to garlic. A food product I used to adore. Go figure.

"Here, it's ready, actually," she says, walking back over to the stove and heaping a mammoth portion onto a plate. "You want salt on it?"

What I want is for the whole thing to be thrown in the trash, honestly. Preferably the neighbor's trash. The neighbor who lives on planet Pluto. That might be far enough away for me to withstand the stench.

But what am I supposed to say? I wonder, as she carries the steaming plate o'puke over to the table. Mom knows it's my favorite and she made it especially for me. Maybe I can take one bite—

Oh no. I'm going to hurl.

I jump out of my seat and bolt to the bathroom. I barely make it to the toilet before my stomach releases all its contents into the porcelain bowl.

Okay. It's decided. I'm definitely not eating the breakfast scramble. Mom's hurt feelings be damned.

"Sunny, are you okay in there?" Mom asks, knocking on the door and sounding even more concerned than she did before.

"She's fine." I can hear Rayne's voice outside the door. Thank goodness. She can cover for me while I brush the vomit out of my teeth.

"She's not fine, honey. She just threw up."

"She's just nervous. We have a huge history test today."

"Are you sure, Rayne?" Hmm. Mom sounds suspicious. I guess that makes sense. I mean for all her peace, love, and flower-child beliefs, she hasn't just fallen off the turnip truck either. She knows I'm an excellent test taker. It's Rayne who has the nervous test-taking fits that she believes exonerate her from going to school on exam day.

"She's right," I say, exiting the bathroom with a smile. "I'm fine, Mom. Just got the old butterflies. After all, this test counts as twenty-five percent of our grade."

"Okay. If you're sure . . ." Mom says, still looking doubtful. "But you know, Sunny, you'd probably feel more confident if you had stayed in and studied last night instead of going out. I didn't even hear you come in."

Shoot. I'd forgotten about that.

"I was over at a study partner's house," I say, crossing my fingers behind my back. "We were going over history and kind of lost track of time."

Okay, before you think I'm a horrible person for lying to my mom, technically I'm not fibbing whatsoever. I *was* at Magnus's "house" last night and we *were* talking about history. The history of King Arthur, the crusades, and vampires, to be exact. But since there really isn't any test to begin with, I think I'm owed some creative license over what I studied to pass it.

For a moment Mom looks like she doesn't buy my explanation. But then she shrugs. "Okay, sweetie. I'm glad you studied. I've got to get to work." She reaches over and kisses me on the forehead and then does the same to Rayne. "Have a good day, girls. And good luck on the test."

I watch as she heads to the front closet to retrieve her handbag. I feel bad lying to her. As far as moms go, she's pretty cool. Not like some of my friends' moms who act more like prison wardens than parents. She's always been the "Friend Mom." The one who promises she'll never judge us for telling her things. The type who'd rather we ask for condoms or birth control than go out and have sex without telling her. She's open and accepting and loving.

But I still don't think she'd get the whole vampire thing. After all, "Friend Mom" does not necessarily equal "Accept That Your Daughter Is Turning Undead and Be Cool with That Mom."

"Bye, girls," she says, waving as she exits.

"Bye, Mom," we chorus.

Now alone, Rayne and I let out nervous laughter.

"That was close," I say, heaving a sigh of relief.

"No kidding," Rayne agrees. "Though I do think she's still a bit suspicious."

"She probably thinks I'm pregnant and having morning sickness or something. Throwing up at the sight of food."

"Nah. She knows you better than that," Rayne says with a laugh. "My little Sunny the Innocent," she coos, tousling my hair.

"What-EVER," I say, making the W with my fingers.

Rayne smirks. "Now if it were *me* throwing up, we'd already be in the car on the way to the clinic."

"Yes, indeed, 'cause you are a skanky ho," I say gleefully. Rayne playfully punches me in the arm. She thinks it's funny, go figure.

"Actually *you're* the skanky ho this time around. The bitch who stole my blood mate," she replies with a laugh. "And speaking of, how was the oh-so-dreamy Magnus last night?"

For some reason her question makes my face heat in a blush. Though judging from how fair my skin is now, it probably doesn't even register a dusty rose.

"He's fine," I say. "Upset about Lucifent, of course. I mean the guy was his sire and all."

"Lucifent was Magnus's sire?" Rayne says, raising an eyebrow.

I smile, happy to finally know something she doesn't. "Yup," I say, and relate an abbreviated version of the tale.

When I'm finished, Rayne releases a long, dramatic sigh. "Wow," she says dreamily. "My blood mate was a knight in shining armor. How cool is that?"

I shrug. "Yeah, he's actually an interesting guy when he's not being all arrogant and rude." I pause, then add, "Which is ninety-nine percent of the time." Don't want Rayne to get the idea that I'm developing some kind of affection for Magnus, since I'm so not. In fact, I think a change of subject is in order here. "Now go toss out that disgusting garlic concoction before I gag again."

"Okay. I'll take it outside." Rayne disappears into the kitchen, and moments later she and the smell exit the house and the air becomes relatively clear again.

As the smell fades, I realize I'm suddenly ravenously hungry. I enter the kitchen, searching for a garlic-free snack. I peer into the fridge. Not much there. Then my eyes fall on a package of hamburger meat in the very back of the fridge.

My mom's a strict vegetarian, you see, and brought me and my sister up that way as well. But my sister could never completely lose her taste for red meat. So once in a while she gives in to her carnivorous urges and enjoys a good burger.

I stare at the hamburger, suddenly realizing my mouth is watering. In fact, I'm suddenly craving it so badly that I think I might be drooling a bit.

Suddenly, my hand reaches involuntarily to the raw meat, as if it's taken on a will of its own. My stomach growls in anticipation. It looks so luscious. So red. So delicious.

I look around to see if Rayne's back. She's probably still burying the garlic mess. I have time. I grab the package and tear it open, greedily grabbing handfuls of raw meat and shoveling them into my mouth, rejoicing in the bloody juices flowing down my throat. I swear, a chocolate peanut-butter sundae with extra whipped cream and chocolate sauce could not taste half this good.

"You know that's a real good way to develop *E. coli*."

I whirl around, mouth full of raw meat, to see Rayne standing there with a smirk on her face. I suddenly realize what I'm doing. Horrified, I spit the meat out into the sink, trying to force myself to throw the rest up.

"Oh my God. I can't believe I just did that," I cry, absolutely mortified. "That's so disgusting."

"It's okay. I'm sure vampires are immune to food-borne illness," Rayne says.

"But it's so . . . gross!" I stare at the rest of the beef, fighting the nearly overwhelming urge to dig back in. "I can't believe I just ate raw hamburger. It's all bloody and slimy and—"

"Don't beat yourself up over it, Sun. You're just giving in to your vampire urges, is all." Rayne shrugs. "Pretty soon you'll have to be moving on to live blood, though."

I narrow my eyes. "I am sooo not partaking of live blood."

"You will if you're hungry enough."

"No. I won't. I definitely won't. Cross my heart, hope to die. I vow on my prom date with Jake Wilder," I promise. "I will never, ever be that hungry."

My stomach growls in response. Uh-oh.

TWELVE

Roses Are Red,
Blood Is, Too . . .

"Sunshine McDonald, please report to the principal's office."

I perk up out of my sleep-deprived coma at my name being called over the loudspeaker system. I'm in trig class, which I hate, and have been hiding out in the back row, head in my hands, trying to do the whole "look awake while sleeping" pose.

I'm so tired. So, so tired. I don't know how I'm going to get through this week, let alone the rest of my existence. If Magnus doesn't find a vampire antidote, I'm doomed to be a high school dropout.

I glance over at the teacher to make sure he's heard the announcement. He must have, as he simply waves me toward the door with a saucy smile. Ew. He's like the fifth male teacher today to flirt with me. This Vampire Scent thing is great for boys my age, like Jake, but when it starts affecting pervert adults it gets a little freaky.

I rise from my seat, thanking Lover Boy with a nod, and he goes back to calculating huge incomprehensible math problems on the board with a big goofy grin on his face. Major ew-age.

I'm happy to step into the hallway, away from class, but I soon realize this might be going from the frying pan to the fire. I have no idea why I'm being summoned to the principal's office, but usually that sort of thing is never good. Then again, I've done nothing wrong. I haven't said or done anything weird. I haven't bitten any of the student body. I did run out of home ec class after the teacher announced we were going to bake cheesy garlic bread, but I later blamed that on my aversion to carbs due to my South Beach Diet.

I arrive at the glassed-in office and step inside, my heart beating furiously. I so don't need to get in trouble on top of everything else.

"Hi, I'm Sunshine McDonald," I say to Miss Rose, the longtime school secretary sitting at the front desk. "You guys called me?"

Miss Rose looks up. She's an older woman, probably in her sixties, wearing a prim little pastel suit with a perfect string of pearls. Got the Barbara Bush look down pat.

But when she sees me, her demure smile morphs into what looks like a lecherous grin.

"Hi, sweetie," she purrs in a low, sensual voice that no Barbara Bush look-alike should ever be allowed to use. "I'm so glad you could come down." She gives me the once-over from head to toe. "You're looking awfully pretty today, dear."

I take a step back, a little shaken. Has she been affected by the Vampire Scent? She couldn't be! It only works on guys and . . .

I start to laugh. I can't help it. The whole thing is just so absurd. So surreal. I can't believe I'm in school being hit on by a secretly lesbian grandma.

Miss Rose frowns at my merriment, looking rather offended. Poor thing.

"Sorry," I say, swallowing hard to contain my chortling. "The principal wanted to see me?"

"No, dear," Miss Rose says in wounded tone. "I had them page you so you could pick up your flowers."

"Flowers?"

Miss Rose gestures to the desk adjacent to hers. My eyes fall on an absolutely enormous bouquet of blood-red roses. There must be at least five dozen in the vase, all meticulously arranged by some expert florist.

"For me?" I ask, mentally cataloging my brain for who could have possibly sent me roses.

And delightfully, the only person I can think of is Jake Wilder.

Of course. It makes perfect sense. He can't stop thinking about me and our prom date on Saturday night. He wants to thank me for saying yes with this "little" token of his appreciation. Something to hold me over until he brings me my corsage.

I walk over to the flowers and breathe through my nose, taking in their soft, powdery scent. Jake's such a wonderful guy. So thoughtful. So sweet. I reach for the card, hardly able to wait to read what I'm sure will be cleverly written poetry, professing his undying love for—

Damn it, the flowers are from Magnus.

I stare at the card, at first so lost in my fantasy world that I think maybe the florist just delivered the wrong bouquet. But no, the card says my name. It's just signed by a vampire instead of my prom date.

So disappointing.

I glance over at the flowers. He probably freaking stole them from the graveyard or something. Jerk. Why would he send me flowers anyway?

I glance at the card again.

Dear Sunny,

I'm so sorry for all you've had to go through due to my dreadful mistake. I'm sure last night was especially traumatic for you. Please accept this tiny token of my apology and meet me at Club Fang tonight, to discuss your situation.

Yours truly,
Magnus

I release an exasperated sigh. Now I have to go back to Club Fang? I'm already way behind on my homework, having gone out the past two nights. You know, turning into a vampire is bad enough without me flunking out of school as well.

But what choice do I have? If I want to reverse this process, I've got to do what he says.

"Sunny, dearest, would you like to come and sit on Miss Rose's lap?" the secretary invites, while fluttering her white eyelashes. "I've been dying to talk to you."

Ugh. That settles it. Club Fang, here I come!

THIRTEEN

The Donor Chicks

I arrive at Club Fang at around eight P.M. Unlike last Sunday, to-night there's no DJ in a bondage cage and no one's doing the foot-stuck-in-the-mud dance to suicide-inducing music. No, tonight the club's been transformed into a hip-looking coffeehouse and wine bar, with its inhabitants lounging at various café tables, looking trendily bored as they suck down frothy cappuccinos and glasses of wine.

I check a few of them out, trying to decide which are the vampires and which are the humans who love them. Since everyone's pale faced, red lipped, and dressed uniformly in black, it's surprisingly hard to tell the creatures of the night from those still among the living.

I see Magnus at the back of the room, sitting at a small table, accompanied by two hot girls. He catches my eye and motions me over. I realize I'm strangely excited to see him, which is very annoying, since that's not the kind of power I want him to have over me.

It's probably just the anticipation of me turning back into a human that's got my heart beating faster and my breath catching in my throat, I remind myself. It's not like Magnus turns me on in any way, shape, or form, that's for sure. Especially, I note, as I get closer, not in that outfit. I mean, who would get turned on by a fitted black T-shirt that perfectly molds itself to his sculpted six-pack abs or a pair of tight black leather pants that showcases—

Okay. Fine. I admit it, I'm attracted. Very attracted. In fact, I'm willing to bet I'm more attracted to this vampire hottie than I am to Robert Pattinson, Chace Crawford, and Brad Pitt put together. So sue me.

Bottom line, attraction does not equal wanting to remain someone's blood mate for all of eternity. Period. End o' story.

As I reach the table, the two girls, pierced and tattooed out to the max, look up and stare at me with unfriendly, black-rimmed eyes. Oh, let me guess, more jealous Magnus disciples, hating me 'cause I'm the guy's blood mate. As if I signed up for the stupid gig.

"Hi," I say, looking straight at Magnus and ignoring his groupies. The guy should consider becoming a rock star like the vampire Lestat did in that Anne Rice book *Queen of the Damned*. He'd probably do very well in the screaming teenage fans department.

"Hey," Magnus greets back, glancing at the girls with a smug smile, looking oh-so-proud of himself. I frown. Does he expect me to be jealous of his fan club or something? Puh-leeze.

"Um . . ." I shuffle from foot to foot. Should I sit down? There's no extra chair.

"Sit," Magnus suddenly instructs, almost as if he's read my mind. Ugh, he can't do that, can he? That would royally suck. Especially since I was just thinking about how sexy he is in that outfit.

Trying to shield my mind and think random non-Magnus thoughts about Marc Jacobs shoes and the square root of pi, just in case he does have some kind of mind-reading abilities, I grab a chair from a nearby table and take my seat.

"Um, hi, I'm Sunny," I say to the girl on my left. "Nice to meet you," I add, holding out my hand to the one on the right. "Do you guys come here often?"

The girl stares at my hand, but doesn't take it. She also doesn't answer my question.

What's her problem? Is she a mute or something? Or just incredibly rude? (Judging from whom I've met so far in the vamp community, I'm betting on the latter.)

"It's okay, Rachel. You can talk to her," Magnus says, oh-so-grandly giving his permission. Jeez. He really does get off on this all-powerful-vampire thing, doesn't he?

Then again, people let him get away with it. Like this Rachel chick, for instance. I mean, Magnus commands and both girls suddenly light up like those animatronic characters at Disney World. What's up with that? Are they trapped under some kind of Magnus mind control or something? Or are they just your typical obsessive Goths, like my sister, willing to do whatever the big bad vamps command?

"Greetings, oh honored one. I am Rachel," says the girl on my left in a reverential, way overly dramatic tone. "And this is my companion, Charity."

"Hiya, Sunny," says Charity, in a surprisingly squeaky valley-girl voice. Wow. I hadn't expected that to come from her blood-red-lipped mouth. "We've, like, heard so much about you."

They have? They've heard about me? That would mean Magnus talks about me. Talks about me to his friends even. Which is interesting, of course, but certainly no reason to have my heart start beating like crazy.

Trying to regain control of my once-again traitorous body, I study the girls more closely. Both have long, impossibly straight black hair, soft blue eyes, and china doll skin. Hmm . . . I wonder . . .

"Are you guys . . . ?" I trail off, not quite sure of the PC terminology. Would a vampire be considered mortally challenged? "Are you . . . ?"

"Vampires?" Rachel fills in.

My face heats. "Uh, yeah." Okay, guess they're cool with the V-word here.

"No," Rachel says, shaking her head. "Unlike you, we are regretfully still attached to this mortal coil."

"We wish, though," Charity chimes in. "That would so totally rock if we were."

"Indeed," her friend agrees, solemnly. "To be a creature of the night would, as my dear friend so eloquently puts it, totally rock."

O-kay, so they're not vampires. But they know about vampires. They're like vamp wanna-bes. Maybe they're part of the training program Rayne was in?

"Actually, we're Donor Chicks," Charity informs me.

"Donor—?" I scrunch my eyebrows. Then realization hits me like a ten-ton truck. I stare from one to the other. "*You're* Magnus's blood donors?"

Wow. Magnus had told me that vampires contracted willing humans to provide them with their blood supply, but I didn't think about the fact that these donors would be very attractive young women. Dinner for Mag boy must be a real gourmet treat.

"Yes." Rachel nods enthusiastically. "We are bound to serve Lord Magnus," she says, smiling over at the vampire in question, looking prouder than a peacock. "Offer him our blood sacrifice so that he may sustain immortal life."

I roll my eyes. What a drama queen. "So what you're saying is you, like, willingly let him suck your blood? Why the heck would you sign up for something like that?" I'm trying not to be judgmental here, but seriously!

"Are you kidding?" Rachel frowns, her expression telling me that I've just asked the stupidest question known to humankind. "It is an honor to provide sustenance to such a powerful being," she explains. "By doing so, we, too, are indirectly taking part in immortal life."

"Plus it's great pay!" Charity interjects. Rachel shoots her an evil look, like it's rude to bring up the more mercenary aspects of their agreement.

But Charity ignores her. "I mean, for a young mom like myself, there's no better way to earn a few extra bucks on the side. Definitely beats waitressing for a living. Now I can take care of my baby, rent a kick-ass apartment, and have enough money to go to college. All without food stamps. It's a total win-win, you know? Maggy here gets his bloody-wuddy," she says, chucking a frowning Magnus under the chin, "and me and my baby get a big fat bank account."

Okay, then. There you have it. I mean, what can I possibly say to properly respond to that little spiel?

"Well, um, I'm glad it's all working out for you," I respond lamely. "Wouldn't be my first career choice, but hey, neither is astrophysics and plenty of people do that for a living and make out real well."

"Girls, could you get Sunny a drink?" Magnus says, speaking up for the first time. "She must be very thirsty."

Without even a pause to question why I can't get up and get my own damn drink, or why both of them have to go for that matter, the Donor Chicks jump up and head for the coffee bar.

"They're, um, cute," I remark, watching them across the room. Charity is giggling about something and Rachel is rolling her eyes at her.

Magnus shrugs. "They're dinner," he says simply. As if he's talking about a pork chop or something.

"They're also human," I protest, not knowing why I feel the need to defend them. After all, they certainly aren't unwilling victims. If they're stupid enough to think that the concept of a vampire downing their blood like some vintage red wine is cool, then who am I to say they're being exploited and used? "I mean, I knew you had donors, but it's just completely weird to meet them in person."

"I can imagine," Magnus says, twirling his wineglass in his hands. "I debated bringing them with me. I don't usually dine out."

Dine out. Hardy har har. "Is that supposed to be a lame attempt at a vampire joke?"

He smiles. "Pun was intended, yes." He takes a sip of his wine. "I usually swing by their houses early in the evening, then go on with my night."

"Ah. A bloody booty call." See, I can make vampire jokes, too. "So no fraternizing with dinner allowed, then?"

"It's not against the rules," Magnus says with a shrug. "We are allowed to associate with our donors if we choose to. In fact, I've heard of many donor-vamp relationships developing and lasting for years. But my particular donors are, how do I put this?" he asks, glancing over at the giggling girls. "A bit overwhelming at times."

"I see." Well, I guess that means he's not attracted to them.

That's a relief . . . or not. Actually not. In fact, for the record, I think it'd be totally fine if he were attracted to them. If he had a relationship with them, even. Because after all, I couldn't care less who he's dating.

No, really.

"So why did you bring them here tonight?" I ask.

He grins. "For you. I thought you might like a bite to eat."

"Ha, ha. Very funny."

"I wasn't making a joke this time."

I screw up my face. "Ew! I'm *not* drinking anyone's blood." Then I blush as I remember the incident with the raw meat in the kitchen this morning. I really hope he can't read my mind, 'cause that was way embarrassing.

"You *have* to drink blood. You're a vampire."

"No. I don't have to and I won't. I'll just order a burger if I get hungry."

"A burger won't—"

"An extra-rare burger with lots of blood."

Magnus shakes his head. "A burger is all empty calories," he says. "You need to be nourished with human blood."

"I am not drinking blood. End of story."

"You should just try it. You'd probably like it."

"I won't like it. I know I won't."

"You probably didn't think you'd like brussels sprouts the first time you tried them either," he reasons.

"I still don't like brussels sprouts, just FYI. And I certainly will never, ever, in a million years like the taste of human blood."

Before Magnus can respond with some other idiotic reason why I should partake in this cannibalistic behavior, the Donor Chicks return, carrying a goblet of red wine.

Saved by the Goths.

"Here you go," says Charity, thrusting the drink at me. "Your merlot."

I take a sniff. It smells delicious. Not that I'm some wino, but this particular brand has a warm, spicy smell. I shouldn't be drinking wine. Especially not on a school night. Mom would absolutely kill me if she found out. But then again, I'm already dead, right? (See, I'm good at this vampire humor thing!)

I take a sip.

Mmmm. Thick and hearty. Must be a very good vintage.

I take another sip. This is good stuff. Really satisfying. Warms my stomach almost immediately, washing away all the stress and frustrations of the day.

On my third sip, I look around the room. Funny, I would have totally guessed that a makeshift coffeehouse like this would serve only the cheap stuff. Like blush from a box or something.

Um, in fact, now that I think about it, why would a coffeehouse serve wine at all? Would they even have a liquor license?

Then it hits me.

Oh.

My.

God.

I spit my mouthful of "wine" back in the glass, my stomach heaving in disgust. I feel like I'm going to be sick. I look up at Magnus, who is smiling smugly from across the table. It takes every ounce of willpower not to slug him one.

"You tricked me!" I cry. "This is blood, not wine, isn't it?"

"I knew you would like it," he says simply.

"You told me it was merlot," I accuse Charity.

She grins. "Lord Magnus asks that we call it that. It sounds more . . . civilized," she says with a giggle. "And, like, if you're out in public, you can't be talking about drinking the B-word 'cause people will lock you up and throw away the key."

I feel a little like locking myself up and throwing away the key at this very moment. I can't believe I just drank some random Goth girl's blood.

I can't believe I liked it.

I can't believe I'm staring at the glass, wanting to take another sip.

"Ugh. What's happening to me?" I moan.

"Look, Sunny," Magnus says, leaning over the table and meeting my eyes with his own deep, soulless ones. "You'd find things a lot easier if you'd just start embracing your inner vampire."

"But I don't want to be a vampire!"

He sighs. "You've made that exceedingly clear, believe me. However, until we manage to stop your transformation, by all accounts you *are* becoming a vampire. Therefore, you must do the things that vampires do. And if you do not drink blood, you will very simply waste away and die before you get the opportunity to change back."

Okay, I guess he has a point. I glance around the coffeehouse, making sure no one's watching me, then take a tentative sip of the blood in my wineglass. Soon, I'm gulping it down with wild abandon. Gross, I know. But I can't seem to help it. It just tastes so yummy.

"Very good," Magnus says, as if praising a one-year-old for eating her first Cheerios.

"Yeah, yeah," I mumble between gulps. "Whatever I have to do." I am so not admitting how delicious I find the drink or how I'm dying for a second glass.

"Thank you, ladies," Magnus says, turning to the Donor Chicks. He pulls out a wallet from his back pocket and hands each a wad of cash. Guess vamp blood payment is an under-the-table type gig. "You are free to go."

They take the money and giggle once again as they kiss Magnus on each cheek.

"Thanks, Maggy," says Charity. "You're the best."

"I will see thee tomorrow evening," Rachel adds. "Till next time, my divine immortal one."

Oh, puh-leeze. This girl makes Rayne seem normal.

Without further ado, the girls wave good-bye to me and exit the coffeehouse. Magnus watches them go, then turns to me.

"Like I said . . ."

". . . a little overwhelming," I finish, nodding. "I totally see your point."

"So," Magnus says, clearing his throat, "I've done some research."

I lean forward in my chair, excited. "And?"

He pauses. "Do you want the good news or the bad news?"

Why do people always ask that? It only prolongs the suspense, don't you think? And really, what difference does it make which one you bring up first?

"The good news, I guess." After all, if I know the good news, then I'll be in a better mood to deal with the bad news.

"The good news is that according to the ancient texts I've researched, there is a way for the vampire transformation process to be reversed. A way for you to turn back into a human."

"Woot!" I cry, raising a fist in the air in triumph. That is good news! "I knew there had to be a way!"

Overjoyed, I can't resist the urge to lean across the table and give the surprised vampire a big smacking kiss on the cheek. "You rock, Magnus! Thanks so much! I knew you could do it."

He waves off my attempted embrace. "I haven't told you the bad news yet," he reminds me.

"Bring it on, then. No kind of bad news can wreck my day now."

"According to my research, the only way to turn you back into a human is to purify your blood. And the only substance I know of that can do this is a drop of blood from the Holy Grail."

The Holy Grail? Holy crap!

FOURTEEN

The Holy Freaking Grail?!

I stop celebrating, hands stuck in perpetual freeze-frame cabbage patch dance, and stare at Magnus.

"The Holy Grail?" I repeat, realizing my voice has risen to a screechy hiss. "The HOLY FREAKING GRAIL?"

Magnus dips his head in a nod. "I told you it was bad news."

"How the hell are we supposed to get a drop of blood from the Holy Grail? Does the Holy Grail even exist? I thought the Holy Grail was something that was made up by the Church . . . or Steven Spielberg." I slam my head against the table. "I'm doomed. Doomed, doomed, doomed. Doomed to walk the earth as a creature of the night forever. Doomed to drink ditsy donor blood for all eternity."

"Chill out, Sunny," Magnus commands, sounding a bit ticked off at my admittedly overdramatic display. "The Grail does exist. I've seen it with my own eyes."

I look up, hopeful once again. "You have?"

"Indeed."

"So then you know where it is?"

Magnus pauses. "Erm, not exactly."

I knew it! I just knew he'd say that. "DOOMED! I'M DOOMED!" I cry, commencing with further head-banging.

"Will you keep your voice down?" Magnus hisses. "You're upsetting the others."

I lift my head and look around. Sure enough, I've pretty much got the whole Club Fang giving me the evil eye.

"You know, not everyone sees being a vampire as a dooming prospect," scolds a black-caped, bleached-blond teen who looks alarmingly like Spike from the *Buffy* show. "In fact, some of us quite enjoy it."

Oh brother.

"Um, sorry?" I venture, deciding to go the humble, ignorant route. After all, come Saturday night I'm going to be one of the blood-drinkin' gang forever and ever, and I don't want to start off on the wrong foot. "I meant no offense. I'm sure it's a very pleasurable way to spend eternity and all. It's just, well, not really my cup of tea, you understand."

"Whatever," the Spike guy replies, turning back to his companions. "God, I hate vampire newbs!" he adds under his breath.

"So ANYWAY," Magnus interrupts loudly, before I can give "Spike" the finger, "I hadn't finished what I was going to say before you erupted into premature mourning."

"Oh. Sorry," I mutter. "Go on."

"As I was saying, the Holy Grail is not a myth. It's a real object of power. The cup was used by the Christ during his Last Supper, then retrieved by Joseph of Arimathea, who filled the cup with Jesus' blood after he died on the cross."

Filling a wineglass with the blood of the dead. Nice, normal guy, this Joseph of Arimathea. Then again, after just gulping down a goblet of *Château de Rachel et Charity*, I realize I am not really one to talk.

"The Grail was hidden away in Israel for many years, until the British knights came over during the crusades. They stole it and brought it back to England."

I drum my fingers on the table, impatient for Mag to get to the point. Honestly, I don't think I need to know the whole history of the world here.

"Fascinating. Really," I say, as the vampire pauses for breath. "Now can you just tell me how we can retrieve the thing already?"

He ignores me, of course, and drones on. He'd make a great history teacher. He's almost as boring as Ms. Dawson. "Somehow the ancient relic fell into the hands of the Lady of the Lake, Nimue, who lived on the island of Avalon. And that's where it's believed to be to this day. Buried far under the ground in a secret cave under the hill of Tor."

Now we're getting somewhere. "So is Avalon even a real place? Does it still exist? Can we get there and retrieve the Grail?" I know I'm asking questions faster than Magnus can answer them, but I'm way too desperate to help it.

"Yes, no, maybe," Magnus answers, matter-of-factly. "In that order."

"Um . . ."

"Yes, it was a real place," he clarifies. "But the priestesses of the past are long gone. It's not even technically an island anymore. Over the years the waters have turned to marshlands and the marshlands have since dried up. What used to be an island is now connected to the mainland of England."

"Gotcha."

"Present-day Avalon lies in a place called Glastonbury. A small, quiet village in the southwest of England."

"Do you think the Grail is still there somewhere?"

"Perhaps." Magnus strokes his chin thoughtfully. I love how he has just a tad of dangerous stubble lurking on his otherwise boyish face. I wonder if vampires have to shave. "I have heard rumors of an ancient druidic order that still makes its home in the village. They guard their secrets closely, but perhaps with the right persuasion, they may share their wisdom."

"So that's good, right?" I ask hopefully.

"I won't lie to you, Sunny. It's a definite long shot."

"Long shot, but not impossible shot." I'm determined to be Glass-Half-Full Chick here.

"Correct."

"So," I say, wanting to sum it all up. "All I have to do is fly to England, head to Glastonbury, find the members of an ancient hidden druidic order, and persuade them to take me to the Holy Grail, where I will be able to drink a drop of purifying blood and stop the transformation of me into a vampire."

"All before Saturday night at midnight," Magnus adds, looking at his watch.

I sigh. Things are looking not so half-full all of a sudden. I might have to change my name to Glass-Half-Empty Chick from now on. Actually, make that Glass-Drained-Dry Chick in this case.

First off, how the heck am I going to get to England? I can't exactly suggest an impromptu trip to my mom. She'd have all these ridiculous objections—her job, my school, no one to take care of our cat, Missy, etc., etc. Not to mention the fact that the old hippie has this outdated belief that airplanes are gas-guzzling monstrosities that wreak havoc on the environment and should not be flown except in emergencies like Grandma's funeral when there was no time to take her hybrid Toyota Prius.

Nope, the chances of me jetting off to jolly old England before Saturday at midnight are slim to none.

"Guess you can start calling me Vampire Sunny," I say with a desolate sigh. I take another mouthful of the blood wine. Might as well start developing a taste for the stuff.

"Hold on there," Magnus says. "You're not giving up that easily, are you?"

I look up from my glass. "I'm not living in a fantasy world, Mag. I'm not holding out false hope. There's absolutely no possible way I can swing by Glastonbury before Saturday night. I'm just being realistic."

Magnus picks up his own goblet and swirls the liquid around, staring at it for a moment. Then he looks at me. "I'll take you," he says, after a long pause.

I stare back at him, trying to ignore the sapphire blueness of his eyes. "What?" I ask, even though I heard him perfectly. It's simply that I can't believe what he said.

"To England. To Glastonbury. To Avalon. To find the Grail."

"You'd . . . you'd take me?" I repeat, knowing I'm not sounding like the most intelligent person at the moment. But still . . .

Magnus shrugs. "Sure. The coven has a few private jets. I can borrow one tomorrow night and we can head over." He sets down his glass. "I honestly don't know if we can find the Grail while we're there, but we can at least give it the old college try, right?"

I nod slowly, blown away by what he's just proposed. I mean, surely he has better things to do than to spend the week on a wild goose chase for the Holy Grail. And yet he's perfectly willing to set aside his plans to help me out.

"That's so . . . nice of you," I say, lamely.

He reaches over and takes my hand in his. Gah! His touch sends chills down my arm, through my body, and down to my toes, like some kind of crazy electrical current. I resist the urge to squirm.

"Sunny," he says, tracing the back of my hand with a finger. Okay, he needs to stop doing that. Right now. "I hope you know I feel bloody awful about what I've put you through. If there's any way I can make it up to you, reverse the curse I've put you under, I want to do that."

I feel my insides melting, like a lime Popsicle in the sun. "Th-thank you," I murmur. "I really . . . appreciate that." I sound totally lame, but what else can I say?

He catches my eyes from across the table. I want to look away, but for some reason find myself totally mesmerized. He really does have amazing eyes. I wonder if he was born with them or if it's something you get as a perk from becoming a vamp. I supposed it would be a pretty good consolation prize. Lose your soul, gain captivating, irresistible eyes. Yeah, that would be cool, actually. Maybe you also get to lose weight and look like a supermodel. Blood would be pretty low in carbs, right? High in protein, rich in iron . . .

We're still staring at one another. This is getting a little weird. I should say something. Look away. Not start thinking about what

I'll do if he reaches across the table, cups my chin in his hands, and kisses me senseless.

'Cause the scary thing is I think I might let him. In fact, I think I might kiss him back.

And that would be a very, very, very big mistake.

"Magnus!" cries a tortured-sounding voice. "There you are."

Magnus turns to address the voice, eliminating any kissing possibilities. Phew. What a relief. After all, I don't want to start any kind of relationship—physical or otherwise—with a creature of the night, especially not one like Mag. Though I do admit, he's a lot nicer and nobler than I first gave him credit for. And he is rather good-looking . . .

I shake my head to get rid of my crazy thoughts and focus my attention on the guy who's approached our table.

"Jareth," Magnus greets our visitor, tight-lipped. Is he disappointed that our potential kissage was so rudely interrupted as well? Nah, I'm imagining things. "How are you this evening?"

"How am I?" Jareth asks with much incredulity. He's tall and good-looking in a Jude Law, British kind of way. Looks about eighteen, but is probably more like eight hundred. "How am I?" he repeats. He pulls up a chair and sits down. "The mighty leader of our coven has been tragically cut down and you ask me how I am?"

"We are all completely devastated by the loss of the master," Magnus agrees cautiously.

"Are you? Are all of you?" Jareth demands, scanning the room with eerie phosphorescent green eyes. See, I really am thinking the eye thing comes from the vampire curse. Who has such cool eyes in real life? (Well, besides that blind chick from season three of *America's Next Top Model*—not that I've ever watched that silly show. Really.) "For a people in mourning, you seem to be having a bloody good time."

He's got a point. No one here at Club Fang looks particularly broken up about the fact that their fearless leader was effectively dusted just twenty-four hours before. Sure, they're all wearing black, but I have a feeling that's more an everyday fashion statement than anything to do with paying their respects to Lucifent.

"We all grieve in our own ways, I am sure," Magnus replies evenly. "Some more openly than others."

"Bah! I would not let them show such disrespect myself," Jareth scoffs. "But I suppose you've got your own style of ruling. Speaking of, when do you plan to officially take command of the coven?"

What the . . . ? I whip my head around to stare at Magnus. What is this guy talking about? Taking command of the coven? Magnus?

Magnus shrugs. "I have some important business to attend to overseas," he explains. "When I return to the States, I will take my reign."

Holy crapola. Is he saying what I think he's saying? Magnus is taking over Lucifent's gig as king of the vampires? I had no idea the guy was that high up on the food chain. I figured he was just some everyday vampire type, but no! He's royalty. How cool is that?

Hmm, I wonder. Does this mean if I end up having to remain a vampire forever that I get to be queen of the vampires? 'Cause that would be kind of cool. Especially if there's a tiara involved. I've always had a thing for tiaras . . .

"Do not stay away too long," Jareth advises sternly. His glowing emerald eyes really are a bit disconcerting. "There are others who would take advantage of your absence to legitimize their own rights to the throne."

"I am aware of their ambitions," Magnus says softly. "And I promise you, I do take them quite seriously."

"Very well, then," Jareth says, evidently satisfied by Mag's answer. "While you are gone, we will publicly throw our support behind you. It will not stop them, but perhaps it will delay their momentum."

"I thank you for that, brother." Magnus reaches over to pull the other vampire into an embrace. Midhug, he whispers something in his ear that for the life of me I can't make out. Not that I'm trying to eavesdrop on them or anything. I'm just curious. And hey, if I'm going to be stuck being queen, I figure I have the right to know all this stuff.

"You will make a fine coven master," Jareth says, after parting from the hug. He rises from his seat and salutes Magnus. "I have much to do, so I bid you farewell. Good luck with your overseas adventure and I hope to confer with you on several matters when you get back."

"I shall look forward to it," Magnus says diplomatically, mirroring the vampire's salute and bowing his head.

Once Jareth's gone, I turn to Magnus, ready to get the 411 on the whole king thing.

"So what's the deal?" I ask eagerly. "You're like king of the vampires now? How come you didn't tell me? I mean, you'd think that might have come up in conversation."

Magnus shrugs. "I didn't think vampire politics would interest you."

"Vampire politics, no. My blood mate being king of the coven, hell yeah."

Magnus raises an eyebrow. "*Your* blood mate?"

I can feel my face heat into a major blush. Why did I just call him that? I didn't mean to. It just kind of slipped out.

"Um, yeah. Well, temporary blood mate, anyhow, right? Until we find the Grail and all."

"Ah." Magnus nods. If I didn't know better, I'd say he almost looks disappointed. Which is totally weird since I know that he doesn't want me as his blood mate any more than I want him to be mine. "Of course."

"So what's the deal?" I ask, going back to the subject at hand. "Are you king or what?"

"Technically, yes. I am next in line for the leadership position of our coven," Magnus says. "I was Lucifent's first fledgling, and therefore his most direct blood link. By vampire law, that makes me master."

"Wow. How cool is that?" I cry. "King of the vampires. That's gotta be a good gig. You must be so psyched."

Magnus shakes his head. "Not especially, no," he says. "The position carries a lot of responsibilities and much danger. There are those, both in the outside world and right in our own coven, who seek to destroy the leader to further their own political agendas."

"Yeah, I heard Jareth say that. So there're going to be guys out to get you? Like vampire guys, not just the Slayer?" Hmm, maybe being king of the vampires ain't such a good gig after all.

"Yes. There will be 'guys out to get me,' as you so eloquently put it," Magnus says with a rueful smile. "But I am not concerned. With Jareth's men by my side I am well protected."

"Are they like bodyguards?"

"Soldiers. Jareth is the general of our army."

"Ah, I see." Wow. This vampire thing is super-organized. It's like this whole underground society, with kings and soldiers and evil guys up to no good . . .

Magnus rises from his seat. "We've dallied long enough. I must make preparations for our trip to England tomorrow."

"Okay," I agree, standing up and grabbing my purse off the floor. I glance at my watch. "I've got to get going anyhow or I'll miss curfew. Can't exactly jet off to England if I'm grounded."

We head out of Club Fang and into the night. I remember the first time we wandered through the parking lot just a few nights ago. At the time I had only thought about getting it on with a hot guy. Ha! If only I'd known what I was in for, I'd have gone shrieking into the night.

At least I think I would have.

"So if you're really going to have to take the throne and all and there are bad, power-hungry vamps that would love to usurp your power and become kings themselves, do you honestly have time to go traipsing off to England to help me find the Holy Grail?" I ask, turning to look at Mag. His already pale skin looks almost lustrous under the moonlight. I don't know how one vampire can be so delicious. It's so unfair.

"Don't get me wrong," I add. "I'm psyched to have your help, since there's no way I can do it on my own. It's just that, trying to be Unselfish Girl and all, it seems you've got a lot on your plate."

Magnus smiles—that gentle, reassuring smile he uses only occasionally, but each time it melts me a little. I can't believe I had thought he was an asshole when I first met him.

"You are my blood mate," he says simply, finding my hand and squeezing it with his own. "I would die for you."

Gah! A little warning before the touching would be nice. Mainly so I can resist the overwhelming urge to morph into a jiggly pile of Jell-O, thank you very much.

"You'd . . . die . . . for me?" I manage to choke out. I've got to lighten the mood here. "Technically aren't you already dead?"

He chuckles at that and pulls on my hand so I end up facing him. We're way too close now. Way overstepping the three-foot-bubble rule. I can feel his breath on my face. His hands moving to my waist. I draw in a raspy breath, trying to sustain some semblance of control.

"Um," I say, suddenly not at my most articulate. My heart is beating out of control and I feel like I'm going to keel over. How can one guy have so much sex appeal?

Then I remember. The Vampire Scent. I'm not really attracted to him whatsoever. It's just those pheromones of his that have got my juices flowing. Ha!

I pull back. "Is there a way you can turn off the Vampire Scent thing?" I ask. "'Cause it's kind of throwing me off my game here."

He laughs and yanks me closer, our bodies now flush against one another, my curves molding into his hard, flat planes of stomach muscle. He feels so good I can barely stand up.

"As my blood mate, you are immune to my Vampire Scent," he whispers in my ear, tickling the lobe with his breath. "Any attraction you feel is all your own."

See? I truly *am* doomed.

"Eh, please. You've totally got it wrong. I don't, er, feel any attraction," I manage to say, reluctantly pulling myself away from his embrace. "I mean . . . um . . ."

He releases me with a grin. "Right. No attraction whatsoever. Good to know." He doesn't look like he believes me for one second. Which is understandable, since I don't even believe myself.

"I've, um, got to get going," I say, stepping backward a few steps. In fact, I need to ditch this scene ASAP—before I throw myself at him and succumb to the passions of the night. (Wow, do I sound like a romance novel or what?) "Don't want to piss off my mom and get grounded for missing curfew for the third night in a row."

Magnus nods. "Of course. I understand." I strain to see if he looks disappointed, but he's keeping a complete poker face. "It is probably for the best. I have much to do."

"Great. Okay." So why do I feel this deep sense of disappointment all of a sudden? What did I want him to do, grab me and drag me back to his lair and have his wicked way with me against my will? He's a gentleman. A retired knight in shining armor, trained in the code of chivalry. Not some barbarian caveman with no respect for women.

"So when do we leave for England?" I ask, turning to walk toward my parked car. Magnus follows, a few steps behind.

"As soon as possible," he says. "I shall arrange for the private jet tonight. Meet me at the Manchester Airport tomorrow at four P.M. and we will go from there."

"Okay," I say, fishing through my purse for my keys. I unlock and pull open the front door. "Then, till tomorrow, I guess."

"Till tomorrow," Magnus repeats.

We both stand there for a moment, as if each is unwilling to be the first to walk away. Why does this have to be so awkward?

Finally Magnus turns to leave.

"Mag?" I call after him.

He stops and turns back to look at me. "Yes?" he asks in a low rumbly voice that totally turns me on all over again.

"Thank you."

He nods slowly and starts walking again. I hear him mumbling something under his breath. Something I can't quite make out. But something that sounds an awful lot like "Anything for you, my love."

But I'm sure I'm just hearing things, right?

FIFTEEN

But I'm a Vampire, Not a Druggie!

I arrive home only three minutes after curfew. I probably broke every speed limit in the book to make it, but I figured if any cops were going to start writing tickets, I'd stick them with my Vampire Scent. It has to be said, that sure is one useful supernatural power. (Except of course when it turns on lesbian secretaries and weirdo perv teachers. That I could do without.)

I unlock the front door to my house and step inside. The place is completely dark. I wonder if everyone's already in bed. Though I suppose Rayne's probably still awake, typing away on her computer as usual. Which is good 'cause I've got to work out a plan with her. Since I can't exactly tell Mom I'm skipping town for a couple days to make an impromptu trip to England hoping to find the lost cup of Christ that will purify my blood and remove the vampire taint, my dear sister is going to have to cover for me.

I enter the hallway, trying to tiptoe. No need to wake everyone up. But my Keep Quiet plan is immediately foiled when I accidentally step on a loose, creaky flagstone. Damn.

A light switches on in the kitchen, making me jump back in surprise, my heart leaping to my throat.

"Sunny? Is that you?"

I breathe a sigh of relief. Just Mom. For a split second I was thinking the Slayer might have figured out where I live and was having a midnight snack while waiting to dust me.

Then again, it's very possible that a curfew convo with mom could be more painful.

"Yeah, mom. It's me." I glance longingly at the stairs that lead up to my dark, cozy bedroom. The fluorescent kitchen light is giving me a headache, even from here. But I know there's no way I'm going to escape a lecture at this point.

"Do you want some Tofutti?" she asks. "I'm making myself a dish."

"No thanks," I say, reluctantly heading into the kitchen. Only my mom would consider ice cream made out of tofu a special treat. I prefer Ben & Jerry's Chunky Monkey myself, and hey, don't those guys work to save the planet, too?

I plop down at the breakfast bar and rub my eyes with my fists. I'm so tired. I haven't had a good night's sleep since this whole thing started. At the same time, I feel really wired and I doubt I'll be able to get any sleep tonight either. At least until dawn, and then Rayne will have to drag me out of bed. I wonder if I can fake sick and avoid school . . . I really need a good day's sleep.

"Are you sure you don't want any? I have some sugar-free carob syrup to put over it," Mom says, holding up the jar. I cringe. I didn't like that imitation hippie chocolate stuff before I became a vampire. I'm certainly not going to develop a taste now.

My mom finishes squirting carob on her Tofutti and puts the bottle and container back in the fridge and freezer, respectively. Then she sits across from me at the breakfast bar and spoons a large scoop into her mouth.

"Mmm," she says, licking her lips. "You don't know what you're missing."

I laugh. "Oh yes, I do. Remember, you forced us to eat this stuff as kids. I didn't taste real ice cream till fourth grade."

"Yes, and that was only because Evil Aunt Edna corrupted you. One mouthful and you became a hopeless junk food junkie," Mom says with a sigh, taking another spoonful. "And you never looked back."

I smile. I know she's not really upset. She raised Rayne and me to be our own people. To have our own thoughts and dreams and ideas. And diets. She taught us her way, but never insisted we follow it. She's cool like that.

"So how did your test go today?" Mom asks, studying me with eyes that on the surface look completely innocent. But I know she's asking a weighted question.

"Um, fine. Fine," I mumble. I really suck at lying. Unlike Rayne, who could enter the Lying Olympics and win the gold medal, hands down. I mean, I thought twins were supposed to have identical DNA, but somehow Rayne got the Good Liar gene and I got stuck with the Face Gives Everything Away one.

"Mmm-hmm," my mom says, sounding more than a bit skeptical. "And your night tonight? Did you have a good night?"

"Yeah, it was okay," I say, praying for no follow-ups. But it seems the interrogation gods have no plans to show me mercy.

"Where did you go?"

"Um, a coffeehouse in Nashua." Figure I might as well be as truthful as possible, without mentioning the whole vampire thing, of course.

"I see." My mom presses her lips together for a moment. "And what did you do there?"

"Drank coffee . . . ?" Well, duh.

"And who did you drink this coffee with?"

I squirm in my seat. "Er, a few friends."

Please don't ask who, please don't ask who, please don't ask who.

"Who?"

Damn.

"Um, there was Rachel and Charity . . ." *Who gave me a goblet of their own blood to drink before taking off,* I imagine telling her. *Wasn't that just so nice of them? And then Jareth showed up. Vampire General, you know. Out to protect Magnus, king of the vampires and my blood mate for eternity, unless I can swing by England*

tomorrow to pick up the Holy Grail. You don't mind if I skip
school for that, do you?

I wonder how many milliseconds it would take for her to dial the
men in white coats?

"Rachel and Charity?" Mom repeats, tapping her temple with
her index finger. "Don't think I've heard you mention them before.
Do they go to school with you?"

"Man, what is it with the third degree, Mom?" I retort, unable
to hold back my guilty annoyance a moment longer. "I mean, since
when do you care who I hang out with or what I'm doing?"

Jeez. I take back all that cool mom stuff. Every single last coolness point awarded over the years. Gone. Tonight, she's as much a
pain in the butt as the rest of my friends' moms.

"Since when do I care?" she repeats, raising her eyebrows. Uh-
oh. I so don't like the raised eyebrows thing. It never turns out good.
"You want to know since when? I guess it'd be since your sister told
me you were studying at the library all night. Alone."

Oh.

Damn it, I knew I should have called Rayne on her cell on the
way home to find out if she'd taken it upon herself to cover for me.

"Oh. Right," I say. I've got to save this or I'll be grounded and
it's going to be a heck of a lot more difficult to get to England with
Magnus. "We were studying. Drinking coffee and studying. This is
sort of a library-slash-coffeehouse kind of place, really. It's the new
'in' thing, actually. Everyone says coffeehouses are the new libraries.
Like you get your caffeine and then you study. It's great and—"

"Sunny, are you on drugs?" Mom suddenly asks, point-blank.

I stop talking immediately, but I think my mouth is still hanging
open in shock.

"Am I on . . . drugs?" I repeat incredulously. She's got to be kidding me, right?

"It's a simple question."

She's not kidding. I can tell by the oh-so-serious expression on
her face. I can't believe it!

"I know it's a simple question, but why would you ask it?" I
demand, very insulted at this point. "Do I *seem* like I'm on drugs?"

My mom shrugs. "Actually, yes, you do. You're out till all hours of the night and you lie about where you are. You throw up first thing in the morning. Your eyes are completely bloodshot and your pupils dilated. Your hands are trembling and you're paler than Rayne with her pancake makeup on. So, yes, I have to say, you do seem like you're on drugs."

Okay, fine. She's got a point. But still . . .

"I'm not, though," I deny, knowing I sound totally lame. But how can I defend myself without spilling the crazy truth, which she'll never believe anyway?

"Sunny, you can tell me if you are," Mom says, putting down her Tofutti spoon. "I know that many teens experiment. I myself dabbled plenty back in the seventies. Pot, acid, you name it, I probably tried it. But if you're going to partake, you need to do it safely. And I want to make sure you're not doing anything dangerous. I love you and I don't want to lose you."

I seriously want to bang my head against the table in frustration. I can't believe my mom thinks I'm doing drugs. And I have no idea how I'm going to convince her otherwise. I mean, everything she's listed is basically a symptom of me turning into a vampire, yet I can't very well tell her that.

"I can assure you, Mom," I say, swallowing back my annoyance. I know she's just trying to help, but I'm tired and cranky and just want to go to bed. "I am not, nor am I planning to be anytime in the near or far future, on any kind of drugs."

My mom sighs deeply, running a hand through her long graying hair. She always jokes that Rayne is the cause of all her premature grays. Tonight, I think she's putting the blame on me as well.

"You know, I had hoped we'd have the kind of mother-daughter relationship where you'd feel free to talk to me about this kind of stuff," she says sadly. "I know it sounds cliché, but I wanted to be your friend as well as your mother. Someone you'd share things with and know that I wouldn't judge you for them. I wanted to have a different kind of relationship with you and Rayne than I had with my own mother."

"You do. We are friends," I cry, reaching over to place my hand over her forearm, succumbing to a major guilt attack. "I do tell you everything. I love you, Mom. It's just honestly, this time there's nothing to tell. I'm simply not on drugs. Period. End of story."

My mother nods slowly. I can see a tear slip from the corner of her eye. Great. Now I've totally upset her. But what can I do? I can't tell her the truth this time. There's no way. But by keeping silent, I'm making it seem like I don't trust her.

Gah, this is so hard.

"Sunny, I hate to do this to you," Mom says, swiping her wayward tear on her sleeve. "But I feel it's for your own good."

Uh-oh.

"If you're not on drugs, then you're obviously sick or something. 'Cause you don't look good. So I need you to stay in until you start looking better."

"You're grounding me?" Crap. I can't be grounded. I have to sneak off to England tomorrow. How can I sneak off to England tomorrow if I'm grounded?

"No, not grounding, exactly."

"But I can't go out."

"Right."

"At all."

"You can go to school . . ."

"So how is that not grounding?" I demand.

She shrugs. "I guess it is. I just always hated that term. It sounds so . . . totalitarian."

"Then why be a fascist dictator?" I try.

"Sunny, please." My mother rubs her temples with her forefingers. "It's late. I'm tired. You have school tomorrow. Go to bed."

"Fine. Whatever," I retort. I jump off the bar stool I was sitting on and head toward the hall. "Some cool mom you turned out to be," I mutter under my breath, secretly hoping she can hear me.

SIXTEEN

The Great Twin Caper

I trudge up the stairs, totally bummed out, and hang a left toward Rayne's bedroom, praying she'll still be awake. If anyone will know what to do in a sitch like this, she will. After all, she's the original bad girl in the McDonald household. I'm just playing catch-up.

I see a crack of light under her door and lightly knock. "Rayne? Are you awake?" I whisper.

"Yeah, of course. Come in."

I push open the door and enter the room. She's got it dimly lit with a black light, and cutouts of bats and spiders on cottony webs glow green on her walls.

She's sitting at her computer, with some kind of role-playing computer game up on her screen. She signs off as I enter and invites me to sit on the bed with her.

"So how'd it go?" she asks eagerly. "Did Mag come up with a way to turn you back?"

"Yeah, sort of. He researched and says he's found something that will purify my blood and remove all the vampire taint for good."

"Great!"

"No, not great, actually. I mean, great that he found something, but not so great that the something in question isn't exactly sold at Wal-Mart."

"Great stuff never is." Rayne shakes her head. "So what is it? Eye of newt? Mummy dust? Vial of slime from the Bog of Eternal Stench?"

"Worse. Blood from the Holy Grail."

"Ouch." Rayne pulls her feet up on the bed so she's sitting cross-legged. "How the heck are you going to get hold of that? Does the Grail even exist?"

So I relate all that Magnus told me about the Grail, its supposed resting place in Avalon, and our impending trip. She looks impressed.

"First a tour of the vampire coven, now a holiday in jolly old England. You're so lucky," she says when I'm finished. "I'm totally jealous."

"Please. I'd so rather have you go in my place," I say with a sigh. "I have no idea how I'm even going to get there."

"I thought you said Mag had a private plane. That's amazingly cool that he has a private plane. I bet it's all luxurious with beds and everything. You know, if I had the opportunity to be with Magnus on a private plane with beds on it, I'd be an official mile-high club member before we landed. Maybe even before we took off." She grins evilly as I swat her on the knee.

"Yeah, yeah," I say, rolling my eyes. It never ceases to amaze me that whatever the subject matter at hand, Rayne can think of a way to relate it to sex.

"What? You don't think I could do it?"

I laugh. "Are you kidding? I'm just shocked to learn you've never done it before. I figured you'd be a mile-high platinum member in good standing, Slut Girl." Now it's Rayne's turn to swat me. "Hey! You hit way too hard!" I protest, rubbing my abused knee.

"You know, for a vampire, you're a real wimp, Sun," Rayne says with a laugh as she collapses on the bed, staring up at the ceiling. Like mine, hers is also lit up by glow-in-the-dark stars affixed during our misspent youths. "So when are you going to England?"

"Well, I'm supposed to leave tomorrow night. But I don't know how I'm going to get out of the house. Mom's evidently decided that I'm some crackhead and has subsequently put me under house arrest."

"Are you kidding me? Mom's grounded you? Wow. She must be really worried." Rayne sits up. "After all, she's not exactly the grounding type."

"I know, I know," I groan. "But she thinks I'm all on drugs or something. 'Cause of how I look and stuff."

"Puh-leeze. You on drugs? Come on!" Rayne snorts in disgust. "She knows you better than that. I mean, I can see her saying *I'm* on drugs. But you? Give me a break."

I shrug, for once not arguing with her over her Sunny the Innocent spiel. I just wish Mom shared her opinion. It'd make things a lot easier.

"So now I'm royally screwed," I say. "I don't want to incur the wrath of the Momster, but my life as I know it depends on this trip to England. I have no idea what I'm gonna do."

"Hmm." Rayne taps her finger on her knee in thought. "Well, why don't I be you?" she suggests at last.

"Huh?" I scrunch up my eyes in confusion. "You mean like you go to England with Magnus?"

"Please. I wish. But no," Rayne says, shaking her head. "What I mean is I can pretend to be the grounded you. And you can pretend to be the me that wants to go sleep over her friend Spider's house. Then you can really sneak off to England."

"You have a friend named Spider?" I ask, raising an eyebrow. "Is that a male friend or female one?"

"Um, well, a little of each, actually. Long story. But Sun, you're missing the point here."

I try to shake the image of the androgynous "Spider" and focus. "So," I recap, "you'd be willing to sit home and play grounded me while I jet off to England to find the Holy Grail?"

Rayne shrugs. "It's a sucky gig, I know. But I sorta feel responsible for getting you into this mess. So sure. I'll be the grounded you."

"Don't you think Mom might catch on? I mean, it'd be ten thousand gazillion times worse if she figured it out. And then you'd get in trouble, too."

"Hello? Earth to Sunny!" Rayne says, waving a hand in front of my face. "In case you don't remember, we are so identical that a superpowerful creature of the night couldn't even tell us apart. You think nearsighted, hippy-dippy Mom will have the slightest clue?"

I think about it for a moment. "You have a point."

"Of course I do," Rayne says, bobbing her head in enthusiasm. "It's perfect. I'll just act real boring and goody two-shoes and she'll never know the diff."

I have to bite my lip not to respond, reminding myself that she's totally saving my life here and I need to cut her a little slack in the tact department.

"Okay, then. It's settled," I say. "Tomorrow morning, you tell Mom you're staying with Spider and then once we're in school we'll switch clothes."

"Sounds like a plan," Rayne says, eyes shining. She loves stuff like this. She pauses for a minute, then adds, "Though I have to say I so wish *I* were going to be the one traveling to England with Magnus."

I look over at her, surprised. "You don't still have a thing for him, do you?" I ask cautiously, trying to sound casual.

Oh, please don't say you have a thing for him, I mentally beg. *That would so not be good.*

My mind wanders back to our night. Magnus stroking the back of my hand. My body pressed against his. Our almost-kiss. I wonder what Rayne would say if she knew about my extracurricular Magnus activities. Would she be mad? If she's still crushing on him, then I have a pretty good idea that she would be. And I don't want to incur the wrath of Rayne.

My twin sighs, long and hard, and throws herself dramatically onto the bed. "Of course I do," she moans. "He's meant to be my perfect match. I mean, I don't know if he told you, but they don't just randomly hook up vamps and humans as blood mates. There are scientific studies and everything. It's very complicated. And after all that, the Council decided that Magnus and I should be destined to spend eternity with one another. And now, because of a stupid, stupid mistake, he's stuck with someone who doesn't even want him."

"I—" I start to protest, then bite down on my lower lip. *Definitely don't want to go there, Sun.* "How do they determine blood mate compatibility?" I ask instead, trying to sound completely detached.

"DNA. Your DNA is compared to the vampire's to determine compatibility," Rayne explains. "You'd know this if you read my blog."

"Yeah, yeah, read the blog, I know, I know," I mutter. But inside I'm thinking something completely different.

Because one thing you may or may not know about identical twins is that they also have identical DNA. Which means technically, if Magnus and Rayne are perfect blood mates . . .

So are Magnus and I.

SEVENTEEN

Swapping Spit with the Sex God

Amazingly enough, the next morning, things start off going exactly to plan. Rayne tells Mom about her sleepover at Spider's and Mom makes offhanded comments like "Okay" and "Have fun." She doesn't even ask who or what a "Spider" is, thank goodness.

Nope, she's way more interested in reminding me that I'm still very grounded. (Though she uses the phrase "resting at home until you feel better" instead of the G-word—something she must have read in the *Hip Mama Handbook*.) But whatever the terminology, the bottom line is the same: I'm to come home directly after school. I am not to pass Go. I am not to collect $200. (After all, I might use it to finance a big crack rock for breakfast, right?)

I try to act all agreeable and normal and non-druggie-like, which turns out to be more difficult than I anticipated, mainly due to my exhausted, bloodshot eyes refusing to open all the way in our bright, sunshiny kitchen. Bleh.

Luckily this morning there's carrot and buckwheat pancakes sans garlic on the menu and I manage to wolf them down without puking. They do nothing, however, to stop the ravenous thirst for blood that's been raging inside me since I first opened my eyes. You know how when you've got your period you crave chocolate like crazy? I've got that kind of craving for blood this morning, but times about a million.

I want blood. I need blood. I'd do almost anything to get it. Gross, I know, but what can I say? Hi, my name is Sunny and I'm a bloodoholic.

At one particularly low point, I find myself mesmerized by a particular vein in my mother's neck. Imagine, here's me, watching it, fantasizing about the delicious, syrupy blood flowing freely inside it. The vein pulses, almost as if it has a life of its own, and I envision sinking my teeth into it and just sucking away like mad.

Then Mom catches me staring.

"What?" she asks, touching her neck self-consciously.

"Nothing, sorry," I say, dragging my eyes away from the tempting little pulse. I can't believe I've just been caught eyeing up my mother like she's a piece of prime rib.

I need serious help.

To prevent further embarrassment, I excuse myself and head to the bathroom, locking the door behind me. I peer into the mirror. Wow. If I were my mom I'd think I was on drugs, too. I look like crap. My face is even paler now—like White Witch of Narnia pale—and my lips are blood red. If I end up remaining a vampire for eternity, I'll never have to restock on lipstick.

My eyes are dark and bloodshot and my pupils are totally dilated. I try squirting a little Visine in them, hoping it will do the trick, but I'm not sure it makes much difference.

And then there's my teeth. Little fangs that slide in and out at will. So weird.

At school I'm a walking zombie. Seriously, if I don't get this vampire thing straightened out soon, I'm going to end up flunking out. There's no way I can concentrate on what the teachers are saying in my current state. And I'm utterly unable to focus my eyes under the fluorescent lights, meaning I can barely read the pop quiz questions from English class.

When the final bell rings, I'm thankful to head to the girls' locker room, where I'm supposed to meet Rayne to change clothes and start The Great Identical Twin Switcheroo.

Unfortunately, before I can make it to the girls' only haven, I'm stopped by a boy.

Not just any boy, however. I'm stopped by Jake. Jake Wilder, to be exact.

My heart flutters a little as he steps in front of me, his dark, brooding eyes raking over my body like I'm some gourmet dessert and he hasn't eaten in a week.

He wants me. Badly. His desire radiates from him.

I shiver.

"Sunny," he cries, his normally deep, velvet voice sounding a little hoarser than usual. "Where have you been?"

I cock my head in confusion. What is he talking about? I've been at school. Like always. "Um, hi, Jake," I say, a little warily. "What do you mean, where have I been?" I steal a glance at my watch. Magnus's plane leaves in one hour and I've got to change clothes first. But I can't exactly blow off the Sex God, now can I? After all, what if he has some important prom thing he needs to ask me about? Like what color my dress is so he can get a matching cummerbund, or something.

Crap. That reminds me—I don't have a dress yet! Haven't exactly had any time to shop for one. You know, this vampire stuff is really wreaking havoc on my everyday schedule.

"I've been looking everywhere for you. It's weird, but . . ." Jake runs a hand through his already seemingly tousled hair. Honestly, he looks a little ill. But then again, I look like death warmed over, so I'm really not one to talk. "I can't stop thinking about you. Even when I'm sleeping . . ." He pauses, red-faced. "I have these dreams where you—"

"Okay, Jake," I interrupt, putting a hand over his mouth. "We're headed deep into TMI territory here." Even though secretly I would love to hear about Jake Wilder's erotic dreams, especially if they involve me, I think I might regret it in the long run . . .

Suddenly, without any kind of warning, Jake grabs me by the

waist and pulls me close to him, covering my surprised mouth with a deep kiss. For a moment I can't breathe. At first I think this is because I'm so turned on by the fact that I'm being kissed by a Sex God. Then I realize Jake's crushing my rib cage.

"Mmhmm," I protest.

Jake loosens his hold and his desperate, breathless kisses travel from my lips down my neck. I do my best to scan the gymnasium, hoping no one's around to see us—I'm so not into PDA. Still, for Jake Wilder, I should probably make an exception.

As he nibbles on my neck, his hands rove up and down my back, almost clawing at me, as if he can't get enough. I am so blown away that he's doing this, I've been rendered speechless. I can't believe Jake Wilder is groping me in the middle of our high school gym. If you had told me I'd be accosted by Jake Wilder in our gym a week before, I would have laughed and laughed and said things like, "Yeah, right" and "Good one!"

Then again, I probably wouldn't have bought the whole vampire thing either. I've got a much more open mind now.

"You smell so good," Jake whispers, his traveling lips now touring my ear. "You're so beautiful."

"Um, thanks?" I say, not quite sure what to do or how to react. I sneak another glance at my watch, then scold myself for doing so.

What am I doing? Who cares if I'm a few minutes late? Magnus is a thousand-year-old vampire. He has eternal life. So technically speaking, he's got all the time in the world. And who knows how much longer I'll be able to make out with Jake Wilder? I mean, once I turn into a human again, I assume he'll go back to not acknowledging my existence. I've got to take advantage of his intoxication.

Then again, that's kind of sick, isn't it? I mean, how can I enjoy a make-out session with someone who's not really into me—who just *thinks* he is? Suddenly, the kisses aren't sexy. Just kind of gross. And sloppy, too, now that I'm being honest. I mean, who really, at the end of the day, enjoys a slimy tongue jammed into her ear? Even if it is a tongue belonging to the resident school Sex God.

I gently push Jake away. "I'm sorry," I say. "But I have to go."

"Please don't go!" he begs, his deep, soulful eyes boring into my skull. Yikes. How hard is this? The man I've loved from afar for two years now is begging me to stay like some kind of lovesick puppy. "Sunny, I want you," he says, reaching over to brush a lock of hair out of my face.

I take a step back, using every last ounce of willpower. "You don't," I say firmly. "You think you do, but you really don't."

Jake's face crumples with a look of devastation. "How can you say that?" he asks.

"Sorry Jake, gotta go." I pat him on the shoulder. "Things to do, people to see, you know how it is. I'll catch you around though."

Crushed Sex God nods desolately. "We're still going to the prom, though, right?" he asks.

"Of course," I say in my most reassuring voice. *If once I reverse the vampire thing you still want to go with me*, I add silently as I say my good-byes and head into the locker room.

And that seems to me a big fat "if."

EIGHTEEN

Leaving—on a Vamp Plane

Rayne is waiting for me in the locker room.

"What happened?" she asks. "You look all bedraggled-like."

"Jake Wilder happened."

Rayne raises an eyebrow. "Ooh, Jake Wilder. Is that a good thing, then?"

"Sort of. I guess. Well, not really." I lean against the nearest locker and sigh deeply. I'm so confused. "It was weird, actually. I mean, don't get me wrong—I have no moral issue with Jake sticking his tongue down my throat, believe me. But still, the whole time he was doing it, I couldn't help but think how he doesn't *really* like me. How he's just bewitched by the Vampire Scent thing and has no idea what he's doing. And suddenly, the impromptu make-out session didn't seem so exciting."

My twin nods in sympathy. "Sorry, Sun," she says. "I can see how that would suck. But hopefully you'll be back to normal before you know it and then you can see once and for all if Jake likes you as a person. Who knows," she adds, "maybe the vampire thing is just a coincidence and he's really been pining for you from afar for years and has finally worked up the courage to talk to you."

"Right. And maybe someday you'll end up being an investment banker with a minivan, a husband who wears paisley ties, and three Gap kids."

Rayne snorts. "Touché."

"It doesn't matter anyhow," I say, pushing myself off the locker. "I've got to concentrate on my mission. Jake and his weird new obsession must wait. Turning back into a human takes precedence."

I slip out of my jeans and tank top and hand them to Rayne. She in turn offers up a long black skirt and peasant blouse that reek of patchouli.

"Make sure you wipe all the goop off your face," I remind her as she slips into my jeans, complaining how awful they make her thighs look. "Mom's never going to buy the idea of me channeling Taylor Momsen."

"I know, I know," Rayne says. "Relax, will you? It's going to be fine. We're not going to get caught. You'll get to England no problem, find the Grail, turn back into a human, and live happily ever after with dopey, puppy-dog Jake Wilder."

"One can only dream," I answer with a dash of dramatic flair. I pull the peasant blouse and skirt on and glance at myself in the mirror. This is not a good look for me. And Magnus, safe and sound in some very now-looking Armani ensemble, is going to have a field day.

Not that I care what he thinks, obviously.

After the clothes swapping and face washing, Rayne drives me to the airport where I'm to meet Magnus. I'm not very talkative on the way there, mainly 'cause I'm still very nervous about this whole thing. I mean, think about it for a second. I'm now leaving the country with a man I barely know, who incidentally happens to be an immortal creature of the night.

Not exactly your typical 7-Eleven Cherry Slurpee run.

All too soon, Rayne pulls up to the private hangar where Magnus says the coven keeps its jet. I had this strange idea in my head that Air Vampire would be a black plane with a blood-red interior. But I guess that would be too obvious, 'cause the real-life vehicle in question just looks like your typical, nondescript private plane.

I hug Rayne good-bye before exiting the car.

"Good luck," she whispers. "Take good care of Magnus for me."

"I will," I say, getting that lovely guilty feeling back in the pit of my stomach. Maybe it's just my thirst for blood. I hope Magnus has a good supply on board, 'cause I feel like I'm going to pass out from hunger.

I get out of the car and head for the plane. A man in a pilot's uniform greets me with a friendly smile.

"Hello," he says in a clipped British accent. "You must be Ms. McDonald."

"Yup, that's me," I reply. "But you can call me Sunny."

He gestures to the stairs leading up to the plane. "You may board at your convenience, ma'am."

I glance around the tarmac. "Where's Magnus?"

"Inside," the pilot informs me. "He is taking a nap at the moment."

Ah, that makes sense. I thought it seemed too early—too daylight—for him to be up and about. He must have holed himself up in the plane before dawn and made plans to wake up midflight, once the sun's retreated from the horizon.

I head up the stairs, turning to give one last wave to Rayne. The nervous feeling starts nagging at my stomach once again. But I squash it and attempt to step confidently into the plane.

I forget my nerves completely when my eyes fall on the jumbo jet's interior décor. Just like the coven, this place reeks of luxury. Decked out in gold and velvet, it's a display of wealth that's almost obscene. There are soft leather armchairs and ridiculously huge plasma TVs. Bottles of red wine (blood?) chilling in silver buckets and state-of-the-art laptops sitting on etched-glass desks. This is truly the Ritz of the airplane world.

"Please have a seat and fasten your seat belt," the pilot says, coming up behind me. "We'll be taking off shortly."

I comply, still blown away by all the extravagance. Being a vampire sure has some perks. Then again, Mag is the next in line to be king. I wonder if the plane is available to all the vamps or just the ones in high places.

I switch on the television, delighted to find it has every movie under the sun. I pick a light comedy, eager to be distracted, and settle into my uber-comfy seat. A minute later, I'm out like a light.

"SUNNY?"

I open one eye, then the other, slightly annoyed at being disturbed from my slumber. Magnus is peering over me, a slight smile playing at the corner of his mouth.

"Are you going to sleep all night?" he asks, poking me lightly in the shoulder.

"Grumph," I reply, trying to roll to my other side to ignore him. Unfortunately, like a good girl, I'd fastened my seat belt so I have limited maneuverability.

"Wake up. We're here," he instructs.

"Here?"

"In England. The town of Bristol, to be exact."

"What time is it?"

He glances at his watch. Rolex, of course. "It's just before three A.M. local time. We've got to get to our safe house before the sun rises."

I yawn, stretching my hands above my head. "Safe house?" I ask. I can't believe we're in England. That I slept through the whole flight. I didn't even get a chance to enjoy all the luxuries the plane had to offer. Darn. Maybe on the way back . . .

Magnus nods. "You know I can't get caught out in the sunlight. I've arranged with a local vamp holiday house for us to stay with them until nightfall. Then we'll travel by car to Glastonbury. It's about an hour trip."

"Oh. Okay," I say. I had forgotten about Magnus's aversion to the sun. This meant our trip was going to have to take longer than I anticipated. I had stupidly assumed we'd get to England, grab the Grail, and head straight back to America, arriving just after school ended. Hopefully Rayne will be able to keep up the twin charade a bit longer.

I unfasten my seat belt and follow Magnus out of the plane.

There's a limo (of course!) waiting and a properly dressed chauffeur opens the door for us to climb inside.

Once settled and on our way, Magnus turns to me. "So how are you holding up?" he asks, to his credit sounding genuinely concerned.

"Fine."

"No. I mean, really," he insists. "It's okay. You can tell me. I'm sure it's been a bloody terrible experience for you. It's hard enough for those who have been properly trained. But to go through all this completely unprepared . . . Well, I can only imagine how hard it must be."

I nod slowly. "It's really strange," I admit. "My mom thinks I'm on drugs. I've got all these weird cravings. I feel sick to my stomach all the time. It's hard to see under fluorescent lights and the sun beats down on my skin as if it could blister it at any moment. And," I add, reluctantly, "I feel like I'm dying of thirst."

There. I said it. I admitted I wanted—make that needed—blood. I'm officially a freak of nature. But then again, so's he.

Magnus nods sympathetically. "I'm sure you're ravenous by this point. I had some wine for you on the plane, but I didn't want to wake you. Figured you needed all the sleep you could get." He pats me lightly on the knee. "Hang in there. When we get to the coven, we will be able to feed."

Oh goody. I can't wait.

NINETEEN

Vampire Hotel

Ten minutes later, we pull up to an old English manor. An ancient scary-looking one like you always see in the movies, with wrought-iron gates and scads of unhappy ghosts going around and haunting everyone. But Magnus assures me the vampires who live here keep the place clean of any sort of poltergeists.

The interior of the mansion is less ostentatious than the American coven. It's also not underground, which means all the windows have had to be boarded up to make sure no sunshine slips in. An old vampire (I mean, they're all old, technically speaking, but this one actually has the liver-spotted hands to prove it) greets us, bowing low to Magnus.

"Well met, good sir. I hear you will be taking over The Blood Coven," he says in a low, respectful voice. His accent reminds me of the ones you hear vampires use in the movies. Like from Transylvania or something.

Magnus returns the bow. "Indeed. But first I must attend to some important business in Glastonbury. So I do thank you for allowing us weary travelers a place to rest."

It's so interesting to me how formal vamps are when they chat with one another. It's like there's some secret vampire-speak they've all mastered. Then again, I guess in the era when they were growing up human, that's how people really talked. They probably prefer it and only learn slang to keep up appearances among mortals.

"Of course. It is an honor to host you and your blood mate," the grandpa vampire says. The tux he's wearing totally screams Dracula wanna-be, but I'm not opening my big mouth this time. I mean, really. For all I know, the guy *is* Dracula.

Drac escorts us down the hallway and up a large winding flight of stairs. The place looks very badly kept up, to tell you the truth. There's cobwebs everywhere. If I end up stuck as a vamp forever, I'm living in the luxury New England coven instead. Way more my style.

The doors to the bedrooms look like vaults in a bank, each with its own keypad lock. Drac picks a door, seemingly at random, and enters a code. The door swings silently open into a blackened room.

Magnus bows low again. "Thank you, my good sir," he says.

Drac returns his bow and then retreats down the hall. Magnus ushers me into the room.

Where there is only one bed.

"Um." I scan the room. "Hmm."

"What's wrong?" Magnus asks, shutting the door behind us. He's standing directly behind me, and I can feel his breath on my neck, which is a tad disconcerting. I step into the room to add space between us.

"Doesn't Drac have a second bedroom? I mean, this is a mansion, right?"

"Drac?" Magnus repeats, raising an eyebrow in question.

I blush. Forgot that was just my nickname for the guy. "You know, our illustrious host."

Magnus grins. "He does look a bit like the legendary Dracula, doesn't he?" he admits. "We all used to tease him about that in our younger days . . ."

"Um, can we walk down memory lane later, Mag? Right now we need to concentrate on the big picture," I interrupt. I don't mean to be rude, but there's a pressing issue to be dealt with here. "We have one room. One bed. And two of us."

Magnus nods. "Indeed. I am sure our host has assumed that we would share a bed, as we are blood mates, after all."

"Well, we all know what assuming does, right? Makes an *ass* out of *you* and *me*."

"I'm sorry, Sunny. But if I were to ask him for a second room, it would raise far too many questions. Questions that might undermine my newfound position as coven master."

"Ah," I say, realizing what he's saying. "So if you were to say you screwed up and did an unauthorized bite on some poor innocent girl like me, then people might say you're unfit to be king?"

He nods. "Indeed. And while I do not relish the idea of taking over the coven, it would be better that I do so than to let those seize control who do not have the coven's best interests at heart."

"Gotcha," I say. "So we have to play loving blood mates in front of the other vamps."

"Basically, yes."

"And that means sharing a bed."

"Yes."

For a moment I wonder if he's lying. Just making it up so he can be in a position to get his groove on with me. But then, that's a huge charade to come up with just for a little booty call. And really, he doesn't seem the type to have to trick his dates into bed, not with his looks and appeal.

"Okay, fine," I say. "We'll share a room."

"I can sleep on the floor," he volunteers, going all knight-in-shining-armor chivalrous again.

I shake my head. "I appreciate the gesture, but there's no need." I gesture to the bed. "It's like king-sized plus. I'm sure we can both fit comfortably on it."

"Okay. If you're sure."

"Yup. Positive. And speaking of beds . . ." Even though I just woke up a short time ago, I already feel sleepy again. I kick off my shoes and crawl under the covers on the left side of the bed.

In turn, Magnus pulls off his shirt, revealing those killer abs that make me drool every time, then joins me in bed, keeping his distance on the right side.

So now we're in the same bed, but chasms apart. And while I freely admit I've never shared a bed with a guy, even platonically, it doesn't seem that weird. And I completely trust Magnus, for some unknown reason, not to do any funny business.

"Get some rest," the vampire says, turning over to his side to face me. "We're going to have a busy night tonight finding the Grail."

"I will," I say, yawning. I cuddle into my plush feather pillow. This bed is truly deluxe and I feel suddenly very warm and safe. "Thanks."

"You're welcome," he says simply. Then he smiles a sleepy little smile and my insides involuntarily go to mush. "I am happy to do it."

"No, I mean for everything," I babble on, not quite ready to shut my eyes for some reason. Not quite ready to stop looking into his beautiful blue eyes, if we're being completely honest here. "You've got a ton on your plate with the whole taking over the coven thing. And bringing me here to England on what could be a total wild goose chase is probably the last thing you wanted to do this week."

He reaches over and brushes a strand of hair from my eyes. "It's no bother. Really."

"You know, Magnus," I say, feeling warm and cozy from his touch and for once deciding not to fight the tingly feelings. "You're really a nice guy. If I *did* want to be a vampire, you'd totally be my first choice for blood mate."

He smiles again, though this time I'm half convinced his eyes look a little sad. "Go to sleep, Sunny," he whispers, leaning over to kiss me softly on the forehead. "Go to sleep."

I do.

TWENTY

A Rave Mistake

I sleep like a rock and wake on my own when the sun sets, feeling well rested, though ravenously hungry. I open my eyes. Somehow in the middle of the day, Magnus has shifted in his sleep and is currently lying with his arm draped over me, spooning me into him. Surprised at the nearness and more than a bit uncomfortable, I squirm out of bed, waking him in the process.

He rubs his eyes sleepily. "Is it nighttime?" he asks.

I glance at the bedside clock. "Yup. Eight P.M. on the dot." I wonder if he has any idea I was just in his arms. Hopefully not, as that would be *très* awkward.

"Excellent." He rises from bed and grabs his shirt from the floor, pulling it over his head. "Time to head to Glastonbury."

Since we've both slept in our clothes, there's not much getting-ready time and moments later I follow him out of the bedroom and down the stairs.

"What's Glastonbury like, anyhow?" I ask as we step outside the mansion. The limo is still waiting for us, go figure. I wonder if the driver got any sleep.

"It's a very quiet village, home to many artisans and spiritualists," Magnus explains as we get into the limo. "Quaint, actually. A pleasant holiday spot for most tourists."

"Cool." I always wanted to visit one of those stereotypical English country towns, with stone cottages and antique shops.

"Once a year they have a major festival with big-name musical acts," he continues. "The crowds descend on the town in droves. Usually more than a hundred thousand people show up, if you can believe it. They camp for three days in a field, listen to music, dance, and do God knows what drugs. It's meant to be quite insane."

"Sounds cool. When's the festival?"

"Oh, they don't hold it until the end of June or so. Never in May."

I frown, disappointed. "Too bad. It sounds like a blast."

"Believe me, it's for the best. With a hundred thousand people crowding the town, the druid order makes itself scarce. We'd never find them and thus never find the Grail."

"Oh. Well, then I guess it's a good thing it's not that time of year." Obviously, getting the Grail is much more important than partying at some big English rave.

"Indeed."

"Still, it would have been kind of cool to see. A hundred thousand people standing in a field, all one with the music. You don't get that in America."

Magnus pauses for a moment, then says, "If you really want to see it, I can take you in June, if you like."

I glance over at him, completely taken aback. Is he making post-vampire plans with me? Does he honestly think we'll be hanging out with each other after I turn back into a human? Is it even possible to keep some kind of relationship . . . friendship going between a vampire and a human? And if it is possible, is that what I want to do?

Do I want to keep hanging out with Magnus after I've been re-humanized? I've only known him a few short nights, but if I'm being completely honest here, I do kinda like having him around. He's funny and interesting and loyal and chivalrous, and yummy as anything. What's not to like? Then again, what will I do when he eventually gets assigned another blood mate? Will he drop me like a hot clove of garlic when the Council assigns him a real, willing partner? His true queen? And how will I deal with that?

No, I decide to myself. It's better to make a clean break of it. Once I turn back into a human, that's it. I'm severing all ties. Forgetting vampires even exist and going on with my normal boring everyday life.

"Um, Sunny? You know what I was just saying about taking you to the festival?" Magnus says, interrupting my whirling thoughts. I glance over. He's staring out the tinted window.

Okay, here goes. Time to make the break. I swallow hard. "You know, Mag, you really don't have to—"

"I think we may see it after all."

"Huh?"

Magnus leans back into his seat. "Look out the window."

I scramble over him to cup my hands over the glass and peer outside. Then I gasp.

The festival, it seems, has been moved up a month.

Everywhere I look, there's people. All types of people. Young people. Old people. People with dreadlocks. People with mohawks. People dressed in designer clothes and people dressed as Goths. Hippies, ravers, stoners, metalheads. All swarming the streets with sloshy plastic cups of beer.

"Oh my gosh," I cry. "The festival is . . . now?" The second I voice the question I realize how obvious the answer is. We're in the middle of a swarm of people.

I sink back into the leather seat. Great. Just great. I make it all the way to England and it just happens to be on the one day of the year when the druids I'm seeking go into hiding. Once again, my lack of luck astounds me.

"Wow. This sucks," I say mournfully.

"Indeed," Magnus agrees, as always not the most optimistic of blood mates.

"What are we gonna do?"

"Well, there's no way to find the druids in this mess," he says, peering out the window again. "They'll have gone underground. We'll just have to wait it out."

"But it's Thursday night. And I turn into a vampire on Saturday. That doesn't give us much time."

Magnus reaches over and squeezes my knee. I know he means it to be comforting, but it's totally not. "I know, Sun," he says. "It's a complete disaster. I'm so sorry."

I look out the window again, feeling the tears well up in my eyes and drip down my cheeks. Of all the unfortunate things to happen, this has got to be the worst. My one chance for redemption has been ruined by a massive flock of English raver kids. Don't they have school? Don't they have lives? Why are they here, set on ruining mine?

I try to resign myself to life as a vampire. It won't be that bad, will it? I mean, I'll have riches beyond my wildest belief, unimaginable powers. That'll be fun, right? And hey, if we're being honest here, sunshine is completely overrated. As is college. And getting married and having a family. And . . .

Oh, what's the use? No matter how you slice it, this absolutely blows. I don't want to be a vampire. I'm sure it's a fine lifestyle choice for some people. But it's just not me.

The sobs come in full force now. Choking, rasping gulps of sorrow that rack my body. Soon, I'm crying so bad I'm actually shaking. All this time I've held out hope that somehow the process could be reversed. And now that I know I'm doomed, the magnitude of my situation hits me like some Acme anvil in a Road Runner cartoon.

This sucks.

This totally sucks.

This totally, utterly, and unbelievably sucks.

Suddenly I feel arms around me, pulling me away from my dark pit of despair and enveloping me in a warm, safe embrace. I press my head against Magnus's shoulder and just let him hold me as I cry. Let him stroke my back with his fingers as I choke out my sobs.

"Shh, shh," he soothes. "It's going to be okay."

"It's *not* going to be okay," I cry. "I'm going to be a vampire forever."

"That's not necessarily true," he whispers. "We can find a way. Or wait till the festival is over. The place could be completely evacuated tomorrow, which would give us plenty of time to find the Grail."

I sniff, wishing I had a Kleenex to wipe my nose. I hate getting all slobbery like this. I pull away from Magnus's hug, so I can look him in the eyes. He gazes back at me, solemn and concerned.

"You really think we have a chance?" I ask, brushing the tears away with my sleeve.

He nods slowly. "I do," he says. "And Sunny, I don't want to sound negative here, but even if we don't, which I don't think will happen," he adds, probably in response to my crumpling face, "but worst-case scenario," he reaches over and cups my face in his hands. I suck in a breath. "I want you to know that I won't abandon you. I won't leave you to fend for yourself. If you have to stay a vampire, I promise you now, I will be your blood mate in every sense of the word. As long as you want me or need me, I will keep you safe. You don't have to be afraid. I will never leave you."

This promise, this confession, this ultimatum from the beautiful creature in front of me is almost too much. My heart breaks and soars all at the same time. I don't know whether to throw up or throw my arms around him.

"Th-thank you," I murmur. "That means a lot to me."

He doesn't reply. Well, not with words anyway. He just leans in and kisses me.

TWENTY-ONE

He Did the Mash,
He Did the Monster Mash

It isn't like our first kiss, the one out in the parking lot of Club Fang. That was a kiss full of lust. Of empty passion between two strangers who knew nothing of one another. And it isn't like the kiss Jake Wilder gave me just before I jetted off to England. That was, admittedly, a bit on the sloppy side.

This kiss is different. It's impossible to describe. At least not without sounding like someone out of my Aunt Edna's romance novels.

So I stay still for a moment, simply enjoying the softness of his lips moving against mine, forgetting for a moment all my pain, my worries, my fears, and just relaxing into his embrace. Taking in the strength and reassurance his mouth is offering me. (Okay, maybe I *am* stepping into romance heroine-speak for a moment, so sue me.)

And then, against my better judgment, I kiss him back.

For a moment, we are one. Tasting, touching, loving one another. There are no longer human-vampire cohabitation issues. Just two individuals who feel the undeniable need to connect with one another on a kind of base, intimate level.

Insert major dreamy sigh here.

He pulls away first, blushing furiously. I notice blood tears leaking from the corners of his eyes before he brushes them away.

"I'm sorry," he mutters, turning to look out the window. "I shouldn't have done that."

I stare at him for a moment, unable to speak, knowing that whatever I say next will turn the tide of our relationship forever. I realize my fingers are clawing at the leather seats and I release my hold.

I think of the possibilities. If I stay vampire, there's no reason we can't hook up, right? I mean, we're blood mates; our DNA is compatible to spend an eternity with one another. And after all, if I'm stuck as a vamp, there's no one I'd rather be stuck with than sweet, perfect, caring Magnus who kisses like a god.

By the same token, if I do manage to regain my humanity (and let's be honest, that's plan number one), would it be realistically feasible to keep such close ties to an immortal creature of the night?

Seriously. I mean, what would it be like to have a vampire boyfriend? As far as I can imagine, it could never work. We couldn't get married, for one. (What would he put on the marriage license as his date of birth?) And after a few years, I'd start growing old and he'd stay looking like a teenager forever. What would people say to an aging sixty-year-old woman with a handsome teenage boyfriend? (Well, besides "ew" anyway.) I mean, the whole Demi and Ashton thing is weird enough. This would be much, much worse.

And then there's the blood mate issue. The Council will eventually assign Magnus a new, proper blood mate. Someone to spend eternity with who won't grow old and complain about her arthritis. And what am I supposed to do then? Make it a threesome? Somehow I doubt Mrs. New Blood Mate would be down with that.

Nope, there's no way around this. It's not going to work. And it's probably better to pull off the Band-Aid all at once, as they say, rather than slowly prolonging the torture. Stop myself. Stop him. Stop this budding relationship now—before I'm in too deep. Before I find myself in love or something equally ridiculous like that.

"I think we need to concentrate on finding the Grail right now," I say firmly, crossing my arms over my chest. I hope I look confident and in control, 'cause inside all that's raging is doubt and confusion. I hold my breath, waiting for his response. Is he going to be pissed? Or beg me to reconsider?

But all he does is nod and I can see his hard swallow. "Of course," he agrees, clearing his throat. "We should most certainly be concentrating on that."

I squeeze my eyes shut. Gah! This is so, so hard. Suddenly all I want to do is throw my arms around him and continue where we left off. Kiss him senseless all night long. But that would be really stupid. Impulsive gratification that would lead to a lifetime of regret.

I can feel him staring at me, his beautiful blue eyes boring into my skull, as if he's attempting to read my mind. I suddenly realize I never did determine whether he had the power to do that. I hope he doesn't. I don't want him to see all the confusion swirling around in my head.

"Well, since we're here," I say at last, determined to switch to a safer, less painful subject, "maybe we should go out and enjoy the festival."

Magnus glances out the window again, looking as if I just asked him to dine on the blood of a garlic farmer. I don't blame him. I'm sure the last thing he wants to do at this moment is wade through a crowd of drunken revelers, taking in the sights like some undead tourist with nothing better to do.

"Never mind," I say, taking it back. Screw it. I don't want to make things worse. Plus, how much fun could we really have in our depressed, mopey states? "It was a dumb idea."

"No, no," Magnus protests, looking back at me, his expression completely unreadable. "It's a rather good idea, actually. You'll probably never get a chance to experience such chaos again. Might as well make the most of it, right?" He tries to smile, but it's definitely a halfhearted attempt.

"Okay," I hedge. "If you're sure . . ."

"Sure, I'm sure. It'll be fun."

I'd actually believe him, if he weren't wearing a death-warmed-over expression on his pale face. But before I can object, he instructs the limo driver to wait here and opens the car door.

"Let's go," he says with what sounds to me like forced cheerfulness.

We step out into the night. Into the crowds. Into the craziness. "Here goes nothing," I mutter, not sure why I thought this was a good idea.

We struggle to make our way through the throng, buy two tickets from a bearded scalper wearing a Tottenham Hotspurs soccer jersey. Then we head through the makeshift gates and onto the field. And it's there that my jaw drops open in wonderment.

Wow. All I can say is *wow*.

Seriously, you've never lived until you've seen a hundred thousand people dancing all at once. The stage appears miles away and the performers look like ants from our location. But that doesn't seem to bother the festivalgoers in our geographic sphere. They're dancing like they've got front-row tickets to the action—bouncing up and down to the music, screaming their heads off, and generally having a grand old time.

I grin, feeling my doubt and depression slink away, replaced by a shared vibe of excitement. I mean, how cool is this? We have nothing like it in America. These Brits really know how to rock out. I'm so glad we decided to get out of the car.

"Well, this is a bit disconcerting, isn't it?" Magnus yells in my ear, evidently not sharing my enthusiastic sentiments. Then again, as a proper, thousand-year-old vampire, I'm guessing this mania really isn't his regular scene.

I, on the other hand, have determined that I'm going to have a good time and he's not going to wreck it for me. 'Cause I deserve it, after all I've been through this week. Yup, I'm now ready to cut loose and stop thinking about all the bad stuff and just get down on the dance floor. (Or grass floor, as the case may be.)

And that means Magnus is so not allowed to be the old fuddy-duddy stick in the mud that I can see he's planning to be. We need to put our differences aside tonight. Enjoy ourselves and our unique surroundings. After all, this could be a once-in-a-lifetime experience. I want to enjoy it.

So I grab him by the hand and drag him into the midst of the throng. "Dance!" I yell at him, not sure he can hear me over the music. I start bopping to the beat myself, hoping he'll get the picture.

He rolls his eyes and stands still for a moment, perhaps calculating how many vampire coolness points he'd lose for getting his groove on at the Glastonbury Festival. Knowing what I do about the Vampire Code, I'm sure raving's considered "behavior not becoming" for the incoming king. But still . . .

"There's no one here to see you," I remind him. "And I'll never tell!" I grab his hands and start dancing around him, trying to force him to move. At first he stands there like a stone statue, then slowly starts nodding his head to the beat. Then, other body parts follow.

At first he's awkward, just going through the motions. But by the time the next song starts up, I can tell he's getting into it. By midtune, he's totally boogieing down.

"Whoo-hoo!" I cry, throwing my arms around him in a big hug. I probably shouldn't be doing things like that, seeing as I'm trying to keep our relationship on a platonic level. But at that moment, it feels like a perfectly normal thing to do. And hey, we're still friends, right? And friends hug. No big deal. I squeeze tighter. "I knew you could do it!" I say in his ear.

He laughs. "Bloody hell!"

And so we dance. And hop. And twirl. At one point we dance together, clutching onto one another like deranged prom dates. I can tell from the looks on the other ravers' faces that this kind of twosome "old-fashioned" dancing isn't really festival approved. But I don't care. Having Magnus's hands on my waist, spinning me on the grassy dance floor, feels too good for me to worry about what other people think.

After what seems like hours of cardio, we collapse, laughing and sweaty and exhausted, onto a nearby grassy clearing that is remarkably free of people.

"Whew!" I cry. "That was fun."

"Indeed."

Magnus lies down on the grass, staring up into the darkened sky. I join him. It's a beautiful night. The moon hangs low and full and is almost orange in its intensity. Perfect temperature and a clear sky, glittering with pinpricks of light. Nice. You know, if I do end up stuck as a vampire for all eternity—never again setting foot under the sun—at least I'll always have the stars to keep me company.

"I haven't been dancing in probably eighty years," Magnus admits. "Not since the Roaring Twenties, I shouldn't think."

"Really?" I'm surprised. That's a long time not to get your groove on. "Not even at Club Fang?"

"Not really my thing," he admits. "Just 'cause I'm a vampire, doesn't mean I'm into the Goth scene."

"Yeah. I suppose that makes sense," I reason. "Like why go around dressing in black and wishing you were dead, when technically you already are."

He grins. "Exactly."

"Well, your first time dancing in nearly a century—how did you enjoy it?"

"Very much so. I think I might only wait a decade or two to try it again," he says dryly. I shove him playfully on the shoulder.

"Whatever, dude. We're so dancing again in like five minutes' time and you know it!"

"Are we now? Well, if you say so, it must be true."

I roll onto my side to face him and he does the same. "Come on, admit it. You had fun. You're dying to do it again."

"All right, all right. It was quite enjoyable," he says with a small smile. "But don't say a word to anyone back at the coven. I'm trying to build up credibility for my takcover. And I hardly think 'getting my groove on,' as you so delicately put it, will impress many as to my leadership abilities."

"Who cares what they think? I mean, screw them! What business of theirs is it what you do in your spare time? Are you vamps not allowed to have fun or something?"

He sighs. "Vampire politics are very complicated. And our systems have been in place for nearly a thousand years. Most of our kind are very set in their ways and do not take kindly to modernisms or vampires who try to stay with the times. It's unfortunate, though," he adds after a pause. "I believe our species is missing out on a lot of good nights out."

"Well, when you're king you can change all that."

"It's not that easy. But we shall see." He reaches over and brushes away a lock of hair that's fallen into my sweaty face. I wish he wouldn't keep doing that. I find it way too romantic for comfort. "You have a great outlook on life, Sunny," he says, softly. "I could learn a lot from you."

I can feel myself blushing and have no idea how to respond. "Thanks?" I venture at last.

He smiles, but doesn't speak. For a moment we just stare at one another. I wonder if he's going to kiss me again, but he doesn't make a move. He's probably afraid to, seeing how I reacted the last time. Instead he just lies there and watches me with his sad, blue, beautiful eyes.

I can't stand it.

"I love this song! Let's go dance," I exclaim, jumping to my feet. I don't really love this song. In fact, I'm not even sure what song it is. Or what band, for that matter. But I've got to break the spell somehow and this is the only way I can think to do it.

I grab him by the hand and yank him up. He laughs and together we weave back out into the crowds. Soon we're dancing again and I'm relieved to note that Magnus seems to have abandoned his dark thoughts and looks actually rather happy as he moves to the rhythm of the night.

IT SEEMS LIKE only minutes later, but must be hours, when I look up at the sky. The horizon has pinkened with predawn light. "We'd better get going," I tell Magnus. "We don't want to be caught in the sun."

"One more song?" he begs. "I love Coldplay."

I laugh. Gone is the cool, slightly ironic vampire he pretends to be. Now he's a kid in a candy store. Eyes shining. Alive. (Well not technically alive, but you know what I mean.) Mission accomplished.

"Fine by me. You're the one who's going to be burned to a crisp," I tease.

He sighs. "You're right, of course. Let's go."

We head back to the limo, which miraculously is still waiting for us. Guess if you pay someone enough, he'll stick around till Judgment Day. So cool. I would love one of these chauffeur set-ups to bring me to school and back everyday. Fetch my lunch from the local pizza joint and have it hot and waiting for me at lunchtime.

The chauffeur opens the door for us and we climb inside. If I had a limo, though, I'd redo the boring interior. Maybe throw up a few disco lights or something. Make it really fun. Hmm, I wonder if MTV ever pimps these kinds of rides.

The chauffeur gets in his side and puts the key in the ignition. Soon, we're speeding back to Château du Vampire.

"That was so much fun," I say, after a long yawn, sinking back into my leather seat. I'm so sleepy all of a sudden. I guess hours upon hours of dancing in a field will do that to a girl. Not that it wasn't totally worth it.

"Indeed," Magnus agrees. "I had a fantastic time. More fun than I've had in centuries." He smiles his shy smile. "Thank you, Sunny."

"Anything for you, Maggy," I respond, trying to keep the mood light. I can't bear to have him go all mushy again. It'll ruin all my work to keep things platonic.

I close my eyes, pretending to sleep, mainly to avoid looking at him. But even with my eyes squeezed shut, I can feel him on the other side of the limo. His stare. His desire for me. I don't know if it's a blood mate thing or what, but I can feel it radiating from his body.

He wants me. I'm sure of it. As sure as I am about Marshmallow Peeps being the best candy in the universe. And if I'm being completely honest here, I want him, too. In fact, I'd like nothing better than to cuddle up next to him and sleepily exchange sweet kisses and caresses all day long.

But I can't. I can't give in. I must stay strong. Break this all off now, before it's too late. Before I fall in love.

I open one eye and steal a glance over at him. He smiles at me.

Oh God, what if I already have?

TWENTY-TWO

Ancient Druid or
Mad Football Hooligan?

When I awake that night, it's raining hard. And I can hear the wind whistling through the trees. I climb out of bed, careful not to wake Magnus, and pull back the heavy drapes to look out the window. This is the stereotypical weather everyone says England always has, I guess.

Suddenly I miss America with a vengeance. What am I doing here? In a foreign country, spending the night dancing in a field like a crazy person, with only a vampire to keep me company? This isn't me. I'm normal. Average. I don't do things like this.

I just want to go home.

But I can't. Not until we get the Grail. Otherwise this whole adventure has been for nothing. Otherwise I'll be stuck as abnormal for eternity.

I look at my watch. Eight P.M. I wonder how Rayne is doing, handling Mom. Pretending to be me. She sounded a little bored of the charade when I called her early this morning. But she said not to worry. That she'd take care of everything.

She never stresses out or overthinks anything. She just goes with the flow and doesn't care what people say. I envy that in her.

"Sunny?"

I turn back to the bed. Magnus is sitting up, rubbing his eyes sleepily. Guess I woke him up after all.

"Hey," I say, quickly exchanging my view of him for one of the ground, mainly to avoid seeing him shirtless and sexily mussed from sleep. Seriously, when I wake up in the morning (or evening in this case) I look like death warmed over. He looks like Brad Pitt at the Oscars.

"Hey yourself."

Wow. This is kind of awkward, really. Things still feel so unsettled between us.

"So, um, do you think the festival's over?" I ask, trying to stay on neutral ground.

Magnus nods. "Yes, I heard someone say Coldplay was the final act. So I'm sure everyone's either left or is sleeping it off somewhere."

"So do you think that means that the druids could be back then?"

"Hopefully. We shall certainly try to find out."

"Cool. Well, what are we waiting for? Let's go."

Magnus gives me a funny look, but doesn't comment at first. Is it that obvious that I just want to get him dressed and out of the bedroom ASAP?

"Sunny, I think we need to talk," he says at last.

Talk? Sudden panic grips me like a vice. I don't want to talk! If we talk, he's going to tell me something I don't want to hear. Like that he's in love with me. Or that he wants me to stay a vampire with him. And then I'll have to choose. And I don't want to choose. Choosing is so overrated.

I mean, what if I make the wrong choice? Go with my feelings and decide something stupid, like staying vampire forever? Then what if after a few months we start not getting along so well? He's staying out late and partying with the boys. And I'm stuck in the coven kitchen, crying in my bowl of blood. He comes home drunk and tells me that his feelings have changed. "It's not you, it's me," he'll say lamely. And then he'll leave again. And I'll be stuck, alone. A vampire without a blood mate. And I'll wish I'd never given in and sacrificed my humanity, all because I thought a vampire looked yummy without his shirt on.

Okay, I'm projecting a bit here, but you get the point.

"Can't we talk later?" I plead. "I really want to see about getting the Grail first."

Magnus's face falls. I can see his disappointment clearly. But all he does is nod. "Fine," is his single-word answer.

He gets out of bed, slamming things around as he gets dressed. Letting me know, in not so many words, that he's ticked off about my avoidance issues.

Well, tough. He'll have to deal. I need that Grail blood. That's my number one priority right now. Relationship talks can come later.

Soon, after showering and dining (don't ask, I don't want to talk about it!) we find ourselves once again making our way to Glastonbury in a speeding limo driving on the wrong side of the street. We're both silent. Both staring out the windows to avoid looking at one another.

We approach the town limits. This time, however, there are no roadblocks or crazy drunken teens to keep us from our mission. This time we can drive right up to the main street of the once-again sleepy little hillside town.

We step out of the limo and instruct the ever-patient driver to wait. I look around. The place is utterly charming—your stereotypical little English village with pubs and art galleries and cozy tea shops that are spelled *shoppe*. Of course, everything's closed for the night (except the pubs, which are packed with locals, most likely celebrating the fact that the damned festival is over for another year).

I whirl around, taking it all in. "This is so adorable! I love quaint little towns like this." I peer into a darkened window. "It'd be so cool to come here in the day and really explore the place."

"Well, if we don't get moving, you won't have that luxury ever again," Magnus reminds me in a completely unwarranted grumpy tone. Ugh. What crawled up his butt and died?

"Okay, okay," I say, abandoning the shop window to follow him down the road, which is lined by tall, skinny town houses. "Where are we going, anyhow?"

"Here," Magnus says, stopping abruptly in front of one of the nondescript town-house doors.

"Here? How do you know it's here?" I scratch my head. "It looks like every other house we've just passed."

Magnus points to the brass knocker on the door. "The door bears the sign of the goddess," he informs me. "Druids live here."

"Oh. Okay." *Just shut up, go along, and don't ask dumb questions, Sunny.* "So are we going to just knock and ask whoever comes to the door about the Grail? Do you think they'll know? Do you think they'll tell us if they do?"

Magnus gives me a look. Shut up. Dumb questions. Right. I'll just go check out this lovely flower box.

The vampire grabs the brass knocker and taps out a couple of short, then long knocks. I want to ask him if it's some secret druid code he's tapping, but I've learned my lesson on the dumb questions thing.

Moments later the door creaks open and a wizened old man with a long gray beard sticks his head out. I stare at him. He looks exactly like Gandalf the Grey of *Lord of the Rings* fame. How cool is that? Finally, after the disappointing images of the Slayer and the vampire leader Lucifent, someone who actually looks the part.

"Can I help you?" he asks in a deep, rumbly English voice.

"We seek audience with the Pendragon," Magnus answers. "Can you help us?"

Gandalf's eyes narrow. "What would one such as yourself seek with our Order? You are not of this world."

Wow. He can tell that just by looking at Magnus? I wish I'd had that ability when I first met the guy. Then I wouldn't be in all this mess.

Magnus bows his head low. "I am quite aware that I am a damned creature of the night, my lord. However, I have a great need that I hope can be addressed. And may I remind you, 'tis not the first time our two faiths have joined one another in noble purpose."

"You speak true." Gandalf opens the door wide. "Step inside, my son."

Hmm. So the druids and the vamps have hooked up in the past? I wonder what that was about? I mean, you've got your druids, who are nature-loving tree huggers. Then you've got your vampires, who like to drink blood and lavish themselves in luxurious underground palaces. Not a big common bond, as far as I can see. But hey, what do I know?

We step inside the house and walk down a narrow corridor and into a quaint little parlor. Gandalf (who introduces himself as Llewellyn the Pendragon, which is evidently some kind of leadership position in the druid world) invites us to sit down and asks if we'd like a "spot o' tea."

"Though I understand it is not your drink of choice," he says to me with a wink. Ugh. Grandpa Druid isn't trying to hit on me, is he?

After we tell him we're cool with the whole tea thing and would just prefer to get down to business, the old druid sinks into one of the parlor chairs and leans forward, elbows on his knees, saying he's eager to hear our request.

So Magnus goes through the whole spiel. My accidental bite. How he's been trying to reverse the transformation. How only a drop of pure blood from the Holy Grail can do the trick, yada, yada, yada.

"I see," Llewellyn says when he's finished. "And you are under the impression that we know where the Grail is buried."

"I had hoped," Magnus agrees, "that you would be so kind as to lead us there."

"We have been chosen by the Goddess herself to be the Guardians of the Grail for millennia," Llewellyn says, his voice cold and formal. "'Tis a task we take seriously. Allowing an unpure, undead being near the holy chalice would be blasphemy."

My heart sinks at his words. Oh great. He's going to be difficult about this, isn't he? Figures. We get this far and then we're totally shot down. I just know I am doomed to walk the earth as an undead forever. Perfect.

"I understand," Magnus says. "Though perhaps a tithe, made to the Goddess, the great Earth Mother, would ease her mind about such a trespass."

Llewellyn frowns. "Do you dare bribe me, vampire?" he asks, angrily. "You should know better than that. Our Order is based on love and nature and purity. We are not mercenaries, able to be bought with something as common as coin."

"A tithe of one million pounds," Magnus adds in an even voice.

My mouth drops open. So does Llewellyn's, though he quickly shuts it again.

"Let me . . ." He clears his throat. "Let me consult with the Goddess in our Sacred Grove. I shall return with your answer."

He rises from his seat and exits the room. Once he's gone, Magnus turns to me.

"Lesson number one. Everyone has their price," he says. "Even those who commune with nature must still pay rent and buy food at the market."

I giggle. "But a million pounds, Mag?" I ask, remembering the amount he offered. "That's a lot of money. Almost two million American dollars if I've got the conversion right. Are you sure you want to give a million pounds?"

"You are worth it."

Gah. What do I even say to that? I can't deal when he says stuff like that. I mean, in one sense I like it. It gives me that whole chills-tripping-down-my-spine thing. But in another, I realize it's dangerous. I can't succumb to his charm. I must move on with my life.

"Yeah, yeah," I reply at last, using sarcasm to deflect his sentiments. "Whatever."

Eager to change the subject, I bounce up from my seat and head over to the door that Llewellyn has just exited. I put my ear to the wood. (Aren't druids supposed to be one with the trees and thus against objects created through their demise, like wooden doors? It'd be like a Hindu chowing on cow or my vegetarian mom wearing leather pumps.)

"It's a million pounds, dude!" a voice on the other side is saying. A voice, in fact, that sounds remarkably like Llewellyn's, were he to use words like *dude*, which before now I would not have guessed him to do. "Is that bleeding fantastic or wot?"

"Yeah, but wot we're supposed to be is Guardians and stuff," another male voice argues. "You know. Sacred Mission and all that?"

"Eff that, mate. Do you know what kind of flat in London we could get for a million pounds? We could spend every night at the pub downing Stella, watching footy on the telly, and picking up fancy birds. It'll be brilliant."

Hmm, somehow I'm thinking he's not talking about bluejays and robins here. So much for Nature Boy and his Holy Orders. I'm actually a bit disappointed. But if I've learned one thing on this crazy vampire journey, it's that no one is really like you'd imagine them to be. And, of course, in this case, the old leader of an ancient druid order turning out to be a money-grubbing hooligan greatly works out to our benefit.

"A'right," the other voice agrees. "But let's show 'em the Grail real quick. In-and-out like, before the rest of 'em wake up from their festival 'angovers and we have to share the quid with those tossers."

"Too right."

I leap back to my seat, just in time for "Llewellyn" (BTW I'm pretty convinced now that's a fake name; he's probably really called Bob or something) to walk through the door in the most regal, ceremonial manner. Heh.

"Good people of the earth," he begins, back to speaking like he's a cast member from *Lord of the Rings*. "I have returned from my consultation with the Good Mother, who once bore the very earth from her womb."

I stifle a giggle. Yeah. Good Mother, a.k.a Cockney friend in the kitchen, same diff.

"And?" Magnus prompts.

"And she has—" He pauses for dramatic effect. Honestly, these druids are almost as bad as the Goths. "—decided to grant your request. On the account that your mission is to purify and redeem the blood of a virgin who has been cruelly ripped from innocence by a damned creature of the Other World."

Okay, I know his speech is total BS, but excuse me, how the hell does everyone know that I'm still a virgin? Really, I want to know. Is there some stamp on my forehead I can't see? Some secret handshake I don't know?

"Please tell the Good Mother that we are eternally grateful for her extreme generosity," Magnus instructs, before I can tell the druid to stop casually throwing around the V-word. The vampire holds out a briefcase I hadn't noticed him carrying. "And that I hope this tithe will further the good work that she pursues."

Or allow two local guys to drink and get laid, in this case, but hey, it all works for me.

Llewellyn accepts the briefcase, his eyes shining with his greed, and opens it. Inside lie stacks upon stacks of high-numbered bills.

"Holy fu—" he starts, then catches himself. "Yes, this tithe will be most pleasing to Her Goodness." He closes the briefcase and tells us he will return. Then he exits back into the kitchen.

Magnus and I exchange amused glances. "I still think he would have taken much less of a . . . donation," I say.

The vampire shrugs. "I would have given him much more."

I blush again. He's been so good to me. "Thank you, Mag," I say. "It really means a lot to me."

"I know," he says in a very serious tone. "It means a lot to me as well."

TWENTY-THREE

Grail Hunting

About fifteen minutes later we're climbing down a dark spiral stone staircase, deep underground, with Llewellyn as our guide. Still holding on to that false nature image, he insists on using a torch to light our way. But whatever. As long as we get there, I guess.

"This passageway leads underneath the mighty Tor," our druidic tour guide explains. "It was dug a thousand years ago by our Order's ancestors."

Wow. Real fascinating. You know, this guy could get a job as a tour guide for the Tower of London, once he blows his million on booze and chicks.

We reach the bottom of the stairs and come to a wrought-iron gate. Llewellyn reaches into his robe to pull out an antique-looking key, made of gold. No high-tech key codes for these guys, I guess. He fits the key into the lock and the gate creaks open, revealing a low ceiling over a cobwebbed passageway, leading into the darkness.

In other words, my worst nightmare.

"This way," Llewellyn commands, beckoning with a long-fingernailed hand.

I stare down the passageway, trying to control my breathing. I'd kind of forgotten how claustrophobic I am. My heart starts pounding in my chest as I watch the torchlight dance off the low-hanging earthen walls. I'd give my left arm, firstborn—anything—if only I could get a halogen headlamp or something.

"It's okay," Magnus whispers in my ear. He grabs my trembling hand. "Relax."

Easy for him to say. Harder for me to do as the walls seem to close in around me. My mind plays out scenarios of earthquakes and floods and other natural disasters that could cause the tunnel to collapse and bury us alive.

I realize I'm digging my nails into Magnus's palm and I loosen my hold. "Sorry," I whisper.

"It is said that Joseph of Arimathea once traveled these passages," Tour Guide Llewellyn presses on, completely oblivious to my stress. "Wanting to discover a safe place to store the cup of his cousin, Jesus Christ, whose blood he had collected as he lay dying on the cross. He felt that blood this pure and holy could be put to good use someday."

"Good thinking, Joey my boy," I mutter.

"He did not feel that, with the persecution of the Christians in the eastern lands, the artifact would be safe. So he entrusted it to our Order. And we have guarded it since."

Yeah, until today, when you sold out poor Joey for a million bucks.

"The cup itself is affixed to a massive stone and cannot be moved. But I have prepared two vials made out of the purest crystal, for you to fill."

"You must wait for Saturday night to actually drink," Magnus whispers. "According to what I have read."

Darn. So it's not an instant reverse-o-matic kind of thing. Figures. But still, I finally have hope. And that's what's important.

We reach a massive door made out of stone. Using another ancient-looking key, Llewellyn unlocks it and the door swings silently open.

We step inside and I draw in my breath, all thoughts of claustrophobia disappearing in an instant.

I don't know how many of you have seen *Indiana Jones and the Last Crusade*, but in that movie, he gets to the room where the Holy Grail is stored and there are a million different ornate cups and he has to figure out which one is the real one, 'cause if he drinks from the wrong one he'll die. And it turns out to be the plainest cup of them all.

Well, let me tell you, that's just another one of Hollywood's misconceptions.

For one thing, the room we enter appears to be made entirely of gold. Gold floor. Gold ceiling. Gold walls. And there's only one cup. One Holy Grail. And it's certainly not plain by any stretch of the imagination. It sits front and center, affixed to a massive boulder as Llewellyn mentioned, and is the most ornate cup I've ever laid eyes on. It's gold. There are jewels affixed to it. It's darn fancy, this Holy Grail.

"The Grail," Llewellyn says with a flourish of his hand.

I look over to Magnus to voice my excitement. I notice he's suddenly sweating bullets. Actually sweating blood, if you want to be literal about it. He's also breathing hard and his face is corpse white.

"Are you okay?" I ask. I haven't seen him this affected since I teased him with the cross the first night—

That's it! Being so close to such a religious artifact must be driving him nuts. Poor guy.

"I'm . . . fine," he says in a tight voice. "Just . . . get . . . the blood."

Llewellyn pulls out two clear vials from a pocket in his robe and walks over to the Grail. Magnus makes a soft choking sound and I reach over to squeeze his hand. If I'd known how much this would bother him, I would have suggested I go alone.

I turn back to Llewellyn and watch him dip the vials into the cup, filling them with a dark, crimson liquid. Then he seals each vial and hands one to me and the other to Magnus.

"Wait, Magnus can't—" I start. I don't want the vial to burn his hand or something.

"I'm fine, Sunny," Magnus says, accepting the vial. "It's sealed."

Oh. Well, who knew? I turn the vial in my hand. "This thing

isn't very breakable, is it?" I ask. "'Cause it would suck to get all the way home and have some kind of carry-on luggage accident."

Llewellyn shakes his head. "It is made of crystal and is thick and strong. However, I gave each of you a vial, in case some unfortunate incident should occur."

Well, that was nice of him to think of a contingency plan. But hey, we just gave the guy a million pounds, so we should be expecting good service, I suppose.

"Great." I stuff the vial in my shirt pocket. "Then are we all set here?" I take one last look at the Grail, wishing I'd brought my camera phone. I could have sold the photo to some museum and recouped the million we spent. Um, that Magnus spent, anyhow.

"Come, let us leave the sacred place," Llewellyn says, heading to the door. "It looks as if it is causing your friend much pain."

He's right. Poor Magnus. We should get the hell out of here ASAP before the guy has a seizure or something. So I follow Llewellyn out and we head back through the passageway. I realize my heart is pounding again. But this time, it's not pounding with claustrophobic fear. This time it's pounding with joy.

"We did it!" I whisper to Magnus, reaching over to give him a hug. "I'm going to get to be human again!"

So why doesn't the vampire look very happy?

TWENTY-FOUR

Thanks for the Memories

The trip back to the good old U. S. of A. is uneventful. In fact, I sleep most of the time, waking only as the plane touches down. I'd have probably even slept longer if Magnus hadn't roused me and urged me to hurry.

"There was some stormy weather over the Atlantic," he explains. "Which made the trip longer than usual. We have little time before the sun comes up to get home."

I nod as I rub the sleep out of my eyes. "Okay," I agree.

Magnus hands me a squeeze bottle. "Breakfast," he says. "For here or to go."

I accept the bottle with a laugh. "You forgot to ask if I'd like fries with that."

He smiles and motions for me to follow him out of the plane. I do and soon we're in his deluxe Jag, zooming through the predawn streets towards my house.

He's quiet during the drive. I feel like I should say something, but I'm not sure what.

"Thanks for helping me get the Grail blood," I say at last. I've already thanked him like a million times, but I am truly grateful for his help, so I guess once more can't hurt. I certainly couldn't have done it without him. Getting to England would have been difficult enough. Coughing up nearly two mil to offer to a football- and beer-loving druid would have been utterly impossible.

"Not a problem," he replies, concentrating on the road in front of him instead of me. I notice his hands are gripping the steering wheel just a tad too tightly and I wonder what's up. But before I can ask, he pulls up in front of my house.

"So, um, I'm supposed to drink this tomorrow?" I ask, rummaging through my jacket pocket for the vial. I turn it over in my hands, admiring the way the crystal catches the Jag's dashboard lights and sparkles.

Magnus nods. "I can meet you somewhere, if you want. To be with you when you drink," he adds. "It's probably going to be a bit . . . disconcerting to change back. I could help you through the discomfort."

"Sure," I say immediately. That's so nice of him to offer. Then I remember. "Oh wait." Damn it. "I'm actually going to be . . . at the prom," I finish lamely.

Magnus raises an eyebrow. "You're still planning on going to the prom?"

"Well, yeah." I shrug. "I mean, I can always drink the blood in the bathroom or something. Or maybe spike my cup of punch?"

"I just figured . . ." Magnus starts then trails off.

"What?"

"Well, it being your last night as a vampire and all . . ."

My heart aches as I realize what he's implying. He wanted to hang out. Spend one last night with me. But while I'd love nothing more, I have to stay strong. Break this off now. Get back to my real life as a human. Go on my date with real-life Jake Wilder and forget my vampire blood mate ever existed.

"Sorry, Mag," I say, trying to sound like I don't care at all, even though nothing is further from the truth. Still, I figure it'll be easier for him to deal with that way. "I've got a date and I can't break it.

It's with Jake Wilder, this guy I've had a crush on for like a millennium. One of the most popular boys in school. I can't exactly back out now. It'd be social suicide."

Magnus's face falls. He looks absolutely crushed. I'm a bit surprised. I mean, I knew we shared time together and a hot kiss, but could he really be that attached to me? Could he really feel as strongly about me as I do about him? I remember suddenly that he had wanted to talk and I'd never given him a chance to say what he wanted to say.

I shake my head. Too late now. It doesn't matter. Very soon, I'm going to be a human again. And once I'm a human, there's no point in continuing a romance with a thousand-year-old vampire. I must sever ties now, once and for all, and get on with my human life. A life that will hopefully include hooking up with the luscious Jake Wilder.

So why do I feel so reluctant to do this? Why does my heart suddenly feel like it's being squeezed in a vise?

"Look, Mag," I say firmly, pushing all the doubts out of my head. "I really do appreciate all the help you've given me this last week. But it's time for me to move on. I've got a life. A human life. I can't be chilling with the undead once I get back to normal. Let's be realistic here. We both know this will probably be the last time I ever see you. So thanks for the memories and I wish you well with getting a new blood mate and all."

Ugh. I sound so cold. So mean. So not me. But what else can I say? *Oh, Magnus, I love you so much and my heart is breaking inside*? No. Because then he might ask me to stay. To remain a vampire forever. And I can't make that choice.

"The . . . sun's coming out," he says at last, his face hardening into a mask of indifference. "I've got to go. So, if you don't mind exiting the vehicle . . . ?"

"Oh." Pain stabs at my heart. Was I secretly wishing he wouldn't buy my words? That he'd say, "No, Sunny, I can read your mind and I know you really love me and therefore I refuse to let you go." That's ridiculous. I don't want him to say that. I want him to let me go. Right?

I can feel the tears well up behind my eyes. A dam ready to burst. So without another word, I open the door and get out of the car. I don't turn back to look at him. I don't say good-bye. Because if I did, I know I'd never be able to walk away.

Instead, I run into the house like a coward, not turning around until I'm safely inside. Peering out the window, I watch his car peel out of the driveway and speed off into the dawn.

Then I burst into tears.

TWENTY-FIVE

Twin Sisters Suck

"So did you get it?"

I whirl around, my heart jumping to my throat at the sound of the voice behind me. I'd been so wrapped up in my tortured thoughts and tears that I hadn't heard Rayne approach.

"Sunny?" she says, looking concerned. "Are you okay?"

I nod, unable to speak without choking on the sobs stuck in my throat.

"You didn't get the Grail, did you?" Rayne concludes. "Oh, Sunny, I'm so sorry. I know how much you were counting on that." She approaches me, arms outstretched, inviting me into a sisterly hug. "But really, being a vampire won't be as bad as you think. And I'll help you every step of the way."

I shake my head. "You . . . don't understand," I manage to say. "I got the blood from the Grail."

Rayne drops her arms and looks at me quizzically. "You did?" she asks. "You really got it?"

I pull the vial from my pocket and hold it up for her observation. "I really got it."

"That's great! I'm so happy for you! You must be thrilled." She studies my face. "Though you don't look thrilled. You look, I don't know, like you've lost your best friend or something."

I shrug. "I'm fine."

"And you're crying."

"I'm not."

"Sunny, you're a vampire. You cry blood tears. Not exactly subtle."

I put a hand to my face and then looked at it. Sure enough, it's stained red. Ew.

"Okay, so I'm crying. Tears of joy, probably."

"Yeah, right. You think I just fell off the naive truck? I'm your twin sister, remember? Psychic connection and all that. So come on, spill. What's wrong?"

"You're going to think I'm being really, really stupid."

"That's never stopped you from telling me stuff before," Rayne quips. I glare at her. "Sorry. Come on, try me. I promise I won't think you're being stupid."

"Well . . ." I glance out the window again, at the empty driveway where Magnus's car had sat just moments before. "Don't get me wrong. I do want to turn back into a human . . ."

"But?" Rayne prompts.

"But . . ." I start, then burst into another set of tears.

"But you're in love with Magnus," Rayne says somberly.

I stare at her. "How did you . . . ?"

"Call it intuition, I guess. Or that psychic twin link thing I mentioned. Or maybe it's just that you're so freaking obvious about it. In fact, I think even a trained monkey could pick up on your heartbreak vibes right about now. Maybe even an untrained one."

"Oh, Rayne, it's terrible," I cry, ready to let it all out. "I love him. I really do. He's sweet and nice and chivalrous and sexy and funny and I just love him to death." I sniff back my sobs. "Um, no pun intended."

"None taken." Rayne nods. "And all true. So what's the problem?"

"That he's a vampire, duh. And after tomorrow night I'll be a human." I rub my eyes with my fists, wishing I had some tissues.

"Sunny, don't take this the wrong way or anything, but . . ." Rayne pauses for a moment, as if carefully choosing her words.

"Did you ever consider . . . not going through with the change? Remaining a vampire so you can be with Magnus?"

"No. No way. I don't want to be a vampire."

Even if it means spending eternity with the guy you're in love with? a voice in my head asks. I shake it away.

"Are you sure?" Rayne presses. Unfortunately, unlike the voices in my head, I can't shut her up as easily.

"Yes. I am sure. Very sure."

I'm not sure at all.

"There are lots of benefits to being a vampire, you know," Rayne says, continuing her pitch, undeterred by my halfhearted assurance. For a moment I wonder why she cares so much. I mean, since when did it matter to her whether I'm undead or alive? Rayne usually cares about nothing but herself. And I know she wants Magnus as a blood mate, so what does it benefit her that we stay together? Weird.

"Riches beyond belief . . ." she drones on.

Maybe she figures if I stay a vampire then she'll have this "in" in the vamp world. Especially since my blood mate is the new king and all. Maybe she figures she'll be able to cut in line, get on the short list to be assigned a new blood mate. That has to be it. There's no other reason she'd be trying to talk me into staying a vampire.

Anger wells up in the pit of my stomach and starts traveling up my throat. She's so selfish. She cares nothing about me and my wants. My dreams and hopes and fears and future. She is simply thinking of herself and what would most benefit her.

"Magical powers . . ." she adds to her list of Top Ten Reasons Sunny Should Stay a Vamp.

Bitch.

Total bitch.

"Freedom to travel anywhere you like. Even Australia . . ."

I can't take it. Not now. Not like this. Next thing you know she's going to bring up her blog again. So help me if she brings up her blog again and the fact that I haven't read it . . .

"If you'd read my blog you'd know that—"

GAH!

"Screw your damn blog, Rayne!" I explode, too furious to worry about waking Mom anymore. "And you know what? Screw you, too. You have no idea what I'm going through. You have some warped notion that this is all fun and games. Well, it's not."

"Sunny—" Rayne tries to interject.

But I'm on a roll and I find I can't stop shouting. "It's not fun to be a vampire. You don't get to see the sun. You don't get to eat garlic-and-chicken pizza. Your mom grounds you because she thinks you're on drugs and you're made to feel bad beyond belief if you have some crazy desire to get your old life back. Well, I refuse to feel guilty for wanting to be a human. For liking the human me and not wanting to sacrifice everything I am to be transformed into some crazy immortal all-powerful being."

I'm raging now. I know I should shut up, but I can't. "Look, Rayne. I want to be a human. I want to have a normal life. I want to go to the prom with Jake Wilder and have a great time with him! I want to dance the night away like a regular high school student and forget this whole mess ever happened.

"I'm sorry if *my* wishes for *my* life don't coincide with yours. I'm sorry if my turning back into a human inconveniences you. But you know what? That's tough luck. This is my life and I'll do whatever the hell I please. So why don't you just eff off and leave me alone!"

Rayne stares at me for a moment, as if she can't believe I just exploded on her. Not surprising since I can't believe it myself. I so didn't mean to go off like that. It just . . . happened.

"Do you have any idea what I've been through, trying to cover for you while you've been gone?" she asks in a tight voice. "Mom practically called out the National Guard when I didn't come home from Spider's for three days. But did I confess? No. I kept up the charade till the bitter end. Now *I'm* the one who's grounded." She turns to stomp off, still muttering under her breath. "Last time I try to help you out, you ungrateful little witch."

Guilt washes over me like a tidal wave. Talk about misplaced aggression. I just completely chewed her out for no reason whatsoever. 'Cause I'm not mad at her, I realize suddenly. I'm mad at myself. And all the stupid decisions I've made.

"Rayne. I'm sorry—" I try.

She whirls around, shooting me daggers with her eyes. "Don't be," she says, her voice cold and venomous. "*I'm* not." She turns back and starts up the stairs. "Oh and one more thing," she adds, pausing halfway up. "Seeing as you've decided not to stay blood mates with Magnus, you don't mind if I have a go, do you? After all, he was mine first."

My heart sinks to my toes. Could this get any worse? "Sure," I mumble, staring at the ground. "Whatever." What else can I say? I've decided to sever ties with Magnus but I don't want anyone else to date him either? That would be completely unfair. And, as she said, she did have him first.

"Excellent," Rayne says in a triumphant voice as she continues up the stairs. "Thanks, Sun. I can't *wait* to tell him the good news. I'd call him now, but I think it'd be much, much better to meet up face to face. Get him alone and . . . mmmm. De-lish." She grins evilly as she turns the corner and disappears from my line of sight.

I slump into a nearby armchair, sobbing. I try to think about how great it's going to be to return to normal life. How wonderful the prom will be, intimately dancing with Sex God Jake Wilder. Maybe he'll ask me up to his hotel room. Maybe I can shed my Sunny the Innocent cloak once and for all. Maybe he'll fall in love with me and we'll get married and have babies and live happily ever after.

But the fantasy is bittersweet. Because no matter how hard I try, I can't shake the new visions dancing in my head. Rayne hooking up with Magnus. Him kissing her all over and whispering how much he loves her. And for millennia afterward they'll hang out together, drinking blood and talking about the old days. Once in a while they'll bring up that week long ago when he accidentally bit her pathetic twin sister by mistake. Of course, by then I'll be long dead. Worms chewing on my decomposing body.

Oh, what am I going to do?

TWENTY-SIX

Prom Preparations

"I'm so glad you're feeling better, sweetie," Mom says, as she fusses over the waffles she's made for me Saturday morning. "I was getting worried about you. But the last few days you seem just like your old self again."

I cringe with guilt. Rayne did such a great job pretending to be me that she got in trouble herself. And what did I do? Rip her a new one because she tried to help. Nice, Sunny.

"Yeah, I feel much better," I say. "Must have gotten over whatever bug I had."

It's true. For some reason, I've suddenly seemed to have lost the creature-of-the-dead crackhead look I started out with and now have this porcelain-doll-of-perfection thing going on. Yup, for the first time in my life, I have absolutely flawless skin. Even my annoying freckles have seemingly faded overnight. Hallelujah! That's almost worth remaining a vamp for, in and of itself.

"I'm so glad," Mom says, bringing over a plate of waffles and setting them in front of me. Yuck! Do I have to pretend to eat? I tentatively pick up a fork and pick at the spongy texture. "I didn't want you to miss the prom."

Ah, the prom. I can't believe it's tonight! I don't even have anything to wear! I'll have to hit the mall ASAP.

"Yeah, I can't wait," I say, taking a bite. Bleh. It tastes like cardboard. "Jake's picking me up in a limo."

"Ooh, that's so cool," Mom squeals. Turns out even hippy-dippy save-the-world moms get excited over these silly high school milestones. "You must be really excited."

I nod, trying to look excited, which shouldn't be as hard as it is. After all, going to the prom with the hottest, most popular guy in school is a dream come true, right?

So why am I dreading it so much?

THAT AFTERNOON I surf the clothing racks at a fancy mall department store, looking for something appropriate for my dream date with Jake. It's funny. A week ago, I'd have told you this was the highlight of my life. Going to the prom. More importantly, going to the prom with a Sex God. But instead, I can barely muster up the enthusiasm to try on a gown. And every time I pick one that I think looks halfway decent, I can't help but wonder what Magnus would think of it.

Stop thinking about Magnus, I scold myself for the umpteenth time. It's over. I'm never going to see him again. Well, unless Rayne starts dating him, that is. Then I guess he'll be hanging around a lot. Which is completely fine and doesn't bug me in the least.

Yeah, right.

I finally settle on a pricey black number. Something sexy and slinky and very anti-Sunny. After all, girls who have dates with Sex Gods should look the part. And, a nagging voice in the back of my brain reminds me, on the not-so-remote chance that Jake has only been influenced by my Vampire Scent, once I turn back into a human I'm going to need to impress him. This outfit should do the trick.

I hope.

I bring the dress up to the counter and try to pay the clerk, but he refuses to take my money.

"No, sweetie," he says, handing me back my debit card. "This one's on me."

I should have picked Armani. Taken advantage of the Vampire Scent while I've still got it. If I could keep one vampire power once I turn back, that would be it. So very useful.

I ARRIVE BACK from the mall with barely enough time to get ready for the event. My mother tells me that Jake's called three times to make sure I'm still going. That I'm still going with him. That I don't mind him picking me up in a limo at seven P.M.

Yes, yes, and yes, though I'm not thrilled by the limo thing, to tell you the truth. It reminds me too much of my mode of transportation while on my recent trip to England. Or, more pointedly, what happened between Magnus and me while we sat in the vehicle in question. But what can you do? I can't exactly tell Jake I'd rather take my mother's Toyota because limos remind me of making out with vampires.

Pathetic, I know.

Once I'm satisfied that my hair and makeup are as good as they're going to get on such short notice, I head back into my bedroom to slip into my dress. Wow. One awesome thing about being a vampire on prom night—flawless figure! Maybe it's due to the fact that I haven't been hungry for human food. Or maybe blood doesn't have a lot of carbs. But for whatever reason, I think I've lost about ten pounds this week. And if you're going to lose ten pounds and then put on a dress, this dress is the one to put on. It molds itself to my body like it was made just for me.

Woot! I'm going to look sooo good.

Seriously. I'm not one for bragging, but as I study myself in the mirror, I realize I'm suddenly superhot. Like Paris Hilton hot, if Paris were five foot four. I just hope I don't turn back into a pumpkin at midnight when I drink the Grail blood. That would royally suck.

• • •

"DONE CHECKING YOURSELF out?"

I whirl around. Rayne is standing in the doorway, a scowl on her face.

"Go away," I growl, shooting her a glare before turning back to the mirror. No need for her to ruin what's sure to be the best night of my life.

"Wait. Sunny," she says, ignoring my order and stepping into the room. Gah. I knew I should have installed a lock on my door. "Are you sure you want to go through with this?"

"Go through with what?" I ask. "Going to the prom with Jake? Of course I'm sure. It's what I've dreamed about since I first laid eyes on the guy freshman year."

"No. Not that. The . . . other thing."

"Are you kidding?" I ask, incredulously. I cannot believe that after all of this she's *still* trying to get me to change my mind. As if. "Believe you me, Rayne. I am so ready to skip out on the vampire world. In fact, I wish it were midnight right now. I'd be downing that Grail blood like it's a Cherry Slurpee from 7-Eleven. And you know how I live for Cherry Slurpees from 7-Eleven."

"And what about Magnus?"

My heart sinks. Why did she have to bring up the M-word? I'd never admit it to her, of course, but I've been missing the guy like crazy. Wondering what he's doing. How the coven takeover is going. If they've crowned him king yet. And more important, if they've assigned him a new blood mate. And whether that blood mate happens to be my twin sister.

I know Magnus was mad at my decision to go to the prom, but deep inside, I guess I'd hoped he wouldn't drop off the face of the earth. That he'd still be in my life. I don't know *how* exactly. After all, he's not the type to swing by for tea. Or to call up and ask me out to dinner and a movie or something.

But still . . .

Anyhow, it seems as if that wasn't meant to be. After peeling out of my driveway last night, he's not called or e-mailed or IM'ed or anything. He's just disappeared from my life like he'd never been in it at all.

Not that I mind. I'm glad, actually. It's better this way.

Kind of.

Okay, not really.

"What about Magnus?" I repeat. "Who cares about him?"

I do! I do!

Shut up, heart. You don't count in this case.

"Oh," Rayne replies in an odd voice. In fact, if I didn't know better, I'd think she sounded almost disappointed. Which wouldn't make the least bit of sense, considering she's the one hoping to play Rebound Girl with him. My disinterest should be good news for her. She can have her way with him and live vampily ever after and I won't say a word in objection.

"Okay, then," Rayne adds after a long pause. "If you're sure."

Jeez, what is her problem? "Look, Rayne," I say, a little annoyed, mainly because I have no idea what she's getting at and all this thinking about Magnus is doing nasty things to my insides, "as fascinating as this conversation has been, I'm running a bit late. So if you don't mind, I'd like to cut the chitchat and get ready for my date with Jake."

"Oh. I see. Okay. Fine. Whatever." Rayne immediately turns and stomps out of the room.

I turn back to the mirror, feeling a little guilty for being so rude. What's wrong with me lately? She's my twin sister. The person I grew up with. The one who knows me better than anyone.

"Hrmumph," I huff as I pick a stray piece of blond hair off the dress. That just goes to show you. If she knew me better than anyone, she'd know that I'm fully vested into changing back into a human tonight. That I'm in love with Jake Wilder. Not Magnus.

Nope. Rayne doesn't know me at all.

TWENTY-SEVEN

Desperate Prom Dates

Jake's prompt. He's rented a limo. And he's dressed in a divine tux. What more could I want in a prom date? He comes to the door and he has a corsage. His cummerbund is black like my dress. He smiles at me and calls my mom "ma'am," and he doesn't even bat an eye when she explains her crazy government conspiracy theory that terms like "ma'am" were put into place to keep women barefoot and pregnant in the kitchen. (Yeah, I don't get her sometimes either.)

In short, Jake is perfect. A dream come true.

So why can't I muster any enthusiasm?

He tells Mom he'll have me back at a decent hour. He allows me to get into the limo first. He offers me a glass of champagne in a fluted glass.

If you looked up *perfect prom date* in the dictionary, Jake's handsome mug would be staring right back at you.

So why am I stifling the urge to yawn?

"To the most beautiful girl at Oakridge High School," he says, as we clink glasses.

"Why are we toasting Mary Markson?" I ask with a giggle.

He scrunches his eyebrows in honest confusion. "I meant you, Sunny," he stammers. "I'm sorry, I guess I should have been more clear."

"Um, I know that," I assure him. "I was just making a joke." A pretty obvious one, I would have thought, but I decide to cut him some slack. I can tell he's nervous. Isn't that too funny? Oakridge High's resident Sex God is nervous around little old me. Who would have thunk it?

I lean back in my seat and take a sip of my champagne. This is nice. Speeding to the prom in a deluxe limo with the most delectable guy in school sitting right across from me. I steal a quick peek. He really is so hot, with those brooding eyes and killer bod. De-lish. And he's all mine.

"I'm so glad you decided to come to the prom with me," Jake continues, giving me a once-over that can only be described as reverent. "I was so scared to ask you."

Imagine! Me scaring a boy! A boy like Jake Wilder scared of me! Too, too funny.

"I'm glad you did," I say, dipping my eyes to appear demure. "I've liked you for a while now."

"Really?" Jake looks surprised. "It's funny, I didn't know you existed until that day in drama."

Ah, there's the icy water of reality dumped on my head. I take a big gulp of champagne, wishing it was blood. I realize I'd been secretly hoping he'd say he'd been lusting after me all year. Then I could report back to Rayne that he really does like me for me and not 'cause of some weird vampire mating call.

But, um, not so much, it appears. Oh well.

"When we were on stage and I kissed you, it was just like my whole world changed in that instant. Everything I was, everything I wanted from life—all disappeared in a flash of light. At that moment, I realized that I could easily spend all eternity with you."

O-kay then. This is getting a bit on the creepy, stalkerish side, I have to admit. I mean, don't get me wrong—having the love of my life spout sonnets of devotion to me while drinking champagne in a luxury limo is extremely cool and all. But knowing he's only doing it 'cause I've inadvertently bewitched him kind of sucks.

I ask you: Is it so hard for a boy to like me for me? To adore and speak passionately about the real life Sunshine McDonald, not her vampire alter ego?

You mean like Magnus does? that annoying voice in my head asks. *The one guy you know is not influenced by the Vampire Scent?*

No. Not like Magnus, I tell the stupid voice. I really hope it goes away with the rest of the vampire stuff. *I want a human boy to feel that way about me.*

Jake reaches over and starts stroking my knee. "Did I mention how beautiful you are?" he asks.

I stifle another yawn. This is going to be a long night.

WE ARRIVE AT the prom and parade around the parking lot so all the parents, who evidently have nothing better to do, can clap and cheer and take photo after photo. Of course when they get to me, it's worse. All these balding, potbellied dads start giving me lecherous grins and making "whoo-whoo" noises, much to the chagrin of their wives.

Major ew-age. The heck with free clothes; now that I've got old men leering at me, I'm thinking this Vampire Scent thing has got to go.

After the processional, we walk into the hotel that is hosting the prom. It's pretty nice. Gold-accented walls, crystal chandeliers hanging from the ceiling, and a huge dance floor. On stage there's a DJ spinning Top 40 dance remixes. By the far wall there are tables piled with buffet trays and a beautiful dessert cart. Pretty class act.

"Over here!"

We turn to see several very popular seniors beckoning us over to their table. At first I think they must be mistaking me for someone else, and then I remember I'm with Jake. And just 'cause he's been blinded by my Vampire Scent doesn't mean that he's suddenly lost all coolness points with the in crowd. Suddenly I feel much better.

I, Sunshine McDonald, somewhat geeky sophomore, will be spending the evening with the A-list.

"Hi Jake, hi Sunny," the aforementioned A-list cries as we sit down at their table. Wow. They even know my name. How cool is that?

"Sunny, you look beautiful," says Rick, the captain of the football team, who sits to my left.

"Yes, you're like the most beautiful girl in Oakridge," agrees Sam, the basketball player across the table.

I can feel my face heat. Wow. These A-listers are so nice. So welcoming. So . . .

So pissing off their girlfriends.

Uh-oh.

I look around the table. All the guys are drooling and all the girls are giving me the most evil stares known to humankind. Crap. This Vampire Scent thing can really backfire if you're not careful. Free dresses from smitten clerks—good. Making the entire cheerleading squad want to kick your ass—very, very bad.

"Jake, let's dance," I say, even though we've just arrived and there's barely anyone on the dance floor. I mean, dancing before dinner? How uncool can you get? But I'm desperate to get away from this table before the girls go all Charlie's Angels on me.

Luckily Jake is, of course, still bewitched by me and will do anything I say, even if it's social suicide. So though I'm positive we look absolutely ridiculous all alone on the dance floor, he obeys my command. Even more luckily, Jake's still the most popular guy at Oakridge. So as soon as he gets up to dance, half the senior class follows suit.

Me. A trendsetter. I could get used to this.

The DJ throws on a slow song and Jake proceeds to pull me close. I nestle my cheek in his chest, enjoying the feel of his lanky, muscular body pressed against mine, his chest rising and falling with his breath.

Ah. This is nice. Normal high school stuff. Exactly what I've been craving.

Well, that and the pulsating vein on the side of Jake's neck. But

I won't go there. I will not, under any circumstances, bite my prom date. At least not in public.

"You're so beautiful," Jake murmurs into my ear. "So, so beautiful. You've got me completely addicted."

Sigh. Great, here he goes again. I wish he'd just shut up. I mean, I like hearing that he thinks I'm beautiful, don't get me wrong. It's just that every time he says it, I'm painfully reminded of the fact that in real life he's, as the self-help book says, just not that into me. That, in reality, this is all an illusion that will end as soon as I drink the Grail blood and turn back into a pumpkin.

Cinderella, I feel for you, girl.

Whoa! My head spins as Jake suddenly decides to get creative on the dance floor. He dips me backward without any kind of warning. As I scramble to keep my balance, my eyes fall on a surprising prom guest.

Make that two very surprising prom guests.

I regain my balance and break away from Jake's embrace. "I'll be back," I tell him, patting him on the arm and trying to appear composed. "I just want to go say hi to someone."

Say "hi" or "what the hell do you think you're doing here and why did you bring him?" to be exact, but Jake doesn't need to know the sordid details of my upcoming convo.

"Hurry up, babe," he says, dipping his head to plant an unexpected, way-too-PDA kiss on my lips. "I'll miss you every second you are gone."

"Hurry. Right. Okay," I agree as I back away. Once I'm at a safe distance, I turn and make great strides to the punch bowl.

I'm going to kill her. I'm going to kill her. I'm going to kill her. I'd kill him, too, if he weren't already dead.

"What are you doing here?" I hiss at my sister, who's dressed (surprise, surprise) in a lacy black Gothic princess dress that's completely inappropriate for prom.

Rayne scowls. "Nice to see you, too, sis," she says.

"You're not a senior. You're not on the guest list."

"Really. Go figure. Maybe I—ohhh," she makes an overly dramatic shriek, "maybe I sneaked in." She fans her face with her hands.

"Oh, shock, horror. Call the police. I broke into Oakridge's senior class prom. Past all the teachers and Homeland Security spies. All the way to the punchbowl. Watch out, senior class . . . there's an evil sophomore in your hotel."

I roll my eyes. "You're so not funny. And you still haven't answered my question."

"Which was?" Rayne asks sweetly.

I hate her. I absolutely hate her. Can you emancipate yourself from your twin sister? If so, I'm definitely filing the paperwork Monday morning.

"Why. Are. You. Here?" I ask, spelling it out slowly, through clenched teeth. "And. Why. Did. You. Bring. Him?"

"Him?" Rayne asks in a ridiculously innocent voice. As if she hasn't a clue who I'm talking about. "Oh, you mean Magnus?" she concludes. "Well, I needed a date and he wasn't doing anything and . . ."

I squeeze my hands into fists, not quite convinced I shouldn't wind up and smack her. The proximity of the senior class advisor, Mr. Moody, is the only thing that's stopping me at the moment.

"This is *my* night," I growl at her. "*Mine*. I am on a date with the hottest guy from Oakridge High. And I refuse to let you spoil this for me."

"I'm not spoiling anything. We're just here to dance and drink punch."

"Yeah, right. I know you too well, sis," I spit out. My stomach is churning with fury. "You came to rub it in. To flaunt it in my face."

"Really, Sunny, you should work out these anger issues of yours," Rayne says with a *tsk-tsk*. "I have no idea what you're talking about, but you sound like you need some serious help." She grabs the ladle and pours herself a cup of punch. "Go back to your date and enjoy the prom. Magnus and I will stay out of your hair."

"Yes, don't worry, we'd never want to ruin your dream night," Magnus agrees, coming up from behind Rayne.

The second I lay eyes on him everything inside me starts doing crazy things all at once and I feel like I'm going to pass out. My hands start shaking. My stomach is nauseated. My heart aches. Tears form at the back of my eyes and I suddenly find it difficult to breathe.

He looks so good. Dressed to the nines in a dashing tux. He's chopped his long hair to ear length, long layers in the front hanging casually in his face. His amazing blue eyes look even bluer, if that's even possible. But the warmth I've found comfort in is long gone. Instead he gazes at me with an icy stare.

Gulp.

It takes everything inside me not to throw myself in his arms and cry and cry and hope that he'll hold me and comfort me and tell me everything will be okay. But he won't tell me that this time. He'll shove me away and wrap his arm around Rayne's waist to show me that *she's* his new blood mate now. And later they'll go back to the coven and giggle at how ridiculous I acted at the prom and how clearly I'm still holding a torch for Magnus, even though I'm the one who technically broke up with him first.

I glance back at Jake. My dream date. He and his buddies are slapping each other on the back, having a grand old time. One guy passes around a silver flask filled with God knows what kind of alcohol and Jake takes a long swig. Then they giggle some more, evidently oh-so-pleased by their juvenile delinquency. I cringe, wondering what Magnus thinks of their immature behavior.

I suddenly feel very old and jaded.

I look back at Magnus and Rayne, blinking back tears. How could I have been so stupid? How could I have let Magnus go? He's everything I ever wanted in a boyfriend. He's sweet and loyal and nice and funny and oh-so-handsome. He did everything in his power to assist me on my quest to regain my humanity, even though it was against his best interests.

And I've been so ungrateful. In fact, I didn't even properly thank him for all he's done. I just said, "Thanks for the memories, dude," and ditched him like a bad habit as soon as I got what I wanted and he could no longer help me. I wouldn't even agree to meet up with him tonight, for a proper good-bye.

I am the biggest loser on the planet. I don't deserve him. In fact, I don't deserve anyone. I deserve to be an old maid, living all alone, with fifty cats to take care of.

I steal another look at Magnus and suddenly all the stupid excuses I've been making about why it'd never work out between us seem ridiculous and naive. And suddenly all the reasons I've wanted to stay human seem inconsequential.

I want to be with Magnus. No matter what I have to give up.

It'd be worth everything.

Even my soul.

But it's too late.

Isn't it?

Rayne looks from Magnus to me and back to Magnus again, her expression unreadable.

"I've got to pee," she suddenly announces, without ceremony. And before I can say, "Do what you have to do," she's already gone.

Leaving me alone with Magnus.

Was this her plan all along? Could my evil boyfriend-stealing twin actually be a saint in disguise?

I wonder . . .

I stare at Magnus. He stares back at me. You could cut the tension in the room with a knife. I realize it's up to me to make the first move. I was the rejecter in this whole mess. He opened himself up to me. Told me how he felt. And I threw it all back in his face. I am the one who needs to make serious amends.

And I'm ready to do so now.

"Magnus, I'm—"

"Sunny, there you are!" Before I can protest, arms wrap around my waist from behind. I whirl around. Jake grins at me, looking like a lost, slightly drunk puppy dog.

I look back at Magnus, who is watching the scene with cool eyes. This is not good.

"I've been looking everywhere for you, my love," Jake says, squeezing me tight. *Gah! Go away, dude! You're screwing up everything.*

But Jake doesn't go away. Instead he leans into me and starts messily kissing my neck. "Oh God, I love you so much, Sunny," he murmurs too loudly. Way too loudly.

Magnus's eyes narrow. "I've got to get going," he mumbles.

"No, Mag, wait!" I cry. But he's already halfway out of the room. Vampires can really move when they want to.

I've got to reach him. To tell him how I feel before it's too late!

"I beg of you, Sunny, my love, please never leave me!"

"Oh, eff off, Jake!" I cry, while squirming to get away. I know full well I'm damning my one and only chance to be A-list in high school. To date a Sex God and be the envy of all my friends. But I totally don't care. In fact, I don't care if I turn into the biggest social reject Oakridge High has ever seen.

As long as I get to talk to Magnus.

But Jake isn't letting go without a fight, so I give him a little persuasion.

In other words, I stamp on his foot. Hard.

With spiky heels.

And vampire strength.

He lets go, yelping in pain. I hope I haven't put an actual hole in his foot. Oh well, no time to check now.

I sprint to the ballroom exit. This is like Cinderella in reverse, though I'm sure Magnus isn't going to leave a glass slipper behind. Maybe a Prada loafer . . . ?

I'm outside before I catch up to him. He's walking through the parking lot, his head bowed and his steps slow. He looks like he's lost his best friend.

What he doesn't know is that his best friend wants him back. Badly.

"Magnus!" I cry.

He stops in his tracks, not turning around. I rush over to him, grab his hands. I'm so out of breath it isn't even funny. I really need to clock in some quality time at the gym when all this is over.

"Magnus," I repeat, panting. We lock eyes. His look so sad, it breaks my heart. "I'm sorry. I didn't mean—"

"Sunny, I—" he says.

And suddenly we're talking and crying and laughing all at the same time. Apologizing, explaining, begging for forgiveness.

"I love you, Magnus," I say after we both pause for breath. "I didn't realize it. Or maybe I did, but I didn't want it to be true. I thought it would be way too complicated. And I was too concerned with being normal. But I don't care anymore. I love you. And I want to be with you. Forever. No matter what it takes."

"I love you, too, Sunny," he says, reaching over and brushing a bloody tear from my eye. "Accidentally biting you was the best mistake I've ever made in my life."

Aw. He's so sweet. So wonderful. So—

So kissing me.

Our mouths clumsily find one another, desperately seeking everything from the other person. Seeking and finding, I might add. Finding acceptance. Desire. Love. The works.

It's so wonderful I can barely stand it. He loves me. Magnus loves me. It's unbelievable for me to even comprehend how great that is.

As we kiss, his arms wrap around me and pull me close to him. We fit perfectly together. Like we were made for one another. And maybe we were. After all, I know we have compatible DNA.

I honestly wouldn't mind kissing him all night. Never going back into the prom. Never having to face my crazy, obsessed date. Make this my new reality and forget everything about the world. If I had Magnus at my side, I'm sure I could do it in style.

Then Magnus pulls away, glancing at his watch. At first I'm irritated. Like, hello? Does he have somewhere he needs to be or something?

"It's almost time," he says.

I cock my head in confusion. "Time? For what?"

"For you to drink the Grail blood."

"But . . ." I scrunch my eyes. "I'm not . . ." Didn't he listen to a word I just said? I love him. I want to be with him. And that means giving up my humanity for him, obviously. Doesn't he want me to?

"Not?" His turn for the confused look.

"No, Magnus." I shake my head. "Don't you get it? I'm not going to drink it. I'm going to stay a vampire so I can be with you."

He frowns and takes my hands in his, bringing them up to his chest. I can't feel his heart beating, but that's probably only because he doesn't have one.

"No, Sunny," he says firmly.

"Huh? What do you mean, no?"

"I won't allow you to remain a vampire for my sake."

"But . . ." Doesn't he want to be with me? Or was this all some kind of sham? I can feel my heart tearing apart inside. "But I love you," I say, almost afraid to admit it again.

He smiles softly and leans forward to kiss me on the forehead. "I love you, too," he whispers. "That's why I can't allow you to remain a cursed creature of the night. I want you to have the gift of life I never had."

"But I thought you said you liked being a vampire."

"It has its moments," he says with a shrug. "But at the same time, it can be a lonely life. And forever is a long time to live." He pulls me tight into an embrace. "I don't want you to suffer like I have. I want you to be you. The human you that I love."

"But then, but then . . ." I can't seem to form a sentence. This is not going the way I had planned at all. Not that I had really planned it out, but if I had, this wouldn't be the scenario. In my planned version, he'd be thrilled that I wanted to stay a vampire. We'd crush the blood vial and retreat to his coven and be one with one another, forever.

That's it! That's what I need to do.

I pull out the vial from my purse and before I can have second thoughts, I slam it on the ground. Then I smash it with my foot. Blood and glass go flying, staining my once-adorable stilettos.

I swallow hard. There. It's done. Over. *Finito*. No turning back now.

I am a teenage vampire.

"Why did you do that?" Magnus cries, looking horrified.

"Because I want to be a vampire," I say stubbornly. Oh God,

what have I done? What possessed me to do that? Panic sets in fast and furious.

"But you don't," Magnus insists, not making it any easier. Why can't he just be happy? Why can't he throw his arms around me and say he was hoping I'd do that? That I've made him the happiest vampire alive and he can't wait to spend eternity with me. Or do something besides stare at me with an incredulous look on his face, saying things like, "But you hate being a vampire."

"I've changed my mind," I say firmly. No need to show him my doubts and fears and overall freak-out. "I've grown to enjoy the whole vampire thing over the past few days. And I think it'd be a charming way to spend eternity."

"You're just saying that because you think that's what I want to hear," Magnus says, sighing deeply. "But you don't really mean it. Sunny, I know you too well."

Jeez. This is not turning out how I'd hoped it would. At all. Where are all the tender embraces? The taking me back to the coven and celebrating my new unlife?

"Well, what's done is done," I say, attempting a casual shrug. "No turning back now." I stare down at the Grail splatter on the pavement. I wonder if I got on my knees and licked . . .

No. That's ridiculous. It's gone. It's done. I'm a vampire and I'm more than thrilled about it.

"Do you want to go . . . inside?" Magnus asks abruptly. "Maybe dance or something?"

Dance? I stare at him in disbelief. How can he think of dancing at a time like this? I've just sacrificed my whole humanity and all he can think of is getting his groove on?

I shake my head, too depressed for words. "No, I'm good," I say, though, of course, I'm not really. Not really good at all, if you want to know the truth.

"Okay," he says. "Do you mind if I do? I have to . . . use the little vampire's room."

I smile halfheartedly. "I'll wait here."

I lean against a nearby car, watching him as he heads back inside. I love him. So, so much. I have no doubts about that. And I really do want to be with him forever. So why am I so depressed? I made my decision. There's no turning back now. Sure I sacrificed my humanity, but it was for the guy I loved. So totally worth it.

I'll probably learn to love being a vampire. I'll get assigned my own Donor Chicks. (Or maybe hot Donor Males, heh, heh!) I'll travel the world. Rule as queen by Magnus's side. We'll vanquish evil slayers, etc. Sounds like a blast. Much better than high school.

Of course transitioning is going to be a bit difficult. I can never tell my mom—she'd just lock me up in a place where doctors would stick tons of needles in me and do all sorts of crazy experiments like I'm some kind of lab rat. Ugh.

No, it'd be better if my mom thinks I'm dead. I'll fake a car crash or something. Those always seem to happen around prom time anyhow. Sure, she'll be sad at first. But then she'll eventually grow to accept life without her daughter. And anyhow, she'll still have Rayne. Well, until Rayne gets to the top of the waiting list again and becomes a vampire herself.

Sigh.

At least I'll get out of going to high school, I remember, brightening a bit. All those pop quizzes and complicated projects? Never again. Though I will miss performing the starring role in *Bye Bye Birdie*. Wow, my being dead is going to really screw up the play. As far as I know there's no understudy to the understudy. I may have inadvertently caused the whole school play and everyone's hard work to collapse. They'd totally kill me, if I weren't already pretending to be dead.

And then there's field hockey. But my teammates will be fine without me. Well at least against everyone but Salem. Salem's pretty tough.

And lastly there's Audrey. My best friend. She's going to be really shocked when she comes back from Disney World on Monday and finds out I've dropped out of school, field hockey, and drama. Oh, and that I'm dead, too, of course.

Wow. Who would have thought so many lives would change if I weren't around? Go figure. Nice of me to suddenly come to this realization after it's too late.

"Sunny, are you okay?"

I look up. Magnus has returned from his trip to the bathroom and is staring at me with a very concerned look on his face. At first I have no idea why, then I realize I'm crying. Stupid blood tears.

"I'm fine. Wonderful. Very happy," I say, swiping at my face. I don't want him to think I'm having second thoughts. Not that I am, really. At least not about him.

He closes the gap between us and takes my head in his hands. Running his fingers through my hair, he pulls me close and kisses me. Suddenly, I'm feeling much better. Concerns about school and parents and friends evaporate as I enjoy the sensation of his lips on mine.

I can do this. I can stay a vampire. Stay with Magnus. Be happy and live a fulfilling eternal life.

His kisses trail down my face to my neck. I love neck kissing. And being a vampire's girlfriend, I figure I'll get to experience a lot of it.

And then a searing pain shoots through my entire body.

"Ow!" I cry, pulling away. "Why the hell did you just bite me?"

TWENTY-EIGHT

Boys That Bite

I jump away, my hand to my neck like so much déjà vu.

"That hurt!" I cry. In fact, it hurt a lot worse than the first time he did it, a week ago at Club Fang. The Club Fang bite was just a pain in the neck, so to speak. This one feels like poison is shooting through every vein in my body—my head to my toes to my fingertips.

"Sunny, sit down," Magnus commands. Dazed and in massive pain, I allow him to drag me down to the curb. I struggle for breath.

"What did you do to me?" I cry. I feel like I'm dying. Not that I know what dying feels like, but I'm pretty sure this can't be far off on the pain scale. My head hurts. My body aches. I feel sick to my stomach. It's awful.

Magnus pulls out his implanted teeth and presents them to me. "I'm sorry, Sunny," he says solemnly. "I thought it was for the best."

"What was?" I sob, begging the pain to go away. My whole body is practically convulsing like I'm having a seizure. "Did you poison me?"

He sighs and opens his other hand. I stare at it, then up at him.

The other Grail vial.

And it's empty.

I put two and two together.

"I'm sorry, Sunny," Magnus says. "I know you say you want to be a vampire, but honestly I don't believe you. In fact, I'm willing to bet a gallon of blood you're just saying that because you want to be with me."

I hang my head in shame. The physical pain has subsided somewhat, but the mental anguish is just beginning. What can I say? Of course, he's right. But I don't want him to think that's any reflection on my feelings for him.

"So I guess it wasn't meant to be," I say with a sigh. Great. Now I'm happy to be turning back into a human, but depressed as all hell about losing Magnus.

"What wasn't?" Magnus asks gently.

I look up in surprise. "You and I. Together."

He smiles that signature sweet smile of his and takes my hand. I tremble as he strokes my palm.

"Are you kidding?" he asks. "Vampire or human or, hell, if you decide one day you're going to become a werewolf or fairy, I'm not letting you go."

For a moment I'm tempted to ask if there really are werewolves and fairies out there as well as vampires, but then the full impact of his words hits me.

"Really?" I ask, choking out the words through my happy tears. "You want to be with me anyway? Even if I'm not your blood mate?"

He nods. His eyes are full of love.

"But it'll be hard to . . ."

"We'll make it work."

"And what if you get assigned . . . ?"

"You don't have to worry."

"But what if the other vamps—"

"I'll take care of them." Magnus places a finger to my lips. "The lady doth protest too much," he quotes.

I grin sheepishly. "You just met me?"

He laughs, then his face turns serious.

"Sunny, I love you. No matter what. We will make things work.

I have full confidence in our relationship." He pauses, then adds, "You may not be my blood mate, but you certainly are my soul mate."

Aw. In fact, major aw-age. I love him so much.

Then, before I can come up with something equally endearing to respond with, he kisses me. A lot. I'd give you details, but I figure it'd just be way TMI and really, who wants that? Plus, a girl has to have some secrets, right?

Just suffice it to say, I happily kiss him back.

Human to vampire. Vampire to human.

Hey, it works for us.

Blog Entry 407
Author: Rayne McDonald

So there you have it. My sister, Sunny, is officially a member of the human race again. (And yes, her freckles are back, nyah-nyah!) She and Magnus (who was really never my type anyhow! I need someone wayyyy more dark and brooding) are officially an item. Boyfriend and girlfriend. Vampire and human. Doesn't matter, they're nauseatingly happy together. And Magnus has installed himself as official Master of the Blood Coven, Eastern U.S. region. All's well that ends well, right?

Well, not so much.

To make a long story short, here I am walking through the hallways of Oakridge on the Monday after the prom, feeling pretty good about myself. Giving the finger to various meathead jocks, avoiding the teachers who want to put me in detention for skipping class to go smoke over at "The Block," flirting with the new kid who's wearing an Interpol shirt. (He's not that cute, but evidently has good taste in music.) You know, your typical Raynie day.

Suddenly, out of nowhere, some old guy grabs my arm and starts dragging me into a side corridor. "You must come with me," he says in an urgent voice.

I'm just about ready to go tae kwon do on his ass, but then I realize it's Mr. Teifert, Sunny's drama coach.

"Dude, I think you've mistaken me for my twin," I say, as he drags me down into the auditorium's backstage area. "I'm Rayne. Sunny's the one in your play, not me."

The teacher pulls on the door and slams it closed with a loud ominous clanking sound. Hmm, cool sound effect. I could use that in my film. (Did Sunny tell you I'm a budding filmmaker? I'm going to be the next Tim Burton or David Lynch, just FYI.)

"I know who you are, Rayne," Mr. Teifert says, scratching his balding head.

I raise an eyebrow. "Oh. Then maybe an explanation of why you dragged me in here might be in order, don't you think?"

He nods. "Yes, yes, of course." He takes a deep breath. "Now brace yourself. This may be a little difficult to take in at first . . ."

Um, he isn't going to tell me he's in love with me, is he? That would be extremely gross. I mean, sure, I dated my English teacher for two weeks last semester, but he was a sexy twenty-two-year-old Australian who liked Nietzsche. Mr. Teifert's practically ancient—at least forty, I'd say—and so not sexy or cute or Australian. Besides, once I caught him singing show tunes, so I'd been thinking he might bat for the other team.

"What I'm going to tell you may come as a bit of a shock," he continues in an extremely serious tone.

Jeez, enough with the drama, drama-teacher guy.

"Shock. Awe. I gotcha. Spit it out." After all, I'm late for class. Not that this would normally bother me.

He clears his throat. "Very well then. Once a generation a girl is born who is destined to slay the vampires."

I stare at him. "You know about Bertha?" I ask incredulously. "You know about vampires?" Okay, he's right. I am shocked. And awed. And all that. I had no idea this geeky old balding teacher had any clue about the Otherworld. I guess that's why he acted so weird when Sunny and I were joking around in the auditorium last week.

"Bertha, um, has had some blood pressure problems," he stammers. "She's temporarily retired from the slaying biz."

"I see . . ." I say slowly. Too much drive-through super sizing for Bertha between slays, I guess.

"No, I don't think you do," Mr. Teifert says. "What I'm trying to tell you, Ms. McDonald, is that you are next in line."

"Next in line?" I swallow hard, not liking where this is going. "Next in line for what, exactly?"

Mr. Teifert smiles and holds out his hand. "Congratulations, Rayne McDonald. You are the chosen one. Slayer Inc.'s new official Vampire Slayer."

To be continued . . .

STAKE THAT

ONE

Blogfast Sux!!!!!!!!!

THURSDAY, MAY 31, 8:30 A.M.

ARGH, I am sooo pissed right now!

As you know, I've been keeping this blog for like EVER in an effort to document my transformation into a vampire. I've shared with you my notes from my Vamp Certification 101 class, told you all the juicy details about my hot vampire blood mate-to-be, Magnus. Heck, I've even posted excerpts from the *Biting Humans for Fun and Profit* manual.

But what does my blogging site decide to do the week everything is supposed to go down? IT decides to go down, TOO! The whole last week's worth of entries . . . vanished into thin cyberspace air. *Grrrrrrrrr!!!!!*

Okay, deep breath, Rayne. There's nothing you can do about it except send threatening hate e-mail to Blogfast.com. And then the vindictive little geeks who run the site will probably delete your whole blog altogether instead of just last week's entries. Better to just recap and deal.

But still. Major *grrr*, if you ask me.

Okay. Of course you're all dying to know: Am I a vampire? After all, the last blog entry of my own *Neverending Story* not eaten by

The Nothing was written the night I was scheduled to be transformed. I was headed to Club Fang (the coolest Goth club in the known universe) with my twin sister, Sunny. (Yes, yes, we're Sunshine and Rayne. Hippie parents and all that. And we've already heard all the jokes, so please don't bother.) There I was to meet my blood mate, the drool-worthy vampire Magnus. He was supposed to bite me and then we'd spend eternal life together as vampires, which, FYI, is a pretty sweet gig. I mean, we're talking riches beyond belief, amazing powers, and best of all *NO HIGH SCHOOL*. w00t!

Problem is that's not exactly how it all went down. Instead of biting me, Magnus the Mentally Challenged bit my twin sister, Sunny, instead. We're like, identical, you know, but still! You'd think he would at least have double-checked that he had the right girl before going to the point of no return. After all, we're talking Real Life Extinguishing Event here, not some *Parent Trap* movie starring Lindsay Puke Lohan.

And let me tell you, Sunny, who had no idea up until then that the whole vamp world even existed, was *so* not pleased to be informed that due to a "bloody" bad case of mistaken identity she would now spend eternity as a pasty, blood-gulping creature of the night. (Her words, not mine!) And Magnus the Moron was freaked out beyond belief that he was going to get in trouble with the boss, Lucifent, for performing an unauthorized bite. (After all, she wasn't even blood tested first for diseases. Not that my innocent little twin sis would ever have diseases!) Luckily for Maggy, Lucifent got dusted soon after by Bertha the Vampire Slayer. So Mag not only got off scot-free, he became the new Master of the Blood Coven and high priest of the eastern vampire conglomerate of the United States of America. Life is strange.

So, long story (somewhat) short, the two of them decided to see if they could stop the transformation. Ended up having to go to England to get a drop of pure blood from the Holy Grail. It's too long and boring to tell, but I made Sunny promise to write it all down so maybe when she does I can post it here or something. Bottom line: They were able to stop the vamp process and my sweet little sis is now a member of the human race again. Of course, in the process, her and Magnus fell deeply in love and now they're doing the interspecies dating thing.

Which leaves me back at square one. No hot blood mate to spend eternity with. No riches beyond belief. Just an American History paper that I didn't write because I'd assumed I'd be an immortal drop-out before the due date. Can we say, "Rayne's Life Sucks Big Time?"

Bleh. I'm too depressed to write. More later.

POSTED BY RAYNE McDONALD @ 8:30 a.m.
THREE COMMENTS:

Ashleigh says . . .
OMG, Rayne! That totally sux that Blogfast ate ur entries. U should, like, totally sue or something. I was on vacation with the fam & figured I'd catch up on ur adventures when I came back and now I've missed everything! Booooooo!!

ButterfliQT says . . .
Thank god your sis got 2 turn back 2 a human! From what you've written about her, I think she'd make a totally sucky vamp!!!! (LOL—sucky vamp! hehe)

Rayne says . . .
I'm sooo with you, Butterfli. I mean, the girl didn't appreciate the idea of immortal life and big bucks one bit! She was more interested in who was gonna take her to the prom. Puh-leeze.

DarkGothBoy says . . .
Hey. U R Hot. Screw Magnus. He sounds like a tool. I'll be your blood mate any day. IM me—DarkGothBoy.

Rayne says . . .
WhatEVER, dude. I'm looking for a REAL vampire, not some poseur who gets off on blood suckage.

TWO

Drama with the Drama Teacher

FRIDAY, JUNE 1, 5 P.M.

You are *never* going to believe what happened to me today.

So it's Monday. And I'm walking through the hallways of Oakridge High, feeling pretty good about myself, right? I mean, I decided to try to have a positive attitude about the whole thing. Sure, I missed my op to become a vamp this time around and had to get back on the waiting list for the next blood mate, but it wasn't like I'd lost my chance forever. And besides, Magnus may be hot, but he's so not the type of guy I'd want to spend eternity with. (I want someone *waaaaaay* more dark and brooding.) So in a way, I figured, it all worked out for the best.

So, as I was saying . . . I'm walking through the halls, giving the finger to various meathead jocks like Mike Stevens—football quarterback and loser extraordinaire—avoiding the teachers who want to put me in detention for skipping class to go smoke over at "The Block," flirting with the new kid wearing an Interpol shirt. (He's not that cute, but evidently has good taste in music.) You know, your typical Raynie day.

Then suddenly, out of nowhere, some random old guy grabs me on the arm and starts dragging me into a side corridor.

"You must come with me," he says in an urgent voice.

I'm just about ready to go tae kwon do on his ass, but then I realize it's Mr. Teifert, Sunny's drama coach.

"Dude, I think you've gotten me mistaken for my twin," I say, as he drags me down into the auditorium's backstage area. "I'm Rayne. Sunny's the one in your play, not me." This mistaken-for-my-twin thing has so gotta stop.

The teacher pulls on the door and it slams closed with a large ominous clanking sound. Which, FYI, is a totally cool sound effect. I could use that in my next film. (For those of you just joining us, I'm going to be the next Tim Burton or David Lynch, just FYI.)

"I know who you are, Rayne," Mr. Teifert says, scratching his balding head.

I raise an eyebrow. "Oh. Then maybe an explanation of why you hauled me in here might be in order, do you think?"

He nods. "Yes, yes, of course." He takes a deep breath. "Now brace yourself. This may be a little difficult to take in . . ."

At first I totally think he's going to come up with some sicko declaration of love or something. Which would have been extremely gross. I mean, sure, I dated my English teacher for two weeks last semester, but he was a twenty-two-year-old sexy Australian who liked Nietzsche. Mr. Teifert's practically ancient—at least forty, I'd say—and so not sexy or cute or Australian. Besides, once I caught him singing show tunes, so I've been thinking he might bat for the other team.

"What I'm going to tell you may come as a bit of a shock," he continues in an extremely serious tone.

Jeez, enough with the drama, drama teacher guy.

"Shock. Awe. I gotcha. Spit it out." After all, I'm late for class. Not that this would normally bother me.

He clears his throat. "Very well then. Once a generation there is a girl born who is destined to slay the vampires."

I stare at him. "You know about Bertha the Vampire Slayer?" I ask incredulously. "You know about vampires?" Okay, he's right. I am shocked. And awed. And all that. I had no idea this nerdy old teacher had any clue about the Otherworld. I guess that's why he acted so weird when Sunny and I were joking around in the auditorium last week.

"Bertha, um, has had some blood pressure issues," he stammers. "She's temporarily retired from the slaying biz."

"I see . . ." I say slowly. Too much drive-thru super sizing for Bertha between slays, I guess.

"No, I don't think you do," Mr. Teifert says. "What I'm trying to tell you, Ms. McDonald, is that you are next in line."

"Next in line?" I swallow hard, not liking where this is going. "Next in line for what, exactly?" I mean, sure, if he's going to say next in line for the senior class play iPod giveaway, I'm his girl. But somehow I think he might be going in a much more unpleasant and less tuneful direction.

Mr. Teifert's smile doesn't quite reach his eyes as he holds out his hand. I stare down at it, not ready to shake.

"Congratulations, Rayne McDonald," he says. "You are the chosen one. Slayer Inc.'s new official vampire slayer."

I gape. "What the—"

Oh, crap. My mom's calling me to dinner. More later . . .

POSTED BY RAYNE McDONALD @ 5 p.m.
THREE COMMENTS:

Angelbaby3234566 says . . .
OMG, Rayne! How can u leave us hanging?!?! Come back and tell us the rest! How can u be a vampire slayer?????

DarkGothBoy says , . .
Hey—serves you right, you snotty beeyotch. Now you'll WISH you hooked up with me. No vamp will touch you with a ten-foot pole. Sux2BU.

Rayne says . . .
Don't worry, GothBoy—I'd rather become a nun than touch your, um, pole.

THREE

Destiny Bites!

FRIDAY, JUNE 1, 7 P.M.

I'm back. Sorry for the interruption. Mom has been militant about the whole family eating together ever since Dad left us. (Don't even get me started!) She would have freaked if I didn't show up for our nightly meal of tofu burgers and baked cardboard—er, French fries. I think she gets lonely, especially now that Sunny and I have a car and we're always off doing our own thing. She needs to start dating again. I mean, she's a total hippie—but seems downright Quaker when it comes to free love.

Anyway, back to "the slayer" thing.

I stare at Mr. Teifert. "Sorry, dude," I say. "I so cannot become the slayer. No freaking way. I mean, I'm in the vamp inner circle here. I have vampire friends. My sister is dating the new Blood Coven Master vamp. I'm on the waiting list to become a vampire myself. How can you expect me to all of a sudden go all Terminator on them? That just doesn't fit into the Rayne five-year plan."

There are several armchairs on stage, set up for the production of the senior class play *Bye Bye Birdie* (which Sunny is starring in, BTW). Mr. Teifert motions for me to sit in one of them, but I shake my head. I'm not interested in sitting around and chatting with this psycho.

"I'm out of here," I say, turning to exit stage left.

"Wait," he calls after me. "You must listen to what I have to say."

"Dude, I don't have to listen to a damn thing," I retort, but something inside me makes me stop walking. Curiosity, I guess. I mean, desirable occupation or no, it's not every day one gets told one has a "destiny." Especially by the drama coach.

Mr. Teifert sighs, running a hand through his wild black hair. "Actually, you do, Rayne."

"What's that supposed to mean?"

"I'll tell you, if you'll sit."

Grr. I mean, what am I, a dog or something? I reluctantly turn back and head toward center stage. I plop down in the nearest chair, which is way more uncomfortable than it looks. The springs dig into my butt and I hope this big revelation of my destiny isn't going to take too long.

"So tell me already," I say.

Mr. Teifert takes the seat across from me. He leans forward, hands on his knees. "You know me as a high school teacher. But I am also senior vice president of Slayer Inc. We're a human-run organization that tracks the vampire community and makes sure they stay in line."

"And if they don't, you dust them. Very diplomatic."

Mr. Teifert sighs. "Yes. There are times when that becomes our only option. But we do try to use other, more civilized methods first."

"Um-hm."

"But if all else fails, if the vampire in question refuses to follow the code, then we must remove him."

"Like you did with Lucifent?" I accuse, remembering how Bertha the Vampire Slayer recently took down the former master. "What did he ever do to you?"

Teifert shifts, as if his seat is suddenly uncomfortable. "That's confidential," he says. "But trust me, we had our reasons."

"Okay, fine," I say. Obviously this was going nowhere. "Not

that I agree with your methods, but let's move on. So if, like, once a generation there's a slayer born and Bertha is that slayer in mine, how come you're picking on me?"

Teifert snorts. "Please. This is the twenty-first century. You don't think we'd have a backup?" He shakes his head. "Sure, in the old days they only chose one. But then when that one was killed by a vampire or something they had to wait a whole other generation before they could start policing the covens again. Completely impractical. So nowadays we select several girls at birth."

"So if I die in my duties, you just swap me out? Kind of harsh." Suddenly I have sympathy for Bertha.

"Our goal is, of course, to keep you alive. And we will do everything in our power to do that."

"You're talking like I've already agreed to do this," I point out. "I haven't. And I won't, actually. I'm on a waiting list to become a vampire and I'm thinking that becoming an official slayer would definitely put me at the back of the line."

"I'm sorry, Rayne," Mr. Teifert says, in actuality not sounding the least bit apologetic. "But you don't have a choice."

I narrow my eyes. "What do you mean 'I don't have a choice'? *Of course* I have a choice. I can just, like, choose. To slay vampires or to let them live. And I choose life. Well, not life exactly, seeing as they're technically already dead. Undead, I guess, but—"

"When you were born, you were injected with a dormant nanovirus by a Slayer Inc. operative working in Mercy Hospital," Mr. Teifert interrupts in an oddly calm voice. "If you refuse to fulfill your destiny, we will be forced to activate the virus and you will, I'm afraid, suffer a very painful death."

I'm sure my eyes are totally bugging out of my head now as I stare at him. Nanovirus? WTF is a nanovirus? This has got to be a joke, right?

I realize my palms are totally sweaty all of a sudden. And my fingers have become real trembly. Fear pokes at my heart. Has Teifert already activated the virus? Am I dying as we speak? OMG, I could be literally dying. Right here, right now!

Or am I just being all Hypochondriac Girl? Like the time I swore

I had come down with Ebola after reading about it in Social Studies. I mean, I had all the symptoms. Headache, muscle ache, red eyes, fatigue, stomach pain . . .

The school nurse had not been impressed, informing me that those were also symptoms of a hangover. As was the distinct smell of vodka on my breath. Guess I should have brushed my teeth a few more times after Spider and I embarked on our "do these fake IDs work" adventure the night before.

But I'm not taking any chances. Especially since it feels like my throat is starting to close up. My vision is getting spotty. "Please!" I beg. "I want to live. Turn it off! Please, turn it off!"

Mr. Teifert rolls his eyes. "I haven't turned it on, Rayne. But I must say I am quite impressed by your dramatic prowess. Ever consider the theater?"

Oh.

Vision returns. Throat loosens. I no longer feel the urge to go toward the light. Phew.

"Come with me." Mr. Teifert rises from his chair and beckons me to follow. I reluctantly stand up and trail behind him as he heads to the back of the stage, behind the cheerily painted background flats, behind the interior curtain, behind the cage that holds all the lighting controls. Just when I think we can't go back any farther, we come to a small, nondescript door I'd never noticed before.

Mr. Teifert pulls out a large old-fashioned golden key and slips it into the lock. Before opening the door, he glances from left to right. To see if we're alone, I guess. Then he turns the key. The door creaks open.

I can practically feel my heart pounding against my chest cavity as I follow him inside. At this point I'm thinking, what if the guy just made up the whole Slayer Inc. thing? What if he's really some psycho axe-wielding teacher who likes to chop up teenagers and then eat them in the back room? Have any other students gone missing from Oakridge lately? Hmm. When was the last time I saw Tubby Toby? He had a lot of meat on his bones . . .

I'm about ready to run screaming back onto the stage, when

Teifert flips a switch and the room becomes bathed in a dull orange glow. I glance around, my breath catching in my throat. Suddenly, I'm too fascinated to leave, even if I now have an even better reason to do so.

Weapons. Lots of weapons. In fact, I'd bet my Dr. Martens combat boot collection that none of you have seen so many weapons in one place before. (Well, if you don't count museums, which I don't, as those are ancient weapons behind glass. Not the ready-to-chop-off-someone's-head-at-a-moment's-notice variety like these are.) There are intricate medieval swords, shiny axes (gulp!), and a large collection of jeweled daggers.

"Tools of the slayer," Teifert explains. I glance over at him. Under this lighting he no longer looks like a dorky drama teacher. In fact, if I didn't know better, I'd say he had some kind of weird glow about him. A glow of . . . power.

"I can use these?" I ask, running a hand along the helm of the sword. I start imagining myself wielding the mighty blade. Just like that cool senior Jen Taufman who belongs to the Society of Creative Anachronism and does medieval battle recreations on the weekends.

"Uh, no," Mr. Teifert corrects, sinking all my dreams of becoming a twenty-first-century knight in shining armor. Figures. He pulls open a drawer and rummages around. "Not right away, anyway. To begin with, you'll use this."

I stare at the item in his hand. That? That's all I get to vanquish evil and slay immortal creatures of the night?

"Uh, that's just a chunk of wood, dude."

"It's a stake," Mr. Teifert clarifies. "You must know about staking vampires, Rayne. Even Hollywood's got that part right."

I roll my eyes. "But those stakes are at least smooth. Pointy. Elegant almost. I bet you just found that thing outside on the ground in the woods."

Mr. Teifert inspects the rough stick in his hand. "That's because it's not finished yet. Each slayer must carve her own stake. Embed it with her own essence. That's what gives it its power."

"Oh, joy. So not only do I have to go out and fight evil villains, but I have to take up woodworking, too?"

The drama teacher sighs deeply. "I never said becoming the slayer would be a field trip to a Justin Bieber concert."

"Good. Because I'd rather stab myself with an unfinished stake than attend one of those," I inform him. "Die a slow painful death. It'd still be better. I can't believe you think I am a friend of the Bieb's. I mean, I know you adults all think we teens look the same, but hello?" I gesture to my outfit. "Black-wearing, night-worshipping Goth girl here. I so have better taste than that."

"Um, right. We're getting off topic here," Teifert interrupts. Good thing, too, cause I had a lot more to say on the subject. I mean, talk about insulting!

The drama coach holds out the stake. I take it, reluctantly, worried that the nasty thing is going to give me splinters. "Um, thanks," I mutter, not quite sure of the appropriate response to the giftage of a piece of wood.

"Look, Rayne. Try to see the job as an opportunity," Teifert tries again. Jeez. The man doesn't give up. He'd make a great Army recruiter.

"An opportunity to murder innocent creatures of the night that pose absolutely no threat to the human race? Rock on." There's more than a hint of sarcasm in my voice, as you can probably imagine.

"Now that's where you're mistaken, little girl," Mr. Teifert says, narrowing his eyes and going all authority figure on me. "Not all vampires are so-called 'good guys,' as you seem to believe. And those who are living a peaceful existence have no reason to fear our organization. It's only the evil vampires that we wish to keep in line."

"Okay, fine. Only the bad guys. What about my sister's boyfriend?" I ask. "Is Magnus a goodie or a baddie?"

"We are pleased at Magnus's rise to power. We feel he will be a great master, actually."

Oh. Well that's a relief. Don't have to worry about pissing Sunny off. Nanovirus or not, dusting one's sister's BF would so be against the twin code of honor.

"Okay. So if I were to take this gig," I say cautiously. "Not that I'm necessarily saying yes, but if I do, who'd be my first victim?"

Mr. Teifert reaches into his leather briefcase and pulls out a file. He flips through the pages until he comes to an eight-by-ten photo. He holds it up so I can take a look.

My eyes widen and a chill trips down my spine as I examine the photo. The vamp in question just looks evil. Seriously evil. He has jet-black hair—parted down the middle and hanging to his shoulders—a trim goatee, pure white skin, and piercing ice-blue eyes that seem to bore into my skull. Sort of resembles a young Trent Reznor from Nine Inch Nails. If Trent had huge fangs protruding from his bloodred lips, that is.

"Maverick," Mr. Teifert whispers.

The name has power. Like the bad guy in *Harry Potter*. Hearing it sends chills down my spine. I stare at the picture. The eyes seem to taunt me. Begging me to come closer . . . closer . . .

"Okay, okay!" I cry, turning my head away. "I've seen enough."

Mr. Teifert slips the picture back into the file. "Maverick owns the Blood Bar downtown. It's an underground nightclub where humans can go and pay to have their blood sucked by a vampire."

"Um?" I raise an eyebrow. "Ew?" I mean, I'm a big fan of all things vamp, but that just sounds creepy and wrong.

"Yes. 'Ew' would be an appropriate reaction, I think. It's not exactly a high-class establishment. Strictly for the extreme fetish crowd."

"So people get off on that? Getting sucked dry by a vamp turns them on?"

"Evidently. It's become quite the hot spot."

"And you want to shut them down."

"Not exactly. While we don't approve, as a rule, of these unlicensed bite shops, we understand that humans are doing this of their own free will, making it a victimless crime. And normally the vamps that work there are all tested for diseases before becoming employed. So while it's a bit . . . distasteful . . . we tend to turn a blind eye."

"Then what . . . ?"

"Maverick has been very vocal about his displeasure at Magnus taking over the Blood Coven after Lucifent's death. We believe he may be up to something. We need you to infiltrate the Blood Bar. Pose as a human who'd like to get sucked. Figure out what Maverick has planned and then, if you get the opportunity, stake him."

Huh. That doesn't sound so bad actually. In a way, I'd be helping the vamps. The good guys anyway. And saving the life of my twin's BF. I'd be a hero. Maybe my good deeds would actually push me to the front of the vampire line. Then Slayer Inc. could just get the next chick in line to be the once-a-generation slayer.

Also, there's that whole nanovirus in my bloodstream thing that's awfully convincing. Well, if that's even true. Which it might not be. Come to think of it, it does seem a tad far-fetched, don't you think? Like some story an adult would make up to get a teen to do whatever he says. Still, I'm not taking any chances 'til I find out for sure. Maybe Magnus will know the deal.

I square my shoulders, firming my resolve. "Okay," I say, hoping I sound more brave than I feel. "I'll do it."

POSTED BY Rayne McDonald @ 7 p.m.
FOUR COMMENTS:

CandyGrrl says . . .
> OMG, Rayne! That's so crazy! I can't believe u of all people r now the slayer! Ur like some superhero or something! Do u get powers like Buffy? And more important, do u get to hook up with Spike? Yum!

Rayne says . . .
> Hmm . . . dunno about the powers. Forgot to ask. As for Spike, I certainly wouldn't kick him out of bed if he were to crawl in one night. ☺

TheyROut2GetMe says . . .

Don't you think it's a little dangerous to post your
"secret" mission on your blog for everyone in the known
universe to read? I mean, what if Maverick Googles
himself and learns about your plans?

Rayne says . . .

Uh, hello?! You think I'm stupid? You don't think I
changed names to protect the innocent—or the guilty in
this case? [Though Maverick is a way-cool name for an
evil vampire, don't you think?] And the Blood Bar's real
name is much more creative and Gothy sounding. But
yeah, "Maverick" can Google himself until the bats come
home—he ain't stumbling across my blog.

FOUR

Gamer Grrls

SATURDAY, JUNE 2, 2:20 A.M.

It's wicked late—just popped on for a minute. Was playing World
of Warcraft—this online video game—with Spider, my best friend.
Spider plays a gnome mage (like a pint-size magician) and I play this
fierce human warrior chick. It's the best game EVER and we play
all the time. Mom claims I'm totally addicted, but, hey, I could say
the same to her about her repeated watchings of BBC's *Pride and
Prejudice*. She <3's Colin Firth with a vengeance.

Anyway I told Spider about the whole slayer thing over chat.
Rather then recapping, I'll just paste in the transcript:

> **RAYNIEDAY:** OMG, Spider, the weirdest thing
> happened today!
> **SPIDER:** The cheerleaders invited you to join their
> ranks?
> **RAYNIEDAY:** Um, no.
> **SPIDER:** Football captain Mike Stevens asked
> you out?
> **RAYNIEDAY:** Heh. No. And uh, ew, BTW.

SPIDER: Then I'm sorry, it's not the weirdest thing. Maybe it's up there in weirdness, sure, I'll buy that. But THE weirdest thing? I think not.

RAYNIEDAY: Hehe. This is even weirder. I'm telling you.

SPIDER: Watch out behind you! An orc!

**Spider casts fireball on Orc. 450 damage.
**Rayne slashes at Orc. Orc dodges her blow.
**Orc hits Spider for 1,324 damage.
**Spider dies.

SPIDER: D'oh! I hate being the mage. I'm always the first to die. How come you never die? I'm the one doing ALL the damage and you just rack up the experience points.

RAYNIEDAY: 'Cause I'm wearing armor. Duh. You're going into battle wearing, like, some silk robe. Hello?

SPIDER: Yeah, I'm, like, freaking tissue paper here. Come get the mage, everyone. Pick on the poor squishy mage!

RAYNIEDAY: ANYWAY—while you run back from the graveyard, I've got to tell you what happened!!!

SPIDER: Hmph. No sympathy. Fine. Fine.

So I tell Spider about Mr. Teifert. Slayer Inc. My destiny. Etc., etc.

SPIDER: Wow. That's so crazy. What are you going to do?

RAYNIEDAY: IDK. Slay Maverick, I guess? I mean, if he's out to get Sunny's BF, then that seems like the right thing to do.

SPIDER: But isn't that totally dangerous? I mean, what if you get made into a bloody snack?

RAYNIEDAY: Gulp. Thanks. You're making me feel so much better.

SPIDER: Just trying to be realistic.

RAYNIEDAY: I know, but I, like, don't have a choice here. They've got the nanos in me. If I don't help them, they'll kill me. And I'd so rather be a living snack than dead meat.

SPIDER: Guess you've got a point there. Still, be careful, okay? I mean infiltrating a vamp nest and trying to stake their evil leader? That sounds harder than passing Trig without sleeping with the teacher.

RAYNIEDAY: Heh. So THAT'S your secret. :P

SPIDER: Hehe. I don't "sine" and tell.

RAYNIEDAY: Very "cosine."

SPIDER: At least I don't go off on "tangents."

RAYNIEDAY: Uh-huh. ANYWAY—I'm going to head to the Blood Bar 2morrow nite. I'll IM you when I get back, k? If I don't IM, tell Sunny what happened and maybe Magnus can send in the big guns.

SPIDER: You haven't told Sunny to begin with?

RAYNIEDAY: . . .

SPIDER: Um, don't you think you should?

RAYNIEDAY: No effing way. Cause, like, what if she tells Magnus and Slayer Inc.'s wrong and Mag and Maverick are best buddies? Then Magnus could go warn Maverick and I'll totally get nanoed. Then I'd definitely fail Trig—teacher sleepage or no.

SPIDER: I guess you've got a point.

RAYNIEDAY: No, I've got a stake, LOL.

SPIDER: Hehe. Okay, fine. Go slay some vamp butt. Good luck. I'm back from the graveyard, BTW. Rezzing now.

RAYNIEDAY: Uh, you might want to wait—

****Spider resurrects.*
****Shaman hits Spider for 975 damage.*
****Spider dies.*

SPIDER: NOOOOOO!!!!!

RAYNIEDAY: Sigh. And on that note, I'm logging. Got a busy day tomorrow. Evil vampires don't just slay themselves, you know.

POSTED BY RAYNE McDONALD @ 2:20 a.m.
THREE COMMENTS:

DarkGothBoy says . . .
You play World of Warcraft? Wow, you're such a cool chick. I'm on the Stonemaul server. Have a level 80 paladin. w00t! Are you into role-playing? We should totally cyber sometime.

Rayne says . . .
Um, remember that ten-foot pole thing? That counts for your virtual "lance" as well. Just. Not. Touching. Virtually or in real life. Get a life and stop reading my blog.

Spider says . . .
Jeez, Rayne, you had to put in the part about me dying? Couldn't you have cut and pasted that part out? Obviously it's so not relevant to this story and you make me look like a total nooblet in front of the WHOLE WORLD. And for the record, whole world people, I'm a really good player. It's just that Rayne sucks as a bodyguard. SUCKS, I tell you! It's so her fault that I'm always dead.

FIVE

The Blood Bar

SATURDAY, JUNE 2, 8 P.M.

I must be brief—I'm actually writing this from my iPhone from inside the Blood Bar!! Let me tell you, this place is creepy with a capital C! Or ghetto with a capital G. Or some kind of capital word for weird, sick, and twisted. (Which, I guess, would be three capital words: Weird, Sick, and Twisted, duh.)

First of all, I had to go through the total crackhead section of town. Wandering past pimps and prostitutes, drug dealers, and bums to find it. I half thought I'd get attacked and killed before I even got to my destination. Some slayer I'd turn out to be if I got myself killed by some punk mortal before I even got to stake my first vamp.

At least I look good. After all, one does not enter a vampire den unprepared and so I made a special effort to Goth things up even more than usual before I came. I've got on this black lacy corset top under my leather jacket, a black vinyl miniskirt, fishnets, and knee-high platform boots. The outfit, in conjunction with my overly blacked-out eyes, red lipstick, and powdered white face, makes me look pretty kick-ass, if you can excuse the vanity for a moment.

I find the address. A nondescript brick building. Which I guess makes sense. Obviously they're not going to have some neon sign out flashing "Get Sucked Here!" or anything. But this joint is beyond subtle. In fact, I'm not even sure if I have the right place—until a street-light glints on a tiny stained glass window embedded into the door . . . the shape of a drop of blood.

Bingo.

Not quite sure what to do, I knock. This big, burly bouncer type guy creaks open the door from the other side and looks down at me with suspicious eyes. I meet his gaze, hopefully appearing less freaked out than I am. I mean, the dude looks like Vin Diesel if Vin Diesel took steroids. Yeah, that big. Except unlike the tanned action hero, this guy is pasty white. So, like a ghosty Vin Diesel on steroids. Which throws me a bit. Usually the vamp wanna-be crowd is all scrawny and lanky.

"What do you want?" he asks in a grumbly, growly voice. Hmm. Not exactly the rising star in the customer service department. Good thing I'm a slayer and not a secret shopper or I'd so be knocking off points already.

"I, um, am interested in being, uh . . ." Jeez, what's the correct terminology here? "Sucked?"

"I don't know what you're talking about."

I shake my head. Oh, so he's going to be like that, is he? "Yes, you do. You totally know. You're just pretending you don't because you're afraid I'm some cop or something. Well, I am not a cop. Obviously. I mean, since when do sixteen-year-olds become cops?"

"I don't think you're a cop. I think you're underage. We don't serve minors."

D'oh.

"Ha-ha." I laugh. "Did I say sixteen? Silly me. I meant twenty-five. Look, I even have an ID that proves it." I reach into my black canvas messenger bag and rummage through the front pocket for my wallet. Grabbing my fake ID, I present it to Vamp Diesel, hoping he won't notice my trembling hands.

"You're from Kentucky?" he asks, squinting at the photo (so not me). "And you're five eleven?"

"Only when I wear my stilettos."

He rolls his eyes, not looking all that convinced. "Run home and play with your dolls, um"—he glances at my ID—"Shaniqua." He snorts, handing me back my license. "This is not the place for you."

Okay, that's it. No more Miss Nice Rayne. I drop my eyes to the ground and flutter my lashes. Then I look up at him with my best Angelina Jolie imitation, pre–Brad Pitt/mommy era. "I don't play with dolls," I say, making my voice sultry and deep. "I play with vampires." I reach up and drag a lazy finger down the front of his massive chest. He stiffens immediately. Heh. Men are so easy.

"Well, I guess your license does say you're twenty-five . . ." He hedges.

"I am twenty-five. Twenty-five and three quarters, to be exact." I smile coyly, reeling him in. "Now, please let me in. I'm *dying* to be sucked."

At first I'm not sure if he's going to go for this, but he surprises me by opening the door wide and gesturing me forward. I give him a little bow and step over the threshold.

"Fine, fine. But behave yourself," he instructs. "Don't make me sorry I let you in."

"I will," I promise. "I mean, I won't. Make you sorry, that is. I will behave. You won't even know I'm here. What's your name, anyway?"

"Francis. And I run the door most nights."

I rise onto my tiptoes to kiss his cheek. "Thank you, Francis," I say. "You won't regret this."

"I already do," he says, his face turning a slight pink color. Close as vamps get to blushing, I suppose. "But go in and have a good time before I change my mind."

I thank him once more, then head in. The door leads to a dark hallway, the walls painted with strange Celtic-looking designs that glow under the black lighting. Under my feet is a plush crimson rug. Weird, ambient mood music floats through the smoke-filled air. I guess the Blood Bar feels it's exempt from the no smoking laws of the rest of our state. Which makes sense, really, as lighting up is just where the sinning *starts* here.

The whole thing is truly spooky and I have half a mind to turn around and run back out the door screaming. But something compels me to keep moving forward. To see this through.

I reach the beaded curtain at the far side of the hallway and go through into the main bar. The place is decorated like a Valentine's Day card. Everything is red. Red velvet couches, red shag rugs, red walls, and red lightbulbs in the chandelier. The fuzzy lighting makes it hard to get a good look at the other patrons. Some are sprawled out on couches in a relaxed, almost sleepy manner. Others are sitting on the edges of their seats, looking tense. All of them look like junkies—underfed, drawn faces, trembling hands.

This one guy standing over in the corner looks particularly foreboding. He appears fiftyish and is wearing a well-fitted black tux. Sandy-haired, high cheekbones, and an athletic physique, he has a sort of elegance about him that the other gaunt Blood Bar inhabitants lack. If I hadn't seen a photo of Maverick, I would have pegged this guy as the bar's owner, given the proprietary sense he exhibits as he surveys the lounge, arms crossed over his chest. But while he's definitely vampish, he's no Trent Reznor look-alike, so he can't be the big baddie we're here to find.

He catches me looking at him and gives me a small nod. Freaked out, I quickly drop my eyes. The last thing I need is to start drawing attention to myself.

"Do you have an appointment?" A sultry female voice behind me makes me turn around. A tall, voluptuous woman with long black hair to her waist has focused her huge violet eyes on me expectantly, a clipboard in her hands. She wears a crimson corset top and a long silky black skirt that's gotta be vintage or I'd so be asking her where she got it.

"I, um, do you take walk-ins here?" I stammer, caught off guard. She frowns. "We certainly do not."

"Well, good. Because I, um, have an appointment." I squint down at her appointment book. Good thing I have excellent eyesight. "I'm Jane Smith."

She glances down at her clipboard. "Do you mean *James* Smith?"

Hmm. Maybe time to see the eye doctor after all. "Yeah, that's me. James Smith. Evil parents really wanted a boy. Anyway, I go by

Jane now. To my friends, anyway. Do you want to be my friend? I need more friends, actually. People to call me Jane."

She rolls her heavily made-up eyes. I know she doesn't believe me, but I've managed to annoy her enough that she just wants me out of her hair. Good strategy for dealing with teachers as well, by the way. Works every time.

"Fine, fine. James. Jane. Whatever. You're in room six." She gestures to the wall on the far side of the room. "Behind those curtains."

I swallow hard. This is it. I thank her and head to the back of the room, pulling aside the heavy velvet drapes. Behind it are ten nondescript doors, each with a gold number. I find room six and slip inside.

The room is dark, without any windows. The walls are painted black and thus suck out even the dim lighting given off by a few candles in the room. In the center is a big canopy bed with black linens. Even the floor has a charcoal-colored rug. Maybe they make it black so the bloodstains don't show as easily. The thought makes me a bit queasy and I close the door behind me and retreat to a wooden low-backed chair. What have I gotten myself into? This is totally Spooky World and I'm not just here for a visit.

Suddenly I realize the precariousness of my situation. I'm all alone in a vampire blood bar on the wrong side of town. And no one (besides Spider, and I don't give Spider's rescue abilities much credit) knows where I am.

Some might call this a bad situation to be in. After all, I've got no plan. No idea what to do now that I'm here. What if I have to actually get sucked by some random gnarly vamp? What if I get some kind of awful disease? What if just sitting in here is infecting me?

Can we say Stupid, Rayne?

I take a deep breath, remembering what Mr. Teifert told me. The vamps here are all tested for diseases. I'm fine. I'm safe. From that, at least. And I have my stake, in case I meet with any danger. I reach into my bag, examine the chunk of unfinished wood, then sigh and put it away. Sadly, that *so* doesn't make me feel any more secure.

And that's where I am right about now. After forty-five minutes of waiting, my anxiety level has gone down and my boredom level has gone up. This is worse than the doctor's office. Nothing much to do. I've already checked my e-mail, played Angry Birds, texted with Spider. And now I'm writing my blog.

Oh, wait! Someone's coming. *Ooh*, this is it! More later.

POSTED BY RAYNE McDONALD @ 8 p.m.
ONE COMMENT:

SunshineBaby says . . .
Rayne! Are you just making this stuff up to see if I'm reading your blog? You're not really a slayer, are you? I mean, you'd come tell me if you were suddenly a slayer, right? You can't keep something like that from your twin sister. Especially when the twin in question is dating a vampire. Which, I might add, is sort of your fault to begin with. Not to mention that the Blood Bar place sounds really dangerous. But I'm guessing this is just a joke to freak me out. I hope . . .

SIX

Jareth

SATURDAY, JUNE 2, 11 P.M.

I'm so getting my hair dyed black. Tomorrow. I'd do it tonight if I could find a drugstore that was still open. Just get a bottle of dye and dump it over my head. Something. Anything. Just so I don't look exactly like Sunny.

Sorry. Getting ahead of myself here.

So last I wrote I was in the Blood Bar, waiting for the vamp who's supposed to suck me, right? And it was a long wait, let me tell you. But finally the door opens.

The guy who enters the room is nothing like the other vamps I saw hanging out in the sitting room. The half-starved, junkie looking ones. This guy, while definitely a vamp with gorgeous fangage, is like a Jude Law clone. I know! Drool, right? Seriously, the dude's got the same dirty blond hair, beautiful green eyes (though his are rimmed with black eyeliner—yum!), and high cheekbones. He's tall. He's lanky. He's wearing a black wife-beater tank and tight black pants. His buff arms tell me he clocks in mucho time at the gym, but at the same time, he's simply toned, not bulky and meatheady like the bouncer, Francis, had been.

In other words, he's the most gorgeous Goth guy I've ever seen.

And he's a vampire, too. Which automatically makes him not a poseur, like, uh, some of you. (Cough, cough, DarkGothBoy.)

Anyway, I'm all staring at him, totally and officially and instantly in love. I'm thinking, he can jump me, bite me, have his wicked way with me. Whatever his little black heart desires. He can take me on midnight strolls through ancient, ivy-walled cemeteries and kiss me senseless under the waning moon. Forget whiny, annoying Magnus. Sunny can have him. I want a blood mate like this guy.

"Hi, I'm Jareth, and I'll be your biter tonight," he mumbles in a deep, British-accented voice. OMG, yes! He's English, too! Major w00t! At this point I'm thinking this guy is way too good to be true. I wonder if he already has a blood mate, but I can't imagine he'd be working in a place like this, if he did. Maybe he's a lost soul, waiting for the love of a pure heart to redeem him like you always read about in those Christine Feehan books.

I watch intently as he wanders to the far side of the room, not yet glancing in my direction. He lazily sinks into the bed, extending his arms spread-eagle across the width of the pillows. His movements are slinky, almost catlike in their grace. He closes his beautiful emerald eyes and smiles the most seductive smile known to mankind, his fangs slightly protruding from his mouth. Aha! Now we're talking.

I wonder if he's really as attractive as I think he is or if he's using the Vampire Scent on me. Vampires have this pheromone thing going on that makes them irresistible to humans. Probably how they rose to such power in this world. One grin and we're putty in their fangs.

"If you have any special requests, please tell me now and I'll do my best to accommodate you," he purrs in a throaty voice, shifting in the bed a bit, eyes still closed.

Gulp. This guy oozes sex. He's practically dripping with it. I so want to jump him. Even more than I wanted to jump Ville when I went to see HIM last fall. And that's saying something.

I shake my head. No, no, that will never do. One, this vamp's not really interested in me; it's his job to turn me on. I don't want to be like the fat guy who falls for the hooker. Two, he's one of the bad guys, duh. So even if he did—for some unfathomable reason—take an interest in me, I so can't start hooking up with one of Maverick's men. Then I'd have to war against my sister and her BF and that seems kind of lame. Not to mention I'd be nanovirused by Slayer Inc. A lousy situation all around.

"Um, hi, Jareth," I say, realizing he's waiting for an answer to his special requests question. Not that I can think of any. Well, not that I should say aloud anyway. Hmm, maybe I should at least introduce myself. "Nice to meet you. I'm—"

"God!" Jareth interrupts as his eyes flutter open and he looks straight at me for the first time. Though with that accent, it comes out more like, "Gawd."

"Uh, no," I correct, though not unpleased at the idea. I like this guy's style. "I'm not God. At least I'm pretty sure I'm not. Though sometimes as a kid I used to pretend I was Aphrodite. You know, the goddess of love? But really, I'm just—"

"Your Majesty! What are you doing here?" he asks, scrambling off the bed and bowing low from the waist. "This is no place for you."

Oh-kay then. I stare at him, confused as all hell at this point. Is this some kind of weird role-playing they do here? Creepy. "Uh, no," I correct, "I'm not a queen or anything, either. I mean, sure, again, I wish. But really I'm just—"

"I know very well who you are, Majesty." His lips curl into a snarl, his green eyes now a dark and stormy sea. He looks so angry. I take a cautionary step back. What have I gotten myself into? Does he know I work for Slayer Inc.? Is he going to alert the whole Blood Bar? Am I utterly screwed?

"Uh . . ." I manage, not at my most articulate.

Jareth grabs me by the shoulders, his nails digging into my skin, his gaze boring down on me. I'm shaking like crazy and am this close to bursting into tears. Some cool slayer chick I am. The way he's got me pinned I can't even whip out my stake. "Why did Magnus send you? Does he not trust me to get the job done?"

What? I look up at him, meeting his eyes for the first time. Did he just say "Magnus"?

"You know Magnus?" I ask, my voice totally croaky.

This could be bad. Very bad. Is my sister's boyfriend actually mixed up with the evils after all? Does this mean I have to slay him? Sunny will be so pissed if I slay her boyfriend, baddie or no. But then, I guess in the long run I'd be doing her a favor, right? Saving her from the Dark Side. Like when Luke killed his father, Darth Vader. Sort of. Okay, not really exactly the same.

He gives me a strange look. "Of course. I'm General Jareth of the Blood Coven Army. But you know that."

"I do?" I rack my brains. Then realization smacks me upside the head. Duh, duh, duh. "Oh! You think that I'm—"

"You know, I must say, I'm quite offended," Jareth rants, releasing my shoulders and running a hand through his hair. "I can't believe Magnus doesn't trust me. Sending his blood mate in to spy on me. And did he really think I wouldn't recognize you? After that night at Club Fang?"

"Dude, you have the wrong idea," I interrupt. "If you'd just calm down, I'll explain. I'm not Sunny. I'm—"

"Insulting. Unbearably insulting. I must go have a word with him this very second." Jareth pushes by me and heads out the door, slamming it behind him.

"I'm Rayne!" I cry after him. "Her sister."

But he's already gone.

I sigh, plopping down on the bed. These mistaken identity things really need to stop. First there was the whole Sunny getting my blood mate and almost becoming a creature of the night, now this. Definitely time to dye my hair black. Or develop an eating disorder like one of the Olsen twins once did. (Though that would force me to give up French fries.) But I have to do something. Anything to keep me from looking exactly like my sister.

Especially now that she's the Vampire Queen and I'm the slayer.

POSTED BY RAYNE McDONALD @ 11 p.m.
FOUR COMMENTS:

ButterfliQT says . . .
　　Wow, Rayne. I can't believe u went into that place by
　　urself. Weren't you afraid they'd, like, kill u or something?

Rayne says . . .

Butterfli, we cannot all live our lives in fear. Some of us
have destinies to fulfill. And, um, thanks for reminding me
about the potential deathage. I really appreciate the
support and encouragement . . .

Anonymous . . .

Hey, Destiny Girl—you make yourself all high and mighty,
but as far as I see it, you're still at square one. You
haven't figured out anything about Maverick or his plans.
You suck.

Rayne says . . .

First off, if you've got something to post in my blog, post
it as yourself. Don't hide under anonymity. That's, like,
way lame. Second off, this isn't some TV drama, where
everything's solved in forty minutes between commercial
breaks. Let's be realistic here. It's gonna take a few visits
before I save the day. But never you fear, oh Anonymous
One. I will succeed. After all, I am Rayne, The Vampire
Slayer.

SEVEN

Jareth the Jerk-Off

SUNDAY, JUNE 3, 10 A.M.

Quick entry before breakfast as I didn't get to finish telling you the whole story last night. Was way too exhausted.

I leave the Blood Bar—not much more I can do tonight—and drive home. I'm exhausted at this point and just want to crawl in bed and get some shut-eye. But as I walk up the steps to the house, I hear a distinct *psst* coming from the bushes. I turn to look. It's my sister, Sunny, hiding in a bush.

I scrunch my eyebrows. "What are you—?"

She puts a finger to her lips and motions for me to follow. She leads me across the front lawn and to an elegant black stretch limo I hadn't noticed parked across the street. I climb inside after her and shut the door. The driver, obscured by a smoked-out glass window, pulls out.

I look around the limo. Whoa. Very elegant. Very vamp. The seats are crushed red velvet and there are crystal decanters filled with crimson liquid. Liquid I can almost guarantee is not some fine merlot.

Something inside of me aches a bit. You know, it's so not fair that this is Sunny's life and not mine. I did everything I was supposed to and now she's reaping all the rewards. I should have the riches, the powers, the gothed-out limo. The hot blood mate.

Speaking of, Magnus is sitting beside Sunny, all decked out in Armani as usual. I can see why she digs the guy. He looks just like Orlando Bloom in *Pirates of the Carribean*. Long black hair, pulled back, deep soulful eyes. (Though that might just be a trick of the light seeing as the guy has no soul. . . .)

I turn to my side and sigh when I see Jareth, the vamp from the Blood Bar, sitting next to me. Still dressed in his Goth best, a serious frown on his otherwise delish face. I sigh again. Great. He obviously sold me out. Sunny's going to be *sooo* pissed I didn't tell her the 411 about the whole slayer thing before heading out.

"What's going on, Rayne?" Sunny demands. Dressed in flip-flops, jeans, and tank top, she looks so out of place in the elegant, Gothic vampire limo. Annoys me to no end the fact that she now belongs here more than I do, let me tell you. At least they didn't fit her with a crown or something. Though I guess technically she's not Magnus's queen unless they get married, right? Can vampires even get married? I can't remember if that was covered in the training. I guess if they did it'd be more country club than church. . . .

Sorry. Digressing. I know.

"Uh, what do you mean?" I ask, not quite sure why I'm even attempting the innocent routine. There's no way she doesn't know.

"Jareth says he saw you down at the Blood Bar," Magnus clarifies. He has a sexy English accent, too. According to Sunny he was once a knight in shining armor for King Arthur in Camelot. I wonder if Jareth was as well. Not that I care.

"He assumed you were me," Sunny adds.

"Hmm. I wonder why," I say sarcastically, still mad at him for scaring me so badly back at the bar. "Oh, wait. Could it be that he didn't shut up long enough to listen to one word I had to say? Could it be that he was too much in a hurry to run and go crying to Magnus before I even had a chance to explain?" I narrow my eyes and shoot daggers at Jareth. Jerk-off. Getting me in trouble with the vamps. So help me if this interferes with my position on the blood mate waiting list. "Thanks, dude, for selling me down the river. Two seconds and we could have cleared this whole thing up. But no. You had to *assume*. And you know what *assuming* does, don't you?" I elbow the vampire in the ribs. "Makes an 'ass' out of 'you' and 'me.' Or however that stupid phrase goes."

"I wouldn't mind you turning into an ass," Jareth growls in his throaty voice. "Then at least you couldn't speak."

"Oh yeah?" I cry, my blood boiling at this point. I'm, like, this close to smacking the guy upside the head. Or whipping out my stake, even. That'd show him. No one should be able to talk to me like that and live. "Well . . . then I could, um, bray, and I bet that would be even more annoying."

"I'd take my chances."

"Jareth! Rayne!" Magnus scolds. "This childish bickering is not helping us get to the bottom of this."

"You're right," I agree. Then when Magnus isn't looking I stick my tongue out at Jareth. He scowls back at me. Ugh, what a loser, right? And that "ass" comment was completely uncalled for. Especially since back at the Blood Bar he wouldn't let me get a word in edgewise while he ranted and raved and pulled out his hair. I take everything back about him being a sexy guy I'd want to have vampire babies with.

"Why were you at the Blood Bar, Rayne?" Sunny asks, her voice all concerned and big sister like. Technically though, I'm the older one. By seven whole minutes. Just cause she's dating some guy who's, like, a thousand years old doesn't mean suddenly she's more wise and mature. "And that thing in your blog? About being a vampire slayer? Was that just a joke? Cause if that was a joke, it wasn't very funny."

Oh, I see. NOW she reads my blog. Now that she's back to being a human and it makes no difference whatsoever. I begged her to read the thing when she was about to turn vampire. As you know, it has a ton of important info about the process. But no! She had better things to do. Like make out with her cheeseball prom date Jake Wilder.

I swallow hard. Explanation time.

"It's not a joke. Your drama coach, Mr. Teifert, is really vice prez of Slayer Inc. And he's tagged me as the next slayer." I lean back in my seat, crossing my left leg over my right, somewhat enjoying the shocked looks on everyone's faces. Especially Jareth's. Heh. I bet he wishes he didn't make enemies with me now. Now that he knows how dangerous I can be. One wrong move and BAM! Stake that!

"Why would he pick you?" Sunny asks, the first to recover her voice.

I shrug. "I don't know. He was all saying it's my destiny or something."

"Can't you just refuse?"

"That's the messed up part," I admit. "He claims he's put some nanovirus in my bloodstream that will be activated if I refuse to perform my slayerly duties. I don't know if it's true or not, but I don't want to take any chances, you know?"

"Nano what?" Sunny asks, scrunching up her freckled nose. "That's crazy. He's got to be pulling your leg. Maybe he overheard us talking and . . ."

"I'm afraid not, Sunny," Magnus says, reaching over to put a slender white hand on her knee. My virginal twin squirms a bit under his touch. She wants him, I can tell, but she's fighting the run to second base. I wonder how long it will take Maggy to score that first home run. "That's Slayer Inc.'s typical MO. They have operatives in every major hospital who tag infants in the maternity ward who they deem to be potential slayers."

Ugh. So the nano thing probably is true. Great. I was so hoping Mag would laugh it off and tell me Slayer Inc. had no real hold on me. Evidently not so much.

"But Rayne can't kill vampires!" Sunny interjects. "I mean, she wants to be one! And . . . and what if she has to kill you?" My twin looks close to tears at this point. She had a run-in with Bertha, the old slayer, once upon a time and it scarred her for life.

"You know, you're going to score lousy on the reading comprehension part of the MCATs," I say. "You obviously only skimmed my blog entry."

"Well, I'm sorry. My twin sister announces to the world that she's the next Buffy. I'm supposed to spend time reading between the lines?"

"Listen, Sun," I assure her, trying to play nice. "They only want me to kill the bad vampires. Not the ones who coexist peacefully with humanity. For example, Magnus here. He's one of the good guys. So I'd never be asked to slay him."

"Oh." Sunny sniffs, still frowning in bewilderment. "Well, that's good, I guess." She glances over at Magnus. He smiles at her and reaches over to brush a lock of hair from her eyes, then kisses her softly. Bleh. Enough with the PDA. I steal a glance over at Jareth. He's staring out the window doing the brooding thing.

"Um, anyway," I say, clearing my throat. "They've asked me to go undercover in the Blood Bar. I'm supposed to do recon on this baddie vamp called Maverick. Evidently he's up to no good. Wants to do something takeoverish to Magnus here. So actually, I'm helping the cause."

"Well, there's no need for that," Jareth butts in, turning back from window stareage. "I have 'the cause,' as you call it, completely under control. I certainly do not need assistance from an operative of Slayer Inc."

Oh, right. Of course he doesn't. After all, he was doing such a fine job on his own this evening, what with running out of the Blood Bar practically screaming simply 'cause he met a girl that looked like his boss's GF.

"Let's not be so hasty, Jareth," Magnus says slowly. "Perhaps Rayne can be of some use."

"Yeah," I say, making a "nyah, nyah" face at Jareth. "I'm very . . . useful."

"I can't imagine," Jareth mutters.

God, I've never met such an arrogant, pain in the butt vamp in all my sixteen years. Not that I've met boatloads or anything, but still.

"Here, as Sunny would say, is the 411," Magnus interjects, and I chuckle, despite myself. It so sounds funny to hear a former knight in shining armor, now Master of the Vamps, use twenty-first-century slang. "Slayer Inc. is not the only group concerned about Maverick's extracurricular activities. I, too, have gotten intelligence that leads me to believe that he has some kind of plan brewing as well. I've sent Jareth in undercover to do some reconnaissance. That's why you met him in the bar. He was working for me."

"And it was all going very well before *she* came along," Jareth mutters under his breath.

"Uh, hello?" I say, waving my hands in his face. "The 'she' in this scenario is sitting next to you!" I am so not going to take his BS.

"Jareth, I know you're frustrated because you lost a night of recon due to Rayne's appearance," Magnus says, staving off Jareth's retort before it can leave his lips. "But I think if we look at the long-term situation, this could actually work out in our favor. As a human, Rayne will be given a different view of the Blood Bar. Between the two of you, we can probably get a very decent picture of what's going on down there. I think you should work together."

I raise my eyebrows. Hold on one gosh-darn second. Work together? Magnus wants me to work together with this guy? Bleh.

I glance over at Jareth, who looks even less pleased at the idea than I am.

"I can't work with . . . the slayer!" he cries, spitting out the job title as if it were poison. "Never in a million years." He looks to Magnus, his piercing green eyes pleading. "I can do this myself, Your Majesty. I am your general. I command your army. I don't need some high school kid tagging along. She'll only get in the way."

"Rayne is more than just a high school student. She's the first slayer in a thousand years to have gone through all the vampire training. To have an insider's look into our world."

"But—"

"This could be the beginning of a great partnership between Slayer Inc. and our kind," Magnus continues. "I'm not going to ruin that opportunity because of your personal hang-ups. I'm sorry about what happened, Jareth. But that was long ago. If we are to survive as a species, we must learn to adapt. Rayne can be helpful to you. And I expect you to accept her help."

"Never!" Jareth growls. "I will never accept the help of a slayer. Magnus, you are a fool if you trust them. Look what happened the last time. And look what they did to Lucifent." The limo pulls up at a red light and Jareth reaches for the door handle. "I am overdue for my feeding," he says, as if that's really the reason he's bailing. Before anyone has a chance to speak, he's out the door and into the night.

I lean back in my seat, pressing my head against the leather interior. Suddenly I'm very tired. And I'm not entirely sure I know what's going on. This slayer stuff is still pretty new. And now we've thrown an unwilling vampire in the mix. Super.

"Don't worry," Magnus says. "Jareth can be pigheaded at times, but he's a fine solider. A professional. He'll come around."

"Cool," I say with absolutely no enthusiasm. "Can't wait to be coworkers with the guy."

POSTED BY RAYNE McDONALD @ 10 a.m.
TWO COMMENTS:

Angelbaby3234566 says . . .
If u ask me, that Jareth guy sounds like a big baby. What's his deal anyway? He should be honored to work with u! U rox!

DarkGothBoy says . . .
See? He'd rather jump out of a speeding limo then spend time with you. I told you the slayer thing would screw with your love life. Shoulda hooked up with me when you had a chance, Slayer Girl.

Soulsearcher says . . .
Obviously this Jareth guy's got issues. I wonder what he has against slayers? You think he's got some deep, dark, painful secret? I just love vampires with deep, dark, painful secrets. Maybe you'll be the one girl who can redeem his lost, tortured soul and the two of you will fall desperately in love and live eternity as a holy bonded pair. (Insert dreamy sigh here.)

Rayne says . . .

Oh yeah, deep, dark, painful secrets are SUCH a turn-on. But no, I just think Jareth is a big, arrogant loser. And he'd probably rather start dating a Chihuahua than have me redeem his lost, tortured soul.

EIGHT

OMG!

SUNDAY, JUNE 3, 11 P.M.

OMG, OMG, OMG! I just got some news that will totally blow you away! I'm so freaking out I can barely type. And that's saying something.

It all came about after Sunny IMed me from her room across the hall. Transcript of convo is as follows:

> **SUNSHINEBABY:** Hey, you awake?
> **RAYNIEDAY:** Yeah. Just finishing up playing videogames with Spider.
> **SUNSHINEBABY:** Ah. You and your gaming. You're such a geek.
> **RAYNIEDAY:** And this is from a girl who likes Dave Matthews.
> **SUNSHINEBABY:** How many times do I have to tell you? It's normal to like Dave Matthews.
> **RAYNIEDAY:** If you say so, geek.
> **SUNSHINEBABY:** Sigh. Anyway . . .
> **RAYNIEDAY:** Yes. What's up?
> **SUNSHINEBABY:** Nothing. Just wanted to say sorry

for going all ambushy on you earlier, but when Jareth came to Mag he was totally freaking out. So Mag figured it'd be better to just all sit down and work this all out ASAP.

RAYNIEDAY: Yeah, that's cool. I'm all for that. Don't know about Jareth though.

SUNSHINEBABY: Yeah, totally. I wonder what his deal is.

RAYNIEDAY: You didn't ask Magnus?

SUNSHINEBABY: I tried, but he just said basically that Jareth has intimacy issues.

RAYNIEDAY: Don't we all.

SUNSHINEBABY: LOL.

RAYNIEDAY: It's too bad he's such a jerk. He's super hot. Totally blood mate material. Unless he already has one.

SUNSHINEBABY: No, according to Magnus, Jareth has always refused to accept a blood mate.

RAYNIEDAY: Really? I thought that was what all vamps wanted. Waited a thousand years to have.

SUNSHINEBABY: Shrug. Dunno. Evidently not Jareth.

RAYNIEDAY: I bet something really terrible happened to him. Like really, really bad. Maybe even by a slayer. Maybe he had a blood mate before and the slayer whacked her. His heart was broken and he swore he'd never love again.

SUNSHINEBABY: Yeah. That'd be soooo romantic.

RAYNIEDAY: Or he could just be an a-hole. Like Dad.

SUNSHINEBABY: Ohhhh!!!

RAYNIEDAY: ?

SUNSHINEBABY: I totally forgot to tell you!!!!!

RAYNIEDAY: . . .

SUNSHINEBABY: Dad's coming!

RAYNIEDAY: What the hell are you talking about?

SUNSHINEBABY: For our birthday! Dad's coming for our birthday!

RAYNIEDAY: Yeah, right.

SUNSHINEBABY: No. I'm serious. I e-mailed him last week and asked him if he'd come to our birthday party. And he wrote back yesterday afternoon. Then the whole Blood Bar Jareth thing went down and I totally forgot until just now.

Okay, time out on the IM transcript to give you a little 411 on the 'rents and the Dad situation. You see, our mom spent her formative teen years in New York City, during the 1970s. Which means she should have been all into disco, Studio 54, and glittery nightwear, right? Partying it up, doing lots of speed, having sex with strangers. Whatever those disco divas used to do. But no. Not my mom. My mom decided to leave the city to head out to this commune upstate. A place where they wore woven clothing and milked cows and sheared sheep. I'm still thinking there were heavy drugs involved to make her want to get up close and personal to smelly, hairy barnyard animals, but probably more the hallucinatory hippie dippy drugs rather than coke or something.

Anyway, at the commune she met my dad. He was trying to "find himself" even then. And he thought a beautiful, blond and barefoot hippie like my mom would be just the ticket to his happiness. He wooed her off the farm, bought her a house in the Massachusetts suburbs, and knocked her up with twins. My mom totally worshiped the ground he walked on, even though mostly he spent his time walking all over her.

About four years ago, he told Mom he felt "trapped" and he needed time to "find himself." At first, I kind of understood. After all, our town is pretty dull. But I became a little doubtful of this pilgrimage to self-realization when I learned the method of travel was a brand-new red Corvette; his Mecca was evidently the holy city of Las Vegas; and his secretary, Heather, was along for the ride.

We haven't seen him since. Not that I've wanted to. In fact, up until now I've always said I'd sooner join the cheerleading squad and go out with quarterback Mike Stevens than bond with dear old Dad. And that's saying something.

RAYNIEDAY: So let me get this straight. You e-mailed Dad?
SUNSHINEBABY: ☺
RAYNIEDAY: And you asked him to our birthday party?
SUNSHINEBABY: Yup, yup.
RAYNIEDAY: And he said . . . YES?!?!?
SUNSHINEBABY: Isn't that awesome? I'm so excited I can hardly stand it.
RAYNIEDAY: I can't believe he said yes. He never comes to these kinds of things. We haven't seen him in years. Are you SURE he said yes?
SUNSHINEBABY: I'll forward you the e-mail. Hold on. . . .

To: SunshineBaby@yours.com
From: RMcDonald@vegasbaby.com

Hiya kiddo,
Great to hear from you. Sounds like you're doing well in school. Congrats on your role in the senior class play. Maybe you'll be the next Lindsay Lohan.
    I can't believe you two are turning seventeen. I remember when you were tiny screaming babies running around in diapers. How time flies.
    Anyway, I just checked my Day-Timer and it doesn't look like anything's going on the weekend of your party. And I was able to find a cheap flight on JetBlue. So count me in! I'll even bring the birthday cake. There's a bakery down the street from me that's to die for.

Thanks again for thinking of me.
Love,
Dad

RAYNIEDAY: Wow. I can't believe it. I don't know what to say.
SUNSHINEBABY: I know. Me neither. I just sent the e-mail figuring that it'd guilt him a bit into remembering he had daughters that he never communicated with. I never in a billion years thought he would actually say yes and come.
RAYNIEDAY: He could still blow us off . . .
SUNSHINEBABY: No way. He bought a plane ticket and e-mailed me the itinerary. And he rented a hotel room downtown. He's definitely coming.
RAYNIEDAY: Wow. I can't believe it.

Anyway, the chatting goes on, but that's the important bit. Sunny ends up signing off to go to bed and I go back to writing this new blog entry. It's a bit hard to type, even now, what with my hands all trembly from the news.

Dad. Coming here. For our birthday. A combination of dream come true and scary nightmare. I wonder what he'll be like. If he'll have gotten fat or bald. If he still has that ticklish spot behind his right ear. If his favorite food is still mac and cheese. If it'll be like he never left or if it'll be weird and awkward. Will he remember all our inside jokes? The stories he used to tell us?

The storytelling is the best part about Dad. Sunny and I would curl up in my parents' big king-size bed, each resting our heads on one of his shoulders. He'd spin fantastical tales. Fantasy, horror, comedy, adventure. Every night he'd have a different story, but the heroines were always the same. Two princesses, Sunshine and Rayne, who went about saving the world. Even when I got too old for those kinds of stories, I'd always beg for more.

Back then Dad was my superhero. My idol. The person I wanted to be like when I grew up. He was so cool. And he understood me in a way that Mom and Sunny never could. Him and I used to sit out on the back porch on warm summer nights and have deep discussions about life, the universe, and everything.

And then one day he left. Breaking my heart in the process.

The shrinks tell Mom that's why I am like I am today. Keeping myself at arm's length from people, not trusting anyone to get close. Dressing rebelliously. Having seedy flings with boys I don't care about and then walking out on them before they know what happened.

The question is this: Could Dad be to blame for all of it or was I always destined to be a freak? Guess I'll never know for sure.

Wow. I can't believe he's actually coming next week.

That he's flying on a plane. Staying at a hotel.

That he's bringing birthday cake.

Okay, I am officially freaking out.

POSTED BY RAYNE McDONALD @ 11 p.m.
ONE COMMENT:

Ashleigh says . . .
   That's so kewl ur dad is coming 2 visit. I haven't seen my dad in like 10 years, so I totally know the feeling.

Anonymous says . . .
   Ooh, little Raynie has Daddy issues. No wonder you've turned out such a LOSER.
COMMENT DELETED BY BLOG ADMINISTRATOR

NINE

Black Is the New Black

MONDAY, JUNE 4, 8 P.M.

So want to hear the good news or the bad news?

Oh, forget it. I hate when people ask that stupid question, anyway. It's not like they really want you to choose. They've already got a preferred news-telling order in their heads. They're just trying to prepare you for the shock/horror of the bad news which is ALWAYS in these cases worse than the good news.

Examples:

> **GOOD NEWS:** You got an "A" on your history paper.
> **BAD NEWS:** You have to read it aloud in class.

> **GOOD NEWS:** My Chemical Romance is coming to town.
> **BAD NEWS:** It's a twenty-one and up show and last week some bar confiscated your fake ID.

> **GOOD NEWS:** There's a sale at Hot Topic.
> **BAD NEWS:** It's only on candy-colored big pants rave gear, not that amazingly cool red velvet corset you've been eyeing.

ANYWAY, my good news is that I did it. I went and dyed my hair black. This beautiful ebony color that's so dark and rich it looks almost blue. Now no one will ever mistake me for Sunny in three billion years.

Cheer!

Bad news? Uh, Mom totally flipped when she saw it.

"What did you do to yourself?" she cries when I walk out of the bathroom. (Yes, it was a "do-it-yourself" project—I'm not spending $100 at the hairdresser when they sell the stuff in the drugstore for $8.99.)

"I dyed my hair black," I reply, though I'm pretty sure it was a rhetorical question on her part.

She grabs a chunk of hair, her expression as distraught as when I told her I had pierced my tongue last year. "But you had beautiful blond hair. Why would you do this?"

"Mom, I'm sick of looking exactly like Sunny," I say. "Everyone keeps mistaking me for her and it's getting annoying."

"How can people mistake you two? You dress completely differently," she says, gesturing to my current ensemble of black on black on black.

"I don't know." I shrug. "I agree my superior taste in clothing should tip them off, but evidently not so much. I'm an individual, Mom. I'm my own person. I need to express myself."

"No, you need to obey me. That's what you need to do," Mom returns. Her hazel eyes flash fire. Wow. I haven't seen her this mad since Sunny went vamp and started missing curfew on a regular basis. (Which is SUCH a bigger deal than a little Clairol #70, IMO.) "And you know very well I don't want you dyeing your hair."

"But, Mom—"

"Do you know what kinds of chemicals they put in those dyes?" she demands, hands on hips. "Stuff that can cause cancer in lab rats. And if it can cause cancer in lab rats, what do you think it can do to you?"

I groan. I should have guessed that she didn't really care about the look. After all, she's a pretty unconventional dresser herself. No, my mom doesn't worry about what the PTA will say. She's too wrapped up in her government conspiracy theories in which Men in Black are developing evil hair dye to sedate the human race while the Illuminati take over the world.

Sometimes I wish I just had a normal mom. One who didn't think hairdressers were really the Antichrist, at the very least.

"I'm sorry, Mom. I guess I wasn't thinking."

"Come to me next time if you want to change your look. I've got a great all-natural henna coloring we could have used. Stuff that's made of plant products and is perfectly safe."

"Sure, Mom. I will." Yeah, right. I'm so not getting my hair dyed with henna. Maybe I'd consider a henna tattoo, but that's where I draw the line. After all, let's face it. Safe and effective or not, henna is for hippies.

She reaches over and gives me a hug. "I'm sorry, Rayne," she says. "I don't mean to yell. I just worry about my girls. I want them to be safe."

"I know, Mom. And I'm glad you do," I say, squeezing her back.

I mean it, too. Though she drives me crazy at times, overall when it comes to moms, mine's about as cool as you can get. She's like a "friend mom." Sunny and I can talk to her about pretty much anything (besides hair dye and vampires, of course) and she's completely nonjudgmental. She doesn't sneak into our rooms and read our diaries or go on Facebook to make sure our profiles are appropriate. (I'm Rayne McDonald, BTW, if anyone wants to friend me.) My friend Ashleigh's mom grounded her for like four weeks when she found out Ashleigh had posted sexy pics of herself on Facebook. Not that I have any sexy pics posted, just FYI. (Sorry, DarkGothBoy.)

So yeah, she's okay. If not a little overprotective at times.

After we pull away from the hug, I notice something surprising. "Hey, Mom, what's up with your outfit?"

Wow. The woman who LIVES in bell-bottom jeans or long flowered skirts and peasant blouses is currently standing in front of me wearing a sexy little black dress with high heels and a pearl necklace. I can't believe I'm just noticing it now. Observe much, Rayne?

"Oh, this old thing?" she asks, blushing furiously as she smoothes the front of the dress. "I've had it for years."

"Just FYI, that'd be much more believable if you'd removed the price tag," I suggest, gesturing to her sleeve.

"Oh." The blush deepens as she reaches to rip off the tag in question. "I guess I've just never worn it."

Eesh. The woman is the worst liar in the known universe. "Spill, Mom."

She sighs and motions for me to come into her bedroom. I follow, plopping down on the old-fashioned, four-poster bed that Grandma left when she died. It would be an elegant piece of furniture if Mom hadn't covered it with a Technicolor-hand-stitched quilt from her commune days. Still, I've got to admit, overall the room is pretty cozy and homey. When Sunny and I were little and big thunderous storms would crash through our neighborhood, we always ran to the oversized bed, crawling under the covers with Mom and Dad. Only then did we feel warm and safe.

Um, anyway . . .

So Mom shuts the door behind us and joins me on the bed. She tries to pull her feet up and under like normal, then realizes she has a nice dress on and chooses to cross her ankles daintily instead. I have to bite my lip not to laugh.

"So?" I prod.

"So . . . I've got a date," she whispers, her eyes alight with mischievous excitement. She's totally forgotten that she's pissed at me about my hair.

"A date?" I cry. "That's awesome!"

She studies me, her gaze turning motherly. "Are you sure? I mean, I know that's got to seem a little weird. Your mom dating someone."

"No! It's not weird at all. I think it's great." After all, I've been dying for the woman to get out of the house for years. Pining away in a nunlike existence—hoping the next time the door opens my dad will walk through—is just not a way for someone to live. Even a mom. "So who's the lucky guy? Where did you meet him?"

I wonder for a moment if I should tell her about Dad coming to the b-day party, but decide not to rain on her parade just yet. We've got nearly a week to break the news and I don't want to ruin her big date.

Her cheeks pinken. It's adorable. I love seeing her so excited.

"Actually I bumped into him at the harvest co-op last night," she says. "Literally. We were both reaching for the same frozen chick-pea burgers."

I smile. Obviously love at first sight. With the only other person in the known universe who would actually eat a chickpea burger. "Very nice. And he asked you out?"

"Yeah, we're going for dinner at Abe and Louis in Boston."

I whistle. "Fan-cy."

She giggles. I haven't seen her like this in years. Maybe in forever. I love it.

"Where's this guy from? What's he do for a living?" I ask.

She shrugs. "I didn't interrogate him in the frozen foods section, Rayne."

"Right. Well, definitely find out all the 411 tonight," I say, mothering my mother. "We want to make sure he's the right guy for you. We can't have you going out with just anyone."

She laughs. "Okay, dear. I promise I'll get you the full scoop."

At that moment the doorbell chimes. My mom jumps off the bed and is at the door in a flash. "That must be him," she says, looking back at me with a grin. "Wish me luck!"

I hold up crossed fingers. "Luck!"

She scurries downstairs and I take the opportunity to peek out her window, which offers a good front porch view. There's a guy at the door—dressed in a tux, no less. I can't make out his face, but he seems well built, with a full head of hair. Not hippielike at all, either, which is probably for the best. And the coolest part? He arrived in a limo. Crazy.

Anyway—Mom on a date, and me off the hook for my hair-coloring experiment. Time to head to the Blood Bar and save the world.

POSTED BY RAYNE McDONALD @ 8 p.m.
FOUR COMMENTS:

Spider says . . .
Ooh, Rayne—I can't WAIT to see ur new hair.
You gotta take a camera phone pic and send it

2 me ASAP! And your mom on a date?
Whoa!

SunshineBaby says . . .

Mom's on a date? A date? You let her take off with some
strange guy without even meeting him first? What if he's
some psycho killer? Wasn't there one in the news the
other day? And did they catch him? I don't think they
caught him, Rayne! Mom could be dating the psycho killer
right now.

If she's not home by eleven, I'm so calling the police.
Or maybe by ten. Gah! She needs to start carrying a cell
phone so we can check in with her. I can't BELIEVE you
let her go.

Ashleigh says . . .

Your mom is way cooler than mine, Rayne. I still can't
believe my mom grounded me over my Facebook profile.
I mean, puh-leeze. The pics weren't even that bad. It
wasn't like I was naked or anything. Just hot. But she's all,
like, "Oh, the perverted old men are gonna see them."
Like I'm going to friend some perverted old man. What-
EVER.

DarkGothBoy says . . .

You don't have to post sexy pics on Facebook, baby. Just
e-mail them directly to me. Or better yet, how about
you come over and I'll take some pics for you? I got a
new digital camera for my birthday and I'm dying to try it
out. And, oh? Don't you feel like a loser? Your mom is
getting more action than you are. Tsk, tsk.

TEN

Bite Me, Bay–Bee!

TUESDAY, JUNE 5, 1 A.M.

I've got to stop with these late nights. They're totally killing me at school. Today (or yesterday, if you consider it's once again past midnight) I slept through Algebra II, American History, and three quarters of Art. (*Sooo* embarrassing to wake up facedown in a palette of paint. Took me a half hour to scrub the stuff off.)

Being a slayer is like having a second full-time job. Luckily I'm not really a homework girl to begin with or I'd be so screwed.

But enough about boring old school. You guys want to hear about the Blood Bar, right? Of course you do.

So I wait 'til after dark and then head on over. My buddy Vin Vamp (a.k.a. Francis) is back on the door tonight, which is a total relief. I so didn't want to have to whip out my painfully bad fake ID again and try to act all convincing.

"Hey, Frannie," I greet. "How's the biting?"

"You're back," he observes, folding his massive arms across his chest and staring at me with cool eyes. "Couldn't stay away, eh?"

"Nope! You know me," I say playfully, punching him lightly on the arm. "Well, actually you don't, I guess. But you will. Soon. I plan on becoming a regular. You'll see me every night. We can develop clever nicknames for each other and banter a while before you let me in."

"*If* I let you in."

"See? Banter." I smile sweetly. "We're well on our way to a beautiful friendship already."

Francis tries to hide his smile without much luck. He totally thinks I'm adorable, I can tell. "You know, Shaniqua," he says, still calling me by my fake ID name, "you're really a piece of work." He shakes his head. "Okay, okay. Come on in." He pulls open the door and gestures inside.

But something makes me pause at the door. I look up at Francis's face, studying it closer. While he does seem amused, there's something about his smile. Like it doesn't quite meet his eyes. And I don't mean in some secretly nefarious, up-to-no-good, one-of-the-bad guys way.

He just looks . . . a bit sad.

"What's wrong, Frannie?" I ask. "No offense or anything, but you look like someone just ran over your pet bat."

Francis rubs his bald head with the palm of his hand. He really is a big oafy looking dude for a vampire. "My blood mate is missing," he confesses. "If you must know. And I'm worried sick about her."

I've explained the blood mate thing, right? Well to recap real quick, each vamp, once they hit a thousand years old, gets to turn one willing human into a vampire. They do all this complex DNA testing beforehand to make sure the human and vamp will be compatible. 'Cause after all, they're destined to be together for all eternity, so you want to make sure it's a good match. For example, I was matched up with Magnus originally, before he bit Sunny by mistake. Luckily twins share DNA so those two were still compatible.

Bottom line, a blood mate is sort of like a soul mate, except without that whole messy soul part. So needless to say, the two vamps are usually attached at the hip. Like an immortal BF/GF with no way to ever divorce.

"I'm sorry to hear that," I say, genuinely feeling bad for the guy. I mean, that sucks, right? What if his blood mate met a new vamp and took off to Vegas, like Dad did? Leaving poor Frannie here all alone in the world with major trust issues.

Francis kicks the ground with his toe. Let me tell you, the guy's feet make Michael Jordan look like a midget. I'd hate to meet him in a back alleyway.

Oh, wait, we're in a back alleyway. Uh, never mind.

"Her name is Dana. She works here as a biter," Francis explains.

Of course, I'm all wondering if a bouncer dating a biter is as cliché as a bouncer dating a stripper. But Frannie looks so upset, I decide not to ask. And really, who am I to judge?

"Three days ago, she called in sick. And she hasn't shown up since. She's not been back to the crypt. In fact, I've searched everywhere for her. It's like she's dropped off the face of the earth."

"I'm sure she'll turn up," I say, trying to sound comforting. I pat him on his big hairy forearm. "Don't worry."

He grins ruefully and pats me on the head. "Thanks," he says. "You're probably right. Nothing to be concerned over." He gestures to the door. "Would you like to go in?"

"Please."

I walk inside, once again enveloped by the dim lighting, smoky air, and crimson interiors, this time soundtracked by the band She Wants Revenge, crooning from some hidden overhead speakers. I can't say I'm surprised to learn that vamps dig Emo.

I enter the lounge and approach the hostess.

"Hey, I'm back," I say, trying to act as nonchalant as possible. "Can I get the same biter as yesterday? Jareth, I think his name was? He was uber hot."

I giggle to myself as she checks the list. Jareth's going to be so annoyed when he sees me again. But, hey, I'm just simply following orders. If he has a problem with me, he'll have to take it up with Magnus.

"Sure. He's not with anyone at the moment," the hostess says. "Go ahead to room six and I'll send him in."

Perfect. I thank the woman and head behind the curtain to room six, praying that Jareth doesn't take forty-five minutes to show up this time. I forgot my Game Boy DS and I'm so not the type of girl who can just sit around and twiddle her thumbs contentedly. Besides, we've got a mission to accomplish here. No time for goofing around.

Luckily it only takes about five minutes for the door to open and "Hotness" to walk through.

"Hi, my name is Jareth, and I'll be your— God!" He curses as he lays his eyes on me.

I raise an eyebrow. "You'll be my god? Hmm . . . Well, we'll have to see about that. I mean, it takes a lot to rock my world these days."

His powder-white face pinkens and he quickly changes the subject. Heh. "What the hell are you doing here?" he growls. "I thought I told you I work alone."

"And I thought I told you I don't listen to stupid, pigheaded vampires. And if I didn't, well consider this fair warning."

"Watch out, little girl," Jareth says, looming over me, raising his arms in what I assume he means to be a threatening, evil gesture. "I am a creature of the night. I am not to be toyed with."

I roll my eyes. "Ooh. I'm scared."

He lowers his hands and huffs in annoyance. "Well, you bloody well should be. I could bite you, you know."

"And I could stake you," I say, rummaging through my messenger bag to pull out the chunk of wood Teifert gave me. I stand up and wave it at Jareth's face. "One false move and . . . POW!"

Jareth stares at the stake, then at me, then back to the stake. Then, to my surprise, he bursts out laughing.

"What?" I scowl, so not appreciating his reaction. After all, I am a vampire slayer, right? He should be shaking in his boots just at the mere sight of me.

"What . . . the hell . . . is that?" he asks, between chortles. He's laughing so hard he's holding his stomach.

"A stake."

"That's not a stake. It's a chunk of wood."

"Well, it's . . . not . . . finished yet," I say, defensively, lowering the weapon. "I need to carve it. Embed it with my own essence." Wow, that sounds a lot dumber when it comes out of my mouth.

"Bwahahahaha!" Jareth continues laughing at my expense. "What are you going to do? Give the evil vampires splinters?"

I can feel my face heat with embarrassment, which is *sooo* annoying. How dare he make fun of me? I have been put on this earth to slay his kind. One false move and I'll go all destiny on his ass.

Somehow. Though probably not with this particular stake . . . Grrr . . .

"Shut up!" I cry, unable to come up with one of my infamous Rayne comebacks. "Stop laughing at me."

Jareth sighs, reaching up to wipe the bloody tears of mirth from his eyes. "Oh, Rayne," he says, shaking his head. "You're precious, you know that?"

"Well, you're just lame and annoying." Why does it seem like I've totally lost the banter battle here?

Jareth holds out his hand. "Give me the stake."

Oh, yeah, right. Like I'm going to fall for that one. It may not be finished, but it's the only weapon I've got. I hide it behind my back.

"No effing way."

Jareth sighs. "Just for a minute."

"Why? So you can render me completely defenseless and suck me dry?"

"With that as your weapon, you already are completely defenseless, sweetie."

I sigh. I know he's right. Reluctantly I hand over the stake. Stupid Slayer Inc. for giving me such a pathetic weapon. After all, Buffy the Vampire Slayer got swords and axes and crossbows. Is that so much to ask for?

Jareth turns the stake around in his hands. Then he reaches into his pocket and pulls out a Swiss Army knife. I involuntarily jump back.

"Relax," he says. "I'm going to help you carve."

He clicks open the blade and starts running it across the wood, shaving off chunks. I watch, mesmerized, as a pretty nice stake emerges from the mess.

"I am a sculptor by trade," he explains. "Mostly my carvings are of stone, but the principle is the same." He hands me the stick and knife. "Now you try. Run the blade down, away from you."

I do as he instructs, slicing into the wood.

"No. Like this." He comes around behind me and takes my hands in his and guides me through the next stroke. "There you go," he says in my ear.

Now, for the record, I must repeat here that he is, without a doubt, the most annoying vampire in the known universe and I can't stand him. In fact, if they said he was the last blood mate on earth, I'd choose to remain human just to stay away from him. If he was the last man on earth, I'd turn lesbian. If he was the last person on earth, I'd become a nun.

That said, he really is freaking HOT. And when I feel his cool breath in my ear as he helps me carve, my body totally betrays me and gets all mushy inside. Which is so frustrating! Gah!

"Okay, I, um, think I've got it now," I say, desperate for him to take a step back before I do something really stupid, like turn around and kiss him. "Thanks."

To my relief (and disappointment if I'm being totally honest here) he lets go of my hands and retreats to the bed. He sits down, watching me with his intense green eyes. I have to force myself not to shiver under his gaze.

Focus on the wood, Rayne. Less thinking, more carving.

"There!" I say about ten minutes later. "How does that look?" I hold the stake up for his perusal.

He walks over and takes it from me, examining it with a critical eye. "That's actually pretty good," he says, sounding a little too surprised for my liking. But secretly I'm pleased. "You're a natural."

"Natural Born Killahh!" I quip.

He chuckles. "Let's not get carried away. Just because you can carve a stake, doesn't mean you can stab someone with it."

"Gonna teach me that, too?" I tease.

His face darkens. "No."

The simple word seems to hold a whole lifetime of stories. He's definitely got to have some deep, dark torment and I'm dying to ask him what it is. But we barely know each other and also there's that whole thing about how we don't even like one another to contend with, so I decide to let him off the hook.

"Okay, no biggie," I say with a shrug. "Thanks for helping me carve it though."

"Not a problem," he says. "As long as you promise never to use it on me."

I'm about to crack a joke, but he looks too serious at the moment, so I let it go. "It's a deal," I say instead.

He smiles. "How about we go into the Post-Bite Lounge for a bit," he suggests. "See if we can pick up any gossip."

"Post-Bite Lounge?"

"Yes. You know how after giving blood at the Red Cross you can feel a little light-headed and queasy? Same thing after being sucked. So they have a lounge where they serve cookies and orange juice to the humans before they send them back into the world."

"Ah." Wow, these vamps think of everything, don't they? "Okay, cool. Let's lounge it."

I stand up and head toward the door.

"Uh, Rayne?"

I stop and turn around. "Yeah?"

He pauses, then says, "This is going to sound weird, but . . ."

"Everything is weird at this point. I doubt anything you could say could make it any weirder."

I can see Jareth's hard swallow from across the room. "You don't have a bite mark."

Okay. I was wrong. That is definitely weirder.

I cock my head in confusion. "What?"

"You're undercover as a human who likes being bitten by vampires. You just spent time with a biter. Now we're going into the Post-Bite Lounge. People might notice that you don't have any marks on your neck."

"Oh." I reach up and touch my neck. Hmm. He's right. "You think that'll raise a red flag?"

"I don't want to take any chances. We can't blow our cover. This is too important."

"Right. No. We shouldn't." I chew at my lower lip. "But . . . oh."

I suddenly realize what he's suggesting. Am I up for that? To be bitten by him? I guess I don't have a choice, do I? Sacrifices for the cause and all that.

"Come here," Jareth instructs.

I walk over to the bed and sit down beside him. "Is this gonna hurt?" I ask, realizing I'm trembling. What is wrong with me? I've wanted to be bitten by a vampire for like EVER. Now I'm finally getting my chance. Of course, this type of bite won't turn me into a vampire. You have to be injected with their blood for that. But still . . . how cool, right?

So why am I *sooo* nervous?

"My fangs have an instant numbing solution that's injected at the moment of penetration. You won't feel a thing."

"Oh. Okay," I say, not feeling all that much better for some reason.

Jareth reaches over and brushes my hair away from my neck. I suddenly feel open. Exposed. Vulnerable. I swallow hard and close my eyes. I can feel his breath on my neck as he lowers his head. His lips brush lightly against my sensitive skin and I involuntarily let out a shiver.

"Ready?" he whispers softly. I can feel his lips forming the word against my flesh. It's kind of erotic, to tell you the truth. I bite down on my lower lip.

"Uh huh," I say, my voice suddenly as squeaky as Sunny's.

Moments later I feel a little pressure on my neck. Just a pinch and then . . . ecstasy.

I am so not going to be able to describe to you guys how awesome it feels to be bitten by a vampire. There aren't human words. It's better than Oreo ice cream sliding down your throat on a hot summer's day. Better than slipping into a steamy bathtub on a crisp fall afternoon. Better than curling up by a fire on a freezing winter's night.

It's better than anything I can possibly think of. Not that at that moment there's much thinking going on in my head. I'm just enjoying. Completely and utterly enjoying the sensations coursing through my veins.

It's heaven. Absolute heaven.

My head lolls backward and I let out a moan of pleasure. "Oh, god," I cry. "Don't stop."

But he does. I guess he has to, seeing as he's not out to drain me dry. Not that I'd have minded being drained dry at that particular moment. In fact, I would have embraced my death with open arms if that sensation were to continue. Now I totally understand why it was easy for vampires to survive in the old days when they didn't have blood donors.

Once bitten, totally smitten.

His fangs retract. The electric current zapping through me clicks off like a light switch. The pleasure is gone. The ecstasy evaporates. I feel empty and alone and needy and desperate for more. No wonder this place is so popular. One bite and I already feel completely addicted.

I lift my head and open my eyes, looking over at Jareth. He's wiping his mouth, looking horrified and flushed and flustered beyond belief.

"Uh, there you go. You're bitten," he mumbles. He draws in a deep breath and pulls out a handkerchief, dabbing his sweaty forehead. Evidently the experience did something to him as well. Which makes me feel better, in a way. I'd hate to have succumbed to that rapture, only to find him all nonchalant and superior afterward.

I reach up to feel my neck, pressing my fingers against the tiny bite holes. "That was incredible," I murmur. "Amazing. I've never felt anything like it. Does it always feel that good? Or just the first time?"

"I certainly don't know," Jareth says in a totally unwarranted grumpy voice. He rises from the bed and walks toward the door. "I was only bitten once. When I was turned."

"Oh, right. Of course. Well, let me tell you, that totally rocked my world. You're good at the biteage, dude."

"I beg of you. Don't ever, ever call me dude again."

I sigh. "Sorry. But I was trying to give you a compliment."

"None necessary. It's just business. Nothing more."

"I know, but . . ." Why do I suddenly feel kind of hurt? He's right. This was obviously just for the job. To look legit. Nothing more. But still, it felt so intimate. . . .

I shake my head. *Earth to Rayne. Come in, Rayne.* We don't even like this dude—er, guy. So there is absolutely no reason to be upset. Just get the job done. Impress the council and you'll be assigned a real blood mate. Someone compatible to you DNA-wise. And then you can bite each other 'til the bats come home.

"Okay, fine. Let's go to the lounge."

I follow him out the door and down the corridor until we get to a room labeled lounge. I've got to admit, I'm looking forward to the cookies and orange juice snack at this point. The bite, with all its euphoria, definitely left me feeling weak in the knees. I wonder how much blood he took from me. I wonder if he thought I tasted good. If they even care about that.

I wonder if he wishes he could bite me again.

Not that I care. Really.

The lounge is decked out like the rest of the Blood Bar, in red and black, but it's more relaxing looking than the formal sitting room lobby. There's a lot of smooshy velvet couches and little end tables with tea candles scattered around the room. The candlelight is all the illumination the place has got and so all the inhabitants look a bit haunted and hollow-eyed. Or maybe that's just due to the fact they've been half drained dry a few minutes earlier.

I make a beeline for an empty couch across the room. I plop down, pulling my feet up and under me. Jareth heads to the bar on the far side of the room and returns a moment later with some juice and Ritz crackers.

"No Oreos, huh?" I ask as I take the plate from him and start chowing on the crackers. I slurp down some juice.

"Could you at least try to chew with your mouth closed?" Jareth hisses, taking a seat beside me. I roll my eyes. God, how can someone so sexy be so uptight and annoying? I mean, it's not like we're on a date, right? My actions should not have any reflection on him. And even if they do, who cares? We're at a freaking bite bar in the worst section of town. I say, in this sitch, it's safe to leave Miss Manners at the door.

Choosing to ignore him, I instead glance around the room, hoping to pick up some revealing scraps of conversation that might clue us into Maverick's evil plan. But it seems luck is not being a lady tonight. No one's saying a word.

"Wait a second," Jareth says, his eyes falling on two girls across the room. They're both gothed out and channeling Lindsay Lohan in their scrawniness, but they're definitely human.

"What?"

"I recognize those two. They're donors for my friend Kristoff."

"Yeah?" I ask, peering at the girls. "But that doesn't make sense."

FYI: A donor is a human who voluntarily signs up to be a regular blood source for a vampire. Each vamp has his own stable of donors. This way they don't bite unwilling people, like you see in the movies. It's all very civilized and there are blood tests and contracts and the donors make pretty good dough for their services.

But why would two donors be at the Blood Bar? They already get sucked by their vamp on a regular basis. There's no way they have that much blood to spare.

"That's a huge contract violation," Jareth says, peering at the girls. "What if they came down with some disease? They could infect Kristoff."

"Do you want to say anything to them?"

"No. It's not my place. And it would blow our cover. But I will certainly be reporting the incident tomorrow to Kristoff. He will have to let them go."

I stare at the two girls. They don't look all that well—even for Donor Chicks, who always look slightly anemic. Even under the dim lighting I can see the dark rings around their eyes and a slightly green tone to their skin.

Curiouser and curiouser, as Alice in Wonderland would say . . .

ANYWAY, THAT'S ALL to report for now. More tomorrow, I'm sure. At least Jareth and I seem to have reached some kind of truce. We're never going to be BFFs, but at least we're not at each other's throats. Well, maybe that's a bad analogy . . . I mean, let's be honest here. Annoying or not, I'd let him be at my throat any day of the week. ;-)

POSTED BY RAYNE McDONALD @ 1 a.m.
ONE COMMENT:

AstrydGrrl777 says . . .
You got bit by a vampire! How cool is that? I'm sooooo jealous! What did it feel like? I mean, I know you kinda described it, but we want details! Lots of intimate, personal, embarrassing details! Come on, girl! Spill!!

ELEVEN

I Can't Breathe!

TUESDAY, JUNE 5, 1:33 A.M.

OMG! So I'm like almost asleep and I hear a car pull up. Mom! I jump out of bed and run to my window, hoping to get a good look at the date.

The front spotlight flickers on, illuminating two figures on the front porch. Two figures kissing, to be precise.

At first I'm overjoyed that my mom has found a boyfriend and is at last getting her groove on. But then I look closer. As the boyfriend in question pulls away, I get a good glimpse of his face for the first time. A face I'd recognize anywhere.

And suddenly I can't breathe.

I've got to IM Sunny. Now!

POSTED BY RAYNE McDONALD @ 1:33 a.m.
TWO COMMENTS:

ButterfliQT says . . .
  ARGH! What is it? You can't leave us hanging like that!
  Who is it? It's not your Trig teacher, is it? The one you
  and Spider were talking about sleeping with? That'd be

sooo nasty! Please post more and tell us it's not your Trig teacher!

Rayne says . . .
Don't worry—it's not my Trig teacher. And just FYI, I don't know about Spider, but I'd rather take an F than come within ten feet of Mr. McFee. I don't do balding mullets.

TWELVE

Do Boyfriends Bite?

TUESDAY, JUNE 5, 2 A.M.

No time to explain. Pasting in chat transcript with Sunny to fill you in. This is huge. HUGE! And really, really, really bad!

> **RAYNIEDAY:** Sunny, are you awake?
>
> **RAYNIEDAY:** Sunny, if you're not awake, wake up now! It's important.
>
> **RAYNIEDAY:** SUNNY!!!!
>
> **SUNSHINEBABY:** What the heck are you IM'ing me for at 2am?
>
> **RAYNIEDAY:** I need to talk to you. It's an emergency.
>
> **SUNSHINEBABY:** Uh, okay. But why not just walk across the hall and knock on my door? It's not like I'm in Topeka.
>
> **RAYNIEDAY:** Cause Mom's home. She might hear me.
>
> **SUNSHINEBABY:** She'll hear tiptoed steps, but not the loud, obnoxious IM beeps coming from our computers?
>
> **RAYNIEDAY:** So turn your sound down. Jeesh. You and technology. And hurry up. This can't wait.
>
> **SUNSHINEBABY:** Okay, okay. Hang on.

RAYNIEDAY: . . .

SUNSHINEBABY: Okay, done. Now what's so important?

RAYNIEDAY: I don't know how to tell you this, but . . .

SUNSHINEBABY: Oh, god, Rayne, just spit it out. It's 2am and I've got a field hockey game tomorrow.

RAYNIEDAY: Hmph. This is so much more important than a field hockey game. Mom's dating a vampire.

SUNSHINEBABY: Field hockey is too import— WHAT?!??!

RAYNIEDAY: I told you it was important. But no. You never believe me . . .

SUNSHINEBABY: Wait. Focus. I don't understand? How can she be dating a vampire?

RAYNIEDAY: She just got home. I spied out my window at them kissing.

SUNSHINEBABY: You know, that's pretty rude, Rayne. Whether we like Mom dating or not, she deserves our respect and privacy.

RAYNIEDAY: Are you going to listen to me about our mom dating the undead or just lecture on parental etiquette all night?

SUNSHINEBABY: Fine. Go on.

RAYNIEDAY: So the guy pulls away and I get a good glimpse of his face. And I recognize him immediately. I saw him my first night at the Blood Bar. He was sort of standing in a corner, surveying the place. I'm thinking he works there as, like, a manager or something.

SUNSHINEBABY: OMG! So he's not only a vampire, he's a bad vampire. One of Maverick's men.

RAYNIEDAY: Yeah. That's what I was thinking. He probably thinks by getting close to Mom he can get close to you and then get close to Magnus.

SUNSHINEBABY: Wow. What are we going to do? We can't just tell Mom she's dating Dracula.

RAYNIEDAY: No. But we have to do something.

SUNSHINEBABY: Maybe he's not a vampire. Maybe he's a human who likes to be bit by them. You know, a customer.

RAYNIEDAY: It's possible. But I don't know. And really, it doesn't seem that good either way, now does it?

SUNSHINEBABY: Wow. This is just like what happened on *The Lost Boys*.

RAYNIEDAY: *The Lost Boys?*

SUNSHINEBABY: Vampire movie from the eighties? With Kiefer Sutherland? Jeesh, Rayne, I thought you watched all those movies.

RAYNIEDAY: I try to stick to vampire classics. Bela Lugosi. Maybe some Christopher Lee. Jack Bauer from 24 just doesn't scream VAMP to me.

SUNSHINEBABY: Fine. But you should watch it. Like, tomorrow. It's totally the same thing. The kids' mom starts dating this guy and they think he's a vampire so they try to prove it.

RAYNIEDAY: How do they do that?

SUNSHINEBABY: Um, I can't remember exactly. Garlic. Holy water. Stuff like that, I think. Really good movie, even if they do all have big hair and bad clothes.

RAYNIEDAY: So you're suggesting we try that stuff on the date? Hmm. Not a bad idea. Then we'd have proof. I mean, I'd like to have proof before I go and stake Mom's BF.

SUNSHINEBABY: Yes. Seems wise.

RAYNIEDAY: Sigh. Poor Mom. She was so excited about the guy. It's going to suck to have to slay him.

SUNSHINEBABY: But it's in her best interest. After all, he doesn't really like her. He's just using her to get to me.

RAYNIEDAY: Right. True. We have the best intentions.

SUNSHINEBABY: Anyway—I've got to get some sleep. School tomorrow. Goodnight, Rayne.

RAYNIEDAY: You're such a nerd. I can't believe you can think of school at a time like this.

SUNSHINEBABY: GOOD NIGHT, RAYNE.
RAYNIEDAY: Sigh. Night, Sun.

SUNSHINEBABY HAS LEFT THE CHAT.

POSTED BY RAYNE McDONALD @ 2 a.m.
TWO COMMENTS:

Just Curious says . . .
Wow, what's with you chicks? You're all hooking up with vamps? Is there something in the McDonald family water supply? Is your blood supersweet?

Rayne says . . .
First of all, we are NOT all hooking up with vampires. Me, for example, the one person in the family who WANTS to hook up with a vampire, has had absolutely no luck in getting one near me. All I get are idiots like Magnus, who go off and bite the wrong girl, or losers like Jareth, who have so many issues they can't see the delectable treat right in front of them. No, it appears it's only McDonald women who aren't interested in being with vamps that have any luck in hooking them. So very sad.

Thirteen

Breakfast Bites

TUESDAY, JUNE 5, 12 P.M.

So I wake up this morning bright and early, throw on a black cro-
cheted sweater and a short black skirt. I roll on my fishnet tights
and lace up my combat boots. Then I head to my bathroom for my
morning makeup routine. It takes a lot of time to become "me" in
the A.M. But it's worth it.

Sunny, whose idea of morning preparation involves slipping on
a T-shirt and jeans and running a comb through her hair, is already
downstairs, dressed and picking at some god-awful concoction my
mom whipped up. Mom makes very interesting breakfasts with the
food she buys at the co-op and we're her guinea pigs. When Sunny
had been turning vampire, Mom experimented with this garlic
breakfast scramble. The smell alone sent Sunny scrambling to the
bathroom to retch her guts out. She claims that was just because of
her burgeoning aversion to garlic, but honestly it could have just
been the recipe and Mom's attempt to cook.

"So what's the special of the morning?" I ask, sliding into my
chair. I'm famished. Nothing she can possibly come up with will
make me lose my appetite today.

"Well, it doesn't really have an official name," Mom says, dishing some of the unidentified mush from the frying pan onto a plate. "But the cook at the commune used to refer to it as hippie hash."

Then again, maybe I'll skip first period and hit Dunkin' Donuts on the way to school.

"So how'd your date go?" I ask, trying not to wrinkle my nose as she puts the foul-smelling scramble in front of me.

She sets another plate in front of her own spot and sits down between Sunny and me. I glance over at my sister and notice that while the food is being moved around her plate, it's not going into her mouth.

"Great," Mom says, her eyes shining. "We went out to the nicest restaurant. Of course, it was a steak house. He's evidently a big steak eater. Says he loves them really rare."

I try to catch Sunny's eyes. See? Rare steak. The only thing vampires enjoy eating, as it's so bloody.

"He took you to a steak house?" I ask. Mom's a strict vegetarian, of course. Poor woman. "Didn't you tell him you don't eat meat? That you belong to PETA? That you think the chemicals found in cattle are mind-controlling hormones injected by the government to sedate the human race while big business goes around and trashes our world?"

"It's okay," Mom says, of course completely excusing her date's major faux pas. "I just had a potato and vegetables. It was very good."

Wow. Mom must really have a thing for this guy. She would never go to a slaughter house with just anyone. It's going to be sad to disappoint her. Not that she'll be disappointed when she finds out he's a thousand years old and undead. Oh, well.

"Then what did you do?"

"He took me out to this elegant club where they had an old-fashioned band and dancing. He waltzes like a dream."

Hmm. Probably 'cause he was around when they invented the dance and has had a thousand years of practice.

"But you hate waltzing. And classical music. In fact, isn't your saying, 'If it's not Jefferson Airplane, it's crap'?"

She narrows her eyes. "Rayne, I'm an adult with a wide variety of interests. I had a good time. Don't spoil it because you feel un-comfortable I went on a date."

Sigh. Here she goes. Her voice sounds all tight. I knew she'd jump to that conclusion.

"I'm fine with you having a date. I just want to make sure he's treating you right." And doesn't spend his days sleeping in a coffin . . .

"Well, you don't have to worry. He's the perfect gentleman. You'll see, tonight."

"Tonight?" Sunny's eyes and my eyes meet across the table. I'm sure mine are as wide as hers.

Mom laughs. "Yes, tonight. I invited him over for dinner. I promised I could cook him a tofu steak that's just as delicious as one made from the slaughter of innocent animals."

Wow. I bet the vamp is really looking forward to that! But to-night! That doesn't give Sunny and me any time to plan. Unless . . .

I break out into a coughing fit.

"Oh, man," I say between chokes. "I've had this horrible cough. Just horrible. And I don't feel very well either."

"But you were just—?" Sunny starts in. I kick her under the table. Hard. Her eyes light up. And her coughs start coming.

My mom looks from one hacking daughter to the other. "Are you two okay?" she asks. "It's not the hash, is it?"

It probably would be the hash if either of us had actually shov-eled any of it into our mouths, which in hindsight may have made the sickness a tad more authentic, but too late now.

"No. It's just, I think I'm coming down with something."

"Maybe you should stay home from school," Mom says, looking worried. "Neither of you sound too good."

"No, I want to go to school," I say, pausing to slump in my chair and close my eyes. "I really hate missing school."

"If you're sick, you need to stay home," Mom commands, reach-ing over to feel my forehead with the back of her hand. "You feel warm, Rayne." It's amazing what the power of suggestion can do to a parent. "You, too, Sunny," she says, switching to my twin.

"But I love school, Mom," Sunny whines. Gah! Overkill, much? I kick her under the table again. For someone starring in the school play, she's not much of an actress.

"Mom's right, Sun," I interject, to stop her performance. "If we go to school, it might get worse. We could be contagious even. One day of rest now can save us from a weeklong absence down the road."

Mom takes a bite of her hash and nods. "Unfortunately, I can't stay home to take care of you guys," she says, as if that would be something either of us would want. "I've got to get to work."

"It's okay, Mom," I say, patting her on the arm. "We'll probably be sleeping most of the day anyway."

"I hope so." She rises from her seat, kisses both of us on the tops of our heads, and brings her mostly untouched plate over to the sink. Evidently this time even she didn't like her recipe, not that she'd ever admit that to us. "There's OJ in the fridge and some veggie burgers in the freezer if you get hungry later."

"Thanks, Mom."

"Do you think I should cancel having my friend come over?" she asks, scraping her leftovers into the compost bin. "I mean, if you two are sick . . ."

"No, no," Sunny says, before I can kick her a third time. "We'll feel better by then, I'm sure."

Great. Way to buy us more time, Sun.

"Okay. Well, you let me know," Mom says, sounding relieved. "Call me at work if you take a turn for the worse and would rather just lay low."

So she goes to work and now Sunny and I are home alone. Sunny rinses our breakfast plates and I run up to my room for my secret stash of strawberry Pop-Tarts. After toasting, we rendezvous in the living room, me on the couch, Sunny on the lounger.

"So what are we going to do?" my sister asks, mouth full of Pop-Tart. "He's coming over tonight. That doesn't give us much time."

"Right." I break my pastry in half, licking the strawberry filling. "What about calling Magnus? Certainly he could recognize a fellow vamp."

"Yeah, but it's daytime. He won't be up and about 'til well after dinner."

"Oh, yeah. Duh." I smack myself on the forehead. That was stupid.

"What about you?" Sunny asks. "Aren't you the knower of all things vamp? The proud graduate of Vampire School? Won't you be able to tell on sight whether the guy sleeps in a coffin or not?"

I shrug. "Not necessarily. A vampire can cast what's called a 'glamour' on themselves to make them look human if they need to. That's how they can walk among us and no one's the wiser. And I doubt the guy's going to show up to dinner sporting his fangs."

"Great." Sunny sighs. "What are we going to do then?"

"What about that movie you were talking about again? *The Lost Boys?*"

"Yeah. We could rent that . . ."

"No time. Netflix takes at least a day to deliver."

Sunny laughs. "You ever hear of a video store, Rayne?"

D'oh. "Oh. Right. Forgot about those." Stores that you can go into and rent DVDs instead of having them mailed to your door. How cute and retro. "Do they still exist?"

"I think there's an old one downtown."

"Okay, cool." I pull my feet out from under me. "So you go run to the video store and rent every vampire movie you can find. I'll go on the Internet and research what I can from here."

"It's a plan."

It wasn't exactly a plan, but it was a start. Operation Date with Dracula was on.

POSTED BY RAYNE McDONALD @ 12 p.m.

THREE COMMENTS:

CTU-in-TrainingGrrl says . . .
Wait—you mean Jack Bauer was in movies before he became a CTU agent? Vampire movies? Whoa. I've got to update my Netflix queue ASAP!!

StarrMoonUnit says . . .

Can you post the recipe for hippie hash? That sounds de-lish! I mean, I've had hippie brownies before and mmmmm. . . .

Rayne says . . .

Hey, CTU girl, you are aware that 24 is just a TV show, right? I mean, it's not even a reality one. It's got, like, a script. Jack Bauer is some dude named Kiefer Sutherland and evidently he's been in a billion movies and even dated Julia Roberts back in the day. Sorry to disappoint.

And P.S., StarrMoonUnit? Hate to disappoint you as well, but there's actually no hash in the hippie hash . . .

FOURTEEN

The Not-So-Lost Girls

TUESDAY, JUNE 5, 10 P.M.

The doorbell rings and Sunny and I are ready. In fact, if Dracula himself were to bust through the door, I think we'd actually have a chance of defeating the guy.

First up, we're both wearing necklaces made out of garlic under our hoodies. We've got holy water (which we snuck in and "borrowed" from St. Patrick's Church down the road) locked and loaded into our Super Soaker Triple Shot water guns. I'm wearing rosary beads and Sunny's got on her cross necklace. In short, together we're every vampire's worst nightmare.

"Can you get the door?" Mom asks from the kitchen. While we've been preparing, she's been running around trying to get the meal together. I felt bad not helping her, but we had too much to do on our end. I did agree to stir the vegan marinade (not sure why tofu needs to be marinated, but whatever) while Mom went upstairs to change. That gave me a chance to add a few cloves of garlic to the mix.

"Girls?"

"I'll get it, Mom." Sunny jumps up, ready to oblige with the door opening.

"Wait!" I cry. "Didn't *The Lost Boys* teach you anything?" According to the movie, the boys' plan to determine whether their mom's BF was a vamp was foiled because they invited him into the house. Evidently if you let a vampire in, you're powerless against him. "We must learn from the lessons the bad eighties movies teach us."

"Uh, right," Sunny says, sitting back down. The doorbell rings again. She picks up the DVD case and skims the back. "Though did you really think it was that bad? I thought it held up kind of well, considering it was made, like, twenty years ago."

"Sunny! Rayne! Answer the door!" Hmm. Mom's not sounding as sweet and patient anymore.

Sunny sets down the case. "Anyway, what if Mom lets him in? Does that mean the house is still safe for him? That anything we do won't work?"

I scratch my head. "I don't know. The movie never addressed that possibility. Maybe we should go to the door and refuse him entrance. Just to make sure. Then if Mom lets him in, she'll be the only one rendered powerless."

"Good idea."

We jump up from our seats and rush to the door. We stare at it for a moment, then at each other, both wondering what we would find on the other side. Would he be elegant and poised? Would he try to hypnotize us with mesmerizing eyes? What if he had one of the hounds of hell with him, like the boyfriend in the movie, ready to attack? Or maybe he'd be full-on vamped already, having decided to skip dinner and go right for our necks . . . as dessert.

You never knew with an evil vampire, now did you?

"Okay, let's do this," I say. I take a deep breath, then wrap my fingers around the handle and pull it open, revealing the man on the other side of the door.

Sunny looks at the guy, then at me, one eyebrow raised in doubt. I know what she's thinking. The guy doesn't exactly look like a creature of the night. Out of his tux, he looks more like . . . well, an accountant. Maybe it was the lighting in the Blood Bar that made him look so commanding. Or the tux. Dressed in a pair of beige slacks and a button-down shirt, I gotta admit, he just doesn't give off the same ghoulie glow.

Or maybe it's the pocket protector that's throwing us off.

He's also . . . tanned looking. But, of course, that could totally be faked with Jergens. There's this girl at school, Denise, who always looks like she's been vacationing in the Bahamas, but it's totally bogus. The girl has never been south of Jersey.

In short, the guy looks nothing like a blood sucker. But that could be his clever disguise. One thing I've learned in the vamp world—no one is as they seem. The former Master of the Blood Coven, Lucifent, looked like the little boy from *The Sixth Sense*. The former slayer, Bertha, resembled a hippo more than Sarah Michelle Gellar. And, of course, Jareth, who is uber-hot and channeling Jude Law, is in actuality the most annoying, uptight, jerky vampire in the known universe.

Not that I've been thinking of Jareth. In fact, I'd nearly forgotten he even exists up until this moment. I'm not even disappointed that he had a council meeting tonight and couldn't meet me at the Blood Bar. In fact, I'm relieved. Very relieved not to have to see him again . . .

Sorry, tangent. Back to what happened.

"Hi. I'm David," Mr. Accountant Nerd says, incidentally (or not so incidentally) giving the same name as Kiefer's character in *The Lost Boys*. He's carrying a bouquet of dark red roses. The color of blood, I might add. "You must be Sunshine and Rayne?"

Hmm. He knows our names. Very interesting. Then again, I guess Mom could have told him . . .

"I'm Sunny. She's Rayne," Sunny says, helpfully. I wonder for a moment whether she's been hypnotized to do his bidding and tell him all, then I decide it's just typical Sunny, being overly friendly.

David looks from me to Sunny and back again. "Um, would you like to invite me in?" he asks, looking a little doubtful.

Ah-ha! I shoot Sunny a triumphant glance. He used the exact words! He asked to be invited in! I knew it! I knew he was a vampire.

"It's pretty wet out here," David adds.

Whoops. I'd been so wrapped up in what he looked like I hadn't even noticed the torrential downpour the guy is standing in. Guess at least we could rule out him being a witch. He so would have melted by now.

Still, that doesn't mean the plan has changed any.

"Actually, no. We can't invite you in," I say, trying to sound as apologetic, but firm as possible. "We are not inviting you in."

"Right," Sunny adds. "In fact, we personally, Rayne and I, are denying you entrance to our house. If someone else wants to let you in—like Mom or something—well, we can't stop her. But that doesn't mean we're inviting you in. It's her decision. Which is separate from ours."

"Right. What she said," I agree. "We cannot invite you in to our house. Nothing personal. We just . . . won't. Can't."

"What's going on out here?" Mom comes up from behind us. She surveys the scene. Us blocking the door like two identical sentries. David standing outside in the rain with his wilted roses. "Girls? Why are you standing in front of the door?"

Caught. We jump aside, both with matching guilty expressions.

"The girls were just saying that it was up to the lady of the house to invite me in," says Mr. Smooth, tossing us a little wink.

Mom looks over at us, her eyes narrowed. She's wondering what we're up to, I'm sure, and doesn't look the least bit amused.

"O-kay," she says at last. "Well, please come in, David. Before you get soaked to the bone."

Bingo. She says the magic words and the vampire steps over the threshold and into our house.

Ugh—hang on. Getting IM'ed. I'll write more in a few . . .

POSTED BY RAYNE McDONALD @ 10 p.m.
ONE COMMENT:

ThisVampsGotBack says . . .
You know, you can be very discriminatory when it comes to your narrow definition of an appropriate-looking vampire. First poor Francis, who has a little extra muscle,

and now this David guy, who because he wears glasses is all of a sudden Clark Kent. Vampires are not all Goths. They come in every shape and size and race. I'd appreciate a little more tact when you describe our kind from now on.

FIFTEEN

Dinner with Dracula

TUESDAY, JUNE 5, 10:30 P.M.

Okay, sorry, I'm back. Ready to recap dinner with Dracula.

So we all go into the dining room, which for a moment I don't even recognize. We're not all that formal in the McDonald house, you see, and we usually sit at the kitchen table. The dining room is reserved for big projects like 1,000-piece puzzles or papier-mâché recreations of Custer's Last Stand or whatever school project we're currently working on. It's usually messy and informal and covered in books and jackets and other bric-a-brac.

Mom's totally cleaned house. I actually think I see things sparkling.

I don't know how she managed to work all day and still have time to cook and tidy up. I feel a stab of guilt that we didn't help her, but what could we do? We had major preps to take care of. She'll thank us someday. When we save her from becoming a snack. When she gets to live to see us help clean the house another day.

"Everyone take a seat and dinner will be right up," Mom says, motioning to the table. Wow. Fancy water goblets and matching plates. Who knew we had matching plates? I wonder if she borrowed from the neighbor. And candles! In the center of the table sits a beautiful lilac and candle centerpiece. Did she actually make that? Candles and flowers and matching plates—oh, my! This guy is morphing Mom into Martha Stewart. Too bad he's an evil dark lord of the night or I'd be welcoming his influence with open arms.

Sunny and I watch as David picks his seat. Then we choose seats right across from him, so we can check out his every move. If he even dares to sneeze, we're going to catalog it for future study.

Mom sniffs the air, a puzzled look falling across her face. "What's that smell?" she asks. "Do you guys smell something?"

Ah-ha! I elbow Sunny in the ribs. "Bad breath," I whisper. "That was a sign of someone being a vampire in *The Lost Boys*."

"Puh-leeze. That's just a movie thing," Sunny hisses back. "Magnus doesn't have bad breath."

Maybe not. I've never gotten close enough to smell it. But still, I'm not entirely convinced. And after all, Mom did say she smelled something and it certainly isn't Sunny and me.

"It smells like a garlic farm in here," Mom adds.

Okay. Maybe it is Sunny and me.

"Uh, we ordered in some pizza for lunch," Sunny says. "Extra, extra, extra garlic."

David wrinkles his nose. "Ugh. Sounds terrible," he says with a small laugh. Sunny and I exchange glances.

"I agree," Mom says, giggling like a school girl. I have to resist the urge to roll my eyes. She's got it bad for this guy.

"Actually, I have a garlic allergy," David says, further damning himself to the dark side. "That's one of the reasons I shop at the co-op. I can get foods that don't contain certain ingredients that would cause me to have an allergic reaction."

I exchange an excited glance at Sunny. A garlic allergy? A little bit of a convenient excuse, don't you think? Good way to pass off to gullible humans that you're not a doomed creature of the darkness set to eat our mom.

We're wise to you, Vamp Nerd.

"Well, you won't find any garlic in tonight's dinner," Mom says, having no clue about my secret last-minute add to the marinade. "Or any preservatives. I don't trust ingredients I can't pronounce."

"I agree. In fact, this may sound crazy, but I've always believed that the food industry could be being paid off by the pharmaceutical companies to make people get illnesses like cancer or high blood pressure. The more sick people, the more medication sales." He chuckles, looking down at his plate. "Probably a little out there, I know."

Oh, no. Ohhh, no. Mom's eyes are lighting up like a Christmas tree. Here we go.

"I've always said the exact same thing!" she cries. She turns to us. "Haven't I, girls? In fact, just the other day when Raynie was coloring her hair with some drugstore dye . . ."

I tune her out. I've heard her conspiracy theories one too many times. I can't believe David here thinks the same thing. I didn't know anyone could be as flaky as Mom. Too bad he's an evil blood-sucking beast, 'cause they'd be a great fit.

The oven timer dings just as they're getting to the part where the government is working with alien nations to secretly control the economy of the universe. Mom heads into the kitchen.

"So," David turns to us, all ready to be Mr. Friendly, "what do you girls enjoy doing for fun?"

I'm about to say, "I slay vampires," but Sunny beats me to the punch with a much wiser answer. She grabs the cross on her rosary beads and holds it up to David.

"Mostly we pray to God," she says, smiling sweetly. "Don't you just love my rosary beads?"

David doesn't break out into a full sweat or anything, but he suddenly looks mighty nervous.

"Have you given your life to the Lord Jesus?" I ask, taking my cue and grabbing my own cross. "He died to save your soul, you know." Not that you have one, Vamp Nerd.

David swallows hard. You can totally tell he wants to run screaming from the room. His insides are probably boiling, just from the proximity of the crosses.

He is so definitely a vampire.

I'm just about to ask him if he'd like to say a few Hail Marys with me, but then Mom returns. Which is convenient, in a way, since I actually have no idea how to say a Hail Mary. We borrowed the rosary beads from Old Sister Anne, the retired nun down the street who's been using them to pray for our family's soul for years.

"What are you girls wearing?" Mom asks, looking more than a tad confused.

Caught. Sunny turns beet red and I'm sure I'm the same. "Uh, rosary beads?" I say. "You know, for when we . . . confess?" Is that what you do with rosary beads? We were brought up in an ultra-liberal church where most of the choir members are drag queens and are thus ultra-clueless to the tenets of the Catholic church.

Mom raises a questioning eyebrow, then turns to David. "Kids," she says, shaking her head. "We're actually lapsed Unitarians. We don't use rosary beads."

David smiles indulgently at her. "I'm sorry to say I'm a bit of an agnostic, myself," he says. "You'll never find me setting foot in a church."

Of course you wouldn't, Vamp Nerd. You'd probably spontaneously combust from the pure evilness that is in your soul.

"Well, in some respects, I believe religion has been set in place to sedate the unhappy masses so the government can control our lives," Mom theorizes as she dishes out the tofu steaks and vegan mashed potatoes.

"I completely agree with you," David says.

Oh, god. Here we go again.

Mom sits and the conversation goes back to the bizarre. For a vampire, David has a lot of out-there political opinions. Either that, or he's just trying to impress Mom. Which means he's done his research. Suddenly, this situation becomes a whole lot scarier. I wonder what he knows about me. About Sunny.

I do notice that the guy doesn't eat much dinner. He mostly pushes the food around on his plate. At first I think this could be another sign of vampirism, 'til I notice Sunny doing the same thing and realize it could just be Mom's cooking. I'm not too thrilled with it myself. Plus, he does take a confirmed bite or two.

The two grown-ups are so engrossed in their conversation that they don't notice as Sunny and I slip out of our seats. Mom's too wrapped up in Mr. Conspiracy Theory. In fact, she's almost glowing. I haven't seen her this happy in years. Really blows that I'm going to have to kill the guy.

Oh, well. It's for the best. But first we have to confirm our suspicions. I need to make sure the guy is one hundred percent evil vamp before I go whip out my stake.

We grab the Super Soakers we'd hidden behind the couch. Time for Phase Two.

"Lock and load," I say, raising my gun.

She grins. "I'm so going to soak you!" she cries in an extra loud voice.

"Not if I soak you first!"

For the record, this was Sunny's plan. I personally didn't think anyone would buy that two sixteen-year-old girls would run around the house playing with water guns. Except, I guess, crazy Aunt Edna, who bought them for us. But she also bought us sweater sets in girls' size 6X, so I'm not sure she's aware that we've graduated from kindergarten yet.

The main floor of our house is all connected, each room leading into the next. So we split up. Sunny goes through the living room and I go through the kitchen, all the while yelling threats back and forth.

"Girls? What are you doing—?"

But suddenly Mom knows exactly what we're doing, though, of course, not what noble reason we have for doing it. We're in the dining room, one on each side of Vamp Nerd, spraying each other with water and "inadvertently" spraying him in the process.

He starts screaming like a little girl, putting his hands over his head. Sunny and I stop squirting.

"Argh! I'm soaked!" he cries.

Mom stares at him, then at us. I've never seen her look so upset. She looks like she doesn't know whether to cry or scream. "David! Are you okay?" she asks before turning to us. "Girls! What is going on here?" she demands. "What the hell do you think you're doing?"

"Uh, sorry, Mom. We were just playing around." 'Cause, um,

sixteen-year-old girls always play with water guns at the dinner table. She's so not going to buy this.

David rises from his seat, shaking the water off. We stare at him, waiting to see what will happen. Will his skin start burning off his body 'cause of the holy water? Will he burst into flames?

I watch as red blotches start appearing on the guy's neck, spreading upward to his face. I knew it! The water burned him. He really is a vampire. I resist the urge to give Sunny a high five. The two of us rock. Mom is saved. She will so be thanking us later for this.

"Oh, David, I'm so sorry," Mom says. She grabs a handful of napkins and runs around the table to dab at his soaked clothes. I wonder if it wasn't overkill. Those Super Soakers really put out a good deal of H_2O. "I don't know what's gotten into them." She shoots Sunny and me death glares. "How about an apology, girls?"

"Actually, I'm not feeling very well," David says to my mom. "I, uh, think I should go."

"What's wrong with your face, David?" Sunny demands, not sounding all that apologetic. "Did the water burn?"

David reaches up to touch his face. His eyes widen. "I think I may be breaking out in hives!" he cries.

"Well, holy water can do that," I say, having no idea if that's true or not.

He ignores me. "Was there garlic in that tofu?"

Uh-oh.

"No. Definitely not!" Mom says, looking like she's going to cry. "David, you're really red. Maybe we should get you to a hospital."

"I can drive myself," he says grimly.

"I really don't—" Mom sighs. She gets the hint. "Okay. If you're sure . . ."

The speed by which David heads for the door makes it clear that he's pretty sure. He wants out of here. Not that I blame him. First garlic, then crosses, followed by holy water. He knows the stake can't be far behind. *Adios, vampiro.*

"Good-bye. I'll, uh, call you." He doesn't sound all that sincere.

"Bye, David. I really am sorry."

But David has already left the building.

We win.

Mom sinks into her seat and puts her head in her hands. We wait for her to yell. To scream. But she doesn't. She just starts to cry.

Oh, great.

"Sorry, Mom." What else can I say? I can't explain why we did what we did. Or that it's for her own good.

She looks up at me, her eyes red and her face blotchy. "Why, girls?" she asks. "Why would you do that?" She grabs a napkin and blows her nose. "You could have just told me you were uncomfortable with me dating. You didn't have to terrorize the guy. I really like him, you know?"

Ugh. I breathe out a frustrated breath. Now what? We've just scared off Mom's date, which is a good thing, seeing as he's pretty much confirmed as an evil vampire. But now she's hurt and upset and feels like we've betrayed her.

"He wasn't right for you," I say, putting an arm around her shoulders to try to comfort her. "You'll find someone else."

She looks up. "Wasn't right for me? He's perfect for me!"

Sigh. Just sigh. I open my mouth to try again, but nothing comes out. Sunny is edging out of the room, abandoning me to the tears. Coward!

"Look, girls. I'm not trying to replace your dad," she says. "I just . . . well, I get lonely sometimes. You have your own lives and are always out and I sit in the house by myself half the time. I'm not that old," she adds. "I'd like another chance at love. And I'm asking you guys to be okay with that."

Mom heads upstairs, slamming her bedroom door behind her. I sink into a dining room chair. Did we do the right thing? This is so hard. So, so hard. 'Cause I am okay with that. More than okay. In fact, I want nothing more than for my mom to meet a nice guy and live happily ever after. I just have one requirement. Prince Charming shouldn't be an evil vampire. Is that so much to ask?

Sunny reappears, her face white and her expression uber-serious. She's holding a beige jacket in her arms. David's jacket.

"He left his jacket?" I ask, raising an eyebrow. This could be interesting. "Did you search it?"

She nods slowly. "And I found something in his pocket," she says, handing a folded piece of paper to me. "Look at this."

I take it and unwrap it slowly, my eyes widening as I read. "Oh, my god," I whisper, looking up at Sunny, then back down at the paper.

"Yeah," she says solemnly.

The scrawled writing on the paper looks like a cheat sheet—like something a cheating student would bring to a test. And it's got information. Lots of personal information. About my mom. About Sunny. About me.

And about Magnus.

This is so not good.

POSTED BY RAYNE McDONALD @ 10:30 p.m.
TWO COMMENTS:

CandyGrrl says . . .
Ooh, that's sooo scary, Rayne! Do you think Maverick knows you're out to get him and sent a spy of his own? Good thing you scared the guy away! But what if he comes back?

Angelbaby3234566 says . . .
You know, now that I think about it, I think MY mom's new BF might be an evil vampire, too. I'm so renting *The Lost Boys* and trying your guys' techniques. Heck, even if he turns out to be human, maybe I'll be able to scare him away anyway, which is good enough 4 me.

SIXTEEN

Way More Than Six Feet Under

THURSDAY, JUNE 7, 1 A.M.

That night Sunny calls Magnus and tells him about the David incident. He reassures her that everything will be okay and he'll assign some vamps to guard our house and some others to try to track the guy down. Unfortunately, we only know his first name so it's not like we can look up his address in the white pages. Sigh. I so should have staked him when I had the chance.

The next day my cell phone beeps as I'm getting out of school, informing me I have a text message. I scroll through and find it's from Jareth, of all people. (No idea how he got my mobile number; maybe Mom's right when she says there's just no privacy anymore.) The message itself is short and sweet:

MEET ME AT CLUB FANG @ 7 p.m.

For those of you who don't know, Club Fang is this way cool Goth club in Nashua, New Hampshire, that's also a big vamp hangout. Well, by night, anyway. During the day I think it doubles as a Knights of Columbus hall. Heh. If only the "knights" knew the antics that went on once the sun dipped below the horizon. They'd totally freak.

It's also the place where Magnus first accidentally bit Sunny and turned her into a vampire, but that's not such a fond memory for me so we won't be rehashing that.

I arrive at Club Fang, park the car, and pay my five bucks to go inside. They've got the smoke machines going and much of the dance floor is obscured by fog. Black lights shine down from the ceilings, casting purplish shadows everywhere. At the far end, a DJ spins Goth and electronica tunes. At the moment he's playing the Sisters of Mercy song "Temple of Love," which is one of my favorites. Not seeing Jareth around, I decide I might as well dance for a bit while waiting.

I love dancing. Swaying my body to deep, seductive music. Letting myself become one with the beat. Losing myself in the orchestra of light. I close my eyes and weave my arms through the air, floating through the ambient waves of sound. It's heavenly. All my troubles, all my stress, just float away into the night.

In the old days, like when my mom was a kid, people always danced with a partner. Which is okay, I guess. But then you're worried about the proper steps and the other person's lead and stepping on their toes. When you're dancing with yourself, you have none of these concerns. You can just let go.

The song changes and I open my eyes. Responsibility replaces rhythm. As much as I'd like to dance all night, I've got to find Jareth. I scan the café side of the club, adorned with little tables covered by black tablecloths and lit by candles. Several vampy-looking patrons are sipping what appears to be a deep crimson wine. But the color looks a bit too dark to be your average merlot, if you know what I'm saying. Many have brought their donors with them. Usually pale, thin Goth girls who think it's oh-so-cool to sell their blood to a thirsty vamp. Most of the donors are total vamp wannabes. Ones who failed the certification program to become vampires themselves.

Maybe I should become a donor. Then I'd get to experience that amazing biting experience every night. Then again, that just rings a little too close to prostitution to me. The vamp would just be using me for blood.

No, I can wait. 'Til I'm assigned a new blood mate. Someone completely compatible with me who I can spend the rest of eternity with. Someone whose bites will actually mean something. I want that. I deserve that.

Anyway, no sign of Jareth, so I turn to head back out onto the dance floor. It's there I spot him. At the far end of the room, lit by a black light, his pale skin is almost glowing. He's dressed simply, wearing a white pirate shirt with puffy sleeves and black pants. But he looks like a god as he sways under the light. His eyes are closed, his face a mask of ecstasy and concentration. He's got perfect moves, perfect rhythm. It's almost as if he's part of the music. I know that sounds weird, but it's hard to describe. Suffice it to say he looks beautiful. Absolutely stunning.

The Jareth I know is uptight and annoying. A total ass.

This is not the Jareth I know.

This is the Jareth I want to know.

I weave my way through the other dancers 'til I reach him. His eyes are still closed, and I notice he's wearing eyeliner. De-lish. I love a guy in eyeliner.

Not wanting to disturb his dance-induced trance, I merely pick up the beat myself, closing my own eyes, floating my arms through the air. Finding the music and making love to it. Letting the dark, melodious sounds take me away. To the place Jareth has found. Hoping I can find him there, too.

An arm wraps around my waist and a body presses against mine. I consider opening my eyes, but the feeling is too nice. The heat, the touch, the matching of my movements with his own.

Is it Jareth? It has to be Jareth. And he feels so good. So right. Just as I imagined he would.

I feel myself being pulled deeper and deeper inside the music. A rich darkness consumes me, pulling me toward a strange white light. I take back every single thing I said about it being better to dance alone. It's better to dance with Jareth. One hundred million, billion, gazillion times better.

"You're a good dancer," his voice whispers in my ear.

"You, too," I whisper back, wanting this moment to last forever. Wow. This is so not the Jareth I know, that's for sure. Who knew he was so deeply and darkly romantic. So—

"Rayne, are you going to waste the entire night on the dance floor? Or can we get some work done here?"

My eyes flutter open at the unmistakable voice. I glance at my dance partner. Uh-oh.

It's not Jareth. Not even close. Ew! I've been grinding with some totally random vamp who's not even cute. Gr-*oss*. And uber-disappointing.

I push the guy away, annoyed. I look over to see Jareth staring disapprovingly at me, arms folded across his chest. He looks terribly annoyed.

"Jareth?" My head's still foggy from the dancing. "I thought—"

"If you've had your fun, I suggest we get down to business," he shouts over the music.

"Hey, buddy," says my accidental dance partner. "She's dancing with me."

Jareth rolls his eyes. "She can marry you, for all I care. Have babies. Live happily ever after in a white-picketed suburban McMansion. But for right now, I have important business to discuss with her and she's coming with me."

He grabs me roughly by the arm and proceeds to drag me to the café side of the club.

"Get your hands off me," I protest, annoyed at his possessiveness. If I didn't know better, I'd say he was totally jealous. But that's stupid, right? I mean, we don't even know each other, really. Or like each other. We shared one bite. And it was performed under necessity, not attraction. Well, not total attraction, anyway. Okay, fine. I was attracted. But for him it was just part of our cover. At least I think so.

Still, for some weird reason he's making me feel totally guilty. As if I was, like, cheating on him or something. Which is so stupid. We're totally not going out. We're not even friends. We're just partners thrown together to solve a vampire mystery. After that's over, we'll part ways. Forever. And I do mean forever.

Jareth still looks pouty as he sits down in his seat. I decide to make peace. Even if he doesn't have any right to be pissed at me.

"I was watching you," I say. "You're an amazing dancer."

"Thanks," he says, still sounding a bit on the grumpy side. "It's something I enjoy."

I smile. "Me, too. I sometimes feel like dancing is the only way I can be at total peace with myself. It's like the world stops while you're dancing. And nothing matters but the music."

He pauses for a moment, then agrees. "I know what you mean. Sometimes I come here by myself. When the world is too much to deal with. I can escape for a few hours. Forget all the pain."

He stops talking and stares at his hands. I wonder, not for the first time, what secret hurt he's hiding and whether we'll ever be close enough for him to share it with me.

I decide to confess. Maybe my humiliation will cheer him a bit.

"You know, I had my eyes closed," I say. "Stupidly, I thought that guy who came up and started dancing with me was you."

Jareth looks up, raising a perfectly arched eyebrow. "Me?"

"Yeah." I'm hoping the bar's dim lighting is hiding my blush.

"Would you . . . have liked it to be me?"

Gah! He did not just go there. Now my face is burning. "Uh . . ."

"You're all red, my dear." His smile tells me he's enjoying teasing me, seeing me uncomfortable. Jeez. I should have never confessed that.

"It would have been nice if it was you, yes," I say at last, not wanting to let him win. Let him turn red for a while.

But he doesn't blush. He just looks thoughtful.

"Anyway," he says, apparently wimping out and changing the subject. "You're probably wondering why I asked you here tonight. And it wasn't, unfortunately, to dance with you."

"I figured," I say. "What's wrong?"

He picks up the salt shaker and fiddles with it, not meeting my eyes. "Kristoff," he murmurs at last.

I cock my head. "You mean your vamp friend? The one whose donors you saw in the Blood Bar yesterday?"

"Yes." Jareth nods. "I went to see him this evening. To let him know we'd spotted his donors and that he ought to let them go. I pounded on the door of his crypt, but there was no answer. I waited for a moment, then heard strange noises coming from inside. A . . . whimpering almost. So I broke down the door. I found him in bed, looking deathly ill."

Concern claws at my heart. I'm thinking, "This is very strange."

"I asked him what was wrong. He could barely speak." Jareth shakes his head, looking pained. Evidently this guy is a good friend. "He says the last few days, he's been bedridden. Can't even feed anymore. And all his vampire powers seem to somehow have left him."

"That's weird."

"Very. I've never seen anything like it."

"Do you think he could have caught some weird disease? Like, because his donors were at the Blood Bar? Maybe they were infected by some other vampire and passed along the disease."

Jareth shrugs. "It's possible, to be sure. But unlikely. The Blood Bar is more regulated than one might think. It screens all its biters. I had to go through a rigorous blood test before I was accepted into the program."

"So you think the two things are totally separate? Unrelated?"

"I wouldn't go that far. It's too much of a coincidence. Oh, and even stranger? His donors are dead."

My mouth drops open in horror. "Dead?"

Jareth nods.

"But we just saw them two nights ago. I mean, sure they looked a bit on the pasty side, but . . . dead?" Suddenly this was getting pretty scary.

"Dead," Jareth repeats. "And no one has any idea why."

"Couldn't they do an autopsy?"

"We could, but the humans have them, obviously. I sent some of my men to do recon and they learned that the girls' parents are doing their own autopsy. And, unfortunately, they're both going to be cremated immediately afterwards. So we can't get to their bodies."

"What would you need to find out what was wrong with them?"

"A sample of blood would probably do it. We have some talented chemists in our coven."

An idea forms in my mind. "Do you know where the bodies have been sent to? We could maybe sneak in and get the sample or something."

Jareth raises an eyebrow. "You want to do that?" he asks. "It could be dangerous."

"I laugh in the face of danger," I quip, letting out a loud fake chortle. "Ha, ha, ha, ha!"

Jareth shakes his head, not able to suppress a small grin. Heh. Even he cannot resist Silly Rayne.

"Well, it's not a bad idea. I'm told the bodies are at the funeral home. But they haven't been worked on yet, so they still have their blood. We could go there before the place closes and hide out until after hours. Then we can get the blood sample."

"Sounds like a plan, Stan."

WE LEAVE CLUB Fang and head into the parking lot. Jareth suggests we take his black BMW and obviously I don't argue. Leather seats and satellite radio set to an all-Goth, all-the-time satellite station is my preferred way to travel. We drive to the outskirts of town, to the funeral home. Neither of us say much in the car, but it's a comfortable silence as Peter Murphy croons over the airwaves.

The funeral home is still open when we arrive. Dozens of cars are parked out front. Whoever's having a wake tonight was obviously pretty popular. I wonder how many people would come to my funeral. Luckily, if I turn vamp I'll get to fake my death and see for myself.

My dad better show up or he's so dead. And when he does die,

I won't attend *his* funeral, just to spite him. Not that he'd be expecting me to, seeing as technically I'd have been the first to die.

The vampire stuff can get confusing at times . . .

Jareth parks the car and suggests we go around to the other side of the house. The backyard hasn't gotten the same landscaping attention the front has and we have to push through tangled briar patches to get there, totally ripping up my tights. It's worth the fishnet sacrifice, though, when we find an unlocked window and slip inside.

"Let's find a closet or something to hide out in until the place closes for the night and the funeral guys go home," Jareth suggests.

"Okay." I feel like a guest star on *Six Feet Under.*

We tiptoe out into the hallway and try a couple doors. The first leads to a bathroom and the second to a tiny darkened chapel. (Which would have been the perfect place to hide were it not for the fact that Jareth's feet would pretty much burn off walking on hallowed ground.) Finally, on the third try, we find what we're looking for. A small broom closet filled with cleaning supplies that we'll both fit in.

Barely.

We squeeze in and Jareth pulls the door closed behind us. It's dark. There's no room to sit down and I pray that the wake is nearly over. Jareth's leg brushes against mine, sending a whole host of tingling sensations through my body. Did I happen to mention how hot he is? Half of me totally wants to jump him. Let him take me, right here, right now. I have to keep reminding myself I don't want him. I really don't want him.

"Are you okay?" Jareth whispers. "You're shaking."

Ugh. I'm shaking 'cause he's totally turning me on. But I can't exactly tell him that, now can I? At the same time, the last thing I want to do is let him think I'm scared.

"Low blood sugar," I whisper. "I only had an apple for lunch." I actually had four slices of pizza with extra cheese, but he doesn't need to know that.

"Sorry," he says. "We should have stopped at the drive-thru on the way. Sometimes I forget what it's like to be human. To have feeding needs."

"What about you? You have feeding needs, too, right? But I've never seen you with your donors."

He grimaces. "I don't like the idea of donors. I get my blood by mail order."

I raise an eyebrow. Interesting. "Really? Why?"

"Would you like seeing the cow before eating your steak?"

"Uh, no. But I'm a vegetarian. No cows for this chick."

Jareth chuckles softly, the dim light catching his fangs and making them sparkle. "How are you going to become a vampire if you don't like the taste of blood?"

Good question. One I hadn't really given much thought to. "I figure I'll learn to love it," I say with a shrug. "Sunny was totally grossed out by the idea of drinking blood until she actually tasted it. Then she developed an unquenchable thirst for the stuff."

"I see. Well, then I'm sure you'll be fine," Jareth says. "So have they told you who will be your blood mate yet?"

"No. After the whole Sunny mishap, I'm back at the bottom of the waiting list. Which sucks, pardon the pun. You'd think Magnus, being the master and all, could pull in a few favors for his girl-friend's sister, but evidently not."

"Maybe it's because they haven't found you a perfect match yet," Jareth says. "Remember, your DNA has to be compatible."

"Yeah, I know. Knowing me, there will never be another vamp with compatible DNA. I'll be doomed to be a slayer for eternity."

"That's not true. They'll find you a match. Actually I think you'd make a good vamp," Jareth says shyly. "Though perhaps a very stubborn, aggravating blood mate."

"Heh." I laugh. "So what's your story? You on the prowl for a blood mate of your own?" As I ask the question, I suddenly realize I'm worried about his answer. For some reason, I really, really don't want him to say yes.

He's silent for a long moment, then says, "I don't want a blood mate. They offered me one a few years back, but I refused."

"But why?" I ask. "I thought that was every vampire's dream. To have a partner to spend eternity with."

"Eternity is a long time and it doesn't always work out that way," Jareth says, a bit bitterly. "It's worse to love someone and then lose them, than to never love at all."

"Heh. I know the feeling."

"Oh?"

I feel my face heat. I hadn't meant to be so revealing.

"Ah, nothing," I stammer. "It's just . . . my dad. He took off four years ago to find himself. Haven't seem him since."

"And you miss him," Jareth says softly. It's not a question. Or a judgment. Or even pity.

"Well, yeah. I mean, sure I do. Sometimes. Though sometimes I don't." I know I'm not making a lot of sense, but I'm not really used to talking about this stuff. Especially not to a hot vampire in a broom closet. "But anyway, I guess it doesn't matter now. He's coming for our birthday this week. So I mean, I guess it's all good." I pause, feeling awkward and not knowing what to say.

"Yes. That seems very good," Jareth says, a bit distantly.

"What about you? What's your story?" I ask, so ready to change the subject. "What makes you such a bitter biter?"

"It was a long time ago. It doesn't matter now."

Hmm. Stubborn. But I'll get it out of him. "It obviously does. It obviously upsets you. Maybe it'd feel good to talk about it. To a stranger."

"A stranger like you?"

"Sure. I can't say I'll be able to give wise advice, but I'd be happy to listen. And we've got time."

"But you're a slayer."

"Dude. I'm like a good slayer—"

Jareth suddenly puts a hand over my mouth. I stop talking and listen. Footsteps. Coming closer. Shit. I hope the cleaning crew doesn't need to get into the broom closet. We'll totally be caught!

I look up at Jareth questioningly, having no idea what to do. His eyes are wide and frightened.

"Follow my lead," he whispers.

And then he leans down and kisses me!!!

. . .

UH, SORRY, HAVE to continue this later. Mom's totally yelling at me to get to bed . . .

POSTED BY RAYNE McDONALD @ I a.m.
TWO COMMENTS:

CandyGrrl says . . .
He kissed u!?!?! How can u leave us hanging like this? Tell ur mom this is more important! Gah!

Soulsearcher says . . .
Making out in a funeral home. Sooo romantic. Oh, so romantic.

SunshineBaby says . . .
You kissed Jareth? Dude, I'm your twin! How come I'm always the last to know?

SEVENTEEN

Closet Kisses and a Lot of Wishes

THURSDAY, JUNE 7, 8 A.M.

Quick entry before school since you're all annoyed that I had to cut out at the kissing scene. Believe me, I didn't want to leave you hanging either, but Mom was being totally adamant. I think she's still pissed that we scared off her date. Oh, and speaking of? I think she's still seeing the guy. Grrr. I've got to have a talk with her.

Anyway, where I left off: footsteps approaching and I'm getting ravaged by the sexiest vampire on earth. But forget the footsteps. You just want to know about the ravaging, right? Heh.

You know how I said how heavenly the bite from Jareth was? Well, the kiss he gave me last night was even better, if you can believe it!

Here's how it went down:

His mouth captures mine. I know that sounds funny, but that's exactly what it seems like. Total domination of my lips. I'm so surprised that my jaw drops, which inadvertently allows him full access. And he takes advantage, his lips pressing hard against mine, his tongue finding my own and meeting it with almost a worshipful caress. Obviously it's hard to describe kisses, but think of your best

kiss ever and multiply it by three and a half million and you're probably pretty close. Every nerve ending in my body is like, singing, at
this point. Just like in romance books, there's, like, this electricity
flowing through my veins. Suddenly I don't care why we're kissing
or the fact that we're probably, like, this close to getting busted by
whoever's coming to the closet. All I can think of, focus on, is his
lips against mine.

Half of me wishes you could all kiss Jareth, just so you can feel
for yourselves. The other half hopes that Jareth never kisses anyone
else but me for the rest of eternity.

The footsteps fade and Jareth pulls away, way too soon for my
liking.

"Sorry," he says, his normally pale face bright red. "I just figured
if they caught us, it'd be better to look like we snuck off together,
than were hiding for some other more nefarious purpose."

I nod, not trusting my voice at the moment. I'm madly praying
the footsteps come back so we can go for round two. But I'm just
not that lucky. Whoever it was hits the lights and slams the front
door closed. They're out.

I involuntarily lick my lower lip, nearly desperate for another
taste. So delicious. So, so delicious. My whole body is humming. I'm
dying to just jump him. I wonder what he'd do if I did. Would he
pull away? Be disgusted? Or does he feel the same attraction I do? I
wish I knew.

We stand in silence, still so close that I can feel Jareth's cool
breath on my face. I wonder for a moment why vampires need to
breathe, seeing as they're technically not alive. I'll have to look it up
later.

Five minutes go by. Then five more. It seems like an eternity. I
wish, not for the first time, that we could kiss again. But Jareth
seems to be stuck in full-on listening mode.

Finally he speaks.

"I think they're gone. We're safe," he says. He pushes open the
door and puts a hand around the small of my back to lead me out
into the hallway. Just that small touch sparks a thrill strong enough

to curl my toes. I wonder what it'd be like to get it on with him for real. I probably wouldn't be able to handle it. Would he be rough and demanding? Or gentle, soft, and sweet? And what would he be like afterward? Would he want to cuddle? Or, like most of my past boyfriends, reach for the PlayStation controller, afterward. I'm so over those guys.

Guess I'll never know. And there's no use fantasizing about it, now is there?

Anyhow, we creep through the dark hallway, down the stairs, and into the basement. There, Jareth finds a hanging light and pulls the string, enveloping the room in a dim yellowy glow. I look around, my breath catching in my throat as I recognize what surrounds me.

Corpses. Everywhere I look. Freak-y. I've never seen dead bodies in real life before.

Of course, they don't seem to bother Jareth even the slightest. I guess that's probably because technically speaking he's a living, walking, breathing corpse himself. He heads straight over to the wall, where there's a large filing cabinet–like setup and starts reading the drawer labels. He pauses at one and then pulls open the drawer. Out pops (surprise, surprise) another body. Ugh. I'm so going to have nightmares tonight. This is worse than the time Spider and I had an all-night *Friday the 13th*–watching marathon. Every time I closed my eyes for weeks later I saw hockey-masked Jason lumbering up to me with his machete, ready to creatively murder me for my sex, drugs, and rock-and-roll sins.

"This is one of them," he says, motioning me over. "And she hasn't been drained yet. Excellent." He reaches into his black leather trench coat pocket (way cool) and pulls out a small silver dagger, an empty vial, and a pair of rubber gloves, which he slips on his hands.

"Wait. You're not going to—" I start, stopping only when I realize indeed he is going to do just that. He draws a small slash across her arm and holds the vial underneath to catch the blood. I involuntarily cringe.

He looks up and laughs when he sees my face. "Relax, dear," he says. "She can't feel it. She's already dead."

"I know," I say, annoyed, but more at myself than at him. Some super vampire-chick-in-training I'm turning out to be—afraid of a little blood. What's going to happen when I have to dine on it every night? Maybe I'll do what Jareth does and get takeout. At least that way I can pretend it's wine or something. Though it sort of takes all the romance out of the process.

The vial fills quickly and Jareth plugs it with a small rubber stopper. Then he reaches into his pocket again and pulls out a small cloth, which he presses against the open wound. "To stop the blood," he explains.

"Don't want her to bleed to death, eh?" I quip.

He grins. "Definitely not," he says. "Not to mention the smell of the stuff is driving me crazy. It's taking everything I've got not to lean down and take a sip."

"You'd better not. We don't know what's in that stuff. What if she is the reason Kristoff's out of commission?"

"Exactly. That would be . . . as you humans say . . . so not cool." He says it in a total valley girl voice, causing me to giggle. He really can be funny when he's not being a jerk.

"I'm glad I can make you laugh," he says with a small smile and I totally feel my face going beet red. I have no idea how to respond to him, but luckily it turns out I don't have to. A moment later he removes the cloth and examines the corpse's wound. "Okay," he says. "Let's get out of this place."

We leave the funeral home and Jareth drops me off at my place. The good-bye scene is très awkward for some reason. As if neither of us really wants to part company. And as if both of us want a goodnight kiss when we do. Unfortunately, we're both total chickens and instead of confessing our desires we stumble over our goodnights with much stammering and blushing and I get out of the car and head for the house.

And that's about it. Time for (sigh) me to head to school. TTYL.

POSTED BY RAYNE McDONALD @ 8 a.m.
ONE COMMENT:

NotYourMama says . . .
Wow, that sounds like quite the kiss, girl! I would love to
get me some of that. You let us know if you decide he's
not the guy for you and I'll be all over that *sheeyat*.

EIGHTEEN

Gamer Girls

SATURDAY, JUNE 9, 12 A.M.

After school I go to my room and sign on to my video game. Spider and I are supposed to join our fellow guild members to do an instance. For those of you who think I'm speaking some other language when I go all gamer geek, a "guild" is a group of friends who play together online and an "instance" is like a special dungeon in the game where your characters can kill computer-generated monsters for really good treasure. (If you still don't get it, ask your brother or boyfriend. They probably play and will be overjoyed to go off on a way-too-detailed explanation that you'll get bored of after about half a minute.)

Anyway—Spider and I had a long chat about Jareth while we played.

Pasting the transcript here. The stuff in "whisper" is Spider and my private convo.

> **KELAHDKA:** Everyone in? We ready to start?
> **RAYNIEDAY:** Yup.
> **SPIDER:** Yup.

RUKKU: Yup.
HAX0R: Yup.
KELAHDKA: Okay, here's the plan . . .

SPIDER WHISPERS: So how's everything going with the whole slayer thing? You kill the bad guy yet? Save the world?
RAYNIEDAY WHISPERS: No. ☺ Not yet. But something weird is definitely going on. Some donor girls who visited the Blood Bar died after infecting their vampire with some kind of weird blood disease.
SPIDER WHISPERS: That doesn't seem so good.
RAYNIEDAY WHISPERS: Watch out!

**Spider firebombs Acolyte for 40 damage.*
**Scarlet Monastary Acolyte hits Spider for 450 damage.*

SPIDER: Uh, can I get a heal?
SPIDER: Anyone? Hax?
HAX0R: Hang on. I'm on the phone.

**Scarlet Monastary Acolyte hits Spider for 230 damage.*
**Spider dies.*

SPIDER WHISPERS: Grr. He did that on purpose.
RAYNIEDAY WHISPERS: ☹
SPIDER WHISPERS: It's 'cause I broke up with him, you know. Ever since I broke up with him I never get healed when we're playing.
RAYNIEDAY WHISPERS: You're imagining things. Why would he not heal you? It only delays the whole group. Surely he's not that stupid.
SPIDER WHISPERS: He is that stupid. He totally is. Why do you think I dumped him?

HAX0R: Sorry. Back. Oh, Spider, you're dead?
SPIDER: . . .

RAYNIEDAY WHISPERS: Be nice.

SPIDER: Why, yes, Hax. I died. How sweet of you to take time out of your busy real life to notice.

RAYNIEDAY WHISPERS: Uh, when I said nice . . .
SPIDER WHISPERS: Forget him. Tell me more about the vamps.
RAYNIEDAY WHISPERS: Hehe. I've got MAJOR scoop actually.
SPIDER WHISPERS: Oh?
RAYNIEDAY WHISPERS: . . . I kissed Jareth!!!!

SPIDER: OMG, YOU KISSED HIM!?!
SPIDER: Uh, mistype.
HAX0R: Who kissed who?
SPIDER: I said MISTYPE. As in I didn't mean to type it to you. So eff off.

**Hax0r cries.
**Rukku comforts Hax0r.

SPIDER WHISPERS: God, this party sucks.

KELAHDKA: Okay, we're going to attack the boss now. Here's the strategy . . .

SPIDER WHISPERS: Anyway, you kissed him? Why did you kiss him? I thought you hated him. Or at least thought he was annoying.
RAYNIEDAY WHISPERS: Well, it wasn't like a real kiss. I mean, we were in this broom closet and . . .
SPIDER WHISPERS: Broom closet? OMG, how sexy is that?!

RAYNIEDAY WHISPERS: Uh, at a funeral home . . .

SPIDER WHISPERS: A Goth's dream come true.

RAYNIEDAY WHISPERS: And someone was coming. We were afraid they were going to open the door . . .

SPIDER WHISPERS: . . .

RAYNIEDAY WHISPERS: And so he kissed me. So we'd look like we snuck away from the wake or something if caught.

SPIDER WHISPERS: And . . .

RAYNIEDAY WHISPERS: And what?

SPIDER WHISPERS: Don't play coy with me, young lady. What was it like?

RAYNIEDAY WHISPERS: /blush

SPIDER WHISPERS: LOL.

KELAHDKA: Okay, here we go! Spider, go ahead and fireball these guys. Hax will keep you healed.

SPIDER: kk.

SPIDER WHISPERS: I want to hear more after this battle.

**Spider firebombs Scarlet Henchman for 400 damage.

HAX0R: Uh, my dog's scratching at the door. I'll BRB.

SPIDER: Wait, I already attacked!

**Scarlet Henchman attacks Spider for 430 damage.
**Scarlet Hound of Hell attacks Spider for 200 damage.
**Scarlet Priest attacks Spider for 235 damage.
**Scarlet Rogue attacks Spider for 500 damage.
**Spider dies.

SPIDER: GDAMNIT, HAX!

HAX0R: Okay. Sorry I'm back. Oh, Spider. You're dead again?

SPIDER WHISPERS: Worst priest ever.

RAYNIEDAY WHISPERS: Sigh.

SPIDER WHISPERS: That's it. I'm logging out. I can't take it.

RAYNIEDAY WHISPERS: But don't you want to hear the rest of the kiss?

SPIDER WHISPERS: Oh, yeah. Okay. One more try. But so help me if he doesn't heal me again.

RAYNIEDAY WHISPERS: kk.

SPIDER WHISPERS: You can tell me what the kiss was like while my ghost runs back to my dead body.

RAYNIEDAY WHISPERS: Well, it was the most amazing kiss in the entire history of kissing. Like in that movie *Princess Bride* where they talk about best-ever kisses? This had to be one of them.

SPIDER WHISPERS: That good, huh?

RAYNIEDAY WHISPERS: Yes. Majorly dreamy. You know, Spider, I hate to admit this, but I think I might be in love.

SPIDER WHISPERS: What? With Jareth?

RAYNIEDAY WHISPERS: He seems all cold on the outside, but he's kind of sweet on the inside. And easy to talk to and stuff.

SPIDER WHISPERS: But he's a vampire.

RAYNIEDAY WHISPERS: So what? My sis is dating a vampire.

SPIDER WHISPERS: Your sis is not a vampire slayer. And besides, the guy sounds kind of emotionally unavailable.

RAYNIEDAY WHISPERS: Emotionally unavailable? WTF? You suddenly Freud or something?

SPIDER WHISPERS: No. Freud was the "He reminds me of my father" guy.

RAYNIEDAY WHISPERS: Well, Jareth definitely does not remind me of my father.

SPIDER WHISPERS: Are you sure about that? From

what you've told me he sounds like he's another guy who won't share his feelings or get close to anyone for fear he'll become trapped.

RAYNIEDAY WHISPERS: Jareth isn't like that. I know he's not. He's just been hurt and now he's afraid.

SPIDER WHISPERS: But what is this big hurt?

RAYNIEDAY WHISPERS: I don't know. But I'm going to find out.

SPIDER WHISPERS: Okay, sweetie. Good luck. Just don't get hurt, okay?

RAYNIEDAY WHISPERS: I'll try.

**Spider resurrects.*

SPIDER: Okay, I'm back.

KELAHDKA: Great. We're going to try this again. Spider, you attack and we'll cover you.

SPIDER: Uh, Hax, you're going to heal me this time, right?

HAX0R: Of course. What are you talking about? Why wouldn't I?

SPIDER: Okay, never mind. Here goes.

**Spider attacks Scarlet Henchman for 300 damage.*

HAX0R: Oh. My friend just got here. I've got to go.

**HaxOr leaves the party.*
**Scarlet Henchman attacks Spider for 100 damage.*
**Scarlet Demon Dog attacks Spider for 245 damage.*
**Scarlet Rogue attacks Spider for 567 damage.*
**Spider dies.*

SPIDER: NOOOOO!!!!!!!!!

POSTED BY RAYNE McDONALD @ 12 a.m.
EIGHT COMMENTS:

Hax0r says . . .
Dude! That's bogus that I don't heal Spider. She gets
healed plenty. She's just such a crappy noob mage she
gets pwned anyway. I demand you take this libelous
slander out of your blog before I sue you for everything
you got.

Spider says . . .
First of all, Hax, it's obviously apparent from that
transcript that it is YOU who are the noob! Also, what
the hell do you mean, sue? You can't sue someone over a
video game chat. Grow up and get a life.

Hax0r says . . .
I have a life, thank you very much. A life WITHOUT
YOU.

Spider says . . .
There is no life after me. Heh. Heh.

Hax0r says . . .
U R A STUPID BITCH.

Spider says . . .
U R A PATHETIC A-HOLE.

Hax0r says . . .
That's it! Now I'm going to sue you, too, Spider!!!!!

Rayne says . . .
Hax0r! Spider! Get your own blogs and stop fighting in
mine! I mean it.

NINETEEN

BIRTHDAY GRRL!!!!

SATURDAY, JUNE 9, 7 A.M.

Yay! Today is my birthday!!!! How exciting!!!! Yes, I know I'm exclamation-pointing too much, but you would be, too, if it were your birthday!!!!

First Mom's going to cook a birthday breakfast—and she's promised to make real pancakes without any tofu, barley, or carrots in them. Extra unhealthy with whipped cream and strawberries.

In the afternoon, Spider's coming over, as are various friends of Sunny's. Mom's going to order pizza and we Netflixed a bunch of DVDs. Of course, Sunny's selection will probably have all Matthew McConaughey stuff. But I rented some classics. The original *Dracula*, starring Bela Lugosi for one. Can't wait!

But what I'm most excited about is Dad. I can't believe he's actually coming. I haven't seen him in so many years. I'm so proud of Sunny for getting up the courage to write to him and invite him. I would have never been able to do that.

I wonder what he'll look like. If he's started to gray at his temples. Will he look old? Or maybe just distinguished? I wonder what he'll bring us for presents. I don't even care if he does, actually. Just having him here is present enough.

Ooh, this is going to be the best day, ever! I *sooo* cannot wait for it to begin.

Oops, Mom's calling me to breakfast and I haven't even selected a b-day outfit yet. Gah! Better get a move on . . .

POSTED BY Rayne McDonald @ 7 a.m.
THREE COMMENTS:

ButterfliQT says . . .
Happy birthday, sweetie! Enjoy the time with your dad.

DarkGothBoy says . . .
Happy Birthday 2 u
Happy Birthday 2 u
U look like a vampire
& U smell like one, too.

Spider says . . .
See you this afternoon. Can't wait to meet the dadster.

TWENTY

NO CAKE

SATURDAY, JUNE 9, 10 P.M.

It's ten o'clock. He's still not here. Sunny and my mom have gone to bed. I'm sitting downstairs on the family computer, surrounded by leftover pizza, stupid presents I don't want or need, and NO CAKE.

I hate him.
   I HATE HIM.
   I HATE HATE HATE HATE HATE HATE HATE HIM!!!!!

POSTED BY RAYNE McDONALD @ 10 p.m.
FOUR COMMENTS:

Anonymous says . . .
   Oh, he didn't show up? What a surprise. Poor
   Raynie. Now she's really going to have daddy issues.
   Boo-hoo-hoo. The Goth freak suffers some more.
   Maybe you should go listen to Morrissey and slit your
   wrists.

Anonymous says . . .

Ha-ha! I could have predicted that.

Anonymous says . . .

Oh, the teenage angst. Makes me a little sick. Welcome
to the real world, little one.

Anonymous says . . .

Maybe this will teach you to stop playing your little
vampire games and face reality a bit, sweetheart.

TWENTY-ONE

My Dad's a Loser and I Think
He Should Die

SUNDAY, JUNE 10, 1 P.M.

Dear Diary,

I used to write a blog and post it on the Internet. But let me tell you, it's not fun posting about your life when bad things happen and then have anonymous people post nasty, hurtful comments about you. So screw that. I'm going to stick with a good old-fashioned lock-and-key diary from now on.

Anyway, it's Sunday afternoon. Not that it matters. I don't think I would have gotten out of bed even if I did have school. I'm such a moron. I actually stayed up waiting for the guy 'til one A.M. As if he'd suddenly come through the door at one A.M., arms full of presents and cake, mouth full of apologies for being late.

Obviously that didn't happen. Not that I really expected it would. Not really, anyway.

Did I mention I hate him?

Screw this. That was his last chance. I am never speaking to him again. Not in a thousand years. A million if I end up turning into a vamp and happen to live that long. He's already dead to me. If I came upon his grave somewhere in my vampirish travels I'd spit on it.

I hate him, I hate him, I HATE HIM!!!!

I'm such an idiot. Why did I buy Sunny's crap about him definitely coming? About how it has to be real 'cause there's a plane ticket and a hotel? Last night I called the airport. The hotel. He just never showed up. Stood them up, just like he did us.

Bastard. Effing bastard.

I wish I could just jump on a plane and head straight to his house and confront him in person. Tell him what a lousy father he is and how he doesn't deserve good daughters like Sunny and me. Or something. Anything. Just so I don't have to feel so freaking helpless and screwed up and alone.

Great. Now I'm crying again and I'm so not a crying type of girl. This whole thing sucks. I don't have time to be all depressed either. I've got Slayer Training scheduled at two, if you can believe it. Teifert called me this morning (Does the entire world know my cell number?), leaving a cryptic message about the time growing near. Which is fine by me, I suppose.

I'm more than ready to kick a little ass.

TWENTY-TWO

Stake That!

SUNDAY, JUNE 10, 5 P.M.

Back from Slayer Training. Definitely a mind-blowing experience, let me tell you.

At first everything seems pretty normal. Mr. Teifert and I meet up in the school gymnasium, down by the weight room. The place is deserted, which is probably a good thing. A student and a teacher, alone in a half-lit gym—probably a bit sketchy-looking to your average outsider. And it's not like we can explain the whole slayer/instructor thing to the general public. They're bound to make up a much seedier scenario—one that will get Teifert fired and me expelled. Not so good.

Oh, but get this! Mr. Teifert forces me to change into a pair of Juicy Couture sweatpants and Nikes before starting my training. Says something about my beautiful black silk dress and combat boots combo not being appropriate workout attire. *Puh-leeze*. Oh, and if that wasn't bad enough—this pair of Juicy Couture sweatpants just so happens to be pink! If anyone evil and cruel were to walk by with a camera phone at this very moment, my entire high school image would be irreparably shattered.

After donning the Pepto-Bismol outfit, we start our training. He has me do some weight lifting first (five pounds is about my limit) and then jump rope (three jumps maybe before I get hopelessly tangled), then run laps around the gymnasium. (And when I say laps, I mean lap—singular—before I'm completely out of breath. I've so got to give up smoking.)

He looks a little distraught at my physical condition, but simply motions to the punching bag and tells me to go at it. I smile. Now we're talking.

"Hi-YAH!" I cry as I slam my fist into the punching bag and then follow it with a beautiful roundhouse kick. I lower my head and narrow my eyes and focus on the bag, making it my enemy. If I'm lucky, this Slayer Training will get some of my pent-up aggression out.

Dad. Is. A. Loser. Punch. Kick. Repeat.

"Rayne, focus. You're not in control," Teifert repeats for the ten-thousandth time. "A slayer must find her deep strength. Her inner power. She must become one with the universe."

I stop punching, reaching up to wipe the sweat from my forehead. "Can we cut the Zen crap for a moment?" I ask. "I'm trying to beat this bag to a pulp."

"No, we cannot cut the 'Zen crap' as you say," Teifert says wearily. "Rayne, one cannot become a good slayer through sheer force and anger. You must find the power within your center. Within yourself."

"Maybe I don't have a center. And if so, maybe I should use what I got." I hold up my fists. "Here's where my power lies, Teifert. Look out, vamps, it's Raynie Power time."

Teifert shakes his head. "Where do they find these girls?" he mutters under his breath. "And why do they keep sending them to me?"

Oh, that's nice. "Hey, you chose me, dude," I remind him, lowering my fists. "I didn't ask for this gig." Great, now I'm a slayer reject, too. Go figure. I punch the bag a few more times. Might as well burn some calories while he's bemoaning my slayer suckiness. "Maybe you chose wrong. Ever think about that? Maybe I'm not really slayer material."

"We don't choose wrong. We have a very precise methodology

for picking our slayers. You just don't see the power you have. You're stubborn and you refuse to learn. And therefore your power will remain dormant. Locked inside of you." He grabs the punching bag so it no longer sways with my hits. "Let's try you with your stake."

He motions over to the bench, where I left the half-carved chunk of wood. I roll my eyes.

"Can't I get a real weapon?" I whine, walking over to the stake and picking it up with some reluctance. "A sword maybe? Or a big two-handed axe like Buffy?"

"By carving this stake, you have embedded it with your slayer essence," Teifert explains, completely ignoring my request for sharp metal objects of death. "Now, it has bonded itself to you and will only work when wielded by your hand. Each stake is unique to its slayer."

"Sort of like the wands in *Harry Potter*?" I can't help but ask.

"When you take this weapon into your hands, you will feel the essence of the tree from which it was taken. You will be filled with the power of that mighty oak. The strength will flow through you and make you one with Mother Earth. Only then will you be able to find your center. And get the job done."

"Huh." I roll the stake around in my palm. "And to think this looks like something you grabbed out in the schoolyard."

"Hold up the stake, Rayne," Teifert commands. "And concentrate on its power."

I sigh, then do what I'm told. Otherwise I'll probably be here all day. I raise the stake above my head and focus my eyes on it.

And then things start to get weird.

As I stare at the stake, the world around me starts to lose focus and the wood starts to take on an almost unearthly glow. I watch in awe as it morphs right before my eyes from a chunk of unpolished wood into a sleek, sharp instrument, smooth as glass. I wave it around, hesitantly at first, then with growing assurance. So cool. So, so cool. I wish you could have seen it.

"Am I making it do that?" I whisper. From the corner of my eye I can see Teifert's nod.

"You are the chosen one. The slayer. As I said, we don't make mistakes."

"Wow, that's pretty amazing." I step forward, toward the punching bag, and then stab the wood into it, with all my might. The stake slides through the tough leather like a knife through butter. Whoa! Now we're talking.

I pull the stake out. It's no longer glowing. I turn to Teifert. "Okay, I believe you now," I say. "Who knew I had all this power in me?"

"Who knew you were going to stab the punching bag?" Teifert grumbles, not looking at all impressed by my feat. He walks over to the bag and examines the hole. "Do you know how expensive these things are to replace?"

"Dude! I've just been given magical superpowers to slay vamps and all you care about is your Visa bill?"

Teifert turns back to me. "So you believe now? That with your stake you have the power to slay vampires?"

"Hell yeah, I believe. Just call me Raynie: Vampire Slayer. Able to kill vampires in a single bound." I wave my stake around again, but it fails to light up this time. I'm probably not concentrating hard enough. Gotta remember that when the zero hour comes around.

"Good. I'd like to have additional training sessions with you, but I'm not sure there's time," Teifert says. "How have your investigations into Maverick been going? Have you learned anything?"

"Well, sort of, though we definitely need more info before some conviction," I say hesitantly. "There seems to be some kind of disease going around. We saw some donors of a high-ranking vampire in the Blood Coven at the bar one night—"

Teifert raises an eyebrow. "We? Are you working with someone? It's highly irregular for a slayer to have a partner."

I roll my eyes. "Uh, what about Buffy? She had that whole Scooby gang on her side and that didn't seem to hurt her odds."

"Repeat after me, Rayne. Buffy. Is. A. TV. Character. She. Is. Not. Real."

Sigh. "Look. If you must know, I'm working with one of Magnus's guys. General Jareth. Don't worry, he's on our side. After all, the vamps want to know what's going down at the Blood Bar as much as we do."

"Jareth, huh?" Teifert says thoughtfully. "I think I remember reading about him. He caused some trouble for Slayer Inc. back in the day."

"Trouble?" Oh, great. Me and my big mouth. What if they suddenly want me to dust Jareth? I could never do that. I wonder if this has something to do with whatever secret Jareth is hiding . . .

"Never mind. It's all in the past, anyhow," Teifert says with a dismissive wave. "So fine, you're working with Jareth. And what have you two found?"

"Okay, like I was saying, one night we saw those two donors of a high-ranking coven guy and the next day those same donors turned up dead. And their vampire, Kristoff, is weak and sick and has lost most of his powers. I mean, it could be unrelated, but . . ."

Teifert scratches his chin. "Interesting," he muses. "Perhaps Maverick is trying a less direct approach to infiltrate the coven."

"What do you mean?"

"What if he were somehow infecting the donors purposefully? So they could bring the disease back to their masters. By weakening the inner core of Magnus's coven, a takeover could more easily be accomplished."

"Wow. That's pretty elaborate."

"These vampires have thousands of years to plot this kind of thing. They can afford to come up with detailed plans because there's no need to rush."

"I guess that's true."

"So what do you plan to do next?"

"Well, Jareth and I took a sample of the donor's blood and he's having it analyzed in the lab now."

"That's something, I suppose. But what we really need is a sample of the virus itself," Teifert says. "You should go down to the Blood Bar and find out where they store these viruses and bring one back to me. Hopefully this way we can develop an antidote before too many vampires are infected and Maverick is able to stage his coup."

"Uh, yeah, sure. That should be easy." I make a face, in case he

can't hear the total sarcasm in my voice. "I'm sure they'll be happy
to let me borrow one, once I show my library card."

"Rayne, you are the slayer. Vampires fear you, not the other way
around. Just bring your stake with you. It gives you your power.
With it, you'll easily be able to defeat anyone who stands in your
way."

"Okay, okay. Stake will be at arm's reach at all times." I tuck the
chunk of wood into the back of my sweatpants. "Just like this, but
with a much classier outfit." Could you imagine me wearing Juicy
Couture down to the Blood Bar?

"Rayne, this is serious business," Teifert scolds. "Do not take your
duties lightly. If Maverick is to take control of the Blood Coven, he
could conceivably unite the vampires against the humans and start a
war. A war that mankind is unlikely to win."

Nice, huh? Talk about putting on the pressure. The fate of the
world lies in my hands. Suddenly I feel very weary and depressed.

TWENTY-THREE

Mike Stevens Must Die

MONDAY, JUNE 11, 4 P.M.

Monday. Did I ever mention how much I hate my school? Well, not the school itself. I've got nothing against the bricks or mortar or climbing ivy. It's the cretins that inhabit it that make me want to slit my wrists on a daily basis.

For one thing, everyone's a clone of everyone else. All the girls with their flat-ironed hair, baby doll T's, and low, low-rise jeans. And the guys—they literally have no idea other clothing stores besides Abercrombie and Fitch even exist.

My friend River and her parents moved away to Boston a year ago. She says there are tons of cool skaters and Goths at her new school. That everyone's open-minded and there aren't really any cliques. Here at Oakridge, we've got nothing but cliques. And certainly no Goths besides me. So I'm the designated freak, basically, and everyone knows it.

It's a lonely life, but it's still better than shopping at American Eagle.

I usually don't care. In fact, if anything, I've always enjoyed being unique. An individual. But today feels different for some reason. Instead of mocking the cheerleaders who stride through the corridors in giggling packs, or the lovebirds who press against the lockers, making out and hoping the teachers won't walk by, or the jocks who "go long," passing the football to one another down the hallways, I notice myself envying them all. They look so blissful. So content in their pathetic, shallow high school existence.

And I, I realize suddenly, am totally and utterly alone. I can put on a brave front, ridicule them, whatever, but at the end of the day I'm the one who's the joke. Because they're happy and I'm not. They're free and I've got the weight of the world on my shoulders. All this time I've thought myself superior to them, but really I'm more pathetic.

As I walk down the hall, I feel the stares of the other students burning into my backside. They're laughing at me. They think I'm a weirdo. A loser. And I hate to say it, but maybe they're right. I mean, my own father doesn't even think I'm worthy of a birthday cake. And he was there at my conception.

Anger churns deep in my gut. I harden my face to match their stares, forcing myself not to cry. Screw them all. I don't need them. I don't need Dad. I don't need anyone.

And then I run into Mike Stevens.

I hate Mike Stevens more than anyone at my school. If I'm the designated freak, he's the designated golden boy. Captain of the varsity football team, even though he's a junior. Student body president. Ash blond hair and sparkling green eyes. And a cocky smile that says he knows he's worshipped by half the school and feels he deserves everything life's dished him.

When we were in elementary school and everyone was like everyone else and there were no cliques, Mike Stevens and I used to play in the mud together at recess. When we were six, he kissed me.

That was a long time ago. We don't bring that up much. Actually, ever. In fact, I'm not sure he even remembers, which is probably a good thing.

These days we'd rather hurl mud at each other than play in it. And today he had the perfect weapon. My hickey.

It's not a hickey, of course. It's a bite mark from a vampire. But that's not something I can convince Mike of, obviously. Sigh. I thought the mark had faded enough to stop wearing a turtleneck, but evidently not.

"Hey, my little Goth princess," Golden Boy says to me after first period, leaning against the row of lockers. I pull out my books and stuff them into my black book bag, trying to ignore him, even though he's positioned himself directly in my line of sight. He's all cargo pants and Patriots jerseyed out as usual. "Who's the lucky guy?"

"Not you, that's for sure," I growl. I am so not in the mood for this today of all days. Not when I already feel so lousy about life, the universe, and everything.

He laughs. "Of course not. I don't do freaks."

"Good. Because I don't do Muggles."

At first I think he may miss the literary reference, but evidently even this illiterate fool has read *Harry Potter*. Those books are just way too popular. I may have to give them up for something more obscure.

"So, witch, which warlock gave you the hickey then?"

"It's not a hickey."

"Oh, really," he says sarcastically. "What, did you burn yourself with a curling iron like Mary Markson seems to do every Monday morning?"

Mary Markson and her boyfriend, Nick, have been going out for eons. They're totally most likely to get married. And she does have a tendency to show up to school with a lot of unsavory neck bruises. She insists she's just clumsy with the curling iron, but since she never has any actual curls to back up the claim, we're all a bit doubtful.

"No. Not a curling iron burn. I got bit by a vampire if you must know."

He rolls his eyes. I knew I was safe to say that. He'd never believe me in a million years. "Ah. So that's your type. I should have guessed."

"No. You shouldn't have guessed. You shouldn't have even noticed. What, are you staring at me from across the halls now? Stalking me?" Ever since I humiliated him in seventh grade (don't ask) he's made it his life's mission to make mine a living hell. Sunny thinks he secretly has a crush on me. Which is just . . . ew.

Mike frowns. Evidently I've struck a nerve. "Please. Your hickey is so big Blind Mr. Bannon the Biology teacher could see it."

"Good. I want the whole world to see the bite of my dark lover."

Jareth is not, of course, my dark lover. Or even my light one. Or any kind of lover, unfortunately. (As much as I might want him to be.) But I can't exactly back down and let Mike win.

"So when do you turn into a vampire then?" the stupid jock queries.

"I'm not going to turn into a vampire, moron. I've just been bitten. I'd have to drink the blood of a vampire to turn into one. Duh. And they don't just let anyone do that. There's a waiting list."

"A waiting list? There's actually enough of you freaks out there for a waiting list?" He bends over, hands on knees, and laughs and laughs.

Grr. Did I mention I hate this guy? I notice a few students have stopped in the hallway, pretending to chat, but really wanting to take in the scene. The Goth girl against the jock boy. It's good reality programming. But I'm just not in the mood.

"Dude, don't you have some cheerleaders to seduce or beer to chug? Some nerd to copy off of? I know your life's lame and all, but certainly you must be able to think of a better way to waste it than talking to me."

He opens his mouth to reply, then I see him glance over at our audience. He seems to decide against what he was originally going to say and instead retorts, "Whatever skank," extra loud, to make sure everyone hears him insult me.

Then he hacks up a loogie and spits on me—ACTUALLY SPITS ON ME—before turning to walk away.

I'm so furious I don't even think. I just drop my books and my bag and run after him, slamming my entire body weight against his retreating back and managing to knock him off balance and onto the floor. My hands take on minds of their own as I punch and slap over and over as he struggles to get out from under me. But he's no match for my super slayer strength. If only I had my stake. I wonder if it works on Muggles.

The fight only lasts a minute or two before Monsieur Dawson, the French teacher, pulls me off of Mike.

"Arrêtez!" he commands. "Allez au bureau du principal!" The guy never speaks English. Which is kind of annoying for those of us who take Spanish. But in this case, even foreign-language-challenged me has a pretty good idea what he's saying.

"It's not my fault. She just jumped me. For no reason. Crazy freak!" Mike says, shooting me daggers.

Angrily I smooth out my skirt and glare back at Mike. Bastard. Now I've got detention and Mom's going to be so pissed at me.

"I'm going to get you for this, you skank freak," Mike adds as Monsieur Dawson drags him away. "Just you wait."

I sigh. I just wish I could somehow turn the guy into a vampire so I could stake him through the heart. Him and my father. The two of them should really die.

TWENTY-FOUR

Parents Just Don't Understand

MONDAY, JUNE 11, 8 P.M.

So of course Mom totally freaks out about my detention. Especially since it was due to fighting. As you can imagine, as a hippie she's very into peace. And it's not just peace in the Middle East—that would at least be understandable. She evidently is advocating peace at Oakridge High as well. Puh-leeze. If only she knew what an obnoxious jerk Mike Stevens is. I try to explain how he spit on me, but she starts spouting something about turning the other cheek. As if I want to get spit on my other cheek next time. Ew!

And the worst part is that she doesn't ground me, she wants to have a "talk." Ugh. I hate talks. I'd much rather be sent to my room without supper and kept there 'til I grow cobwebs. Locked in a tower like Rapunzel would suit me just fine. Just as long as I don't have to talk and share my feelings. (And, uh, grow my hair that long. I have a hard enough time with tangles as it is.)

"You've been acting very angry lately," she says, closing the door to my bedroom and joining me on the bed. I stare at my hands. This is so not fair. So, so not fair. "What's bothering you? Is it your father not showing up for your birthday?" she adds, in that horrible pity voice of hers. Grr. Nothing's worse than the pity voice.

"No," I retort. I knew she'd try that. Try to drag Dad into it.

"I know that must have hurt a lot, sweetie. I'm really sorry about that."

"I'm fine," I retort, anger welling up inside me, bubbling in my stomach, and making me feel sick. I knew we should have never told her about Dad's supposed plans to visit.

Mom frowns. "I don't think so, dear. People who are fine don't get into fights at school."

"They do if they're provoked by asshole football players."

Mom winces a bit at the swearing, but doesn't comment on it. "Are you having problems at school, Rayne?" she asks. "I've noticed your grades are slipping as well. You went from honor roll to C student this year."

"Yeah, well I have stupid teachers." Stupid teachers who always favor the jocks and cheerleaders. Stupid teachers who think just because I dress in black I'm doomed to be a dropout and don't give me the time of day. I'm smarter than all those losers I go to school with.

"What don't you like about them?"

Sigh. "Nothing. They're fine. Forget I said anything." The less I talk, the shorter this will take. I'm supposed to meet up with Spider and I can't leave Spider waiting.

"I don't want to forget you said anything. I want you to tell me what's wrong." Mom reaches over to touch me on the shoulder. I shrug away. I know I'm being unfair, but I can't help it. I know if she touches me, I'll start crying. And that's the last thing I want. "I'm your mother, Rayne. And I care about how you're feeling."

Yeah, right. She thinks she cares, but she isn't ready to hear the truth. That her precious daughter is a weirdo. A freak. A social reject with barely any friends and a father who doesn't even bother to show up to her birthday party.

If only that vampire thing had worked out to begin with. I could be miles away from this miserable existence. I could be living in the lavish underground coven with magic powers and riches beyond belief. My days could have been spent reading the classics. Studying philosophy to enrich my world. No schoolwork. No parents. Nothing but bliss.

Instead, I'm stuck here. In my mundane, horrible existence where no one understands me. Mom will never get it. She's too innocent to understand my depravity. She's too sweet to see the chaos that swirls under my skin. And I'm okay with that, actually. It's better that she live her life in her daisy-strewn optimism than know what a monster she created when she had me.

I think I must take after Dad.

"Rayne, I love you," Mom says, trying one more tactic. I know she'll give up soon and in a weird way this disappoints me.

"I know you do, Mom," I say resignedly.

Mom rises to her feet, her hazel eyes looking a bit watery. I feel terrible for putting her through this. For making her deal with me. Part of me wants to jump up and throw myself in her arms. Let her hold me and comfort me as I cry and tell her how much Dad hurt me by not showing up to my birthday. Take her strength since I have little left of my own.

But I can't find the willpower to get up from the bed. To lose face and admit weakness. So I sit scowling. More angry at myself than at her.

"If you ever want to talk, I'm here," she says. "I mean it."

"Thanks," I mumble, staring at my shoes, barely able to get the word out.

Mom pauses at the door. "I'm supposed to go out tonight, but . . . well, if you'd prefer I stay home, I will."

I look up. "Out?"

Mom's face gets red. "With David."

Great. She's still seeing David. Could my day get any worse? "I don't think you should go out tonight . . . or ever," I mutter. "Not with him."

"Rayne, why? He's really nice. What do you have against him?" Mom lets out a frustrated breath. I can tell she's trying hard to be nice to me still, but at the same time she's ready to wring my neck. "Is it 'cause you feel he's going to replace your father?"

Argh! Does EVERYTHING in my freaking life have to revolve around Dad?

"Do you think I'm stupid?" I yell, scrambling to my feet, absolutely furious that she would even say such a thing. God, I wish that punching bag was here right about now. "Do you really think I'm holding out some kind of inane hope that the guy's gonna suddenly show up at our doorstep and want to be a family again? That's crazy, Mom! Really crazy!"

Mom takes a step backward, her eyes wide. I think she's afraid of me. Great. I've made my own mother afraid of me. I am a loser. Such a loser.

"Then what is it, Rayne? What's wrong with David?"

"There's nothing wrong with him. Nothing except for the fact that he's an evil vampire and I don't want him to kill you."

There. I said it. Let her deal with reality for once. I'm sick of sheltering her from the truth and looking like an idiot. Then again, in hindsight, telling one's mother that she's dating an evil vampire is probably not the best way to keep from looking idiotic.

Mom stares at me, her eyes narrowing and her lips pressed together tightly. She pauses for a moment and then speaks slowly and deliberately. "So you're trying to tell me that I shouldn't date David because he's a vampire."

"An evil vampire. If he was one of the good guys, I'd have no issue with it. In fact, I think it'd be kind of cool."

Realization lights on Mom's face. "Is that what you two were doing the other night with the garlic and the rosary beads?" she asks in a tight voice.

"Well, yes. Actually it was. It was a test. And he failed. Or passed— however you want to look at it. Bottom line, he *is* a vampire, Mom. And I don't think it's wise for you to be dating him because—"

"Rayne, this has gone far enough," Mom interrupts. "You obviously need help. I'm sending you back to Dr. Devlin. In fact, I'm going to see if he has any last-minute openings for tomorrow." She turns and storms out of the room, slamming the door behind her.

I slump back into my bed, tears of frustration springing to my eyes. Great. Just great. Now, in addition to Mom risking her life with Vamp Nerd, I'm going to be sent back to Dr. Devlin, psycho psychiatrist.

Let this be a lesson to all of you. No matter what happens, never tell your mom she's dating an evil vampire. It's just not worth it.

TWENTY-FIVE

I <3 Jareth and I Don't Care What U Think!

DIARY ENTRY, TUESDAY, JUNE 12, 8 P.M.

Wow. So much has happened since I last wrote. Where to begin? I doubt I can write this as one big diary entry—it'd take me a week to type. I guess I can split it up into chapters. Not like anyone's reading this anymore. Sigh. I kind of miss my blog. It feels lonely writing to myself . . .

Luckily Dr. Devlin is booked up for about a month so I don't have to waste the evening talking to him about the symbolism of my dreams or whatever. After detention I go straight home and go straight to my room, yelling down that I'm not interested in any dinner before slamming my door and blasting Snow Patrol from my stereo.

I turn off the light and lie on my bed, staring up at the ceiling. When Sunny and I were little we pasted glow-in-the-dark stars up there and there are still a few left, struggling to glow in their old age. It's kind of comforting to look at them. To remember a more innocent time.

I let my mind wander over the past week. The excitement of Dad coming. The disappointment of Dad not coming. The fight with

Mike Stevens. The fight with Mom. The finding out that I have a destiny. The finding out that I have to share that destiny with a vampire who hates me. The realization that the vampire maybe isn't so bad.

I wonder where Jareth is. I haven't seen him since Wednesday night. He told me he'd call me when the results of the donor's blood came back from the lab, but it's already Tuesday and I haven't heard from him. Maybe he decided he'd be better off working alone. That he didn't need me.

The thought brings on the tears again. Jeez. I feel like I've cried more in the last three days than I have the rest of my life combined.

I'm such an idiot. To think Jareth might actually like me. That he might have been jealous when he saw me dancing with that other vamp. That he might have made up that excuse to kiss me in the broom closet just so he could do it. That there might be some kind of future with him.

Dumb, Rayne. Truly dumb.

Of course he doesn't want a future with me. What do I have to offer? Nothing. Absolutely nothing. My own father isn't interested in a future with me. Why should Jareth be?

Bleh.

I force myself to zone out to Snow Patrol, concentrating on the deep, melodious sounds and trying to block out the overwhelming sadness that's threatening to take me. A few minutes later I'm so into the music that I almost don't hear the knock on my door.

"Rayne?"

Mom. Great. I wonder if she's here to yell or to attempt comfort. I wonder which would be more annoying.

"Go away!" I cry, my voice sounding a bit wobbly. I hope she can't tell I've been crying. I don't want to give her the satisfaction.

"That's really nice, Rayne, thanks," she retorts. "And I'll be happy to. I just thought you might like to know there's a boy here to see you."

I raise my head and look over at the closed bedroom door. A boy? What boy would visit me? "Who is it?" I ask, against my better judgment.

"I've never seen him before," Mom says. "He says his name is Jareth. Tall, skinny. A bit on the pasty side? Dressed all in black, just how you like 'em," she adds, and I can hear a small smile in her voice. "Just hope he's not an evil vampire."

I wince a bit at the dig, but know she's doing her best to try to lighten things up between us. "Nah, he's not," I say with all the false bravado I can muster. "He's one of the good guys."

Mom laughs. "So I should send him up then?" she asks and I can hear the relief in her voice after what she thinks is my attempt at humor.

But no time for analyzing. Jareth is here. Here in my house. Soon to be here in my bedroom. Gah! I'm so unprepared. I glance around the room, realizing I have clothes strewn everywhere and that I'm wearing plaid flannel pants and a T-shirt.

"Rayne?"

"Uh, yeah, sure," I say, frantically grabbing discarded laundry and tossing it in the hamper. I'd normally ask if she could stall him for a moment or two, but I don't want her asking a thousand-year-old vampire about where he goes to high school.

I shed my clothes faster than Superman in a phone booth, tossing on a black-and-white plaid skirt and a Smiths concert T-shirt, then run over to the mirror.

Ugh. Even with the change of clothes I'm not looking so hot. My eyes are completely bloodshot from crying and my makeup's all smeared. I run my index finger under my eyes to try to get rid of the excess black. Then I apply more of my bloodred lipstick. Maybe that'll detract from the eyes.

A knock on the door causes my heart to jump in my throat. Why am I so nervous? It's just Jareth. We've been working together for nearly a week now. It's all business. And that one kiss? Well, it didn't mean anything. So there's absolutely no reason to freak.

Another knock. This one louder.

"Come in," I say, rushing back to my computer, as if I've been sitting there the whole time. No need for him to know he was worth reapplying lip gloss for.

He opens the door and steps over the threshold into my room. I've had guys in here before. Mom's cool with it as long as we keep the door open. But this seems different somehow. More dangerous. And since Jareth doesn't know the door rule, he shuts it behind him before walking over and sitting down on the bed. My bed. Gah! Jareth the hottest vampire ever is sitting on MY bed. I wish I had a web cam so I could have recorded the momentous event.

"So the blood test has come back from the lab," he says, launching right into business. "And it's positive."

Gulp. Good thing he shut the door. If Mom heard the words "blood test" and "positive" in the same sentence she'd be carting me away to the clinic before I could explain we were talking vampires, not HIV.

I turn around in my chair to face him. "Positive for . . . ?"

"Wait a moment." Jareth studies me with his intense green eyes. "Have you been crying?"

I scowl. Great. I should have kept my back turned. "No. Of course not. I'm not your typical crying type of girl. Now, tell me about the donor's blood."

Jareth frowns. "Your eyes look red."

"Allergies."

"And your makeup's smudged."

"I dig the Taylor Momsen look, what can I say?"

Jareth shakes his head. He's so not buying any of this. "What's wrong, Rayne? What happened?"

"Nothing."

"You're lying." He gets up from the bed and walks over to me, kneeling down in front of my chair, his earnest eyes searching my face. I turn my head to look back at the computer, mostly because his concerned expression has me this close to bursting into tears again.

"I'm not."

"Tell me what happened. Did someone hurt you?" He takes my hand in his and squeezes it lightly, his thumb caressing my palm. "You can tell me. It's okay."

And that, my friends, is the point that the dam breaks and the tears cascade down like Niagara Falls. How embarrassing. How pathetic. I can't believe I'm so weak. So vulnerable. He's going to think I'm the biggest loser on the planet. Maybe in the entire universe. If there was any chance he was at all interested in me, it's so gone now. I'm just another whiny, teary-faced human girl.

Jareth reaches up and swipes a tear away with his thumb. His touch is cool against my burning cheeks. "Tell me," he says in the most gentle voice you could imagine.

"Okay," I agree, realizing at this point I've got nothing to lose. I close my eyes resignedly and try to find my voice. I open my mouth to tell him the story of Mike Stevens, but something completely different comes out. Something I hadn't meant to share with anyone, let alone him.

"You know how I told you about my dad? How he left us four years ago to go 'find himself?'"

"Yes. Of course."

"Well, he's evidently still lost. I thought he was coming home for my birthday. Sunny and I turned seventeen three days ago and he sent us an e-mail saying he was going to come home to celebrate with us." I swallow hard. "It's so dumb, but . . ."

"But what?"

"I was so excited. My dad's awesome. Or he used to be anyway. And I haven't seen him in so long. I guess I thought maybe if he came . . . if he saw us again. Maybe he'd want to . . . I don't know . . ." I laugh bitterly. "Stick around or something. Or at least plan more regular visits. Sounds so stupid now that I think about it."

Jareth shakes his head. "Not stupid at all," he says. "It makes perfect sense to me."

"Anyway, it doesn't matter. He never showed. He was supposed to bring the cake, too." I laugh bitterly. "We ended up having a birthday party with no cake. Pretty lame, huh?"

"Did he call to tell you why? Did something happen to prevent him from making it?"

"No. I waited up 'til like one A.M., hoping he'd walk through the door. So idiotic." My voice breaks again and I'm sobbing like crazy now. Can we say LOSER? "Sunny e-mailed him the next day. Turns out some other thing came up and he says he forgot to tell us."

"Other thing?"

"Evidently he's got a new wife. And she has kids. One of them had some school play or something . . ." I shrug. "Why go hang with the old family, I guess, when you've got a whole new one?"

Without warning, Jareth grabs me and pulls me into a hug. At first I'm not sure about this, but his arms feel so right, wrapped around me. His hands so good, stroking my back. I give in, burying my head in his shoulder and sobbing my eyes out. Trying to take the strength he is offering me. I'm scared to death at the perfect comfort I receive, but too relieved to pull away.

"I'm so sorry, Raynie," he whispers, smoothing my hair with his hands. "That's a lousy thing to do. He doesn't deserve you as a daughter."

"I wish I could just hate him," I cry, hoping my nose isn't all running on Jareth's black shirt. "But I can't. I still love him. I still miss him. No matter what he does, he's still my dad."

"It's hard when people you love let you down."

"Sometimes I think that's why I don't have any close friends," I say, now in full-on babble mode. I can't believe I'm telling him all this. But his arms feel warm and his touch is comforting. I haven't felt so safe in eons. "I mean, everyone thinks it's 'cause I'm some tough punk-rock chick who doesn't need anyone. But, in reality, I think it's 'cause I'm scared to death. That if I get close to someone, they'll just leave."

"I know the feeling," Jareth says, almost thoughtfully. "More than you can know."

"Oh?" Excitement builds inside me, competing with my sadness. He's on the verge of spilling the Deep Dark Secret, I can tell.

He pulls his head away. "Some other time," he says, pressing his lips against my forehead and giving me a soft kiss.

I stick out my lower lip in a mock pout. "Oh, fine."

He laughs. "I promise."

"I'll hold you to that."

"Don't worry," he says, reaching over to my nightstand and grabbing me a tissue. He hands it to me and I wipe my eyes and nose. "Unlike some people, I keep my promises. Always and forever."

He reaches up and brushes a strand of hair out of my eyes and studies my face. "You're really beautiful," he says. "You know that?"

I screw up my face. "Yeah, yeah." But secretly I'm pleased.

"No. I'm serious." His fingers trail down the side of my face, his nails lightly scraping at my cheekbone. Feels so good. I close my eyes.

And then he kisses me. Yes, the beautiful vampire, the dark general, the one who never gets close to anyone, leans in and presses his lips against mine.

This kiss is different than the one in the closet. This kiss is soft. Gentle. Light. Like a butterfly's wing whisking my lips. I know it sounds weird, but it's almost like a worshipful caress. I sigh a bit as tingly sensations burst from my fingers, my toes—all over my body. I kiss him back, hesitantly at first and then with more assurance. Jareth is a master kisser, nothing like the awkward fumbling boys I've dated in the past. The ones more interested in the technical workings of my bra. The ones who see the mouth only as an obligatory precursor to getting me to take off my clothes. But Jareth seems content just to kiss me. To explore my mouth with his own. His tongue telling a thousand stories, mine delighting in a thousand tastes.

I wonder what he's thinking as he kisses me. Does he have feelings for me? Is this something he's been hoping will happen? Or is this just a gesture meant to cheer me up, to distract me from my pain? Sadly, I have no real clue what this immortal creature of the night actually feels for me and that scares me to death.

Stop thinking so much, Rayne, I tell myself. *You've got a hot guy making out with you in your bedroom. Just go with it.*

But I can't. Not this time. Because I'm starting to develop a deep tenderness for this vampire. And that's pretty damn terrifying. After all, he's told me a dozen times that he doesn't get close to anyone. He doesn't even have donors, for goodness' sake. He never wants a blood mate. He likes being alone. If I fall for him, I'm going to fall alone. And when I hit rock bottom, it's going to hurt like crazy. In fact, I'm not sure I'd even be able to survive. To claw my way up from such heartbreak.

And so, as much as it sucks, I force myself to pull away. He stares at me dully for a moment, as if in a daze, then frowns. "What's wrong?" he asks in a wounded voice that breaks my heart.

"Nothing," I say briskly, scrambling to my feet. I cross my arms over my chest. "So let's get back to business."

"But—" The hurt on his face is unmistakable and I feel like a monster. Still, even though he's a vampire, he's also a guy. And guys can get like that after they've been denied sex. In fact, I'd be willing to bet he doesn't care one lick about me as a person. He just wants to jump me. Just like everyone else. And I'm so not interested.

"You said you got the blood test results back. What did you learn?"

He sighs deeply and then rises to his feet, running a hand through his dirty blond hair. He stares into the mirror. Unlike in the movies and TV shows, vamps DO have reflections and his, I notice, is not one of a happy vampire. But that can't be helped, I guess.

I feel bad, but I tell myself that in the long run, it's better this way. After all, this can't go anywhere. It can't become anything. So just rip off the Band-Aid and move on to the next scene.

"Well, that's the strange thing," he says at last, evidently resigning himself to the fact that he's not getting any more nookie from this chick. "It's definitely contaminated with some kind of blood-borne virus, but we're not exactly sure what. Whatever it is, our scientists believe it's the same virus that's affected Kristoff. Obviously vampires don't die like humans, but somehow the virus has been able to weaken him and take away his powers."

"How is Kristoff, anyway?"

"About the same. Not sick. Not exactly. Just weak. And powerless. It's the strangest thing."

"Poor guy."

"Indeed. And he's not the only one. Several of the coven's top leaders have come down with a very similar illness. And all their donors are dead."

"Wow. That's terrible. So do you think it's being spread through the donors? Remember, we saw Kristoff's donors at the Blood Bar. Could it be possible that Maverick is behind this?"

"I do. In fact, I'd say it's quite probable," Jareth says, nodding.

"It's my theory that this is the way Maverick hopes to overthrow Magnus's rule. By crippling Magnus's strong supporters, he can weaken his command, and then stage a coup."

"Actually, that's exactly what the Slayer Inc. guy, Teifert, says," I tell him. "He suggested we go back to the Blood Bar and see if we can find a sample of the original virus itself. Maybe they have a room where they store it all. Maybe they even have some kind of antidote there." I jump up from my seat, eager to be out of these closed quarters, lest I do something stupid like jump his vampire bones again. "We should go now. Time is a-wasting."

Jareth shakes his head. "I should go now. Not we. You will stay home."

"What? No way! I'm so not staying home."

"This could be dangerous."

"But I'm Raynie the Vampire Slayer," I say, grabbing the stake off my computer table and raising it in the air.

Jareth chuckles. "Oh, yes. I forgot. Very scary."

"Come on," I whine. "Please? It's, like, my destiny and stuff, remember? Just let me come. I need an adventure. I can't keep sitting around moping in my room."

"Okay, fine. But you have to listen to me. Do as I say. No heroics here," he insists. "You may have a stake, but I'd bet my fangs you don't know how to use it."

"Not true. I got some Slayer Training this weekend. I'm now the stake mastah!"

"Ah. Impressive." Jareth smiles. "Can't wait to see you in action."

"So should we head over now?"

"Hmm." Jareth looks at his watch. "Actually it's only eight. The Blood Bar will be open 'til two A.M. and we want to hit them closer to closing time."

"Oh, okay." A bit disappointed, I set the stake back down on the desk. So much for immediate distraction. "Uh, I guess just come pick me up when you're ready to leave?" Hopefully by then Mom will be in bed. I doubt she'd be cool with me leaving the house at one thirty on a school night.

"Actually, I was wondering if you'd like to . . . do something with me first," Jareth says, sounding a bit shy all of a sudden.

I look up, surprised. "Uh, what?"

"Go dancing."

"Dancing? Now?" Wow. That is so not what I expected him to say. Though I don't know what I did expect. A shiver of delight makes its way up my backbone. Dancing. With Jareth. Mmm.

Jareth shrugs. "Yes. Why not?"

Bleh. I know I should say no. Keep ripping off the Band-Aid. Not put myself in a position where the two of us could easily hook up. Dancing is powerful and dangerous and if I want to stay at arm's length it's the last thing I should agree to.

"I don't know. No reason, I guess. It's just—" *Just that I'm not strong enough not to melt when you take me into your arms.*

"Remember what we talked about at Club Fang the other night? About losing oneself in the music? Seeking peace inside the dance?" He smiles at me. "I think someone's in need of a little of that right about now."

Oh. So that's what he means. An unwarranted disappointment floats through me. Bleh. I should have known. He has no secret agenda to hook up with me. This is just a simple cheer-up technique to get my mind back on the job. Well, that's better, I suppose. Safer, at least. And something I can justify doing.

He's still looking at me expectantly and I realize that I haven't given him a verbal answer. "I'd love to," I reply.

He takes my hand and pulls me to my feet, then ushers me to my bedroom door, hand brushing against the small of my back. Gah. His touch really should be illegal. Almost makes me want to skip the dance club and go straight for the bed. Not that that would be a good idea. And besides, I kind of like this almost old-fashioned chivalrous thing he's got going on. So unlike guys my age, who are just interested in getting it on with the Goth freak.

Besides, we've already established that he's just being nice. He probably feels sorry for me and my pathetic little lost-daddy's-girl thing. Ugh.

We tell Mom we're going out and she looks so pleased that I've actually left my bedroom I bet if I told her we were off to smoke crack and get lap dances she would have waved and said, "Have a good time. Just be back by curfew."

We jump in Jareth's BMW and speed off to Club Fang. He turns the music up extra loud, just the way I like it, and I zone out to the crooning sounds of Morrissey. It's nice and comfortable this way. No awkward convo and strained silences. He must sense that I've already shared way more than I ever share and am currently all talked out.

Club Fang is hopping when we get there. After paying the bouncer the cover charge, we walk inside and are enveloped by darkness, illuminated only by irregular flashing strobe lights and obscured by machine-created fog. The bass is up, the music is dark and enchanting, and I'm in Heaven already.

Jareth grabs my hand and together we weave through the crowd of sweaty gothed-out dancers until we get to the center of the room. Then he pulls me close and together we start swaying to the music.

At first I'm thinking, "Danger, danger!" and that I should not be here. With him. Falling deeper and deeper for a guy who doesn't want me for anything more than friendship. But as the music takes me, my reservations start melting away. I'm here. I'm in his arms. I might as well accept things. Take them for what they are and enjoy the moment. Who knows when something so blissful will come around again.

As we dance, my troubles seem more and more trivial. I mean, so what if my dad didn't show up for my birthday? It's not like he's a regular at any other family events. We've been fine without him for the last four years and we'll be fine without him for the next four. And so what if Mike Stevens is a huge dick with an attitude? High school will be the best years of his life. Soon he'll be strapped with five kids, a job that gives him ulcers, and a wife who doesn't understand him.

None of it matters in the long run. Just the beat. The tribal sounds that stir something primitive inside of me. At this very moment there is no past. No future. Just a vampire's arms wrapped around me, his hot body pressed against mine. Heaven.

Jareth seems lost in it, too. His eyes are closed as he sways against me. I study his face as the multicolored lights dance across it, creating alternating shadows and light. I wonder again what he's hiding. What turmoil and hurt lie under his calm exterior. What has made him so angry? What has made him so like me?

Because he is like me, I realize. He hides his torment, conceals his pain, until he can't anymore and then it explodes and he comes across as a nasty, angry person. But he's not really like that. Not inside.

The beat slows and so does our dance. Jareth's eyes open, almond-shaped emeralds that practically glow in the dark. I know I keep harping on them, but I've just never seen such beautiful eyes before and I'm sure I never will again. He reaches down and brushes a lock of hair away from my sweaty forehead.

"How are you?" he asks. And the way he says it makes me believe that he actually cares about the answer.

"Better," I say, smiling up at him. "Much better, actually."

"Sometimes it's good to talk," he says. "But other times you'd rather just lose your mind."

I nod, amazed at how his thoughts totally parallel mine. He really is the perfect guy in so many ways.

Screw it. I might as well face the facts: I'm in love. And there's nothing I can do about it.

TWENTY-SIX

TUESDAY, JUNE 12, 10 P.M.

We park down the street from the Blood Bar and go inside separately. Jareth goes through the employee entrance and I go through the front door.

"Hey, Shaniqua," Francis greets, smiling at me as I approach. "Thought I'd finally seen the last of you."

"Can't scare me away that easily, Frannie," I shoot back with a grin of my own.

"Luckily for me or I'd miss out on all this witty banter."

"Didn't I tell you that I'd grow on you? You should always listen to me. Always."

"Hey. I do. Heck, if you told me to jump, girl, I'd only have to ask how high."

We laugh for moment. Then I turn to more serious business. "So," I lower my voice, "did you find your blood mate?"

His smile dips into a frown. "Yes," he says, shoving his hands in his jean pockets. "It's the weirdest thing. She's evidently been inflicted with some sort of horrible virus. I mean, she's really sick. She can barely sit up. And worst of all, I think she's lost all her vampiric powers. Of course, she's convinced herself that once she's better she'll get them back, but honestly I'm not so sure."

Wow. Another vampire with ties to the Blood Bar who has come down with the virus. There's definitely something rotten in Denmark.

"No one seems to know what's wrong with her. The scary part is, she's not the only sick one. A lot of her fellow biters have been coming down with it. One day they're at work, sucking away like nothing's wrong, the next they're gone, replaced by some vampire we've never seen before. I've tracked a few of the missing vamps down and everyone seems to have contracted the same sickness."

"Have you talked to management?"

"We've tried, but they've refused to speak with our union reps. They say nothing's wrong and that they don't want us to panic the others with our 'delusions.'" Francis rubs his bald head with the back of his hand. "Honestly, I don't know what to do at this point."

I'm not quite sure what to do myself. This is all becoming far too clear, but I'm not sure who I should trust. Would Francis help me? After all, his blood mate has been affected, and he seems to love her an awful lot. But would he go against his employer? Risk his job and life? And what if he doesn't believe me? What if he grabs his Nextel and calls Maverick to report me? I might be able to get away, but Jareth is still inside.

At least I'm beginning to understand what's going on. The biters are evidently given the virus, unaware. Then, they unwittingly pass it off to the donors, who in turn pass it to their employers. The real targets are obviously the higher-up vampires in Magnus's circle. Like Kristoff. People who keep things running at the coven. We're extremely lucky, I realize, that Jareth gets his blood by mail order and doesn't keep donors himself. Otherwise, I'm sure he'd have been targeted as well.

I make my decision, deciding to trust Francis. After all, he's been personally affected by this dastardly plot. And the people getting sick are his friends and coworkers.

"Okay, Frannie, listen up. Here's the deal. In reality, I'm not your typical Blood Bar patron. I've actually been sent here, undercover." I stop before mentioning who actually sent me. The idea that I'm the Vampire Slayer should probably be left as a need-to-know.

His eyes widen. "Undercover?"

"You know the Blood Coven, formerly run by Lucifent and now run by Magnus?"

"Of course," Francis says. "Everyone knows about the coven. My blood mate has been on a waiting list to join for years. I tried to tell her that they don't take people like us, but she never gives up hope."

Ugh. Vampire segregation? Is Magnus's coven actually an elitist op? I so need to talk to him about that when this is all done. That's so not cool that he leaves people out.

"Our boss, Maverick, the guy who owns the Blood Bar, is a member," Francis adds. "In fact, from what he says, I take it he's next in line for the throne or something." The vampire snorts. "The guy's such an arrogant jerk. Who knows if that's true or not."

"Francis, listen to me carefully," I interject. "Magnus, Master of the Blood Coven, believes that Maverick may be staging a takeover. He wants to be in charge. And since he doesn't have enough vamp power to start an outright war, instead we believe he's created some kind of virus. The virus is injected into the high-ranking coven members' donors and then the donors pass it along to their vampires. All of Magnus's loyal subjects become sick and weak. Maybe even Magnus himself. Then Maverick moves in and takes over."

Francis stares at me. "That seems a bit complicated."

"But don't you see? It could totally work. Is already working, actually. Your friends aren't the only ones who are sick. Several coven bigwigs have also come down with the disease."

"But why are my coworkers being infected? They're not even members of the Blood Coven."

"They're the innocents, being used by Maverick to advance his personal gain," I say. "He probably injects them somehow so they'll pass the disease off to the donors." I bite my lower lip, thinking. "But how do they infect the biters, I wonder. Has anything been different lately, Francis?"

He shrugs. "I don't think so."

"Think harder. Some change in routine? Some new policy or procedure?"

I can see the idea lightbulb flash over his head. "The vitamin injections," he murmers.

"What?"

"A few weeks ago some of the biters, including Dana, were told they were going to start getting weekly vitamin shots. To keep healthy. We thought it was a bit strange. After all, vampires don't usually get sick." Francis squeezes his large hands into fists. "That bastard!" he growls. "He infected her! Why, I should go down there and just kill him. Right here, right now."

I shake my head. "Bad idea, Frannie. You'd just get overpowered by the others. And we don't know who we can trust at this point. Some of the employees must be in on this, or else it couldn't be running so smoothly."

"Right. Of course, you're right." He sighs. "So what can we do? I want to help in any way I can."

"Okay, good," I say, relieved to have him on board. "I have a vampire working with me who's been posing as an employee. He's already inside," I explain. "Can you help us get down into the restricted areas of the Blood Bar? We need to find out where they're keeping the virus so we can bring a sample back to our labs for analysis. Our scientists believe if they have a vial of the stuff, they may be able to create an antidote."

"And if your coven creates the antidote, will you share it with us?" Francis asks. "Those of us who aren't members?"

"Of course," I say, hoping that's true. Well, I'll make sure it is. No vamp discrimination in my book. "There will be enough vaccine for anyone who needs it."

"You're a good person, you know that?" Francis asks. "I'm glad I let you in that first day."

"As if you could resist me." I grin. "Now tell me what you think we should do."

TWENTY-SEVEN

The Not-So-Great Virus Heist

TUESDAY, JUNE 12, 10 P.M. (CONTINUED)

Francis proves to be the best hookup ever. I doubt we could have done any of this without him. First, he sends me inside and I request Jareth as my biter. Once Jareth and I are together in our room, we wait. Francis shows up a moment later, costumes in hand.

"Maverick actually owns this whole block," he explains. "And so there's a huge sprawling basement under this building. Most of the areas are restricted, but I always see the employees who work down there dressed in these." He holds out the clothes. White scrubs, complete with surgical masks.

"Cool. Where did you get them?" I ask.

He laughs. "I, uh, borrowed them from some employees I thought needed a little nap. So you'd better do this quick, before they wake up and figure out how to get themselves untied and out of the linen closet."

"Wow, very nice, Frannie." I hold up one of the outfits. "Now we'll fit right in. Thanks so much."

"Anything to help Dana," he says with a sheepish shrug. But I can tell he's pleased by the compliment. "Let me know if I can do something else."

"No. This is great," Jareth says, slipping the shirt over his head. "You'd better get back to the door before anyone becomes suspicious. Rayne and I can take it from here."

"Okay," he says. "The stairs to the basement are at the far end of the hallway. The employees were nice enough to leave their keycards in the pockets of those uniforms." He grins. "Good luck."

He exits the room and we scramble to don our scrubs and masks. Once outfitted, we nod to one another. This is it.

We find the staircase easily and swipe our keycards, then head downstairs. Francis wasn't kidding. The underground is huge, full of windy corridors and closed doors. The dim fluorescent lighting and low ceilings don't make it any more comforting either.

We try a few doors with our keycards, and at first none seem to work. But there are so many doors, I guess it'll take a while to find the right one. Hopefully no one will catch us randomly trying locks. Might seem a bit suspicious.

But luck is with us. Jareth points at an employee dressed just like us, exiting a door at the far end of the corridor. I nod. Together, we casually walk down the hall, keeping our steps at a normal pace, until we reach the door.

This time, the keycards work and the door swings silently open.

We step into the room and my mouth drops open in shock. The place is like a regular laboratory, with Bunsen burners burning, test tubes bubbling, the works. Whatever Maverick's got planned, it's a full-scale operation. He's got a couple employee vamps in the back, dressed as we are with face masks and scrubs, mixing some kind of multicolored powders together. They turn and acknowledge us, then turn back to their work. Phew. The disguises work. Thank you, Francis.

Jareth beckons me over to the left wall, taken up by the hugest refrigerators I've ever seen. He wraps his hand around the door handle and pulls one open. Puffy white freezer smoke billows out.

Inside there are rows upon rows upon rows upon rows of tiny medicine bottles. Like the kind you stick syringes into. Each bottle is labeled with an "M" which I suppose is for Maverick. Or maybe Murder and Mayhem. Or heck, it could stand for Mickey Mouse for all I know. But what was I expecting? A vial with a warning label? *Do not consume this product if you are a vampire or a human who lets vampires snack on them.*

"Let's take two of the vials," Jareth suggests in a low voice. "We'll bring them back to our lab for testing. To see if they match up with what the donors were infected with."

I nod and reach for one of the vials.

"Wait!" Jareth warns, but he's too late. The room suddenly explodes with sirens and multicolored flashing lights.

Uh, oh. Not good.

"Damn it!" Jareth cries. "You must have tripped some alarm." He glances anxiously around the room. The two employees in the back are staring at us. I can't see their expressions under the masks, but I'm thinking the looks aren't of friendly disinterest anymore.

"What do we do?" I hiss, my heart pounding like crazy in my chest. They didn't cover this in Slayer 101.

Jareth pushes me forward. "Run!" he cries. "And don't stop until you're free and clear of this place." He grabs two vials and pushes them into my hand. "Bring these directly to Magnus. Do not stop, whatever you do."

"But what about you?" I cry, realizing he's planning on going all heroic on me and not being sure I want him to. What if he gets hurt? Captured? Killed, even?

Jareth glances over at the two employees, who are making long strides in our direction.

"I'll distract them. Head them off. Hurry!"

"But what if they—"

"For hell's sake, Rayne, for once in your life just do something without arguing!"

And so I do. I dash down the corridor, weaving through the maze of passages, trying to remember which one leads to the stairs. All around me the lights are still flashing, the sirens still wailing. I hope Jareth is okay. What will they do to him if they catch him? What if they inject him with the virus? What if he gets sick? It'll all be my fault for setting off the alarm.

Suddenly I slam face first into a solid wall. A solid wall of flesh, to be more precise. I look up, swallowing hard as my eyes focus on the man standing in front of me. I'd recognize that face anywhere. Those hypnotic, icy eyes. That cruel stare.

Maverick.

"Uh, I'm, well, I work, uh, lost . . ." Panic has effectively robbed me of coherent sentence-forming abilities. Not that for one moment I think even if I could suddenly speak as eloquently as Bono I'd have any better chance of escaping with my life.

Because I'm caught. By the big baddie himself.

But wait! I'm the Vampire Slayer. I can kill him, right? I reach behind me and whip out my stake. The normally dull piece of wood suddenly erupts in a fiery light as I wave it into the air, just like what happened in the gym at school. w00t!

"Don't come any closer," I say in my most menacing tone, wielding the stake like a sword, ready to swing and stab.

Yeah, baby! Who's scary now!?

TWENTY-EIGHT

Maverick Is a Meanie

TUESDAY, JUNE 12, 10:30 P.M.

Sadly, my victory dance is short-lived. Mainly because Maverick refuses to look all scared and worried at the sight of the glowy stake. Even more so when he starts laughing instead of shaking in his boots. Damn it, what does a slayer chick have to do to get a little respect around here?

"Um, you know, I'll kill you," I add, in case he doesn't get the message. Maybe he doesn't understand. When I show up, he should run. "I'm Raynie the Vampire Slayer."

This time, to my utter annoyance, his laughter goes from a small chuckle to a big rolling belly laugh. He raises his arm and suddenly the stake goes flying out of my hand and right into his. He catches it with ease and it stops doing the glowy thing and becomes just another piece of half-carved wood. He tosses it over his shoulder and it clatters to the ground behind him.

Great. Well, so much for that idea. Now what?

They say when you're in this kind of situation, your body gears up for one of two things: fight or flight. Well, without my magical stick, I figure I'll be a pretty pathetic fighter, so I choose option B and turn tail.

Unfortunately, Maverick must have summoned some additional Vin Diesel–looking guards while I was waving my useless stake around and so when I turn, I turn right into them. They grab me and drag me, kicking and screaming, down the hallway and into a small, windowless room, complete with cobwebs and shackles. It screams medieval dungeon and you Goths would love it. Heck, I would have loved it, if I was not pretty convinced that the room was to be my death chamber.

I wonder if Jareth got out. Maybe he did. Maybe he can get help from the coven.

Maverick watches as his men push me into a wooden chair and then chain me to the wall. They're not gentle and the shackles pinch my wrists. Not that I'm much worried about bruising at this point. As long as my heart's still beating, I'm ahead of the game.

"You'll never get away with this," I shout, mainly because that's what you always hear people shouting in the movies when they're in an impossible situation like this. In the back of my mind, of course, I realize that more than likely he *is* going to get away with this. With all of this. In real life the bad guys do live happily ever after. If you don't believe me, take a look at my dad.

"And what, pray tell, do you think I will not get away with?" Maverick asks, folding his thin arms across his chest. He's wearing black leather pants, a vinyl fetish vest, and a velvet cape. A total *Glamour* "don't," let me tell you.

"Poisoning Magnus's people with your stupid blood-borne virus," I say. "We're totally on to you and know what you're doing. And we're going to stop you. Maybe not me specifically, but I am one of many."

"I see," Maverick says, stroking his goatee with his index finger and thumb. "Do you, by chance, know Rachel and Charity?"

At first I have no idea who he's talking about, then something reminds me. "Magnus's donors?" Fear grips my heart as I wait for what he's going to say next.

Maverick smiles a stereotypical evil villain smile. "Yes. Magnus's donors. Charming girls. We had them as our guests tonight at the Blood Bar."

"Why would they come to the Blood Bar?" I ask, trying to puzzle out the last piece. How come all these donors, who already get bitten on a daily basis, are coming to the bar of their own free will? Why would they need to get sucked?

"Easy. Because they're stupid vampire wannabes, the lot of them," Maverick explains. "We forged some blood mate invitations from the coven. They think they're coming here to finally achieve their lifelong dream. To become vampires."

Ah. Pretty clever, though, of course, maniacally evil.

"And you poison them instead. And then send them back to poison their own vampires. You evil bastard."

"You shouldn't keep dishing out these delectable compliments, my dear," Maverick says with a grin. "But, yes, the donors, including Rachel and Charity tonight, have all been poisoned. And as soon as Magnus indulges in his nightly meal, he will be poisoned, too. In a few days he will lose all his powers and thus be unable to run the coven."

"But why? What do you have against Magnus?"

Maverick shrugs. "Nothing, really. Except he's got my job."

"That's BS. It's his job. He's Lucifent's first sire."

"Sure, that's the nonsense he goes around spouting," Maverick says, squeezing his black fingernailed hands into fists. "But it's not true. I was Lucifent's first. But he disowned me back in the nineteenth century because of a minor unpleasantness."

I can't even begin to imagine what unpleasantness he's talking about, or just how minor it really was. But now I do get why Maverick is so out for Magnus.

"So if you're all hell-bent on revenge, why not just go attack Magnus personally? This blood virus thing is a bit on the overly elaborate side, don't you think?"

"I had to create something that would weaken all of Magnus's forces, not just him. If I just killed him, some other annoying leader would step into his place. Like that weepy little moron Jareth or something."

Jareth. Even the name conjures up a small amount of hope inside of me. If he'd made it out alive he could go get help. Get the army to come and rescue me. I could live to fail at slaying another day.

"This way I will have slowly destroyed all his followers from within, before any of those idiots know what hit them. The Blood Coven will be in code red and I'll step in to guide them to a better future."

"And then I'll slay you," I say, trying to keep up the brave front.

He shakes his head. "No. You won't, because you will be dead."

Before I'm quite sure what's happening, he's on me, having crossed the room in a nanosecond, so fast my eyes can't follow. He's close, pressing his body against mine, his sour breath making me turn up my nose. (Maybe the movie WAS right about horrid breath being a sign of a vamp.) He pushes my head to the side, exposing my neck, and leans in, his fangs digging into my sensitive skin.

I cry in anguish as the pain shoots like lightning through my veins, burning with unquenchable fire. It's like nothing I've ever felt. I grit my teeth and try desperately to remember Jareth's bite—the sweetness, the ecstasy—but all I can feel now is the scorching heat, like it's boiling my blood. I swallow hard, trying with all my might not to cry. I don't want him to see that he has won. Even though I'm pretty sure he already knows.

At least it doesn't last long. He wrenches his fangs out of me and I can feel warm blood seeping down my neck. It's gushing out and my hands are tied, so I can't put any pressure on it to stop it. For a moment, I wonder if I'll bleed to death.

Maverick licks his crimson-stained lips. "I've always wondered what a slayer tastes like. A lot sweeter than I expected." He pulls a vial out of his pocket and screws off the eyedropper cap. Squeezing a small amount of the vial's liquid into the dropper, he walks back over to me.

When I realize what he's about to do, I try to struggle, make my neck as difficult to reach as possible. But being chained, I don't have much leeway. He manages to empty the contents of the dropper into my gaping neck wound.

"There," he says, stepping back. "That wasn't so hard, now, was it?"

"What did you do?" I ask through gritted teeth.

"Hmm, for a slayer you're not all that bright," he comments. "You've been infected with the virus, of course. In three days, you will die." He pats me on the shoulder. "And no, there is no magical antidote like you always see in the movies."

I'm suddenly cold, my heart slamming against my rib cage as reality sinks in. Oh, my god. I'm going to die. In three days, I'll be dead. I'll never make it to eighteen. I'll never graduate from high school. I'll never see my mother or sister or Spider again. I'll never see Jareth again.

"But don't worry, love," Maverick says. "I'm not going to keep you chained here for your last days. You'll be free to go." He motions to the two guards standing at the door's entrance. "Guards, release her," he says. "And escort her out."

Well, that was something, at least. I guess. I could say my good-byes. Hug my mother and sister one more time. I wonder if my dying days would be enough motivation for Dad to come by for a visit. I suppose if it didn't conflict with Bratty Stepchild #2's base-ball schedule, I might have a chance.

Tears threaten to fall again and I bite down hard on my lower lip to stop it from quivering. I must stay strong. Let him think I'm fearless. Don't give him the power of seeing me weak.

The guards unlock my arms from their shackles and I gratefully get up from the chair. Maverick is still grinning maniacally at me, so very pleased with himself.

"They will crown me Master of the Coven," he crows. "When they learn I was the one who took down the slayer."

I stare at him, suddenly realizing exactly what I have to do. He's underestimating me. Underestimating who I am. I'm not just any old sniveling girl who will go quietly into the night to lick my wounds. I am the Slayer. The one chosen once in a generation to kill evil vampires.

I have a destiny. And it's time to fulfill it.

I close my eyes for a moment, searching for the strength I need.

Concentrating, as Teifert told me I could. Trying to be Zen and all that.

And then I find it. Something lying dormant, deep inside of me. Almost like a big ball of light, straining against its chains, dying to be released. I squeeze my eyes and channel that light with all that I have inside me and suddenly I explode with energy and power.

I open my eyes. I am the slayer. Here me roar.

A quick roundhouse kick takes out one of the guards. The other I head butt and then kick in the groin as he's reeling backward. I'm punching and kicking so hard, so fast, I'm not quite sure where my body ends and my target begins. It's like I'm on some kind of super-hero autopilot.

And let me tell you, it rocks!

Having knocked out both guards I turn to Maverick. He's standing there, backed up against the wall, looking a lot less smug than before. "You can't kill me," he says, sounding a bit hoarse. "You don't have your stake."

"Stake, schmake," I say, suddenly realizing something. "You ever see the movie *Dumbo*?"

He stares at me as if I have two heads. "*Dumbo*?" he asks.

I laugh, suddenly feeling in complete control of the situation. "Yeah," I say. "Dumbo's a flying elephant. But the thing about Dumbo is, he only thinks he can fly because he's got some stupid magic feather in his trunk. But turns out," I say, circling Maverick, hands raised in front of me, "he doesn't need the feather at all. He can fly all along."

"As charming as this Disney fairy tale is—"

"But don't you see, Maverick?" I interrupt. "I'm Dumbo. Well, except for the big ears. And the actual flying bit. Okay, maybe bad analogy. But the point is, I don't need some special stake to slay you. The power is in *me*, not some chunk of wood."

And before Maverick can reply, I fluidly grab the chair, break off its leg, and slam the piece of wood into his evil heart. He explodes instantly into a pile of dust.

Whoo-hoo! I am the SLAY-ERRR BAY-BEE!!!!!!!

I contemplate slaying the unconscious guards as well, but realize they may just be evil for the paycheck and now that their fearless leader has gone all "ashes to ashes" they may reform and become model vampire citizens. You never know.

The important thing is I did the job. I slayed Maverick. Fulfilled my destiny. Saved the day.

Yay, me!

But then my exultation dampens as I remember that while I may have saved the Blood Coven, I failed to save myself. I drop the stake and fall to my knees, sobbing uncontrollably.

I'm going to die. In three days I will no longer exist.

That totally bites.

TWENTY-NINE

Fangs for the Memories

TUESDAY, JUNE 12, 11 P.M.

"Rayne! Are you okay?"

I look up, trying to focus through my tears. Jareth and another man rush into the room. Jareth throws his arms around me and squeezes me so hard I practically lose my breath.

"Rayne," he murmurs. "You're all right, you're okay. I was so worried!" He strokes my hair and kisses me softly on the cheek. "I got backup. I was coming to save you."

"Silly vampire," I say, laughing through my tears. "I'm the slayer, remember? I can save myself. Well, sort of. But we can talk about that later." Now is not the time to tell him about my swiftly approaching expiration date. We've still got too much to do.

I can feel his smile against my cheek. If only he knew. "Right. Of course. So you finally figured out how to wield your magical stake?"

"Actually, I finally learned that the stake didn't have any magic. When it comes to vamps, any old piece of wood will do."

Jareth pulls away, looking at my bleeding neck. I'm sure it's nice and crusty-looking by now. "You've been bitten!" he cries, reaching out to touch the wound. I stop him before he does. The last thing I need is for him to get infected, too.

"It's okay," I lie. "It doesn't hurt."

"You have done well, Rayne," the man who entered with Jareth says. I look up in surprise. I forgot he was here. "Teifert will be pleased."

My eyes widen as I recognize the guy.

David?

Mom's boyfriend?

"You're . . . but you're . . ."

David laughs. "Yes, it's me, Rayne."

"But how . . . ? Who . . . ?"

"I work for Slayer Inc.," he explains. He pulls out an official-looking Slayer Inc. badge to back up his claim. "As your guardian."

"Guardian? I have a guardian?"

"What, did you think we'd leave you floundering out in the world alone on your first slay?"

"But why didn't you tell me? I thought you were a vampire!"

David laughs. "Is that why you tried to feed me garlic and squirt me with holy water when I came to dinner?"

Jareth raises an eyebrow. "You did what?"

I can feel my face getting *sooo* red. "Well, I didn't know he was my freaking guardian. I thought he was just some evil vampire Mom picked up in the frozen foods section."

David shuffles his feet. "About that, Rayne," he says. "I have to admit, I was told to get close to your family. To watch you and see how you do. Your first slay is a test. So we observe carefully. Anyway, I figured dating your mom would get me into your house, so I could get a better idea of your home life."

"That's a rotten thing to do," I interrupt, not at all happy about this. He may not be a vamp, but I'll find some other way to dust him if he's been screwing around with my mom's head just to get close to me. "My mom really likes you. And you're just using her?"

"Hey! Wait a minute!" David holds up his hands. "Hear me out. As I said, that's how it started. But then I actually met your mother. And she's . . . wonderful."

"I already know that she's wonderful. She's my mom." I scowl.

David sighs. "Look. What I'm trying to say is I like your mom very much. And now that the assignment is over I'd like to be allowed to continue dating her. If that's okay with you."

I scrunch up my eyes, still not quite sure. "Well, we'll see," I say. "Maybe. If she still wants you."

"Thanks," he says. "I'll take what I can get. Don't worry," he adds, "I'll prove to you that I'm a worthy suitor."

His words bring me back to reality and the fact that I won't get to see how this relationship plays out. Because I'll be dead. Long dead and buried, with worms crawling out of my eye sockets.

I turn back to Jareth. He's staring at me with such concern. I wish the two of us could be alone. I've got to tell him about my impending doom. Let him hold me as I cry in his arms.

Then I remember. "Magnus!" I cry. "We've got to warn Magnus!"

"Warn him?"

"Rachel and Charity are infected! If he drinks their blood he's going to lose his powers, just like the others."

Jareth pulls out his cell phone and dials Magnus's number. After a moment's pause he greets his boss and tells him what happened, warning him not to drink from his donors.

He clicks off the phone after saying good-bye. "I reached him in time," he says. "Rachel and Charity had just arrived, but he hadn't taken a sip yet."

I let out the breath I didn't know I was holding. "Thank god."

"Okay, we'd better get out of this place, pronto! Before Maverick's minions see what we've done here." Jareth rises to his feet. He turns to David. "Do you know of an easy way out of here? I hardly think we should walk out the front door."

David shakes his head. "This place is like a maze."

"Don't worry, I'll lead you out."

We all whirl around at the voice in the doorway.

"Frannie!" I cry.

"So did you do it? Did you get the virus?"

"Yes," I said. "And I dusted Maverick, too." Hmm, this probably means Francis is out of a job. Hopefully vamps have good unemployment benefits.

David nods over at the pile of ashes formerly known as Maverick. "Thanks to Rayne here, he is no longer a threat to vampkind."

Francis walks over and takes my hand in his. "Thank you, Rayne," he says. "And I'm sure Dana will thank you, too."

"I told you we'd become friends, Frannie," I say with a half-grin, while inside I feel like bursting into tears. It's not fair. All these innocent people and vampires, destroyed because of one vampire's quest for vengeance against an alleged wrong that was committed years and years before.

Francis squeezes me into a big, rib-crushing hug. The guy would have been strong pre-vampire. "You were right," he says, thankfully releasing me. "And now, if you'll just follow me, I'll get you guys out of here."

We follow. He leads us through twisty underground passages and up a set of creaky wooden stairs and through a door. We step out into a warm summer night. The stars are shining. The moon is full. It seems so unfair that in two nights I'll be dead.

"Good luck," Francis says. "I'm going to inform the other vamps what Maverick has done. I'm sure Magnus will have a lot more followers by morning. He turns to me. "And thank you again, Shaniqua."

"My real name's Rayne," I say, reaching up to give him a big hug. "I was using a fake ID to get into the club."

His eyes twinkle. "Really? I never would have known."

"Yeah, yeah."

We say our good-byes and head to Jareth's BMW. David says he's going to go by our house to check on my mother, guard her against any possible repercussions of the slayage and distract her from the fact that her daughter is out way past curfew. I thank him and watch as he walks off into the night. I'm really glad that he turned out to be one of the good guys. Maybe my mom will finally have a chance to be happy.

Jareth and I get into his car; the warm leather seats feel nice against my aching body. He turns the key and then looks at me. "Do you want to go somewhere in particular?" he asks.

"Can we go to the ocean?" I beg, for some reason getting the strangest desire for the sea. Maybe it's because I know I'll never get a chance to see it again. Hear the waves crashing against the shore, smell the salty air, feel the sand crackle between my toes.

He nods and unquestioningly pulls out of his parking space and into the night. We ride silently, as if both lost in our own thoughts, until we get to the beach, about twenty minutes away. We step out of the car and walk down to the end of the boardwalk, toward the ocean. I kick off my shoes and dig my toes into the cool sand. Jareth slips his hand into mine and strokes my fingers.

"So you did it," he says, staring into the blackness of the nighttime sea. There are a thousand stars out and they twinkle like diamonds in the sky. "You accomplished your mission. You're a real slayer now."

"I guess." I shrug. Time to break it to him. "Though a lot of good it's going to do me dead."

Jareth jerks his head around to look at me. "What?" he cries. "What are you talking about?"

I reach up and touch my neck. The bite has scabbed over and even feels diseased and nasty. "Maverick bit me," I say. "And then he injected the virus into my bloodstream. He says I'm going to die in a couple of days. Just like all the donors."

Even in the darkness I can see Jareth's horror-struck face. "Raynie!" he cries and his voice breaks with emotion. He pulls me into a hug, squeezing me with almost as much strength as Francis. But this hug is one of desperation. "Oh, my darling, no!" he murmurs. "I can't lose you."

"Yeah, well, I don't exactly want to be lost either," I say wryly.

Jareth pulls away from the hug, his beautiful green eyes hardened and angry. "Stop making self-protective jokes," he says. "This is serious. We have to do something."

"What?" I ask. "There's no antidote. Face it. In two to three days, I'll be pushing up daisies." I know I'm being a bitch, but for some reason I'm unable to let go.

Jareth sighs and pulls me down onto the sand. We sit there a moment, not speaking. "You can be so cold and hard," he says at last. "Always putting up a brave front so others don't see your fear. Your vulnerability."

"Maybe I don't want others to see my fear and vulnerability. I mean, it's my fear and vulnerability, right? If I want to keep it inside, then that's my business." I kick at the sand with my foot. "Besides, it's not exactly like you're Mr. Open Up and Share yourself."

"You're right," Jareth says, staring out into the sea. "You and I are a lot alike in many ways. We both have pain in our pasts, which has caused us to put trust in ourselves and not others. But let me tell you, Rayne, from someone who's done it for hundreds of years: It's not a great way to live. And it never gets less lonely." He sighs deeply, lying back into the sand and staring up at the stars. "I never told you why I don't want a blood mate."

I turn to look at him, surprised. This, I was not expecting. Is he ready to spill his deep dark secret at last?

"No," I say slowly. "You never have."

Jareth goes silent. At first I'm almost positive he's not going to speak—that he changed his mind already. But then he opens his mouth.

"Most vampires are turned individually," he says. "But for me, my whole family was vampire."

"Really?" I ask. "That's so cool."

"Yes," he agrees. "You see, my parents and my brother and sister and I were living as peasants in England back during the Black Plague. Terrible time. All our neighbors were dying. The graves were full. You can't imagine the stench of bodies just rotting in the streets, the sulfur from the burnings. We prayed to God that he would rescue us. That he would spare our lives. Well, God sent a dark messenger that day.

"The vamp Runez had come to feed on the sick. Vampires couldn't catch the plague and so it became a good place to feed, without hurting anyone. We didn't have donors back in that day," Jareth explained. "Runez came across my family, huddled in our little hut. Exhausted, hungry, and scared. But not sick. He knew we would soon catch it and suffer terrible deaths. I was eighteen. My little sister was ten and my little brother only four. The vampire felt bad for us and offered us a choice. Immortal life or certain death." Jareth smiled. "Of course, you can guess what we chose."

"So he turned all of you? Isn't that against the rules?" From what I'd read, vamps can only turn one person during their lifetime. Keeps them from having blood shortages like the Red Cross.

"Things were much less organized back then. Vampires roamed the earth, alone and hungry. There were no covens or political parties. We didn't incorporate 'til the early eighteenth century."

"Oh, okay," I say. Interesting. I wonder what (or who) made them all band together. "So then what happened?"

"At first things were great. The five of us escaped the plague and traveled from village to village, taking money from the dead. It sounds terrible, I know. But it was just lying there. Of no use to anyone. Except us. We ended up with enough gold to buy a small castle in southeastern Britain. We bought titles and everyone as-sumed we were some kind of eccentric royalty. It was then that I trained to be a sculptor. I spent my days carving intricate stone statues to sell to castle courtyards and churches. And since I had eternity to perfect my art, I became quite good. My work can be seen all over Europe, even today.

"In any case, everything had turned out better than our wildest dreams. And best of all, we had each other. A family for eternity. At night we'd gather in the great hall and play games and laugh and laugh." He pauses for a moment, releasing a small sigh. "Sometimes I think I can still hear my sister's giggle, reverberating through a hall."

I smile, thinking of my own family. My silly, hippie-dippy mom, my determined, hard-working sister. If I'd become a vampire I'd totally have wanted to make it a family affair like Jareth did. That way I'd get to keep the people I love around forever.

But Jareth's story, I'm beginning to think, doesn't have such a happy ending.

"Go on," I urge. "What happened next?"

"We lived together for centuries, moving around every few years, so as not to arouse the suspicions of the locals. After all, we never grew old. I could, at least, pass for a man, having been turned at eighteen, but my sister and brother were forever children. People began to wonder. And then we'd move." He smiled sadly. "Moving could be tough, but we always had each other. That's all that mattered."

"Right."

"I told you how the vampires came together in the early eighteenth century, right? A great leader, Count Dracul, started the reorganization. He formed covens around the country and assigned each vampire to a specific group. Minigovernments were created in each coven, with the leaders all coming together on one worldwide Consortium. He felt we'd be stronger working together. At first it seemed like a great idea.

"But then, as we grew in strength and wealth, becoming prominent members of society that were numerous enough to control our respective governments, another group rose to stop us." He grimaces. "You might be familiar with them. Slayer Inc."

I grimace back. I'm thinking this is going to be the part where I learn why Jareth is so antislayer.

"Well, Slayer Inc. went to the head vampire consortium and said that while they believed vampires had the right to exist, there should be rules in place so they and humans could peacefully coexist. And they offered to police the ones who did not. I was on the council when the vote came up on whether we wanted to work with them. Since we didn't have a police force of our own and we'd recently seen some really evil vampires causing major havoc, at the time it seemed like a good idea, though not everyone agreed. In the end, the council was split pretty evenly, with me casting the deciding vote."

"In favor of Slayer Inc."

"Yes. It's amazing how one simple vote can change your whole life."

"What happened?"

"Well, after we'd signed the contracts, Slayer Inc. created some rules. Some of these rules were good. We couldn't be running around biting and killing random humans, for example. That's where the donor program was born. Some, however, were . . . not so good."

"What do you mean?"

Jareth swallows hard before speaking. "No children vampires," he says hoarsely. "They said it was an abomination. And that it threatened our secrecy as well, since it's more obvious a child isn't aging."

His voice cracks and he reaches up to swipe a wayward blood tear from his eyes. My heart aches in my chest and I want nothing more than to comfort him, to relieve some of his pain, though I have no idea how. No wonder he holds such a grudge against Slayer Inc. Against me. I'm starting to hate them myself. How could they do that? Kill innocent vampire children? Kill Jareth's brother and sister? What if they had asked me to do the same? Go up to some six-year-old and stake her through the heart? Just like Bertha did with Lucifent. There's no way I could do that. Absolutely no way.

"They came for my brother and sister a week later. We holed ourselves up in our mansion and held out as long as we could. But we ran out of blood and we were dying. Finally, out of desperation, we attempted to fight our way out. It was a massacre. My whole family, besides me, was killed by a rampaging slayer. Because of me and my deciding vote, I lost everyone I ever loved." His voice breaks and he covers his eyes with his hands to hide his tears.

I lie down on my side, placing my head on his solid chest and wrapping my arm around him. He doesn't pull away. "I'm so sorry," I whisper, feeling tears come to my own eyes.

How could anyone move on with their lives after such tragedy? Their whole family slaughtered before their eyes. I try to imagine how that would feel for me—if Sunny and my mother were suddenly cut down for a sin they didn't commit. But I can't. It's just too terrible to comprehend.

Jareth reaches up and strokes the top of my head. His fingers feel light and feathery as they scrape against my scalp. "They believed they were on a crusade against evil," he says sadly. "But my little brother and sister didn't have an evil bone in their bodies." His voice cracks again, and he pauses, swallowing hard before continuing. "They were my everything. My life. My heart. Without them,

I had no purpose," he says wearily. "Living forever went from being a gift of the gods to a curse of eternal damnation."

My heart pangs again and I squeeze him closer, a vain attempt to take away even a smidgen of his pain. Poor Jareth. Poor, poor Jareth. No wonder he's so bitter. No wonder he didn't want to give me a chance. I wouldn't have given myself a chance. There's no way I'd have agreed to work side by side with a member of the organization that mercilessly struck down my entire family. *Everyone I had in the world.*

"Of course, soon after the murders, the vampire consortium realized that partnering with Slayer Inc. had been a big mistake," he adds. "Their contracts were taken away and their organization condemned by our kind. But Slayer Inc. grew anyway. And even today, as you know, they feel they have the right to police us." He shakes his head. "So many vampires have died because of me and my vote. If anything, I'm the real vampire slayer."

"But you didn't know," I protest. "You can't blame yourself."

"I gave them the means to exist. The opportunity to slaughter my family and others. How can I not be blamed?"

"Jareth, you have to stop beating yourself up over something that happened so long ago. We all make mistakes. And yes, sometimes the consequences are worse than others, but in the end, you have to forgive yourself and move on."

Jareth sits up, pulling me with him. He cups my face in his hands and meets my eyes with his own earnest ones. "Look, Rayne. I'm sorry I wasn't exactly friendly when we first met. But at least now you know what I'm dealing with. Partnering with a member of Slayer Inc., no matter how sweet she is, just feels so wrong. Like I'm betraying my family in some way. Like once again I'm casting the wrong vote."

I nod. "I understand. I'd hate me, too, I think."

"But then I started to get to know you, against my better judgment. You're not one of them. You have your own set of rights and wrongs, your own code that you live by. I began to fall in love with you. And that scared me to death."

My heart leaps in my chest. In love with me. Jareth is in love with me. He doesn't see me as the pathetic freak who doesn't fit in. The one whose own father doesn't care if she lives or dies. He knows the real me and he loves me. How totally mind-blowing is that?

"I love you, too, Jareth," I whisper. "So much."

He leans forward to kiss me, but I stop him before his lips reach mine. It's torture to do so, but I feel I must.

"Wait. I don't know how contagious I am," I say. "I don't want you to get sick, too."

His face crumbles and I realize for one moment we both forgot my situation. That it doesn't matter who's in love with who because soon there will be no me to be in love with.

"Oh, Rayne," he murmurs, swiping at the bloody tears that spring from the corners of his eyes.

He doesn't need to say anything else. I know exactly what he's thinking. He finally allowed himself to love again, and now he's going to lose again.

Sometimes destiny is, like, so unfair.

Vampires Suck

THURSDAY, JUNE 14, 3 P.M.

I should have never trusted Jareth. I knew better. I absolutely knew better!

I can't believe I shared all that stuff with him. Opened up for the first time and told him things. Things I haven't told anyone. About my dad. About my failed relationships. About how scared and lonely I am half the time. How I'm sick of pretending I don't care about anything or anyone when I probably care more deeply than anything and anyone I know.

He seemed so genuine. So caring and sweet. He told me his sob story. About his family. Slayer Inc. He told me he was in love with me. He told me he'd stick by my side and not give up. He told me he'd try to find the antidote.

But now he's gone. Disappeared. I'm lying here in my bed, dying, and he's nowhere to be found.

After our night on the beach, the virus kicked in with a vengeance and I've been bedridden ever since, sick as a dog. Everything aches and I'm so weak I can barely sit up. And the only thing I am pining for is Jareth. I want to see him one last time before I die. To feel his hands on me and hear his gentle voice whisper in my ear, telling me everything is going to be okay.

So where the hell is he?

I hate men. Vampires. People in general. You know, in a way I'm effing glad to effing die. At least then the pain will end. The hurt and anguish and suffering that I feel on a daily basis will slip away as I'm carried over the abyss. The soothing waters of death will claim me and everyone will be sorry and they'll cry and say, "Oh what a great girl" when gawking at my body during the wake and funeral. And maybe my dad will show up and he'll be so sorry that he never took the time to know me.

Yeah, my death will serve them right.

THIRTY-ONE

Waiting for Death

THURSDAY, JUNE 14 (CONTINUED)

Sorry about that earlier rant. I was just so mad I could hardly see. Or maybe that's just a symptom of the horrible sickness. It's totally taken hold now. I feel like I have mono and the chicken pox and the bubonic plague, all rolled into one. I'm handwriting this, because I'm too weak to sit at the computer.

My mom is freaking-out worried and she doesn't even know the half of it. She takes me to a dozen doctors and they run a ton of tests, but no one can figure out what's wrong with me, of course, and in the end, they just send me home, having no idea this sickness is fatal.

Luckily Mom has David to take care of her. And he's a master at calming her down. At least I can die knowing I'm not leaving her all alone.

Sunny's a mess, too. Somehow she has figured out a way to blame herself for all of this. If Magnus hadn't bit her by mistake to begin with then I'd be a vampire, not a slayer. And I'd never have been at the Blood Bar, thus Maverick would never have been able to infect me. I try to remind her that then Magnus would have gotten infected through Rachel and Charity and, as his blood mate, I would have gotten infected through him.

In the end, I still die. It seems my destiny. I hope they've got a good backup slayer.

The vamps and Slayer Inc. have been working furiously to come up with an antidote from the virus sample we stole, but haven't had any luck. If they only had more time, they say. But my time is nearly up. If I'm average, I'll probably die tomorrow. If I'm lucky, I may live one more day.

The way I feel right now, I'd rather just die and get it over with.

I've been thinking about death a lot as I lie in my bed, staring up at the ceiling, while everyone hustles around to make sure I have everything I need to be as comfortable as possible. What will it be like? Where will I go? What will people do when I'm gone? Will they follow my wishes and play Bauhaus at my funeral?

My dad hasn't come. That's the most infuriating thing. I thought for sure when Sunny called him and told him I was dying that he'd be on the next plane. I don't know why. Instead he laughed her off and said she was being overly dramatic.

I hate him.

Him and Jareth.

After Jareth brought me back from the beach, he said he had some things to take care of and that he'd be back. But he hasn't been. And as I lie here dying, the one person my heart aches for is not here. I try not to care. I try to rebuild the wall, as that old band Pink Floyd would have advised. Try to regain my black ice princess shell that Mike Stevens always teases me about. The one where I don't care about anyone or anything. But the ice has melted. I'm vulnerable. Cut open and bleeding.

I listen to the Smiths. The Cure. Depeche Mode. The crooning eighties New Wave singers seem to understand. They're the only ones who do.

Jareth tried to warn me. He said he didn't ever get close to people. He's so similar to me in that respect. Afraid of opening up, of caring for another person. And maybe in a way he's right. He allowed himself to care for his family and they were killed. Now, he allowed himself to care for me and I'm about to kick the bucket myself.

In the end, we all die alone. Maybe it's better to have never loved at all.

Sorry, someone's at the door. More chicken soup, I bet. I'll write more later.

Dad. Yes, Dad.

THURSDAY, JUNE 14 (CONTINUED)

Jareth enters the room and comes to sit in the chair beside my bed. His hair is all tousled, his eyes bloodshot, and it looks like he hasn't slept in days. In fact, if I'm not mistaken he's still wearing the same outfit from the night we went to the Blood Bar.

"Where have you been?" I ask weakly. A few minutes ago I would have rather died than questioned him. Let him know I care. But I'm too sick to be strong, kick-ass Rayne at the moment.

"Vegas," he says.

I raise my eyebrows. "Uh, okay. Win anything?" I can't believe he was off gambling as I lay dying. I mean, I know poker is hot and all, but couldn't he have waited a couple days for that straight flush?

"I got what I went for, if that's what you mean."

"What, a lap dance?"

He chuckles. "Even sick, you're still funny, Rayne."

"Barrel of laughs, that's me," I say sarcastically, closing my eyes. I've become real sensitive to light these days and even more sensitive to seeing Jareth.

"Open your eyes, Rayne," Jareth commands.

Reluctantly I obey. Then open them even wider when I see what—I mean who—is standing behind Jareth.

"Dad?" I croak hoarsely. Am I hallucinating now?

"Hi, kiddo. I'm so sorry you're not feeling well."

For a moment, I'm still not convinced he's real as he walks over to my bed and sits down on the side. He's older looking then I remember, a little gray at his temples and in his beard. But overall, he still looks the same. Still looks like my dad.

I turn to look back at Jareth. "How . . . ?" I ask.

Dad smiles down at me. "This man of yours is very convincing, Rayne. He showed up at my doorstep one evening and said I had to come with him. That you needed me."

My heart pangs in my chest. Here I was blaming Jareth for disappearing and all along he'd been out hunting for the one thing he knew I needed more than anything.

"I'll leave you two to talk," the vampire says, walking to the door.

"Jareth," I call after him. He stops and turns back to look at me. "Thank you," I say.

He smiles the sweetest smile and nods, before turning and walking out the door. I smile back, my heart overflowing. God, I love that vampire. At least when I die, I'll die in love.

I turn back to my dad, noticing a few beads of sweat have formed on his forehead even though it's definitely not too hot in my room. He's nervous. Well, he damn well should be, after what he's done. And just because he's here now, doesn't mean I will let him off the hook.

"Thanks for coming," I say, forcing myself to be civil.

"Rayne, I'm so sorry to hear you've been sick. What do the doctors say? Is there anything they can do? A hospital we can send you to? Anything. I'll pay whatever it costs. Just tell your mother to send me the bill. I want you to get better."

He sounds so concerned. Is this what it had to take? I had to die to get his attention?

"The doctors don't know what's wrong," I say wearily. It really is an effort to talk today. "There's nothing they can do."

"Oh, my darling," he says, his voice breaking. "I hate to see you like this."

"You hate to see me at all, apparently."

"What's that supposed to mean?"

"Uh, hello? Birthday party? Balloons and presents and cake? Last week? Any of that ring a bell to you?"

His face crumbles. "I'm a terrible father," he says, staring down at his hands. I realize he's developed liver spots. He can't be old enough to have liver spots, can he?

"I'm not saying that," I protest, though, of course, I have been saying that all week. But it's unbearable for me to see him look so guilty. "It's just . . . well, we haven't seen you in years, Dad. And we were . . . looking forward to it."

A war is raging inside of me at this point. The old Rayne wants to be bitter and hateful and sarcastic and mean. She wants to cut him down and make him feel the hurt that she's felt because of him. To make him think she doesn't give a crap that he didn't show because he means absolutely nothing to her.

But the new Rayne, the one that is loved by Jareth, wonders if she has the strength to be honest with him. To admit that he hurt her and give him the chance to make things right. The new Rayne wonders if he has a reason for his actions. The new Rayne wonders if he, too, walks around with a hard shell of indifference to hide his inner turmoil.

The new Rayne knows that this man gave life to her. And that he may not have always been there, but he's there now. The new Rayne wants to give him a chance.

"You hurt my feelings when you didn't show," I admit, dying inside at the admission. Before today I wouldn't have told anyone that ever. But in a weird way, as soon as I say it, I feel a little better. "I waited for you until one A.M. The others all went to bed. I was sure you'd walk through that door with a birthday cake in hand. I believed in you, Dad. And you let me down."

Dad nods slowly, still staring at his hands. His eyes blink a few times too fast and I wonder if he's holding back tears. Tears! I never, ever thought in a million years I'd see my dad cry.

"Rayne, I can't do anything but apologize to you for that," he says at last, his voice sounding more than a bit froggy. "I feel so terrible. It's just . . . well, I got scared."

I raise an eyebrow. "Scared?"

"I know I've been a lousy dad. Running away from responsibility and family and everyone who loved me. Your mother, who has always been só sweet. You and Sunny, the most wonderful daughters a father could ever hope for. I felt, somehow, that I didn't deserve you. I'm so rotten inside, Rayne. I've done terrible things. And I felt that by leaving I would protect you two from all of that. I knew your mother would take care of you. Raise you right. You didn't need me screwing everything up." He shrugs. "Basically I got scared. Weird, huh? Scared because suddenly people needed me. Because they loved me. Sounds so dumb when I say it out loud."

It's at that moment I realize how much he really is my dad. And it makes me burst into tears. "Dad, I don't need you. But I do love you," I admit. "I've always loved you. That's why it hurts so much when you stay away."

"I've been feeling guilty about the whole thing for so long," Dad continues. "Then your sister sent me that e-mail about your birthday and I realized that was my chance to make things right. I mean, coming to a birthday doesn't make up for four years of wrongs, but I thought perhaps it'd be a start. A chance to reconnect with you two and come back into your lives." He swallows hard. "But then I got the e-mail back from Sunny when I accepted her invitation. She sounded so happy, so excited. I panicked again. I didn't know what I was doing. How I'd be able to face you two after all that had happened. So I took the coward's way out. I didn't show."

He scrubs his face with his hands. "I'm so sorry, Raynie girl. I screwed everything up, once again. And now here I am and you're so sick and I don't want to lose you."

It takes all my strength to sit up in bed, but I do it. Because right at this moment I need a hug. A hug from my father. I put out my arms and he wraps his around me, pulling me close. He squeezes me into the big bear hug I remember as a kid, though today his arms don't seem as strong. Probably because he's shaking. I bury my head in his shoulder and cry.

"I love you, Daddy," I sob. "I don't care what you've done or what you will do in the future. I'll always love you."

"Thank you, Raynie," he says. "I love you, too. No matter what, you'll always be my baby girl."

"Dad?" I ask, as I pull away and lie back down on the bed. Sitting up takes way too much energy. "Will you do me a favor?"

"Anything."

"Tell me a story. Like you used to."

He smiles, his eyes crinkling, and I can definitely see the tears now. "Of course," he says, his voice quavering a bit. "Once upon a time, there lived two princesses—Sunshine and Rayne . . ."

THIRTY-THREE

The Sacrifice

THURSDAY, JUNE 14 (CONTINUED)

After Dad leaves I take a nap, feeling both emotionally and physically drained. But for the first time since I came down with the disease I sleep peacefully. No haunting nightmares. And I wake up feeling better. Yes, I will die, but I will die with much more peace than I had for most of my life.

A knock on the door. I say, "Come in."

It's Jareth.

"How was your dad?" he asks, sitting on the side of my bed. He presses a cold hand against my burning forehead. I close my eyes.

"Wonderful. I'll never be able to thank you enough for tracking him down."

"It was nothing. I'd do anything for you," he says sincerely.

I open my eyes. "Have you heard from the lab?"

He hangs his head. "Yes. Unfortunately they have not been able to come up with an antidote. At least not yet. If only they had more time."

I sigh, resigning myself once more to my impending death. For some reason I had been keeping a small hope alive deep inside that they'd be able to save me in the nick of time, like it always happens in the movies. But I guess, in this case, it was not meant to be.

"Listen, Rayne, there is one possibility," Jareth says hesitantly.

"Huh?" I look up at him.

"I took a lock of your hair and had them test it. You and I are compatible."

"Compatible?"

"As blood mates. We have compatible DNA."

I stare at him, confused. "But what do you—?"

He swallows hard. "I could turn you. Then you would live. Well, not live exactly. Your body would die. But you would be immortal."

"But if you bite me, you'll become weak and lose all your vampire powers. Won't you?"

"Yes."

"But then . . . how . . . ?"

Jareth takes my hand in his and pulls it up to his lips. He kisses it softly, his mouth caressing my sensitive skin. "I love you, Rayne," he murmurs. "You're the first person I've met since my family was killed that I have opened up to. The first person I've allowed myself to care for. You and I are a lot alike in that respect. We live shallow, empty, solo lives because we live in fear of getting too close to another. But together, I think we can do better than that."

He lowers my hand and looks into my eyes. "I want to be with you for eternity. I want to share everything with you."

I can't believe it. I can scarcely believe it. Jareth wants me! Little old screwed up and scarred me. And he wants to turn me into a vampire. My dream come true.

"But what about the virus? Won't you catch it?"

He nods. "Yes. It's most likely that I will. But don't you see?" he cries. "I don't care. I'd rather be weak and powerless and with you than lose you. None of this world means a thing to me if you're not there to share it."

"Really?" Hot tears burn my cheeks and for once I let them fall, unchecked. "You really mean that?"

"With all my heart." He reaches over to stroke my sweaty forehead. "Please, Raynie, don't leave me. Say you will be mine forever."

"But I don't want you to lose your powers. . . ."

He shakes his head, smiling down at me. "Will you stop arguing with me for once in your life and just do what I say?"

I grin. "*Maybe*."

"Then say you'll be mine. Say you'll let me take you as my blood mate. Say that you'll stay with me for eternity."

"If you're sure you want me."

"I'm very sure."

"Then okay." I laugh even though I'm still crying. "What the heck, right?"

He leans down and finds my neck, his breath against my skin. I remember the first time he bit me in the Blood Bar. How good it felt. But the sensation is nothing compared to this intimate moment. What was once just physically appealing is now something more. There's love in his bite and, as he releases the vampire blood into my veins and takes some of my own, his mind opens to me and I can feel all that he feels. Know all that he knows.

I can feel his pain. His hurt and loneliness. I understand his bitterness and his sorrow. But there's something else there now. A radiant hope and joy that's more powerful than the hurt. A flash of soft, glowing light that envelops my body and steals away all my pain.

I pass out and when I wake up I'm feeling good enough to sit up in bed. I see Jareth still sitting by my bedside and I wonder how long I've been unconscious. He smiles at me.

"How are you feeling?" he asks.

"A lot better, actually," I say, surprised. I sit up in bed and don't feel dizzy.

"Good. It may take a few days for my blood to fully bond with your own."

"Yeah. I remember Sunny had a week before the transformation would have been completed."

"Of course, you won't gain any of the vampire powers. We're basically gimped pseudovamps now."

My thoughts sober at this. "I'm sorry you had to do that," I say. "I mean, I hate that I'm responsible for—"

"Are you kidding?" Jareth asks. "This is the best day of my life." He cups my face in his hands and kisses me softly on the mouth. "I love you, Rayne," he says. "And now I can have you for eternity."

"I love you, too, Jareth."

We kiss for a moment, then he pulls away. "Oh!" he cries. "I almost forgot!" He reaches down under the bed and pulls out a box. He lifts the lid.

Chocolate cake. Just like the one Dad was supposed to bring.

"Happy vampire birthday, my dear," he says.

Did I mention how much I love this guy?

EPILOGUE

So that's my story. A few days later I'm good as new and out of bed. My mom is surprised by my miraculous recovery, but David is able to convince her not to look a gift horse in the mouth and bring in the doctors again. Which is good, considering I think they'd probably be pretty freaked out if they started testing me. Of course, in a few years, when I don't look any older than seventeen still, she and I are going to have to sit down and have a little chat.

That should be fun. *Not.*

Sunny and Magnus are overjoyed at my recovery and Mag doesn't even seem that pissed that he's lost his best vampire general. He's got others in line, he says, and is much more interested in Jareth's and my happiness than in some military position. Oh, and bonus—I've convinced Magnus to re-examine the coven's policy for letting outside vamps into the ranks. Frannie and Dana are definitely in. And many of their friends may soon get their membership cards in the mail as well.

My dad stays until I'm fully better and when he leaves, he tells me I'm welcome to visit him anytime and that he wants to be a part of our lives again. And this time I know he means it.

Oh, and one of the unexpected side benefits? I may not have vampire powers, but I also don't have a lot of their downsides. For some reason the virus seems to have bonded with the melatonin in the skin and Jareth and I are able to face the sunlight without fear of burning to a crisp. This is an even bigger deal to Jareth, seeing as he hasn't caught a glimpse of the sun in nearly a thousand years.

And as for Jareth and me, well, we're just great. To think I actually had to lose my soul to find my soulmate. But hey, whatever works, right? And who really gives a care about vampire powers when we have each other? We have a blast just being together. And we make a point to share everything—even when it's difficult. No secrets between us, that's the only way this is going to work out.

Summer passes without event and soon it's time for school to start again. Sadly, since I'm not allergic to the sun, I'm also not exempt from attending high school. But I guess that's okay. After all, I've got eternity. Might as well get myself educated.

So one September day I'm walking through Oakridge High, dressed in my Goth best, making fun of the cheerleaders, ducking away from the teachers who I owe assignments to, etc., etc. Your typical Raynie day. When all of a sudden I hear a *Psst* sound from the side corridor. I turn to look and see Mr. Teifert waving madly at me from down the hall.

"You must come with me," he says in an urgent voice.

I've technically retired from the slayer biz, by the way. The virus made me too weak to perform my duties. But Teifert says once a slayer, always a slayer and you never know when they might need me. And from the look on his face, I'm thinking this may be one of those times.

Great. And here I thought all I'd have to worry about this semester was Calculus.

"What's up, T?" I ask, as I approach him.

"Rayne, we have a problem, and we need your help."

"Of course you do." I sigh. "What is it this time?"

"It's Mike Stevens."

"Mike Stevens?" I scowl at the name of my captain-of-the-football-team nemesis. I'd almost managed to forget about him over the summer. "What about Mike Stevens?"

"He's missing."

"Uh, okay, T," I say. "Let's get something straight here. Mike Stevens missing doesn't necessarily qualify as a problem. I mean, have you met the guy? Some might say a missing Mike Stevens could be the best thing to happen to Oakridge in a long time."

"That's not all," Teifert says. "There's also something suddenly very odd about the cheerleaders."

"Odd about the cheerleaders?" I cock my head. "You mean more odd than usual about a group of girls who want to dance and kick up their legs while wearing short skirts in the middle of a New England November?"

"Yes. And, Rayne, this is going to sound weird, but . . ."

"Dude, after all I've been through, nothing's going to sound weird. Absolutely nothing in the known universe."

"The cheerleaders? They've been heard, uh . . . growling."

Huh. Then again . . . maybe I'm wrong.

To be continued . . .

Turn the page for a special excerpt
from the latest Blood Coven Vampire novel . . .

SOUL BOUND

Coming soon from
The Berkley Publishing Group!

"Take that, you putrid jumble-gutted zombie!" I cry, mashing my PS3 button as fast as I can, letting loose a stream of deadly bullets from my AK47 and splattering zombie brains, blood, and other assorted bodily fluids all over my bedroom television screen. The game dings as I beat my own high score once again and I lean back in my chair, feeling oh-so-satisfied. *Yeah, baby!* No one's better at Vampires vs. Zombies than me. I should enter a tournament. I'd blast all those wannabe-zombie-slaying nerds out there from here to kingdom come without even trying.

I'm about to start the bonus round when there's a knock on my door.

"Come in!" I call, hoping it's my half sister, Stormy. She's the only one who can come even close to beating me at the game and I'd love another chance to kick her eleven-year-old, video game–addicted butt.

Sure enough, the door opens and Stormy pokes her blond head into my room. "Hey, Rayne," she says. "There's some girl here to see you."

"A girl?" My mind races for possibilities, but comes up blank. I've never really been good with making girlfriends in general and I'm almost positive I haven't given my home address to any mortal ones here in Vegas. (Unlike my much more social twin, Sunny, who made, like, ten friends in two days just by breathing the air at Las Vegas High School.) And, of course, no self-respecting vampire would be swinging by for a chat on a Saturday afternoon while the sun is still high in the sky. "Who?"

Stormy shrugs. "I've never seen her before," she confesses. "Though she looks a lot like the girl from *Resident Evil*."

"Video game or movie?"

"The movie. Definitely the movie."

Hmm. I'm pretty sure I'd remember making friends and influencing people who looked like Milla Jovovich . . .

"Well, send her in, I guess," I tell my sister. What the heck, right?

Stormy nods and disappears. While I'm waiting, I go and save my game. It's a little embarrassing to see the game clock pop up and realize how many hours I've been sitting in front of a television set. *But it's for a good cause,* I remind myself. After all, if Slayer Inc. received reports of me hitting the slot machines or dancing up a storm in downtown Vegas they might decide I'm not taking my whole mission to bring down my sister and her boyfriend as seriously as they'd like. Out of sight, out of mind, that's what I say. As far as they know, I'm scouring the world, one step away from my bounty.

I hear the door creak open and turn around to greet my strange visitor. Stormy isn't wrong—the girl does bear a remarkable resemblance to the famed zombie-slaughtering film star. Not only does she kind of look like her, but she dresses like her, too. I mean, it's not every day you see someone sporting a tight white tank top under a green army vest, tucked into little black shorts with garters that cling to ripped thigh-high stockings—even in Vegas. (Unless, of course, Taylor Momsen's in town . . .) The girl tops off the outfit with an amazing pair of knee-high, stack-heeled, black leather boots and two matching black leather holsters, strapped to her perfectly toned and tanned thighs.

But unlike the zombie killer of the 3-D silver screen, these holsters aren't slotted with guns. They contain stakes.

A vampire slayer. I let out a low whistle, wondering where on Earth she scored an outfit like that. Is there some kind of secret online Slayer Inc. uniform shop that sells this kind of stuff that no one told me about? I mean, I'm not all about the army vest. But those boots, man! I'd pretty much sell my soul to slip my feet into those beauties—if I hadn't already given my soul away when I first became a vampire.

Of course, I'm not entirely sure my current not-so-tanned, not-so-perfectly sculptured thighs could carry the rest of the outfit as well as she does. After all, I'm still recovering from all those high-calorie blood milk shakes they force-feed you in rehab. . . .

"Rayne?" the girl asks, looking down at me and removing her mirrored aviator shades. She wears a slightly disdainful look on her otherwise flawless face and I suddenly get a weird feeling I've seen her somewhere before, though for the life of me, I can't figure out where that could possibly be. "Rayne McDonald?"

"That's my name, don't wear it out," I reply automatically, feeling a little defensive. After all, she just showed up at my house, out of nowhere, giving me dirty looks like that. Even if she is the hottest thing known to slayer-kind and I'm three days overdue for a shower and wearing vampire bunny slippers instead of kick-ass boots.

She purses her obviously collagen-injected, over-glossed lips, looking at me with clear disapproval in her purple contact–covered eyes.

"Um, did you want something?" I ask, suddenly eager to get rid of her and go back to my game. After all, those brain-hungry zombies won't just explode themselves, you know.

She sighs loudly, as if she's carrying the weight of the world on her perfectly sculpted shoulders. "My name is Bertha," she says at last.

Bertha?! I burst out laughing. I'm sorry—I can't help it! This uber hottie's name is Bertha? For realz? I had always assumed there was some kind of law against hot chicks being named Bertha. A name like Bertha should be reserved for girls who look like that crazy ex-vampire slayer from back home who—

Oh crap. So that's why she looks familiar . . .

"Bertha?" I cry, scrambling to my feet, trying to hide my shock. "Bertha the Vampire Slayer? Bertha the Vampire Slayer from Oakridge High School?"

Bertha had been the number-one slayer in my neck of the woods, back in the day. She had some pretty major kills to her name, too. She even bagged Lucifent, the former leader of the Blood Coven. Unfortunately, her career stalled out due to her inability to ever meet a drive-thru she didn't want to go through twice. Those pesky blood pressure issues can really put a damper on one's vampire slayer career.

But um, wow. I guess she kicked that problem . . .

"I probably look a little different than when you saw me last," she says, preening a little. I catch her glancing at her own reflection in the bedroom mirror.

I nod. I mean, holy understatement of the century, Batman! This chick did not just get her stomach stapled. She had a complete Heidi Montag makeover. Her once-pockmarked face is now porcelain-doll smooth. Her old stringy hair now flows down her back in silky waves. Her nose is at least three inches shorter and her breasts would make even Katy Perry cry.

"Wow, Bertha," I say. "You look great. Really great." And I mean it, too. Not that I'm into girls or anything. But if I was, she'd totally be first on my list.

She sniffs and I realize she's moved away from the mirror and is now giving me a critical once-over. It's then that I remember I'm currently dressed in *Nightmare Before Christmas* flannel pajamas, wearing no makeup, and haven't brushed my hair since Tuesday. At this point, I'd be dead last on pretty much anyone's list.

But still, there's no need for the judgment here. I mean, it's not like she gave me any heads-up of her impending arrival so I could apply some mascara.

"So, to what do I owe the pleasure of this visit?" I ask curiously.

"I'm sure you didn't fly more than halfway across the country just to show off your extreme total makeover." Though, to be honest, if I looked like her, I'd pretty much make that my full-time job from here on out. Tracking down all those boys who once rejected me, showing off my curves . . .

"Slayer Inc. assigned me to be your new partner."

. . . finding even hotter boys and stealing them away from their cheerleader girlfriends, only to dump them after—

Wait, what?

I stare at her. "My partner?" I repeat. If my heart was still beating, it'd be slamming against my chest right about now.

She nods. "The powers that be at Slayer Inc. felt you might need some . . . motivation . . . in tracking down your sister. So they flew me out here to assist you."

"Motivation?" I cry indignantly. "They think I have a motivation problem?" I give a loud, barking laugh at the ridiculousness of it all. A laugh that cuts short as I realize she's staring smugly at the video game screen behind me. Particularly the game clock, which is still flashing on the screen.

"Oh, that!" I wave my hand dismissively. "That's just practice. After all, you never know when you might meet up with a zombie while out on a Slayer Inc. mission. But don't worry, Berth, my girl. Can I call you Berth? I am unsurpassed at perfect head shots. Seriously, brains just start splattering all over the place at the mere sight of my mighty broomstick."

She raises an eyebrow. "That's very . . . reassuring."

I grab the remote and quickly shut off the TV. "But enough about me. Let's talk about you! What have you been up to? Are you enjoying Vegas so far? Done any gambling? You have so got to try the Krave Lounge on Fridays. Amazing Goth scene. They've got the hottest—"

"Rayne!" Bertha interrupts. "We don't have time for *clubbing*," she says, spitting out the word as if it were poison. "We're on assignment for Slayer Inc. Or perhaps you forgot?" she adds, giving the television set another look of condemnation.

I sigh. Great. And here I thought I had everything worked out so perfectly. I'd pretend to look for Sunny and Magnus and just . . .

well, never find them. Sure, I'd forfeit the million-dollar bounty, but I'd forfeit a billion dollars if it meant keeping my sister safe. No big deal.

Guess Pyrus is smarter than I gave him credit for.

"Now," Bertha says, plopping down on my bed. "Let's talk strategy. Do you have any leads? Any idea where your sister and her boyfriend might have gone?"

I shake my head. Luckily, I can give her an honest answer on that one. Don't ask, don't tell. That's my policy.

"But you're her twin. Don't you have some kind of twin ESP kind of thing? Can't you sense where she is or something?"

"The only thing I can sense is a super-annoying presence currently residing in my bedroom," I retort, annoyed at the whole twenty-questions routine and wishing she'd just go away.

She frowns. "Nice. Real nice. You think you can hurt my feelings? Cut me down and make me run sobbing from the room?" She shakes her head. "Well, sorry, sister, but this is the new and improved Bertha. And she doesn't take crap from anyone." She rises to her feet, staring directly into the mirror. "I'm back. I'm hot as hell, and I'm not going to take it anymore!"

She raises a fist in triumph, then looks at me expectantly. As if she's hoping I'll cheer on her newfound sense of self-esteem.

"Um, yay?" I try. "Go on with your bad self, you hot mama, you?"

She glares at me. "Laugh all you want," she growls. "But you won't be laughing once I have your sister and her stupid boyfriend in handcuffs." She grins wickedly.

That's it! I leap from my bed, grabbing her by her vest. "We'll see about that!"

She smirks and I realize I've walked right into her trap. "Oh, I'm sorry," she says with wide, innocent eyes. "For some reason, I thought you were supposed to be on my team. You know, the team that hired you for the job? The one that has the ability to wipe you off the face of the Earth by activating the nanovirus inside of you if you don't obey their rules?"

Argh. It takes everything I have inside to let her go. But, of course, she's right. I can't let on that I'm more interested in protecting my sister than doing my Slayer Inc. duty. After all, if I'm killed, who will protect Sunny?

Better to bide my time. Pretend to play by her rules for now. And figure out a way to beat Bertha at her own game.

"Of course," I say brightly, gritting my teeth and wishing I could just bite through that juicy little neck of hers and suck her dry. "I just meant, as a superior slayer, I'm sure to get there first."

Her lips curl into a nasty grin. "Oh, right," she says. "Of course you did." She chuckles. "But, you see, that's not going to happen either. Slayer Inc.'s given me a second chance. And I'm going to prove to them I deserve that chance. That I'm the best slayer around—no matter what I have to do." She smiles triumphantly. "Even if that means going above and beyond—and staking your sweet little sister through the heart."

Join the Blood Coven!

Do you want . . .
Eternal life?
Riches beyond your wildest dreams?
A hot Blood Mate to spend eternity with?

We're looking for a few good vampires! Do you have
what it takes to join the Blood Coven? Sign up online to
become a Vampire in Training, then master your skills at
Blood Coven University.

You'll go behind the scenes of the series, receive exclusive
Blood Coven merchandise, role-play with the other
vampires, and get a sneak peek at what's coming up next
for Sunny and Rayne.

BLOOD COVEN VAMPIRES
Check out all the Blood Coven Vampire titles!

Boys That Bite
Stake That
Girls That Growl
Bad Blood
Night School
Blood Ties

And don't miss the next Blood Coven Vampire novel

Soul Bound

Coming Winter 2012 from Berkley!

www.bloodcovenvampires.com
penguin.com

T125.0511

The Blood Coven Vampire Novels
by Mari Mancusi

Boys That Bite

Stake That

Girls That Growl

Bad Blood

Night School

Blood Ties

"Delightful, surprising, and engaging—
you'll get bitten and love it."
—Rachel Caine, *New York Times* bestselling author

Don't miss *Soul Bound*, the next book in the Blood Coven Vampire
series, coming Winter 2012 from Berkley!

www.bloodcovenvampires.com

penguin.com

T126.1010